**IT STILL AMAZED HER** THAT THE EVENTS OF TAKEN PLACE AT ALL.

It seemed yesterday that she had walked into town to meet Lilian, that April day when Dembry's had opened. Since then she had been loved and rejected, had borne a child, given it up, journeyed to the far end of the country, found a new home and started a new job . . .

Thinking of the past made her think, for once, of the baby: she hoped he was happy. She never usually thought of Alistair, but now she forced herself to summon him to mind. If he was still at the Royal Infirmary he would be romancing some nurse or clerk, as foolish as she had been . . . But thinking like this was a waste of time . . . After breakfast she would wrap up and go exploring, adding to her knowledge of London . . . 'I know I'm going to like it here,' she said to herself and went in search of her boots . . .

Denise Robertson, prolific writer of short stories, radio and television plays and radio documentaries, is familiar to millions as the highly acclaimed and popular agony aunt of ITV's *This Morning* programme. She has written many novels, all of which have been highly praised for their sensitivity and depth of knowledge of human experience, as well as for their beautifully observed depiction of the Durham landscape. Her novels include *The Second Wife, The Land of Lost Content, None to Make You Cry, Remember the Moment, The Stars Burn On* and *The Anxious Heart.* Her most recent books are *The Beloved People, Strength for the Morning* and *Towards Jerusalem,* which together go to make up a new trilogy. All these titles are published in Signet.

Denise Robertson lives near Sunderland with her husband, one of her five sons and an assortment of dogs.

# NONE TO MAKE YOU CRY

## Denise Robertson

A SIGNET BOOK

## SIGNET BOOKS

Published by the Penguin Group
Penguin Books Ltd, 27 Wrights Lane, London W8 5TZ, England
Penguin Books USA Inc., 375 Hudson Street, New York, New York 10014, USA
Penguin Books Australia Ltd, Ringwood, Victoria, Australia
Penguin Books Canada Ltd, 10 Alcorn Avenue, Toronto, Ontario, Canada M4V 3B2
Penguin Books (NZ) Ltd, 182–190 Wairau Road, Auckland 10, New Zealand

Penguin Books Ltd, Registered Offices: Harmondsworth, Middlesex, England

First published in Great Britain by Constable and Co. 1989
Published in Penguin Books 1990
Published in Signet 1993
3 5 7 9 10 8 6 4 2

Printed in England by Clays Ltd, St Ives plc

# PROLOGUE

*1977*

# PROLOGUE

When she woke there was enough light in the room to make out the shape of his head on the pillow beside her. She raised herself on her elbow to see the clock: four forty-five. In fifteen minutes the alarm would go off . . . she leaned to stop it and then eased out of bed as gently as she could. If he woke he would try to persuade her back to bed and there wasn't time.

It had been a mistake to let him stay, but it was done now, no point in regrets. She stepped into the shower and lifted her sleepy face to the flow. Afterwards she felt better, tiptoeing back into the bedroom to dress in the specially selected clothes. As an afterthought she wiped the scarlet polish from her fingernails and went back to wash her hands. Today was a day for discretion.

He was awake, and complained, as she had known he would. She bent to kiss his damp forehead, smelling the lingering odours of sleep and love as he moved in the bed. And then she was away before he asked questions she did not choose to answer.

King's Cross was quiet on that Easter Sunday morning. Even the pigeons that haunt the forecourt were reluctant to begin their day. One pecked at non-existent crumbs and then flew back to its roost.

She paused at the indicator board to check platforms, then went to buy a newspaper. She carried no luggage, only an expensive shoulder bag which matched her shoes. Her green coat was sombre, chosen to merge, the gold studs ornamenting her ears were tiny, her hands ringless inside the soft leather gloves.

She read her newspaper as the train threaded the London suburbs and only turned to the window when the city fell away, thinking of her lover still sleeping in the bed she had left behind. Stevenage, Peterborough, Grantham, Newark, Doncaster, York. . . . and then the Cleveland Hills low in the distance, touched now by sun and spreading fold on fold.

She gathered up her bag and gloves, discarded the newspaper and rose from her seat as the train approached Darlasden.

On the platform she checked her watch and decided there was time to walk to the church. Past Dembry's department store, across the market square, beneath the town hall clock, past the fountain, to the chill of the arched doorway and the soft music of a waiting church. Waiting, this year of 1977, as it had waited for the last ten years.

She slipped a silk Paisley scarf from her bag and tied it loosely beneath her chin, then she bent her knee to the altar and took her seat.

Her nostrils pricked at the unaccustomed smell of incense as she lifted her gaze to a ceiling of cerulean blue. 'Forgive me, Father, for I have sinned . . .' She knew the phrase although she was not a Catholic. The church was familiar to her, but its ways were still foreign, even after all the years.

She sat quietly as the Easter congregation swelled, the wooden floor squeaking with each footfall, each kneebob to a distant altar. If someone smiled to welcome a stranger, she gave no response. Her gaze flitted from the Stations of the Cross towards the door, and back again. Soon they would come.

'Let him look well, God. Let him be happy.' She had whispered that before, on other Easter pilgrimages. She did not often pray and the words were faltering. 'Our Father which art in Heaven . . . forgive us our trespasses as we forgive. . . .'

Had she forgiven? She tried to remember who was to blame, but it seemed unimportant now. Perhaps no one was at fault but her.

A priest appeared in a doorway and turned to make

obeisance. His stride was vigorous as he moved to the altar, his lips moved ceaselessly as his hands arranged the implements of Faith. There had been a priest at the beginning, but he was a man grown old in the cloth. *'Forgive me, Father . . .' 'You are forgiven already, my child. God loves the sinner although he abhors the sin.'* The ceiling had been blue then too, fourteen, no fifteen years ago, and her tears had collected in the folds of her neck and run in a trickle between her young breasts.

She smiled a little at the memory, turning towards the door, knowing that at any moment they would come. Light was filtering through jewelled glass. 'Let him look well, God. Let him be happy . . . so that I can go in peace once more.'

The mother came first, still beautiful, shepherding her children, boy and girl, together. The boy wore a grey suit and his face was earnest above a red school tie. He allowed his mother and sister to precede him into the pew. The father followed, greying at the temples, handsome. A man of substance. 'It has gone well for them, God. Thank you for that.'

The priest intoned a prayer, the congregation responded. It was all rhythmic, well rehearsed. Somewhere a child cried but no one minded. Children were welcome there.

The watcher's lips moved as she tried to be part of the celebration, her eyes never leaving the family group. Satisfaction suffused her. She had come, she had seen and once more all was well. They were a happy family. She put her hands to her lips in a gesture of gratitude and settled in her seat.

The second hymn had ended and they were kneeling to pray when she realized that the boy was restless. He turned to look at his sister and there was concern in the tilt of his head. The girl looked back at him for a moment, and then they were bending dutifully to their devotions and she could tell herself that what she had seen was nothing more than comradeship.

All the same, she watched them more closely, saw the mutinous set of the girl's mouth, saw the boy shake his head as though in warning and once put out a hand to

9

console her. The father turned too, to look at his children with anxious eyes. Only the mother prayed on.

It seemed the girl's cheek glistened, as though with tears, and the boy caught his upper lip between his teeth.

Childish voices were singing of the Lamb of God, but there was no peace now. The picture of the happy family had dissolved as though painted on water. The girl turned in her seat, seeming to look directly at the watcher. There was anger in her eyes, and torment!

The music swelled and the congregation gave itself to God, but for the woman there was no such release. She watched, hawk-like, until it was time to file out again into the sunlight. Once or twice, as worshippers jostled for place, she lost sight of them, and when she emerged, blinking, into the open air the family had divided. Father and mother were standing in the porch to exchange pleasantries with other members of the congregation; the girl and boy were walking away towards the gate. She hesitated for a moment and then followed them, moving as close as she dared.

'I can't bear it, Michael. I can't, I can't, I can't.' The girl's voice was rising, and tears had ceased to glisten and were running unchecked down her cheeks.

The boy was trying to keep his voice low and soothing. 'I know, Sue, I know. I don't suppose it was meant . . . Besides, some things just have to be borne.' There was a despairing resignation in his words that chilled her to the bone.

'*Some things have to be borne.*' The phrase ran round and round the woman's head as she watched the family reunite and move to the sleek grey car. '*Some things have to be borne.*' It echoed and re-echoed as she watched the winking tail-light disappear, as she turned to retrace her steps to the station, past the store and the fountain and the town-hall clock.

It was still there as she sank into her seat on the train, closed her eyes and remembered.

# BOOK ONE

*1962*

# 1

## *April 1962*

A cloud hung over Darlasden, a single cloud in an otherwise blue sky. Helen Clark kept an eye on it as she walked into the town centre, praying it would hang on to its contents and not disgorge them on to her one and only decent suit. The label said 'mixed fibres' and she was not sure how mixed fibres would react to rain. She walked quickly because her lunch break from the Infirmary was only an hour and a half, and if she was late back she would be in trouble.

The trees were full of April buds, and daffodils poked defiantly through railings. Helen felt her spirits rise until she remembered what lay ahead. She was going shopping with Lilian, her sister, and she wasn't looking forward to it. Lilian would grumble about prices, about lack of money, about the indignity of being confined to 'club' shops. She would have to carry Lilian's toddler, and if she didn't watch her tongue Lilian would take offence and be in the huff for weeks.

Worst of all she would ask embarrassing questions about Alistair. 'Has he tried it on yet, our Hel? He will! They all do. I mean, what's a high and mighty doctor want with the likes of us? He's only after one thing. Too good for a pitman, are you? You're far too cocky, our Helen, you and your GCEs. You want to watch it.'

That was how it would go, and all the while she would have to trudge behind, Lilian's bags on one arm, Lilian's infant on the other. 'Do I have to go, mam?' she had asked this morning, cramming toast into her mouth in case she missed the bus. She had known what the answer would be. Lilian was six months pregnant, and they must all dance to her tune.

Perhaps the six years between them was to blame for the fact that they had never got on. Once she had thrown a kettle of water at Lilian and been thrashed with her father's belt until Lilian herself had begged him to stop. That was typical Lilian, blowing hot and cold.

As usual, when she thought bad thoughts about her sister, Helen felt guilty. When she was little she had stood at Lilian's knee for fried potato, ultimate luxury from her big sister's plate. And Lilian had bought her her first bikini from Skegness, because she knew Helen's regulation navy swimsuit had become an embarrassment to her.

She must try to be helpful today, and not get her sister riled. Once Lilian met Alistair she would stop tormenting her. He had such a nice way with him, they would all be smitten – even her dad. Her mother had already suggested bringing him home to Sunday tea, but that wouldn't do. Dad lying around the place with no collar on his shirt, putting the Sunday paper over his face when he didn't want to talk. Lilian and her husband Billy wolfing plate-pies and fruit and jelly as though they hadn't eaten for a week, never mind roast beef and Yorkshires at half-past twelve. And her mother in a pinny at the sink all day, when she wasn't trying to keep her precious grandbairn quiet.

When Alistair came home it must be a proper do with cups instead of mugs and her dad in a collar and tie. And pigs might fly, she thought wryly! Once her dad came in from the pit he cast off boots and muffler and that was it till bedtime.

A bus appeared round a corner, its normal green coachwork almost obscured by a banner proclaiming 'Dembry's Superstore: Grand Opening – 16 April 1962. Super attractions, prizes, competitions. Win a Caribbean holiday. Meet the TV stars. Unbelievable prices on five floors. Come along. You'll be amazed!'

A girl in a red satin costume was posing on the bus platform, a ribbon sash proclaiming her to be 'Miss Darlasden'. She had blonde hair that swung to her shoulders.

14

Helen put up a hand and fingered her own hair, black and curling and hardly reaching her ears. The bus slowed for a zebra crossing and she saw that the girl's long thighs were goose-pimpled beneath the fake tan. Fancy having to stand about in a cossie in this weather! Her own legs were comfortably encased in nylon and it made her feel suddenly superior.

There was going to be a posh café in the new store. Alistair might take her there if they got an afternoon off together. She waited for a lull in the traffic so that she could cross the road, all the time thinking of Alistair and the sheer excitement of being his girl. He was tall and thin and freckled and looked like a student, but he was a junior houseman, a proper doctor. They would sit in Dembry's and she would pour his tea from a silver pot.

A board outside a newsagent's caught her eye as she reached the opposite kerb: 'Kennedy invades Cuba'. Cuba! A little island a long way away. Above her the cloud had expanded into a real threat. She swung her bag on to her other shoulder and quickened her pace as rain began to spot the pavement.

Lilian heaved a sigh of relief at the sight of her sister. 'Here, take the bairn, our Hel – I'm dropping. And I'm desperate for a wee. I'd never have come to the town if I'd thought on about this new shop opening. What a crush!'

Outside the small shop doorway where they had met and continued to shelter, crowds were scurrying to get out of the rain. Helen fished for a hanky to wipe chocolate from her niece's face. 'You'll feel better when you've had some dinner, Lil. There'll be a ladies' lav in the snack bar. We could try there.' She looked into the baby's face. 'Nice fish fingers and chips, pet?'

The child nodded without comprehending.

'One and nine,' Lilian said gloomily. 'That's what they charge in the Biz-Bar, and she'll only play about with them. She's a little toy when it comes to food.' Her face contorted and she put up a hand to cover a belch. 'God, I've got heartburn. I got up with it this morning and I've had it ever since. I've told Billy this is the last time I get caught. I'm having me tubes tied if they'll do it. And you want to

15

watch on, our Helen.' Suddenly her eyes narrowed. 'Although I expect being a medical secretary and working at the Infirmary teaches you a thing or two. You'll be too fly to fall pregnant, I suppose.'

She was fishing but Helen was not going to rise to the bait. 'We can't stand here forever, Lilian. I've got to be back by two. If you want to do any shopping we'll have to get on.'

A clown who was advertising Dembry's opening had moved inside its glass portals to avoid a drenching, and was handing out lollipops. 'Sweeties,' the baby said, twisting in Helen's arms. 'Sweeties, sweeties!'

Lilian scowled as she hurried gingerly over the wet pavement. 'I'll smack your legs, our Karen, if you don't shut up.' The baby whimpered her disappointment as the windows of the new store gave way to the windows of the snack bar, and they hustled gratefully inside.

They had to share a booth with a courting couple who gazed into one another's eyes while their cappuccino went cold and settled in the cup.

'Did you see that?' Lilian said, when the lovers went off in search of greater privacy. 'I don't know which one looked the glakiest.'

Helen had thought it all rather romantic but she knew better than to argue. 'Where do you want to go after this?' she asked, poking around in her Cornish pasty for evidence of meat.

'C. & A.,' Lilian said. 'Clothes for the bairn and a shirt for Billy. Then we'll have a look round Dembry's, if we can stand the crush. After that I don't mind. What do you want?'

With exactly one and eleven between her and pay day, Helen's wants were few. 'I don't mind; I only came down to give a hand. I'll have to watch the time though.'

Lilian, enjoying her egg and chips, was inclined to be magnanimous. 'All right, we know you're keen to get back. We know why, an' all.' She grinned. 'What's he like, this lad of yours? He's got a poncy name.'

'It's not,' Helen said defensively, 'it's Scottish. His family's Scottish. His dad's a doctor . . . and his brother. You'll like him, Lil. He's lovely with the patients. He says he might specialize later on . . . you know, orthopaedics or paediatrics, or something . . .'

Lilian had had enough of incomprehensible medical terms. 'He'll let you down, our kid. Don't say you haven't been warned. He'll marry a posh type from his own place, and you'll be left standing.'

But Helen was not to be shaken. 'We'll see, Lilian. Now, if you're finished we'd better get on.'

Edward Portillo left Berwick at eleven-thirty and took the A1 south. Behind, the harbour gleamed in the April sunshine and a line of swans moved across the water as if drawn by an invisible thread. He had never got used to the sight of the swans commuting between river and sea. It was an image that stayed in his head long after he returned to London.

His mother's eyes had smiled when he said goodbye, but her mouth, twisted slightly since her stroke, had trembled. He had asked her once more if she was sure she wanted to stay. 'It's not too late to change your mind . . . old lady's privilege.'

But she had smiled more widely and pushed him away. 'Off you go . . . and drive carefully. I'm going to be happy here with Dorothy, and besides, you'll visit – and phone. We'll hardly realize we're apart.'

He wanted to tell her it was all wrong, this enforced exile, that all he really wanted was for her to come home with him now . . . but his aunt was there, her eyes flitting anxiously between them.

'She'll be all right with me, Edward. I love her too, you know.' Dorothy was his mother's sister and she was trying to be kind. He had kissed both women, then, and driven away.

He switched on the radio as the road turned away from the sea and the beautiful county of Northumberland unrolled. They were still talking about Cuba, describing the build-up to the crisis. He had lost touch with the Home

Service in the last few months, but now he would have time to rediscover its delights.

He thought about the last few months, the terrible fear of the first week after his mother's stroke and then hope returning as she began to speak again. One day she had lifted her hand to cover his as it lay on the bed and he had felt a wave of relief. It was going to be all right! He had brought her home from hospital for Christmas, and invited his girlfriend, Sylvia, to a huge celebration lunch. But his mother could barely lift a fork to her mouth and once she had choked on a mouthful of food.

'You've got to face it, Edward,' Sylvia had said as they washed up. 'I know how much you love her, but you must face facts. You can't cope with her . . . not the way she is now.'

He had known it was true, but it had not endeared Sylvia to him.

Now he looked left and right at fallow fields where horses grazed – good horses with gleaming coats whose owners lived in grey stone houses set amid trees. Northumberland was a wealthy area, according to his aunt, and could boast more castles than any other county. He settled in his seat and relaxed his shoulders. There was a long drive ahead, but with luck he should be in London by six o'clock.

He thought of the empty flat above the silent shop. What would it be like without her? He felt the same sense of loss he had felt in 1940 when his mother had put him, a bewildered five-year-old, on an evacuee train. She had come to visit him a fortnight later and, seeing his misery in the country, had brought him back to London and the bombs. He had cuddled against her in the train, inhaling her familiar scent, letting her fox collar tickle his forehead, revelling in their closeness, vowing never to be separated from her again. She had persuaded him to go on holidays once he grew up, to see the world; but he had always known she would be there waiting when he returned.

Now all that was over. How would he fill the void? There was his music: he would be free to go to concerts again.

Sylvia could be good company when she chose. And he would expand the business.

Thinking of the shop cheered him a little. Its jumble of bureaux and étagères, all with the patina of age; Doccia and Sèvres on shelves; Meissen and the occasional piece of Chelsea; small pieces of Georgian silver; and the Venetian blackamoor torchères that guarded the door to the stairs, and had been there as long as he could remember. He had named them Mark and Antony, and they had been his childhood companions. His father had threatened to sell them if a good enough price was offered, but his mother had made sure they stayed put. His had been a solitary childhood but he had enjoyed every magic moment.

He was entering Durham now and he glanced at the dashboard clock. He would keep on to Darlasden and then take a break. He knew several dealers there, and country areas still had a lot of good old mahogany and walnut. There had not been an opportunity to buy in while he was nursing his mother, but now he would restock and get the business going again.

The signs for Darlasden loomed ahead. He flicked on his indicator, then switched it off as he saw the bus and its gaudy announcement: '*Dembry's, Darlasden's new Superstore. You've been waiting for our opening.* Today's the day! Novelties, attractions! Bring the children to see Pepe the Clown!'

Edward was not in the mood for clowns. He put down his foot and sped on southwards.


'Oh look, a clown!' Diana Whittington was glad of an excuse to enthuse, to let out some of the excitement that had bubbled inside her ever since hearing the obstetrician's verdict. If David had been with her instead of Anne she would have capered back to the car shrieking her glee: 'I'm pregnant. I'm beautifully, wonderfully, irretrievably pregnant. Look at me! Haven't I been clever?'

She was still a little in awe of her sister-in-law, so she'd confined herself to a modest announcement. 'It's true. Eight weeks he says. Isn't that nice?' There was something so comforting about the word 'nice'. It seemed to fit a multitude of occasions. 'Nice tea, nice walk, nice people, nice pregnancy.'

'David will be pleased,' Anne had said, gathering up her purse and gloves. 'And so are we, of course.' She had held the car door for Diana and lifted in her skirt before shutting it.

'She's kind,' Diana told herself firmly but it did nothing to dispel the sense of chill she had felt ever since Anne greeted her when she came to Darlasden. There was something about her sister-in-law, an intense neatness and precision, that made her feel freckled and loud by comparison.

Now, as Anne negotiated the town-centre traffic, her conscience pricked and she tried to express her gratitude. 'It was kind of you to come with me, Anne. David wanted to take me, but I know it makes him feel guilty to skip surgery. And it's nice of you and Howard to give me lunch.'

Anne smiled but her glance stayed on the road, and Diana sat back to watch the clown capering outside the new department store. 'It's certainly something, isn't it? Five floors and three restaurants.' A giant net of balloons was anchored to the roof, straining to fly up and up into the sky.

For weeks they had been deluged with advertising about Dembry's. She already had a charge card in her purse, made out to Mrs David Whittington, which was also nice. After lunch she would go into the baby boutique and buy two of everything, one pink, one blue, just in case. And she would look at cots and prams and furniture for the new nursery, all with Disney figures on the doors.

She stole a furtive look at her sister-in-law. No baby there yet, and Anne a devout Catholic. The first time she had laid eyes on Anne she had thought of the Virgin Mary. Same black hair, neatly parted, same heavy-lidded eyes, same stillness about the body. But no baby after five years? Poor Anne. Perhaps she would give the babywear a miss for today. If there was a problem with Anne's fertility, it wouldn't do to flourish her own.

'I must ring David,' she said, as they got out of the car.

'He thinks I'm pulling his leg. I mean, a baby so soon . . . it's not decent.' Too late she regretted her words but Anne was smiling serenely.

'Of course you must ring him. He'll be delighted. You've got plenty of time; Howard isn't meeting us until twelve-thirty.'

There was a sudden muffled bang, and, turning at the hotel door, they saw the balloons, freed from their net, soaring skywards.

The dining-room in the Swan was low-beamed and dark. A fire crackled at one end and willow pattern gleamed against oak panelling.

'It's quaint,' Diana said, struggling out of her suede jacket and taking the seat which Howard, David's brother, held for her. The menu was hidden inside tooled leather. 'Chef's roast of the day,' she said, 'that sounds good.'

She had spoken to David on the phone in the lobby. 'It's true, darling. November 14th!'

His pleasure had flowed along the line, making her smile fatuously into the tiny mirror above the coin box. 'Yes, I am a clever girl . . . and don't you forget it. No, I'd rather be with you, my darling, but they're being so kind. I'll be home soon . . . sooner . . . I'm going to do some shopping and then I'll run every step of the way. I love you too . . . About a yard. Well, two yards . . . a lot, anyway.'

Now they sipped dry sherries and chose their food. 'Kennedy has invaded Cuba,' Howard said when the menus were laid aside. 'Well, that's the story. The caretaker told me as I left the office. Kennedy said he'd never put US troops into Cuba . . . just last week he said it. So much for promises.'

'Let's forget about it now,' Anne said, moving her knife and fork fractionally into line. 'Mustn't spoil lunch. What did David say when you told him your news, Diana?'

Diana glanced at Howard to see if he looked snubbed, and then tried to play down her own excitement. 'He was pleased. And surprised. We didn't intend to start a family right now.' She sought for words. 'I have so much to learn . . . about your northern way of life, about being a doctor's wife. . . . oh, a hundred and one things. I want to get it right. And now, a baby. I've got my work cut out. You'll have to help me, both of you.'

Anne was still smiling. 'I expect you'll cope. You seem so confident. You'll take it in your stride.'

'She means I'm brash,' Diana thought. 'She says it so nicely but she's being bitchy all the same.' She thought longingly of getting back to David. Two hours, three at the most, and then it would be all right.

Her roast beef was placed in front of her and she pulled a face at the enormous Yorkshire pudding that accompanied it, but Anne and Howard were both pre-occupied with their cutlery. As Diana reached for her knife and fork she realized that she had never seen her brother and sister-in-law exchange an intimate glance. They spoke *of* one another often enough – 'Howard believes the economy will improve' or 'Anne's terribly good with the garden' – but they seldom spoke *to* one another.

Perhaps that's how she and David would be once the newness wore off. At present it was an effort to talk to anyone *but* each other, but that might pass with time, leaving them politely indifferent like the couple across the table.

And then she remembered David's face, so like Howard's in feature but mobile where his brother's was still, breaking constantly into smiles or laughter. She would be all right with David. And his baby. His babies . . . at least six! She murmured her thanks as Howard passed her the salt and pepper, and got on with her lunch.


Lilian had grumbled her way through several of the Darlasden shops and denounced Dembry's new store for not accepting 'clubs'. Helen wondered if she should point out the evils of buying on tick, but knew it would only lead to another row and she was not in the mood for it. Karen had slept ever since the snack bar, lying more and more heavily in Helen's arms, and each dash from doorway to doorway meant a further drenching.

'I'll have to go soon, Lil. I'll get murdered if I'm late, you know that.' Lilian trudged doggedly on and resentment rose up in Helen. It was sinful to dislike your own flesh and blood but sometimes . . .! At last she could stand it no longer. 'I'll have to put the bairn down, Lilian. You're going to get me sacked. And I'll get soaked on the way back.'

Lilian's eyes were hostile as she surveyed her sister's damp suit and let her eyes fall to Helen's suede court shoes, stained and splashed now by the soaked pavements. 'Serves you right. If you wore a mac like sensible folks you'd be all right. Givvus the bairn here, then, if you've made your mind up.'

She made Helen's return to work sound like an act of selfishness, but her face softened momentarily as she gathered her sleeping child into her arms and Helen's conscience pricked. 'I could take some of your parcels to work and bring them round tonight?'

But Lilian was not to be parted from her purchases and Helen spent precious minutes loading them on to her sister's free arm. 'You'll never manage.' Lilian's slightly swollen fingers were raking through the compartments of her big leather purse, counting up the tokens that were left from her 'club'.

'I'll get rid of these and go straight for the bus. Don't worry about me, I'll manage. I've carried more than this before, many a time. You get off, if it's so important. We mustn't interfere with your fancy job.'

That was it, Helen thought, as she half-ran through the town centre: Lilian disliked her for getting on, although she herself could have been far cleverer if she had made an effort. The rain had ceased and the clown was once more cajoling passers-by to enter Dembry's. She felt his huge, gloved hand pluck at her arm but there was no time for chit-chat. Besides, she disliked his mournful face, with its mean eyes and mouth lost in acres of greasepaint.

When the Infirmary came in sight Helen was already ten minutes late. She might manage to sidle in and get into her medical secretary's white coat unobserved, but Sister Baker missed nothing and was sure to catch her. As she passed the porter's lodge Dobson poked his head through the Enquiry window. 'Watch it! She's just gone into X-ray.'

Helen nodded gratefully and turned into a side corridor. It was the long way round but it would avoid passing X-ray and bumping into Baker. The only sister in the hospital who still wore a bow under her chin, Baker had a tongue that could kill at twenty paces, and terrorized the entire staff of the Ear, Nose and Throat Department.

When she was a doctor's wife and wore an ankle length fur coat she would come back on a visit and gloat. She had seen the consultants' wives and she knew how it was done. She was grinning at the prospect of revenge when she saw Alistair ahead of her, white coat flying, stethoscope dangling from his pocket. She loved him so much, and it was not just hero-worship – if he were a dustbin man she would love him just the same. Even better, because he would need her more.

'Hello, you.' He always looked so pleased to see her that it made her legs shake. He moved her into a doorway and fingered wet hair from her forehead. 'You look like a drowned rat. A very pretty drowned rat, but definitely a wet rodent.'

She wrinkled her nose in what she hoped was rodent-fashion. 'Thanks a bunch,' she said, making a half-hearted attempt to push him away. 'You'll get me shot if Baker sees.' Even to her own ears her voice sounded different: if Lilian were here she would say she was putting it on.

His lips were almost on hers. 'Sod Baker.'

She felt his tongue flicker over her closed mouth and drew her head away, uncertain of how to respond. He knew so much and she knew so little.

At the bottom of the corridor a door swung open. 'See you tonight,' he said, grinning, and left her to go on her way.


The bus was crowded and reeked of damp wool. 'Pass along there,' the conductor said, making no attempt to help Lilian with her parcels. There was no respect any more, not even when you were pregnant.

She settled herself into a seat and helped Karen to kneel up by the window. She was hot and sweaty, with her hair streaked around her eyes. Her legs felt like puddings and her coat buttons strained over her swollen stomach. She had not wanted another bairn, not yet. They had so much to do to the house – new units in the kitchen and an inside lav, not to mention carpets.

Lilian paid her fare and settled back for the journey to Belgate. Might as well relax while she had the chance. After this one was born she would put her foot down. If they gave her a tie it would be all right; if not, Billy would have to put a knot in it. He came from a family of big breeders, but there was no call for her to keep it going.

She opened one of the crackling bags and peeped inside. It was nice getting new things. Possessions. When she got home she would take them upstairs and lay them out on the bed. She would be paying for them for a twelve-month, so she might as well get some pleasure out of them.

There was soap and a facecloth from the new shop, just so she could say she'd been there, but its prices would be beyond her in future unless they got round to taking 'clubs'. She was so deep in with the 'club' woman that there was never the money to break free. Like most of the women in Belgate, she was in a trap and she would just have to make the best of it.

They were passing the Royal Infirmary now, and Lilian pointed through the glass. 'See, that's where your Auntie Helen works. In the hospital.' She said it loudly so that the rest of the bus could hear. No harm in letting folks know you had connections.

Somewhere in that great stone building Helen was arsing about in a white coat, making on she was a doctor. She'd always been like that, full of airs and graces, going to the grammar school and getting a posh job. If she married a doctor there'd be no holding her.

Lilian felt bile well up in her throat and reached in her bag for her Rennies. Life was a bugger and no mistake. Still, if Billy got his deputy's ticket she would show them all. And Helen's fancy doctor would never wed her – that sort never did unless it was their own class. He would just play around, and then toss her off like rubbish. That would bring her down a peg or two.

The thought of Helen getting her come-uppance pleased Lilian so much that when Karen got tired of looking at the scenery and began to winge, she cuddled her in and promised her chips and gravy for tea.

It was still a few minutes short of six o'clock when Edward reached Inkerman Mews but he felt as though the day had gone on forever. A light was shining in the garage work-shop and further down Mrs Stepinska was watering her window box.

'You're back,' she said, when he slowed the car beside her, and she shook her head sadly. 'You'll miss your mama, that's for sure.' Suddenly she thrust her trowel at him. 'Stay here . . .' In a moment she was inside her house and out again, bearing a plate of scones. 'There,' she said, proudly, lifting the tea-towel to show what lay beneath, 'still warm. You eat with butter when you get in and think of when mama comes home.'

His mother would never come home and they both knew it, but the gesture was kind and he carried the scones through the shop and upstairs to the living-room, scooping up the mail as he went.

He put scones and envelopes on the sideboard and switched on the television. The talk was all of Cuba, Castro gesticulating, Kennedy's bulldog chin and Kruschev bellig-erent, in all the newsreel footage they were choosing to show. Perhaps there would be world war after all, and they would all be incinerated inside a mushroom cloud? It would be one way out of his misery.

He picked up the phone and dialled. 'No, don't disturb her, Auntie, just tell her I'm safely home. I'll ring again tomorrow.'

While he waited for the kettle to boil he went out on to the tiny balcony and looked out on the darkening back lane and the rooftops beyond. The view made him think of his mother – holding her hand in childhood, sharing things with her in the last few years when they had been alone together. He felt an almost tangible ache at the thought of the distance between them. Was she feeling this same

26

pain? If so, it was not to be borne. He would bring her back and look after her, and damn the shop. She had managed all right with the commode, and there had been the nurse for bathing: he could do it again if need be. Tomorrow he would ring her, and if there was the slightest hint of regret in her voice he would take to the road and bring her back.

Inside the kitchen the kettle shrilled and Edward felt his panic subside. She was safe now with Dorothy and he was a man, not a child. He must make the business pay so that she need never want, so that he could drive up, or better still take the train, as often as he could get away. He must make her realize she was still loved, however much distance there was between them.

He brewed the tea and settled with it in front of the TV. Mrs Stepinska's scones were there on the sideboard, but he didn't feel like eating yet. Perhaps he would ring Sylvia later on and invite her out for a meal. Desire stirred as he thought of seeing her, and it made him feel guilty. All the same, it was five days since they had made love – and that was a long time.

'Anyway, there can't be a war.' Diana said firmly. 'Not now, not when I am actually pregnant. I'll ring the White House and tell them so if need be.'

'Good,' David said, 'that makes me feel a lot safer. Now, give me the rest of that potato thing and tell me about your day. Did you patronize the new store? If so, what did it cost me?'

Diana shook her head. 'I meant to – I mean to – buy nappies, baby dresses, matinée coats, the whole thing. But . . . .' She hesitated. 'Well, I wondered if Anne might be a bit sensitive on that subject . . . So I thought, what's the rush?'

'She's a strange lady, my sister-in-law,' David said, as she refilled his plate. She sensed he did not want to talk about Anne so she didn't ask for explanations. 'Can we have that again tomorrow?' he said. 'It's choss.'

Diana threw back her head and laughed aloud. 'It's what?'

'Choss. Don't you know that word? Where was you brung up?'

'Oh, I'm just a child of the Home Counties. I don't speak your language, didn't I tell you?' She got up from her seat and came round to sit on his knee, laughing again as he pretended to wince at her weight.

'Oh God, I can't support two of you on one leg!'

She stroked his thigh. 'It's a good leg. Very . . . um . . . fleshy.'

'Fleshy? I like your cheek. That, what you are holding, is my sartorius. Come upstairs and I'll let you trace it to its source.'

She hid her face in his neck. 'Can we? Is it all right?'

He was suddenly tender, his joking forgotten. 'If we're not greedy, it's OK. For a long while yet.'

'I *am* glad,' she said, starting to giggle.

He held her away from him. 'You knew,' he said accusingly.

She nodded. 'It was the first thing I asked the doctor. "What about my sex life?" I said,' and then, seeing her husband's horrified expression, 'Of course, I didn't, you idiot. Would I say something like that to a consultant? He told *me*! He said, "Mrs Whittington, I know you're married to a sex-mad GP so I might as well tell you . . ."'

The rest of her words were lost as he attempted to turn her over his knee.

'Oh God,' she said when at last she was upright again. 'I love you so much, and I want this baby so much, it scares me.'


Helen climbed out of the car in the dark back street and stood while Alistair closed the passenger door. There was no one about and she was glad. Her legs felt a bit shaky and she wasn't in the mood for chat. Belgate people were not the type just to pass by, not even in the dark. If anyone came along it would be 'Hello, Helen pet. Is that you? And who's this, then? He's not from hereabouts.'

'OK?' Alistair sounded anxious and she hastened to reassure him.

'I'm fine. I'll have to go now, though. It's late.'

He put his arms around her and steered her into the shelter of the doorway. 'Funny little thing. Always rushing somewhere, always afraid she'll "get wrong". Stop worrying. I'll look after you. You're not at school now, you're grown up. Really grown up!'

He breathed the last words against her hair and she felt her heartbeat quicken. 'Love me?' she asked.

Once more his lips were against her ear, his breath warm on her cheek. 'You know I do. More than ever, now.' When he talked like this, slowly, as though what he was saying was the most important thing in the world, she couldn't resist him. She felt a physical weakness come over her, a kind of yearning.

'Oh Alistair,' she said, and then stopped, uncertain of what came next.

So her mother had been wrong about men losing respect if you gave in. There was a new note in Alistair's voice now when he spoke to her, a tender note that hadn't been there before. Inside the house a door banged and a light went on in an upstairs room, spilling out from the yard and on to the top of the wall. 'I'll have to go,' she said.

'Or you'll get killed,' he teased. 'I won't let them hurt you, you know that. Still, little girls should be in bed. Give me a kiss, and go and get your beauty-sleep.'

Helen watched while his ancient sports car put-putted to the corner and out of sight, then she opened the yard door. It was dark inside, no light escaping from the drawn curtains, but the yard still gleamed from the day's rain. The pigeons coo-ed softly as she passed the cree, and inside the house she could hear the wireless belting out the song that everyone was singing nowadays: 'I want to be Bobby's girl, I want to be Bobby's girl, that's the most important thing to me . . .' She tried to substitute Alistair's name for Bobby but it wouldn't work, and, besides, the music had ceased.

She hesitated outside the door. If she went in and they turned from the fire they would see her face. Her mother always stared at her when she came home, as if to look for signs of guilt. Perhaps it was written there, what she had done tonight, in Alistair's room, in the darkness she had insisted on? She had done 'it', the forbidden thing, but it had not seemed so wrong at the time, not when it was so important to Alistair and when they loved one another. It hadn't been enjoyable either, and in a funny way that seemed to make it, if not right, at least less wrong. She blushed, thinking of the stain on his sheet, soaking now in the sink. 'It'll be all right, silly. I don't have to explain things.' It was true. He was a doctor, a qualified doctor, and he loved her very much. Everything was going to be all right. He had told her that, and he should know.

She heard the yard door creak open and then a dark figure was advancing. 'Is that you, our Hel?' It was her dad. 'What're you hanging about here for? Let's get inside and hear what the Ruskies have done. There's going to be a war, everyone says so down the club.'

Tonight she had lain in Alistair's arms while he explained about Cuba. He had made it seem so simple, talking about Eisenhower and Castro and how President Kennedy was not really to blame for any of it. He was so clever. And then they had done 'it', and little things like invasions had dwindled in the wonder of giving pleasure.

Suddenly she felt good about herself. About everything. She followed her father into the house, prepared to meet her mother's gaze without flinching.

# 2

## *June 1962*

It was lovely to wake on a Saturday morning and know there was no need to get out of bed. Helen rolled on her face, tucked her arms under the pillow, and thought about the day ahead. In a moment she would get up and take her time over getting ready. She was going into Darlasden on the bus to buy a cotton frock – yellow or blue, with a wide, square neck outlined in white. She had seen a dress like that in last week's *Woman* and known she had to have one like it. She would wear it tonight, and when Alistair called for her his jaw would drop at the sight.

The only trouble was that his car would be parked two doors down because he never drove up to the door unless it was dark. 'We don't want everyone to know our business,' he'd said when she teased him about it, smiling and twinkling his eyes to make a joke of it. She had let it go because it embarrassed her to talk about it, but it hurt just the same.

Tonight her mother would say, 'Fetch him in,' and she would start to wriggle and make excuses, knowing that if she asked him in he would find a reason to refuse. Her family were curious about him now, wanting to know about his background, his home town, his likes and dislikes. Apart from which, they just wanted a look at him. And it wasn't simply Lilian being nosey, it was her mam and dad too. 'He's not wed, is he?' her father had said last weekend, bringing his brows down. 'Don't be daft, our dad' she had said, secretly relieved that he was so way-off the mark.

She knew Alistair wasn't married, she knew he loved her, not just from his whispered words when they made love but from the little secret smiles he gave her at work, from the patient way he explained things, from a hundred little signs. She knew he cared for her, but she suspected he might be a snob and it was not a comfortable thought. He asked plenty of questions about a miner's life but he showed no desire to meet one.

She was wondering whether or not to get up when her bedroom door creaked open. 'Hel?' Her father was there in his stockinged feet, a mug of tea in his outstretched hand.

She turned on to her elbow, being careful to keep the sheet up to her neck because her father embarrassed easily. 'Ta, dad. Seems like a nice day.'

The sun was shining through the thin gold curtains, showing up dust that floated in the air, giving the shabby furniture a shine it did not normally have. One day she would leave this room, tread the cold lino for the last time and go to a home of her own. It was a thought at once unthinkable and irresistible, and she pondered it while she sipped the strong tea.

When she got out of bed she crossed to the window and drew back the curtains, tugging gently so as not to dislodge the rod that held them. Outside the sun shone on the long, narrow Belgate gardens. Some were flowered and ornamental; some, like her father's, were criss-crossed with neat rows of vegetables; others were abandoned to waist-high grass, their front gates lost in towers of white bindweed and pink briar rose.

No one in Belgate used their front gates and very few their front doors, unless for access to the garden. The life of Belgate, the ceaseless comings and goings, took place in the back streets. But the gardens were magic places for children. She had hidden there behind the hedge of Michaelmas daisies, grinning as her mother called her. She had planted nasturtium seeds in the border and taken them up every two days to monitor progress. Some at least had survived, and still flamed orange and yellow in a far corner.

She felt a sudden flow inside her, a welling up of love for all that was past and precious, for all that was ahead. She folded her arms, hugging herself as she ran her hands up and down her upper arms. She was loved and she knew how to love in return. Everyone. Not just Alistair, but mam and dad . . . and even Lilian. She turned from the window and lay down on the bed, the better to contemplate the wonder of it all.


Edward watched as the car moved away towards Kensington High Street, then he put down the catch on the shop door and hurried upstairs to make coffee. He was humming as he filled the kettle and plugged it in. He had sold a kingwood marquetry side cabinet at a nice profit ten minutes after opening. The buyer had been a tourist in search of something British to ship home, and Edward had felt bound to point out that the cabinet was German. The man had wavered, but his wife was going to have it wheresoever it had originated, and so the deal was done. After that he had bought in a Lambeth Doulton teapot and some nice spoons. It was only eleven-thirty and already he had had a good day.

While he waited for the kettle to boil he looked out on the back of Inkerman Mews, dissected two-thirds down its length by Gossett's Yard. He had lived there all his life and never discovered who Gossett had been. There was nothing there now except the gable ends of the mews and a huge, empty lock-up garage that had once been a stable. If business went well he might rent it and use it for extra stock.

He was scalding his coffee when the door rattled below. He carried his mug to the landing and bent to peer down the stairs. On the other side of glass and grille Sylvia was peering in. He clattered down the stairs and lifted the latch. 'Coffee?'

She nodded and followed him upstairs, her high sling-back heels clicking as she went.

'Good day?' She stood with her back to the sink, holding her cup in both hands as though to warm them. Her fingers were thin and freckled and scarlet-tipped, and the emerald cotton dress flattered her green eyes and marmalade hair. She looked good and she knew it.

He told her about the side cabinet and she smiled, the slightly lop-sided smile he knew she cultivated. 'How did you bring yourself to part with it?' It was a standing joke between them that he never wanted to sell on, and he smiled. 'It was German . . . marquetry . . . very fussy. Not my style.'

She leaned forward to twitch his collar into place. 'Good, I'd hate you to feel deprived.'

There were undertones in her words and in spite of himself he responded to them, reaching out for her. 'Supposing I were deprived?'

She linked her arms around his neck and leaned back to look into his face. 'I'd do something about it. That's what friends are for.'

They settled for a long and satisfying kiss and then fell to discussing what film they should see later on.

'*The Loneliness of the Long Distance Runner*,' Sylvia said, looking at the previous night's *Standard*. 'Tom Courtenay and Michael Redgrave. It got good reviews. Or there's *Lonely are the Brave* with Walter Matthau and Kirk Douglas. Is that a war film?'

Edward shook his head. 'No, but you wouldn't like it. It's a Western of sorts.'

They settled for Melina Mercouri in *Phaedra* and agreed to meet in the pub. 'My place or yours?' she asked as she rinsed her cup, and he knew she meant them to spend the night together. They did it more and more often nowadays, and it was increasingly important to him.

'Here?' he said. 'We could eat on the way back, or I've got some veal in the fridge.'

Sylvia put her hands beneath her hair and shook it free of her collar. 'Your place it is,' she said. 'I'll bring my toothbrush.'

When she had gone he looked out at the mews. Mrs Stepinska would know that Sylvia stayed the night – nothing escaped her. And if she knew, Papa Stepinski would know, and the Pollocks, and the Drews, and Miss Cartwright above the joiner. So what? He wasn't a child, so why did he feel guilty?

Tonight he would ring his mother before he went out and she would ask about Sylvia with that hopeful note in her voice that spelled wedding bells. Perhaps he should do it just for her? If he proposed, Sylvia would accept. She would make him a good wife; she was a successful fashion journalist and she had a good business brain. Besides . . . he shivered a little thinking of the night ahead and her naked body entwined with his own. He put his rinsed cup to drain, and postponed the question of marriage as the shop bell rang to indicate a customer.


'Put that down, our Karen, or I'll leather your backside.' Lilian had collapsed into a fireside chair and had no intention of getting up, but the threat was enough. Karen replaced the china dog on the what-not and started to cry.

'She's tired,' Lilian's mother said, scooping her grand-daughter on to her knee. 'There now, pet. Mammy didn't mean it. Your gran'll get you some pop in a minute, and a bikky.' The sobs subsided as Karen's grandmother set up a rocking motion, and Lilian felt herself relax. She liked coming home.

'Billy in tub-loading?' her mother said when Karen's thumb had found her mouth and her eyelids were drooping.

Lilian nodded. 'Yes. That's why I brought the bairn out, so's he could get his kip. Any news?'

Her mother's face brightened at the prospect of gossip. 'Mary Beale's fell again. This'll be her seventh if you count two misses.'

Lilian laughed. 'He must be on piecework.' She put her hand on her distended stomach and shifted in her chair. 'By God, I'm not going through it again, I can tell you. I've told Billy. "What if it's another girl?" he says. Well, he's always been mad keen for a boy, but I've told him, two's my maximum, take it or leave it.'

Her mother was struggling to her feet, hugging the now-sleeping child so as not to disturb her. Lilian tried to look helpful but left her mother to manage on her own as she laid the child on the settee and took the knitted blanket from the back to cover her.

'There,' she said, straightening up, 'that's her put down. I'll scald the tea.' She wore a flowered overall over her grey skirt and blouse, sleeveless and crossed over in the front to tie behind. She wore it winter and summer, except on Christmas Day and New Year's Eve, and when Lilian and Helen had clubbed together to buy her two with sleeves and a button front she had thanked them profusely and put them away in a drawer.

'Ta,' Lilian said, when the tea was brewed and poured. 'How's our Hel getting on? Lost her fancy boyfriend yet?'

Her tone was chatty but her mother's face hardened. 'Anything but, Lilian. He's as keen as mustard. Three nights this week *and* he brings her to the door.'

'Have you met him yet?' Lilian asked, knowing the answer but unable to resist a dig.

'Not yet, but there's plenty time. He's a nice young feller by all accounts. Keen on his job . . . Helen says he's well in with the top doctors.'

Lilian's tea had turned to gall in her mouth. 'I've never liked Scotchmen. Billy did National Service with some of them, and he says you can't trust them an inch.'

'I thought that was Welsh he didn't like?' her mother said accusingly, and Lilian felt her cheeks flush.

'Well, Scotch or Welsh, it's the same thing.' She began to heave herself out of her chair. 'Anyway, I've got better things to do than discuss our Helen's affairs. Can I leave the bairn here while I pop down the road? I know she's only a pitman's daughter, but she *is* your grandbairn.'

She was showing her jealousy and she knew it, but she couldn't seem to help it. She caught a glimpse of her ankles, puffy and discoloured, not the trim ankles they once had been. Life was a bugger and no mistake. And Helen had all the luck!

David was home by two-thirty and Diana was waiting in the drive. 'Hallo "mother",' he said, unabashed and she grinned in delight at his words.

'Hurry up, "father". I have a shopping list ten yards long and time is ticking away.'

'I'm so happy,' she thought as he settled her into the passenger seat. 'I'm just *so* happy.' As he drove towards the town centre she laid her hand on his thigh, feeling the muscles move as he clutched and declutched. Once he looked sideways at her and smiled. 'I like you,' she said, and he nodded, his face solemn.

'So you should,' he said.

'Why?' She loved these teasing games.

'Because I'm your husband. Your better half.'

'Huh!' she said and then, 'Well, almost better half.'

'Four-and-a-quarter eighths?' he suggested, knowing she would never quite work that out.

'Hush,' she said instead and patted his thigh in mock reproof.

They parked in the open car-park above the bus-centre and walked down into the market square, hand in hand. 'Where first?' David said, and she looked at her list.

'Dembry's . . . . and then Mother and Baby.'

He took her arm and they walked towards the new store. 'You're not going to go into those awful tent dresses and coats like marquees, are you?' he asked.

Diana nodded. 'As soon as possible.

He groaned. 'I was afraid of that.'

'Do you mind?' she asked, keeping up the joke.

'Horribly. I'll miss seeing the bits I like. I may get withdrawal symptoms and demand a striptease.'

She considered for a moment. 'That could be arranged. But I have to have maternity clothes . . . . it's either that or I wear a sandwich board with "Look! I am preggers" on it.'

David beamed. '*Just* a sandwich board?'

She withdrew her arm as they neared the swing doors. 'Sometimes I wonder about your mind, doctor. It's . . .'

'Earthy?' he suggested and held the door for her to pass through.

'Seriously, though, I would like to look at maternity wear,' she said. 'Just look, so I'll know what's available.'

They were threading their way through the shoppers and he took her elbow. 'My darling, you shall have a dozen voluminous dresses, one for each day of the week and five in the wash, and I will still find you desirable when you are so bulging you can't pass through a doorway. In fact I'll probably be more aroused than usual . . . . if such a thing is possible.'

'Will you hush?' she hissed as they came to the lift.

'Sorry,' he said cheerfully and stared straight ahead as they went upwards, knowing this would reduce her to further giggles.

As they got out at Babywear, he leaned to look at the ticket on a lacy matinée coat, and groaned. 'Ye Gods, if I'd known it was going to be this expensive . . . I'd have done it sooner!' He gave her a quick peck on the cheek and then composed himself for the long shopping session that lay ahead.

'He wants this baby,' Diana thought as the pile on the counter grew. 'He can hardly contain himself, he's so pleased. He wants it, and I am giving it to him because I love him.'

\* \* \*

Edward cleared the counter and tried to show polite interest. 'I thought I'd bring it in here and ask you,' the man said, stripping away the last of the brown paper. And then, apologetically, 'It's an ugly old thing but I thought, before I just chucked it out . . .'

Edward lifted the lid of the rather battered earthenware jar and inspected it closely. 'It's English, glazed in green and there's been gilt scrollwork here on the handles and round the lid.' He lifted the jar and looked at the base.

'There's some lettering,' the man said helpfully. 'My wife wondered if it was a burial urn . . . you know, for ashes. She won't give it house-room.'

Edward shook his head. 'It's not anything like that, it's a leech jar. You kept your leeches in here till you wanted to pop them somewhere for a feed.'

The man looked amazed. 'Leeches . . . well, I never! So it's not worth anything, then?'

He perked up when Edward made him an offer, and left the shop clutching four five-pound notes.

Mrs Stepinska caught the door as it closed and moved up to the counter. 'What a day!' she said, putting her beringed hands flat on the counter. 'Everyone want something for nothing.'

Edward smiled sympathetically and turned to put the new jar on a shelf.

'You never paid good money for that piece of junk?' Her eyes were round with astonishment. 'You come next door, my Stephan give you better kitsch from the dustbin. I've come to see when you go to Scotland. I got something for your mama, just a little something I know she like.'

Edward smiled at her. 'You're very kind.'

Her eyes were dark-ringed and bright, her face a map of all the adventures that had brought her from Cracow to a London flat above the leather workshop that was her husband's livelihood. Her hair was grey and thinning on top but there was lipstick on the wide mouth and a jaunty red scarf at the neck of her black jumper. 'Kind? What's kind. Your mama is my friend, my good friend. Twenty years I known her . . . so I can't send a gift for someone I known twenty years? So when you go to Scotland?'

Edward decided not to bother explaining about Berwick being in England – he had tried it before to no avail. To Mrs Stepinska 'north' meant only one thing. 'I'm going next weekend. By train so . . .'

She was ahead of his thinking. '. . . So it's got to be small parcel.' Her hands, when she held them up to illustrate, were heavy with rings, opals, aquamarines, broad gold bands inset with rubies and sapphires. Leather must pay, he thought.

'Impossible,' he said. 'But for you I'd take something . . .' He held his hands apart . . . 'this big.'

Mrs Stepinska turned at the door. 'Sylvia coming round tonight?'

Edward nodded. 'Probably.'

Her eyes twinkled with implication. 'Ah poor mama . . . she goes for little holiday, her boy gets up to tricks!'

He threw back his head and laughed. 'Mrs S., you're a wicked woman.'

She poked her head back through the door to reply. 'I hope so. When the wickedness is all used up. . . . *phht!*'

Edward was still laughing when he locked the door. It was five-thirty; there would be no customers now, not those who wanted to buy, anyway. Upstairs he switched on the immersion heater and filled the kettle before he settled by the phone. He called his mother every evening before her bedtime, but he would be too late home tonight. As he dialled Trunks he acknowledged the truth, that he didn't like talking to his mother with Sylvia at his shoulder. It was silly. The conversations were innocuous, but when he talked to his mother he liked to think the old intimacy still obtained.

'I'm sorry, your number is engaged.' The operator's voice was tinny in his ear and he put down the phone. He would try again later after his bath.

In the kitchen the kettle boiled over and he went through to make tea.


'Let's see what you've been buying, then?' Lilian struggled to force a smile and held out a hand. 'Come on, I'm not going to spoil it. I only want a look.'

As Helen held up the blue dress with its bow-trimmed neckline, Lilian's heart hardened. It wasn't fair! Even before the bairn she'd never had a waist like that – or the money to buy a dress that would show it off. 'Very nice,' she said at last. 'Mind, I've never gone much for blue. A bit wishy-washy . . . and it doesn't hold its colour in the tub.'

'You dry-clean this,' Helen said absently, busy unwrapping the chocolate bar she had bought for Karen.

'Dry-clean?' Lilian said. 'You're never going to get it cleaned every time . . . you must have money to burn.'

Billy was lolling back on the settee, a bottle of brown ale on the floor beside him, his eyes on the wrestling on television. It was his Saturday afternoon pleasure, freed from the pit, to sit in his stocking feet and watch soccer in winter and anything that came to hand in summer, a glass of beer close by and the prospect of a well-cooked tea before him.

Today his peace was to be rudely shattered. 'For God's sake, Billy, sit up straight! You're lying around there with your beer-belly showing, you'd think it was you nine months gone, not me. What'll our Helen think? I bet her fancy man doesn't slop around on his day off, dear me, no! Marriage? You can keep it as far as I'm concerned. I never get across these doors, and then you lie around the whole weekend like I was running a doss-house.'

Helen opened her mouth to defend her brother-in-law but Lilian was not to be halted. 'And you shut up, our kid. You know nowt, so say nowt. You get off with your fancy dress and get dolled up and go off gallivanting. I'll sit here like I sit every night. I'm just a bloody prisoner.'

Karen began to wail in sympathy as her mother's tears started. Billy had leaped from the settee and was patting Lilian's shoulder. 'Don't take on, pet. It won't be much longer and then you can go anywhere you like.'

Through her tears Lilian could see Helen standing irresolute. That had wiped the satisfaction off her face! Let her see what it was like once you got your man. Bloody purgatory, that's what it was.

'I'll put the kettle on, shall I?' Helen said, shoving the new dress back into its carrier bag.

Lilian nodded. 'I'm just being daft. I'd like a cup of tea.'
The sisters were not given to open affection but Helen
moved towards her now and patted her arm. 'I'll come
round tomorrow and do your Toni for you. You'll need a
perm for the hospital. And I'll bring me nail kit and give
you a manicure. You know you've got the best nails in the
family.'

It was true, Lilian thought, looking down at her swollen
fingers. Her nails were a nice oval. If she didn't have them
in water half the time, they'd be her best feature.

'There now,' Billy said relieved, turning back towards his
beloved telly. He was lowering himself into the settee
when his wife's voice rang out.

'Don't you dare sit down, Billy Fenwick. There's fish out
there wants frying, and you can do chips and open some
peas. Our Helen'll stay, so do plenty. And switch that
bugger off if you can't find a comedy or some music. And
don't think I'm spending every Saturday in once I've
dropped the bairn. You can make your mind up to that.'

When he got his deputy's tickets she was having a car,
supposing it took twenty years to pay it off.


The fish and peas were lying heavy on Helen's stomach
when she took her seat in the cinema next to Alistair.
'Chocs,' he whispered, sliding a small box on to her knee.
She smiled in the darkness and squeezed his hand to show
gratitude. The film was already beginning . . . Tom Courtenay looking very haggard and deprived. If he had someone to love him, he would be all right. She settled down in
her seat and slipped her hand through Alistair's arm as *The
Loneliness of the Long Distance Runner* unfolded.

She had expected a film about open spaces and mara-
thons, but this was a film about misery and she tried hard
to concentrate, wondering why people laughed sometimes
at so much unhappiness. 'Good, isn't it?' Alistair whispered once or twice, and she nodded vigorously and tried
to look intent on the screen.

In the interval he bought her icecream in a carton with a
tabbed lid, and when the lights went down he took the

empty carton from her and put it under the seat. That was one of the best things about him, the way he took care of everything so that you never needed to worry. He would always take care of her. And eventually he would get over his shyness and come to Sunday tea so that all the people she loved would know and like one another.

She was plotting the Sunday scenario when she felt his lips against her ear. 'Is it me, or is this a trifle boring?'

Helen felt her lips curve at the way he said 'boring', the sound going up at the end in the way she loved. Sometimes, with certain words she would get him to say them again just for her pleasure. Now she turned her face to his and whispered. 'It's all right, but we can go if you want?' She had been bored for the last hour but she could never have criticized his choice of film.

They slipped along the row, making their excuses, feeling a sudden freedom as they reached the gangway. The usherette's torch advanced towards them, flashing on the steps that led to the door.

'Not one of Richardson's best,' Alistair said, when they were out in the street, and, when she looked puzzled, 'The director.' He took her arm as they walked towards the carpark. 'Your place or mine?' he said, unlocking the car door.

'What do you mean?' she said.

He put his arms around her and nuzzled the top of her head with his chin until she winced a little. 'Why do you think I wanted to leave a good film?'

Helen shook her head, trying not to worry about the time. If they went back to his room it would be eleven o'clock before she got back to Belgate. At least eleven o'clock.

He was folding her into the car and closing the door, and she knew it was useless to argue. Besides, she wanted him now, wanted to be in his arms, in his bed, hear him saying, 'Helen, Helen. Oh God, Helen.' She lived it all in her head as he drove towards the Infirmary, and when they parked in the shadow of Pharmacy and began to tiptoe into the doctors' residence it was she who led the way.

\* \* \*

Edward and Sylvia were in total agreement about *Phaedra*. 'Pretentious rubbish,' Sylvia said as they walked back to the car.

'A waste of Mercouri,' Edward agreed. 'Do you want to eat first?'

The light from the car-park was shining on her face and he saw she was laughing at him. 'First? What comes after?'

'I didn't mean that,' he said, getting into his seat and leaning to open the passenger door. He hoped she would not want to eat out. He had not been able to get through to Berwick before he left and if he didn't ring, his mother might worry. As he let out the clutch he acknowledged the truth behind his need to telephone, the superstitious feeling that the one day he didn't make contact might be her last.

To his relief Sylvia suggested sandwiches and wine at the flat, and even offered to prepare them.

'I've just got to make a call,' he said and she nodded as though it was the most natural thing in the world.

By the time he got through to Berwick she was moving between kitchen and living-room, putting out coasters and glasses, and then a plate of sandwiches. He tried to keep the conversation with his mother to a minimum, but she sounded breathless tonight and it worried him. 'OK, darling, I'll talk to you tomorrow. No, I'm fine. I'm sorry you were worried but I was at the cinema. Yes, with Sylvia.' He looked up at Sylvia and smiled while at the other end his mother expressed delight at the news that he and Sylvia were still a pair. 'Good-night then. Yes, I love you too.'

He was prepared to be defiant but Sylvia's face was impassive as she handed him a sandwich. 'This pâté's wonderful,' she said, biting again.

'It's Berman's,' he said. 'You know, round the corner in the High Street.'

They ate until the last crumb was gone and then sat on drinking wine, knowing what was coming, both wanting it but too certain to rush. 'Well,' Sylvia said at last, rising to her feet and holding out her hand. 'Either you take me to bed or I call a cab.'

He allowed her to tug him to his feet and moved to hold

her by her shoulders. 'If you're tired, you'd better go home like a good little girl.'

She stretched to his cheek, putting out her tongue to touch his skin lightly and then withdraw. 'I'm never too tired for you. You know that.'

He put on a lamp in the bedroom and drew the curtains, half-expecting to see Mrs Stepinska's curious face pressed against the glass. When he turned, Sylvia was already naked, her red hair tucked behind her ears, her arms by her sides waiting for him. She was proud of her body and he knew she was more experienced than he. He was still a little embarrassed at undressing in front of her. It was better when he too was naked, and could move towards her on equal terms.

# 3

## July 1962

Wednesday was always a busy day in ENT. Two new-patient lists, the Registrar's review clinic and a minor ops list in the little theatre. Helen was glad to be run off her feet, sent scurrying hither and thither by just about anyone with a claim to seniority. Keeping busy helped to dull the anxiety that nibbled and wrenched at the corners of her mind.

She was on her way back from X-ray with dripping wet-plates when she saw Alistair coming towards her. 'Can't stop,' he said, reaching to squeeze her free hand. 'Two Colles fractures in Out-patients. I'm going to anaesthetize for Jack. I'll pick you up at eight – OK?'

She nodded, trying to look cheerful. 'That's fine.'

He raised one eyebrow. 'Somebody been getting at you?'

She shook her head. 'No, I'm fine. I've got to get these back to Sister. See you at eight.'

As she hurried on her way, holding the X-ray plates at arm's length to stop them dripping against her legs, she felt a little cheered by the encounter. Once she told him, it would be all right. He would take care of everything. Hadn't he always promised her that? *'I'll take care of you'* – he'd said those very words, and nothing Lilian could say would change it.

She had thought of Lilian yesterday. It must be terrifying to be trapped inside your own body, feeling it thicken and distort, feeling life inside you, separate life that was ready to scream for acknowledgement.

'Miss Clark . . . when you're quite ready?' Sister Baker's eyes were hostile. She didn't like clerical staff at the best of times, let alone when they went into brown studies.

'Sorry, Sister.' Helen handed over the plates and would have gone to wash the fixative from her fingers but Baker had other ideas.

'Get into the clinic now, and do what you can to hurry Mr Packer up. My nurses go off at one. We must be finished by then. I'll come and tell him that myself when I've dealt with these. You do your best in the meantime.'

A child was crying as Helen eased through the swing doors. She was sitting on her mother's knee, watching as the consultant, auroscope in hand, peered into her brother's ears. The doctor turned to the mother and asked a question but the woman shook her head, uncomprehending. Helen saw the consultant's face darken: he didn't like to be held up. She moved forward and held out her arms to the crying child. It clung briefly to its mother and then allowed Helen to detach it and walk away, leaving the mother free to attend to the doctor's questions.

'There now,' Helen said, shifting the child to her other arm. The little girl's bottom was warm and damp, a web of mucus obscured her left nostril, and her blonde hair was damp and wispy and clung to her forehead. 'There now,' Helen said again, reaching for a tissue. 'We'll wipe your nose and then your mammy'll be ready to take you home.'

The child's eyes were large and blue and watery, and stared into Helen's eyes, unblinking. 'What's your name, pet?'

There was no answer, only the intense blue gaze. Helen

tried again. 'Tell me your name . . . shall I guess? It's Elizabeth?' Half their young patients seemed to be called Elizabeth. The blonde head moved slowly from side to side. 'Well, is it Jennifer?' Another shake of the head.

The child was heavy in her arms, but Helen was elated by her success in stemming its tears. She wasn't good with babies . . . not usually. When she had her own it would be different. Except that there were some people who didn't love children, couldn't love them. She was never really sure that Lilian loved Karen, threatening to thrash her half the time.

The blue eyes were on her, a hint of impatience in them. It was time for another name. 'I know what you're called. You're called Kim!' The mother was moving away from the desk, holding the little boy by the hand, and the consultant was writing on the case notes. Helen should be doing that for him. She thrust the child into its mother's arm and hurried to take her place, uncapping her pen as she went.

She was taking down the notes when she remembered. It was funny how fear could disappear, only to return and terrorize you once more.


Lilian had pegged out the washing and laid Karen's nappies along the fireguard. Now she scalded tea in a mug and added milk. She would have a few minutes in the chair while Karen was playing in the garden.

Through the window she could see her daughter's head bent over the peg-box. She would probably snap the plastic ones, but a few minutes' peace would be worth it. Lilian's back ached, her legs felt like tree-trunks and her thighs were sore where they had rubbed against one another in the heat. July was a bad time to have a bairn, a weary, sweating month at the best of times without being blown up to twice your size. But at least the bairn would have a month or two of sunshine before the winter set in.

The baby would be five months old at Christmas, too young to know what was going on. She would get it a stocking just the same. The catalogue was already marked with strips of paper, so that Karen would not go short on Christmas Day. Lilian was still paying off last year, but that was the way of it. And she was going to get Billy a good coat, grey tweed with a tartan lining. He would say she shouldn't have done it but he would be pleased just the same.

She was lowering herself into the fireside chair when she heard him on the stairs. He had come in in the early hours and shouldn't have been up for hours. 'I couldn't sleep,' he said, padding in stockinged feet to the opposite chair. He yawned and rubbed his eyes as he fumbled for the sandshoes that served as slippers. 'I hate tub-loading,' he said and then, eyeing her mug, 'Any tea going?'

Her feet were aching and her knicker elastic had moved up over her bump so that the gusset cut into her groin, sawing when she moved until it felt as though blood should flow. She was nine months pregnant, and uncomfortable, and it was all his fault.

'You're not expecting me to run after you, I hope? That's all I'm short of, you coming down wanting to be waited on hand and foot. And that bairn out there crying on all the morning . . .' He was getting to his feet, vowing willingness to make his own tea and serve it to her as well, but she was launched now and couldn't have stopped herself even if she had wished.

'That's men . . . get you in the club because they can't be bothered to wear something, and when they've put you on your back they complain. I'm worn out, Billy Fenwick. I can't wait on you, I can barely look after meself, let alone the bairn. By God, if I had my time again I'd be like our Helen. She'll keep her hand on her halfpenny till she's got a ring. That's what I should've done. You're not appreciated when you're easy got, that was my mistake.'

She kept on crying and berating him until he had brewed the tea and brought it to her in a cup with two digestive biscuits in the saucer. 'There now, there's a good lass,' he said patting her awkwardly on the shoulder. 'I don't know why you take on . . . I think the world of you and the bairn.'

Lilian had been about to cheer up, but somehow being

thought the world of was not enough. She bit into her digestive and proceeded to give him a piece of her mind.

The shop had been quiet for a Friday. Only one sale, a Victorian vinaigrette, pretty enough but unmarked, which he had let go for £30. He had been offered a ghastly Art Deco electric lamp which he had politely declined, and he had bought in a French balloon clock with mother-of-pearl inlay and one of its brass feet broken off. Edward put it on a shelf behind his desk for repair and walked to the shop door. The Mews was quiet, one or two people going about their business, noise coming faintly from the joinery shop at the corner of Gossett's Yard and from the High Street, visible at the top end of the Mews. He lived in an oasis and he liked it. How long could it go on, though? No. 2 was now a smart flat with tenants who kept themselves to themselves. Who would be next to move?

Not the Stepinskis. They could use the money a sale would bring but they would not easily surrender. Miss Cartwright was old; she had retired from the Civil Service when he was still a child, so she must be well into her eighties. The ground-floor workshop where her father had plied his trade as cabinet-maker was rented to a joiner. What would she make from it? A few pounds a week, no more. If she sold she could buy a comfortable semi with a garden, in Perivale or Acton. She seldom came down from her eyrie now. He sometimes saw her on her minute balcony but he had not seen her in the street for a long time. He looked at faded brick, at single doors battered by usage, at double doors sagging on their massive hinges. He had thought the Mews would go on forever, but it was changing in spite of him. Once it had been a place that clattered with horses' hoofs; now the people who had inhabited it in his childhood were going one by one.

The thought depressed him and he turned back into the shop, looking at his watch as he went. In a few hours he would be on the train north. The phone rang and he picked it up. It was Sylvia, who seemed surprised to hear he was going north, although he had been telling her all week.

The doorbell jangled and Mrs Stepinska came in with the long-promised parcel. He smiled and waved her forward and then tried to coax Sylvia back into a good mood.

Helen got off the bus with a girl she had been at school with, and they made desultory conversation as they walked. The old intimacy had withered. The girl talked of her job in Woolworths and asked Helen about the Infirmary, but they were both relieved when the time came to part. In a way, the meeting pleased Helen. At the beginning, when she had discovered Alistair loved her, she had wondered how she would ever make the break from Belgate, from family and friends and everything familiar. Now she realized that you grew up and away from childhood. When the time came for her to go to Scotland with Alistair, she would be ready.

Her mother had her tea keeping warm between plates on the range. It was mince with batter pudding and cabbage and potatoes, but Helen was not in the mood to eat.

'Our Lilian's in a bad way,' her mother said gloomily, sitting opposite to check on every bite her younger daughter took. 'The bairn's dropped, so it won't be long, thank God. She cannat seem to pull herself together. The leastest littlest thing, and she's blethering.'

'Well, it'll soon be over,' Helen said, trying to sound concerned. The mince was proving difficult to swallow and all she wanted to do was lie down for a bit. She put her knife and fork down at last and pushed away the plate. 'That's about all I can manage.'

From the fireside her father's collie rose at the prospect of a feed.

'You're not poorly, are you?' her mother said, peering into her face.

'No, I'm fine, mam, just not hungry. I think I'll lie down for a bit.'

It was not enough to stem the flow of motherly solicitude. 'I thought you looked peaky when you came in. I don't know . . . our Lilian held like she is and now you sickening for something. I wish we could be like some families, never ail a thing. There's your father with dust, only they won't admit it in case it means compensation, and you two girls sick at the drop of a hat. It doesn't come from my side . . .'

As Helen made her escape she heard the remains of her tea being scraped into the dog's bowl, and then the snuffling satisfaction of a dog well fed. Dogs were lucky, they had no worries. In the mirror her face looked gaunt and hollow-eyed. Was that what being 'peaky' meant?

She thought of the trouble there would be when it all came out and panic engulfed her, not ceasing until she thought about Alistair and how he would make everything come right. It would be for the best in the end. She stood up and stripped off her work clothes, laying them neatly over a chair for the morning, then she slipped underneath the eiderdown and closed her eyes.

She had a favourite daydream, guaranteed to bring tranquillity, and she employed it now. Once, when she was a child, her father had taken her to a hill near Belgate. It had been a summer day but there was a wind on the hill, sighing and moaning through the long grass, whipping her hair cruelly around nose and eyes. Her father had stood to throw sticks for his dog, but she had lain down on the grass, letting the fronds touch her face, seeing here a scurrying beetle, there a tiny flower, blue and perfect, growing close to the earth. There had been a singing in her ears and a sense of the ground pulsing with life. She had put out a hand to the moist soil and acknowledged its presence.

Now, as her mother clattered below in the kitchen and fears nibbled at the corners of her mind, she summoned up the memory of the hillside to lull her into sleep.


Sylvia went with Edward in the cab to King's Cross. 'I might as well. I'll get the tube from there.' He offered to pay for a cab for her, but she was not in the mood to accept peace-offerings. It irritated him that she didn't understand his need to go north. He owed his mother a lot, a hell of a lot. And besides, he liked her.

She would be in bed when he got to Berwick but she would be wide awake, longing to hear news of the shop and the Mews. He would make her laugh about the Stepinskis and the con-man who had tried to outwit Mr Pollock and received a boxed ear for his pains. She would laugh until tears of mirth ran down her cheeks, and he would wipe them away and then kiss her good-night.

'Edward! Have you gone to sleep? This is the third time I've asked if you want a magazine.' Sylvia was glaring at him and he hurried to collect his thoughts.

'No thanks, I've got the new Iris Murdoch in my case, and I'll probably just watch the countryside until it gets dark. You see all sorts in the fields, pheasants, rabbits, even deer.'

She leaned to kiss him. 'You're quite a man, my darling. Putting a good face on what most other people would consider an intolerable situation. Still, it won't go on forever.' She saw she had made a mistake and hurried to repair it. 'Well, she might come back . . . you've said yourself she's looking well.'

He kissed her goodbye at the platform gate and turned at the carriage door to wave. She made a nice picture, tall and slender, blazing hair above a cream linen suit. When he took her out he knew other men envied him. He ought to feel more upset about leaving her behind. He could have taken her to Berwick: Dorothy had room, and his mother would have been pleased. Still, there was plenty of time for that.

He opened his book, *An Unofficial Rose*, but it was difficult to concentrate and he laid it on the seat beside him as he watched the London suburbs give way to open spaces.


Diana and Anne had talked about David and Howard as boys, about their husband's respective professions, touched briefly on Cuba, and the coming baby, and then had returned to the subject of the Whittington family. Diana was longing to ask what Anne thought of Ma and Pa

Whittington, but something held her back. 'I'm afraid of her,' Diana thought as she waved to Anne's departing car; then she chided herself for her foolishness as she cleared the tea-cups.

'Nice tea-party?' David said, coming up behind her in the kitchen and putting his arms around her.

She leaned back against him, her wet hands held away from his jacket sleeves. 'Hallo, you. Yes, we had a nice girls-together tea-party. I used the china we got from Aunt May and cut very thin sandwiches. I think she was impressed.'

He didn't answer and she turned in his arms. 'Say I'm a clever girl, then,' she said.

He kissed her firmly. 'You're a clever girl,' he said. 'In fact I think you deserve a large G. and T. Well, a large tonic with a dash of gin, as befits your interesting condition. I, being a worker and, as far as I know, unpregnant, will have a large gin with a dash of tonic. I'll put lemon and ice in yours to make up.'

She finished her preparations for dinner and joined him on the small verandah at the back of the house. The garden sloped away towards the beck that marked their western boundary, and there was a swallow skimming the water. 'It's beautiful,' she said.

He had settled himself on the step, his back against her knee. 'What's beautiful?'

She indicated the garden with its mature trees and the beck, shining now in the afternoon sun. 'All of it. It's a perfect garden for children. Room for a swing and a paddling pool, and lots of places to hide.'

'That's the essential,' he said, nodding solemnly. 'I used to hide for hours while Ma went frantic. She brought dad home from the office once . . . I suffered for that.'

'You must've been a little monster,' she said indulgently, ruffling his hair. 'I wish I'd known you sooner. Would you have loved me if you'd known me then?'

He shook his head. 'Probably not, I hated girls in those days. I've changed.'

She laughed but there was a question hovering on her lips. 'Did Howard ever . . . well, play up? It's hard to imagine him as a little boy. He's . . . he's so . . .' She was seeking for an acceptable word but David was ahead of her.

'He's henpecked. He was a normal bloke before he married. Got up to the usual things . . . nothing terrible. He used to come up to Edinburgh in term-time sometimes and join in whatever we had going on up there. It was different for him, taking articles. I felt sorry for him.'

She waited while he refilled his glass, holding her hand over his own. 'No thanks. I don't want to give birth to a dipsomaniac.' His smile of approval was more than worth the deprivation. 'So Anne has changed him?'

He didn't give her a direct answer. 'My sister-in-law is a cold fish,' he said; and then two birds swooped across the lawn quarrelling fiercely, and when the fisticuffs were over it was time for her to go indoors and tend to the meal. She had put on the potatoes and was layering cabbage and onion in a heavy pan when the discomfort began again, low down in her abdomen. She had often wondered why people complained about wind, but now that she had experienced it for a day or two herself, she was less inclined to scoff.

She took a magnesia tablet and pressed her warm hand against her stomach as she stirred the gravy, thinking of David hiding from his mother, just as her son would hide from her one day – and would then run towards her to be embraced.

Lilian heard Billy moving about upstairs and looked at the clock. He was getting ready to go out for a drink, the second night this week. And she was going to be left behind like a great big dummy. A great big clumsy dummy who couldn't even keep her man at home when she was nine months gone.

'Going out?' she said when Billy came downstairs.

'I was thinking about it,' he said uncertainly, anticipation giving way to nervousness as he looked at his wife.

'You can go out as far as I'm concerned,' she said, her tones silken. 'Go out by all means . . . but take your bloody 'jamas with you 'cos you won't get back in here. Not tonight or any other night. My God, if I'd known I'd come to this, I'd have thought twice . . .'

She was into her stride now and Billy started to shrug out of his jacket. 'Don't get yersel' worked up, Lilian, you'll do yourself an injury. I'll stop in. I don't mind. I was only going down the club to pay me subs.'

'I wish I was dead,' Lilian said, subsiding into her chair. 'I might as well be dead. I never get across the doors, I've got nowt, I do nowt . . . I can't stand the sight of meself. Get out, go down the club, find yourself a fancy woman. I'm no good to you . . . you've had the best of me.'

He got down on his knees beside her, his big hands with the blue flecks of a collier clasping the arms of her chair. 'Listen, pet. I'll put the kettle on and make you a nice cup of tea, then I'll pop down the chippy and get you a nice lot. Now, what would you like, cod or haddock? And I'll get you something at the off-licence . . . anything you like, even spirits. I love you, Lily. I cannat bear to see you like this. Get this lot over . . .' He moved his hand lightly over her swollen belly . . . 'get rid of this lot, get a nice little bairn in the pram, and I'll book us up for Butlins. I've got plenty rest days. I'll see if I can take them together, and we'll have a week away? Now, how about that?'

She had cheered up and was waving him off to the chip shop when she felt a wetness between her legs, a wetness that grew and grew until she realized something important was happening.

'Billy!'

He turned in the doorway, his mouth open with shock at the anguish in her voice.

'Fetch me mam, Billy. Get her quickly. I think me waters have broken.'


Helen waited until they had left the pub and were driving towards Belgate. 'Could we pull up somewhere?'

He chortled at her words, calling her a 'bold woman' and steering for a lay-by.

'Now,' he said, when he'd switched off the engine and put his arm around her. 'Now, give me a kiss.'

She had never felt less like kissing anyone. 'No, Alistair, not now. I want to talk to you.'

His arm slackened against her shoulder and he withdrew slightly. 'OK, talk away.'

She had interlaced the fingers of her hands until they hurt and still she couldn't find the words. 'I'm probably being silly,' she said at last, her doubts increasing even as she talked. 'In fact, I'm sure I am . . . it's just that . . .'

He had taken his arm from her shoulder now, and when he spoke his voice was sombre. 'Oh God, you're not pregnant.'

She couldn't bear the cold disapproval in his voice and she hurried to reassure him. 'No . . . I'm sure I'm not. I mean, you said I couldn't be. It's just that . . .' She was embarrassed about detail, until she remembered that he was a doctor and knew more about a woman's body than she did. 'Well, I haven't had my period. It's a week late, and I'm always regular. And I've felt a bit sick the last few mornings . . . only I think that's probably just imagination.'

She wanted him to reassure her, to take her in his arms and tell her that, whatever happened, he would take care of her, but no reassurance was forthcoming.

'Oh God, what a mess. It can't be true, I've been too careful.' There was an angry note in his voice, as though, if this terrible thing were true, it could be nothing to do with him.

Helen felt a little flicker of something inside her, anger or fear, she couldn't be sure which.

'It would be the bitter end,' Alistair was saying, staring straight ahead of him. 'My family would be finished with me. You can't imagine what they're like. Oh God, I hope you're wrong.'

She put out a hand to his arm but there was no response, only a slight stiffening of the muscles beneath his sleeve as though he was suddenly repelled by her touch.

'You'd better take me home,' she said quietly. 'Maybe it'll be all right tomorrow.'

He nodded and started up the engine, but when he

spoke his voice was distant, as though he were talking to a stranger. 'Yes, it's probably a false alarm.' He didn't sound like a doctor, he sounded like a frightened bairn, and she felt a sudden cold dislike of him. However this turned out, things would never be the same again.

Tears pricked Helen's eyes as she walked up the yard, but there could be no hesitation. If she stayed there in the darkness, terror would overcome her. She pushed open the back door and went through the darkened scullery. As she entered the kitchen her mother's finger flew to her lips for silence, and then gestured to the settee. Karen was asleep there, thumb in mouth, a grey blanket tucked around her.

'Our Lilian's time's come,' her mother said softly. 'Her waters broke tonight and she's gone into the Maternity. Billy's gone with her. By, he's beside himself.'

Helen hung up her coat and turned back into the room.

'There's tea in the pot if you want it,' her mother said. 'And I've boiled a bit ham for tomorrow if you want a sandwich.'

Helen sat gingerly on the edge of the settee so as not to disturb her niece. 'Is Lilian all right?'

Her father looked at her over the top of his paper. 'As all right as she ever is,' he said drily and went back to reading.

'There's no call for that, Joe.' Her mother's low voice was tart. 'Not with a girl in a hospital bed. She's highly strung, our Lilian, always has been. And we know which side she gets that from. She's all right though, or will be when she gets it over and done with.' She grinned. 'It's Billy that's suffering. "Never again," he kept saying, "never again." They'll have *him* in a bed if they're not careful. I'll say this for him, he got our Lilian into trouble but he did the decent thing by her, and he's a good provider. There's many a one goes wrong but they don't all try to make the best of it.'

Had her mother's words been meant as a warning, or was it just her guilty conscience that told her so? Long after Helen had undressed and climbed into bed, the words went round and round in her head. She cried into her pillow, terrified that the door might creak, and a voice say, 'That's not you crying, our Hel?'

When the crying ceased she felt cold terror rise up in her. They would look at her, all of them, and know what she had done. The whole hospital would know. Not that she was pregnant: she could bear them to know that. But to be pregnant and publicly abandoned, that was not to be borne.

She slept at last, but woke to a grey room and went on lying there until daylight filled the room, bringing with it no relief.

# 4

Diana waited until the first daylight brought shape into the room and then she wakened David. 'Darling . . . .' He was drawing himself up in the bed and she felt better just knowing he was awake and beside her.

'Yes, what's the matter?' His voice was fuzzy with sleep until he heard what she was saying.

'I had a pain . . . well, more of a feeling, really. A discomfort low down. I thought it was indigestion . . .'

She had thought he might examine her, probe gently at her tummy and tell her all was well. Instead he swung out of bed and reached for his dressing gown.

'Has it worsened? Show me where.' His face was intent as she pushed down the bedclothes and gestured to where the pain was growing, swelling inside her like some obscene fungus. For the first time real fear reached her. She couldn't be losing this baby – not now, when she knew it so well.

But David was already dialling, speaking rapidly, getting an overnight bag from the high cupboard, scooping her things from the dressing-table. 'Chris is going over to Maternity now. He says it's probably nothing, but it's not worth the risk. He'll meet us there.'

'Is it going to be all right?' It didn't sound like her own voice.

'Shush,' he said, picking up her dressing-gown and threading her arms into the sleeves. 'Of course, it's going to be all right. All pregnancies have a hiccup somewhere. By tomorrow you'll be back on course.'

She allowed him to fasten her belt and do up the buttons before she spoke. 'Don't tell . . .' She almost said, 'Don't tell Anne,' but changed it to 'Don't tell anyone yet,' and was relieved when he nodded.

She was sure that when she stood up something dreadful would happen, that it would all fall out of her in a torrent of blood, but there was nothing except the pain holding her groin in a vice.

'Can you manage?' David's arms were around her, half-guiding, half-carrying her to the landing. She looked down into the hall, at the asters on the hall table that she had arranged a few hours ago, humming as she pushed home the stalks. If she died they would live on for a few days until they dropped, petal by petal, and someone cleared them away.

Her teeth were chattering, which was funny because it was almost too hot to breathe. 'I don't want to let you down, David. I know how much you want a baby.'

He was taking her sheepskin coat from the cloakroom and wrapping her round. A rhyme sprang up in her head: *'Bye baby bunting, Daddy's gone a-hunting, Gone to get a rabbit skin to wrap the baby bunting in.'*

In the passenger seat she rocked backwards and forwards, the rhyme going round and round in her head. *'Daddy's gone a-hunting.'* Yesterday he had put shelves up in the nursery, white shelves to hold toys for his son or daughter. If she lost this baby, how would she face him?

'I'm going to be with you, darling. All the time. It's going to be all right, you'll see.'

And then Christopher Milhill was coming towards her, smiling a cautious smile, putting a warm hand on her own cold one; and the smell, the terrible antiseptic smell of hospital, was engulfing her.

\* · \*

Lilian had wept and begged for a sterilization but it had been denied her. 'Now don't be a silly girl,' the midwife had said, putting Lilian's legs into stirrups. 'You'll feel differently when you've got this over. All mothers say they want no more, it's only natural. When you see the baby, all nice and clean in your arms, you'll feel differently.'

From her position on her back, legs in air, modesty stripped from her, Lilian wished a gory death upon the midwife, but she wished it under her breath. It didn't do to offend the buggers when they had you down. All the same, someone was going to suffer for this.

'The sod,' she shouted out as another pain took her. 'Oh, the sods. Jesus Christ . . .' When pain took away her breath she cursed quietly and efficiently in her mind. She would kill them all, the staff, the baby, the other mothers peering round-eyed round the door of the labour room, the man who had queue-jumped in the Co-op yesterday . . . she had him marked . . . but most of all, Billy. 'I'll kill you, Billy Fenwick, *I'll . . . kill . . . you*!'

There was a final, tearing pang, and then a cry and a squirming red thing held aloft for her to see. 'It's a girl! Are you pleased?'

Lilian sucked in the mucus that had travelled from nose to mouth. 'I'm bloody pleased. If it'd been a boy I'd've cut its balls off!'

They all laughed at her, but she had sensed their disapproval as they tidied her after the birth. She had never liked nurses, thinking they were God Almighty in a uniform, and yet no better than her. Damn them all! She would be out of here as soon as she could stand. She moaned as they lifted her on to a trolley and couldn't resist a protest. 'Can't you be careful. That hurt!'

'You want to count your blessings,' the midwife said as they wheeled her back to the ward. 'A healthy baby and no stitches. You're lucky. We've got a lovely woman in the side ward . . . a doctor's wife . . . lost her baby at five months. A perfect little boy, he was, and not a word out of her. Now she *has* got something to moan about.'

They were passing the door of the side-ward now and Lilian turned her head for a view. Nothing was visible but a screen and a nurse's blue dress showing through the cracks. She wouldn't want for attention if she was a doctor's wife! Inside Lilian envy fought with compassion – after all, there was nothing to compare with a bairn of your own. Above the honeycomb shawl her baby's hair showed black and shining. She had a chance to be a bonny bairn. She had nice features, and Billy was a good-looking lad when he took pains with himself . . . the sod!

The news that Lilian had given birth to another girl came with the milk. Billy carried in two pints of silver top and plonked it on the kichen table. 'It's a girl, seven pounds eleven ounces. Spitting image of her mam. Lilian's fine. She says will somebody bring her some paper hankies and a box of Jaffa cakes. You can visit tomorrow . . . husbands and mothers only, the first day.' His face was grey with fatigue but his smile threatened to split his face.

'Congratulations!' Helen said, crossing to kiss his cheek. She liked her brother-in-law. Anyone who could live with Lilian and not commit murder had to be a saint of sorts. 'I'll make you some tea,' she said as he lowered himself into a chair at the table.

There was the sound of footsteps on the stairs that led straight into the living-room and then her mother appeared, clutching her dressing-gown to her and treading down the heels of her slippers in her haste.

'Is that Billy? Oh my God, is she all right?' One look at her son-in-law's face calmed her fears.

'It's a girl, a little beauty. Seven pounds thirteen.'

Helen turned away to hide her smile. The baby had gained two ounces in as many minutes. It was doing well!

When she had brewed the tea she made her excuses and went back upstairs. It was lucky that Billy had turned up when he did, otherwise her mother would have wanted to know why she was prowling the house at six-thirty when she usually had to be prised from her bed on Saturday mornings. She put her mug of tea on the bedside table and climbed under the blankets.

Her mother's questioning could be relentless. She had experienced it before, questions that were repeated over and over again until you screamed out the truth. She could keep the fact of her pregnancy from her mother for a day or two, a week at most. Then it would all come out.

A laugh bubbled up in her chest, a crazy kind of laugh erupting in the quiet room. Oh God, she was frightened. They would kill her. She would be thrown out and everyone would know. Every eye would be on her, knowing she had done something dirty and that Alistair now didn't want her. And mam would remind her over and over again how she had been warned . . . She could never go back to work, and once she left this room she could never come back to it. She thought of her schoolfriends, and how they would gloat over this – sympathy to her face, and then legging it away to pass on the news. 'Heard about Helen Clark? Fell wrong to one of the doctors. Serves her right, she always fancied herself.'

A picture of Alistair came into her mind, Alistair on the day the pregnancy test had been confirmed, his eyes like stones. She had never, she realized now, really believed he loved her; she had always known it would end in tears. But not in disgrace: she had never expected that.

She cried then, putting her face against the tickly eiderdown, crying tears of fear and humiliation that turned into the blessed relief of anger. He would have to help her get away from Belgate, to London or somewhere – anywhere. And when he had helped her, she would tell him to go away. Pour scorn on him, lacerate him with words. Except that nothing she could do would hurt him. She had heard in his voice last night, in the car, the hostile note that said, 'You are nothing to do with me.'

She felt a sudden wetness, and hope reared up in her. It was her period! It had all been for nothing, the fear and the worry. Why hadn't she trusted Alistair? He had promised to take care of her, and he had.

She could hardly compose her face for the trip through the kitchen to the lavatory in the yard. She felt lighthearted with relief, until she had negotiated the yard, snecked the lavatory door and discovered that nothing at all had changed.

There were flowers everywhere by lunch time. Red roses from David with a card that said simply, '*I love you*', yellow roses and freesias from Howard and Anne, '*We are thinking of you*', and tiger lilies and yellow daisies from David's staff at the surgery.

Diana lay on the bed, watching the ceiling, dry-eyed as she had been since it had happened. It had simply slithered away, all her hopes and dreams for the future, flowing out of her as though it had never belonged. There had been no pain, no sense of the baby's detachment. She had held the vision of her son in her head; it was there now, behind her eyes, it would always be there.'

'OK?' David was advancing into the room, his second visit of the morning. 'Love me?' His face was anxious and she tried to smile.

'I'm fine.' Her voice broke then. 'I'm so sorry, David. I'm so very, very sorry.'

He was cradling her in his arms, lifting her from the pillow to rock her back and forwards. 'Don't say that, you idiot. What have you got to be sorry about? It happened, darling, that's all. I've talked to Chris Milhill, and he says we can try again as soon as we like.'

Diana resented that . . . the suggestion that her baby could be tidied away, and replaced by another, more successful pregnancy.

'What's the matter, darling? You don't think this is the end, do you? There's nothing wrong, no earthly reason why you shouldn't have a perfectly healthy baby. Chris says the foetus was perfect . . . it was just one of those things.'

He was doing it again, dismissing his son as though he had never counted at all.

'And we could adopt, if it came to that. I like kids, you know that; all kids, any kids.'

Diana felt a terrible anger, but her voice, when it came out of her, was perfectly calm. 'I could never adopt, David.

I'm sorry but it wouldn't be an option I could consider. I know it works for some people, but it would never work for me. I couldn't love another woman's child.'

He was taken aback and she was glad. She listened as he stammered out apologies for being ham-fisted. 'I'm sorry, darling. I should let you rest . . .' She let her eyelids droop to show he had got it right, and smiled weakly as he tiptoed out of the room.

Helen wandered from shop to shop, sometimes fingering possible purchases, buying nothing. Her feelings oscillated between hope and despair. Any moment her period would start, it would all turn out to be a bad dream, just a warning to take more care in future. At other times she knew, with a sickly certainty, that it had happened – the unbelievable, unbearable thing that would ruin her life. Once she went into Dembry's cloakroom and tried to be sick into the lavatory bowl – but her empty stomach yielded nothing but acid which burned her throat and made her feel worse than ever.

At twelve o'clock she decided to pocket her pride and ring Alistair. He had been shocked at the definite news last night, scared into behaving in a way that was foreign to his nature, that was all. Now that he'd had time to think he would be his old, calm commonsensical self.

She put coins into the meter and dialled the hospital number. 'Dr McKinnie, please.'

The telephonist's voice was guarded. 'Who's calling?'

Helen felt an agitation in her throat. 'It's a personal call.' There was a long pause and she felt forced to add, 'I'm a friend of his.' If the telephonist recognized her voice it would be all round the hospital that she was chasing him. And when the dreadful truth leaked out, that would make it all the worse for her. She was not going to give her name, not for anything.

'Trying to trace him. Hold on please.'

Helen held the receiver with one hand while she scrabbled for change with the other. The weight of it was starting to make her arm ache, and she had fed in two shillings more when the voice returned.

'Dr McKinnie is in Casualty Theatre and can't be disturbed. Can I take a message?'

'No, thank you,' Helen said, a huge relief overtaking her that she did not have to speak to him after all. She pushed open the door of the box and emerged into the sunshine. She was going to cry here in the street and if she did that she might as well write the word 'adulteress' across her forehead.

Ahead of her the garden of St Mary Magdalene's was green, an oasis in the town centre. She walked between laurels and tiny stunted conifers into the cool darkness of the church.

She had never been in a Catholic church before, and for a few moments curiosity was uppermost. It was all there, the things she had only heard about before. Crosses and statues, hundreds of tiny candles guttering at feet of stone, a curtained box for confessing sins, a priest moving about the altar as if unaware of bent heads here and there in pews.

She prayed, formally at first and then with passion. 'Our Father which art in Heaven, hallowed be thy name, thy kingdom come, thy will be done . . . Please God let it be all right. Let it, let it be all right. Let Alistair love me, let me cover it up so no one will know. Let me not get wrong . . . I'm frightened God, I'm frightened.'

When she raised her head, it seemed as though the priest's eyes were on her, forcing her to drop her gaze, but when she looked again he had vanished. She forced herself to say the Lord's Prayer right through, and then made her way out into the crowds that were still thronging the Saturday streets.

She was about to turn into C. & A. for want of something better to do when she heard the voice behind her.

'Helen! Wait on!' It was Dorothy McBain, who had been a big girl when she had been a junior, and was now a staff nurse in Orthopaedic Out-patients. 'I was coming round yours when I got home.' McBain's eyes were bright with superior knowledge. 'I've got a message from Alistair.'

Helen noticed the use of the Christian name and didn't like it. 'He says he's got an hour off tonight. He'll meet you in Luigi's at seven.'

To Helen, McBain's smile was malicious. 'Thanks,' she said. 'Seven o'clock,' and turned into the shop.

He couldn't have told McBain! He couldn't have told anyone! As Helen moved between racks of blouses in blue and pink and yellow she wanted to scream. If they knew, anyone in the hospital, she would die. When she went to the doctor it would go down in black and white! 'Pregnant.' *Someone* would read it and tell; no one kept confidences. She had told things herself, tit-bits: '*Wait till you hear this!*'

There was a singing in her ears and she wanted to be sick, until she thought of seven o'clock. It would be better then, with someone to share the load. She left the shop and went to get the Belgate bus.


Lilian had fed the baby the precious colostrum and handed it, sated, back to the staff nurse. Now she lay and pondered possible names. It wasn't going to be Gladys after his mam, that was one thing. So it couldn't be Isabel after hers, not without causing an upset. Besides, if truth were known, she didn't like the name Isabel . . . the bairn would get Bella or, worse still, Belsy, which sounded rough. Julia was nice, or Juliet. Or Kimberley. Kimberley Fenwick: you could go anywhere with a name like that. And it went well with Karen: Karen and Kimberley. She had a sudden vision of her daughters, tall and slender and beautifully groomed, both in air hostesses' uniforms and seeing a bit of life. They would bring her perfume and Continental jewellery. Everything was dirt cheap over there.

Lilian conjured up such rosy pictures of the future that a passing nurse called out 'Penny for them?' before going on her way.

She got up for the toilet at four o'clock, and apart from a little wobble in her legs she felt fine, shaking off the nurse's arm for the return journey. They were passing the sideward when she remembered the doctor's wife who had not been as lucky as she had been. 'How's she getting on?' she whispered, inclining her head to the door. The nurse said the patient was being a brick and added, 'It's him I feel sorry for, Dr Whittington. He isn't half taking it badly.'

'Dr Whittington?' Lilian had come alert. 'Him from Belgate?'

The nurse nodded as she helped Lilian back into bed. 'That's right . . . at least, that's where his practice is. They live in that big white house between Belgate and Darlasden. The one set back from the road.'

'He's my GP,' Lilian said, sounding almost affronted that she had not been better informed. 'I never even knew he was expecting.'

The nurse was moving away. 'He wasn't,' she said, grinning. 'It was his wife that got pregnant.'

Lilian was not to be outdone. 'And we all know who puts the match to the tinder, don't we?'

She made a mental note to have words with Billy about birth control before she let him near her, and settled back to consider this new information. Dr Whittington's wife! They hadn't been married five minutes; perhaps it was a shotgun affair. Even doctors could get too clever. She thought of Helen, then, and her fancy boyfriend. Something like that would serve her right. Her conscience smote her when she remembered the baby in the nursery next door. Helen had been a bonny bairn, and she had taken her everywhere once. It was only lately they had grown apart. She made a mental resolve to try harder with her sister. After all, if the doctor did do right by her, she might come in very handy for the girls.

At five o'clock she could stand it no longer. She must have a look at the doctor's wife, even if only through the crack of the door. 'I just need the lavvy,' she called out cheerfully to the nurses busy at the top of the ward. 'I'll shout if I need you.'

The door to the side-ward was ajar and she tried to see past the screen. It was useless. She eased her way through the door and stood, ears cocked for conversation. If Sister was busy at the bed, she would get her arse tanned and no mistake. But the room was silent until Lilian heard what was either a sniffle or a sigh. She gathered her dressing-gown around her and advanced.

The girl in the bed was a bit scrawny, but Lilian could tell right away she was classy. 'Hello,' she said, moving to the bed. 'My name's Lilian, and your man's my doctor.'

The girl was smiling now. 'Oh, that's nice. I'm Diana Whittington.'

She said nothing more and Lilian was suddenly uncertain. If things had been different she'd have compared birth weights and possible names, and argued over who had had the worse time. What did you say to someone whose cot was empty? 'I heard about your bairn. What a crying shame.'

Diana's eyes looked watery but she was smiling. 'Yes, we were looking forward to it such a lot. Especially David.'

Inside Lilian, affection blossomed. 'He's a lovely man, your hubby. Always joking, and nice with the bairns. Still, there's plenty time. I knew a woman once tried four times before she struck lucky.' The thought that this was perhaps not the best example came too late, and she tried to repair the damage. 'Not that you'd be like that. And anyway you could always adopt, if it came to it.'

Diana's smile had gone now and she was picking at the counterpane with her left hand. A diamond ring on her third finger was the size of a marrowfat pea, and Lilian had difficulty in looking away from it. 'I couldn't adopt,' Diana said firmly. 'I know some people could, but not me.'

Lilian nodded. 'I know what you mean.' She cast around for some way to comfort her new friend. 'I'll tell you what. I'll poke me head in the kitchen and see if there's any tea going. I bet you'd like a nice cuppa.' She would tell them it was for the doctor's wife if they gave her any lip. And if there was no one about she would make a pot anyway. Billy paid plenty taxes, so by rights she owned all this.

She was about to turn for the door when she saw that the girl's chest was heaving. Her face was still composed but she was crying inside. Lilian felt her own eyes prick. God could be cruel sometimes, and always to the wrong ones. She heaved her hip on to the bed and held out her arms.

'Come here,' she said. 'Come here to me and have a bloody good blub. You've lost your babby, so you're entitled.' Inside her arms the sobbing girl seemed no more than a bairn herself. 'There now, there now,' she said, rocking backwards and forwards, not even flinching when Diana's tears soaked through her nightie and trickled between her breasts.

Alistair was there in Luigi's coffee bar when Helen arrived, and he stood to greet her, and ask what she wanted to drink. 'You got the message then. I was worried.'

She asked for orange juice and he brought it in a tall glass with straws.

'How've you been?' he said. There was concern in his voice, and Helen felt herself thaw until his next question, which was put too casually to be anything else but vital: 'Anything changed?'

'No,' she said, 'nothing's changed,' and applied herself to her drink.

'If it's true,' he said at last, 'have you thought about what you'll do?'

She knew then that there was going to be no help for her. She would have to manage it all on her own, however it turned out.

'No. I can't think that far ahead.

He was shaking his head too, as though in puzzlement. 'I can't work out how it happened. I was so careful.' It was there again, the suggestion that perhaps there had been some other agency at work but his. Helen felt a bitterness so tangible that it threatened to choke her.

'You can't have been careful enough,' she said.

It was as though he had been waiting for a chance to lash out. 'Don't go blaming it on me! It takes two, and you can't say you weren't a willing partner.'

It was true. She had held herself aloof at first, but from fear not from lack of desire.

'Look, Helen.' He reached for her hand and she let it lie. 'I've talked to Sandy. He won't say anything, he's like the grave. He says he can fix it, as a favour for a friend and all that. It's a way out, you've got to admit that.'

A vision of a knitting needle rose up in her mind, steel-sharp, so that she let out a little cry of terror.

Alistair patted her hand. 'I know. I don't like it any more than you do, but it would be for the best. For now. If I was in general practice I'd say, "This is marvellous darling, let's get married." You know I'd say that. But I'm not in practice, I've got at least another two years as houseman and SHO. And then I might take a Registrar's job. You know what my life's like now – I couldn't ask you to share a life like that. Besides, there's my father. You've no idea how rigid he can be . . .'

When Helen got out of his car at the corner she had promised to think it over. It *would* be one way out, and when it was done she need never lay eyes on him again. Never admit again what a fool she had been. Perhaps it was the only way out? She wasn't the stuff of which heroines are made. She could now hardly string two words together for panic, let alone arrange for a birth and take care of a child. Besides, Dad would put her out and Lilian would gloat. It was the thought of Lilian's triumph that carried her over the step, through the kitchen, past her mother's gaze and safely up to her room.

5

Helen left the Infirmary at lunch-time and walked down into town. There was some peace to be found in moving among crowds, standing in shop doorways to gaze intently through the glass, seeing nothing but looking decently occupied. When she came to the church she turned in almost automatically and seated herself in a side pew. She put her hands on the ledge in front of her and rested her forehead against them.

She would have to decide today. Alistair was getting desperate now, and it was showing on his face. People would know something was wrong, and ferret and ferret until they found out. She had seen it happen to other girls, why should she be different? They would call her brazen if she kept the baby, unfeeling if she gave it up for adoption, and a monster if she had an abortion.

Abortion: the word itself was frightening. She had heard it talked about in whispers, her mother and Lilian tearing some Belgate girl to bits, a hush in their voice when they spoke of abortion, avoiding the word and saying 'getting rid' or 'seen to' instead. They had never included her in these conversations, enjoying their status as married women, but she had heard all the same.

She lifted her head until her mouth was against her clenched fingers and allowed a little moan to escape her lips. 'Please God, you can change it even now. You can make it right. Help me.' Her lip was caught between teeth and knuckles and the pain seemed part of the process. For a moment she half-expected to be touched by a miracle, to feel that sudden flow that would signal all was well, but there was nothing. So much for prayer.

She was getting ready to leave when the priest came silently from behind and stood, blocking her exit from the pew.

'Are you all right, my child?'

She was nodding and smiling, putting her bag on to her shoulder, but he wasn't moving. 'Yes, thank you, father. I was just saying a prayer.'

'Are you Catholic, daughter?'

She shook her head. 'No, father. I just wanted . . .'

He was holding up a hand. 'No matter. We're all God's children.' She smiled, wondering how she could get round him and escape into the open air. 'Did I see you here the other day?'

You couldn't lie to a priest. 'Yes, father.'

He had put his hands on the wooden edges of the pews as though to support himself and she saw that they were gnarled and blue-veined, the skin dry and flaky, the nails clean but unkempt. Perhaps he lived alone and no one fed or cared for him.

'Are you troubled, my child?' She would have denied it

but he gave her no opportunity. 'I hear many things, you know, share many burdens. Perhaps I could help? It helps to share troubles. With God always, sometimes with an old priest who has seen many things in his time.' He was moving away from the pew's entrance and she felt her heart leap with relief. 'I'm always here in the early evening, between six and seven.'

She was nodding and smiling, and then her heels were clicking on the tiled floor, the doorway was looming up, a great golden opening, and she was free.


'You're off then?' The obstetrician looked strangely young out of his white coat and without his usual entourage.

Diana smiled. 'Yes, thank you. And please accept my thanks, everyone's been so kind.'

He was tut-tutting and saying it was nothing at all and she could see he was embarrassed. Etiquette demanded that a fellow medical man get Grade A treatment, so he must come here to make his farewells when he would rather be somewhere else with women who really needed him.

As if he knew what was going through her mind he grinned suddenly, looking from her to David. 'I know how it must feel, going home empty-handed. I feel . . . well, a bit superfluous, as though I've let you down. But neither of us is to blame. It was Nature's way of saying, "Not this time", that's all. There really is no reason why . . .'

His voice tailed away and Diana sensed David moving up behind her. Something must be showing on her face or in her body to alarm them. She tried to relax.

'I know you're right and I'm really grateful. Now, please, we're keeping you from your work.'

David was shaking hands. 'Thanks, Chris, you've been a great help.'

Diana nodded and smiled until Christopher Milhill was out of the door, then she turned to David. 'Put my bag in the car, darling. I have to say some goodbyes.'

In the ward she searched for Lilian's bed. 'I'm off now but I wanted to say goodbye.' There was no one around and she leaned closer. 'You've been a great help to me. I'm a stranger to the north and my own family haven't been able to get up here yet. I hope I wasn't too . . . well, gloomy. You should be enjoying this moment.'

In the crib by the bed Lilian's baby slept, and Diana tried to look at it without seeing. She mustn't spoil things for Lilian, however much it might hurt.

Lilian was glowing with pride in her baby and pleasure at Diana's words. 'No, of course you didn't . . . it'd take more than that to upset me. I'm just glad I was here when you needed someone. I won't lose touch 'cos I'll want to know how things turn out. Many a one has bad luck the first time.' She was looking so earnest that Diana expected her to claim a miscarriage herself just to be companionable.

She had not intended to let down her hair with a stranger but in a funny way Lilian had seemed like a ship in the night, appearing in her room, both of them caught up in unique events, never to meet again. At least that's what she had intended. Obviously Lilian thought differently.

'Well, I think your baby is lovely, and I wish you joy of her . . . . of both your children. I'm sure we'll meet again. In the mean time, take care . . . and please put this in the baby's box.' She pressed the two pound notes into Lilian's hand and moved away from the bed, turning in the ward doorway to wave goodbye.


Lilian could hardly wait for visiting hour, so anxious was she to talk of her new friend. She had already told her mother and Billy of the evening encounter and the cosy chats that had followed it. Now, when Billy appeared with Karen, she repeated it, bringing it up to date with the story of today's visit and the two pound notes. 'By, she's a nice lass. It's that sort that loses bairns, and you think of some of them that has them like dogs dropping litters.'

This talk of over-fertility reminded her of something important, but Karen was creating havoc with the fruit on top of the locker. 'Are you going to stop her, Billy, or have I got to get out of this bed?'

When order was restored she returned to the subject.

'Mind, Billy Fenwick, I hope you're doing something about yourself. I'm not going through this again, don't say I didn't warn you. You don't get in my bed till you've bottomed it.'

Billy was looking uneasy. 'What d'you mean?'

'You know full well what I mean, Billy. If I've told you once I've told you twenty times: I'm having no more bairns, and it's up to you to make sure of that. Otherwise you don't get near me.'

'Well, what shall I do?'

If it hadn't been so serious she would have laughed at the look on his face. 'What shall you do? I see. Three years married and you still don't know how it works. I don't remember you needing a guide-dog when you tried it on the first time. You seemed to know how to go on then.' Suddenly she was curious. 'How did you find out about it . . . an don't say "what", or I'll clip your lugs. Karen, put that down or I'll . . . be a good girl, pet, and I'll let you see your little sister before you go home. Billy, you heard what I said?'

'Why, the lads. You know what it's like in the school yard. I learned off them. And I know about well, contraceptives . . . it's just . . .' He leaned forward. 'Well, you can hardly just walk in and ask, can you? And if you get them off the barber they all look at you.'

Lilian groaned, thinking of the burdens women were called on to bear, and made a mental note to ask Dr Whittington for help. 'Pick that bairn up, Billy, and I'll ask them to fetch the baby.' Her face softened as Billy lifted Karen to see into the crib when the nurse wheeled it to the bottom of the bed. 'Where's daddy's little girl, then? Look Karen, there's our . . .'

Before he could utter the fatal word 'Gladys', Lilian spoke. 'We're calling her Diana. Diana Fenwick, it's got a nice ring.'


Edward had completed an inventory of the back shop and sat now with the lists in front of him. A lot of it was junk, there from his father's time or even before. A lot of treen and brass, out of fashion for ages now, miscellaneous porcelain, and some poor-quality but showy plates. The big ones would go to the catering trade now that Delft-racks were all the rage. There were quite a few weapons and some militaria, probably good – but he had decided not to handle that side, so they could go to a dealer.

He had almost made up his mind that he would special-ize in good but moderately priced furniture, Georgian, Edwardian and the better Victoriana. His father had been a magpie, attracted by anything and everything that was older than he himself. His mother had carried on the tradition. Now it was time for change.

He looked through the shop window to the Mews. This morning he had learned that the Pollocks were going, selling to the same developer who had bought the adjoin-ing property. The selling price had taken him by surprise: £40,000, twice what he would have expected. If those prices were maintained or even raised, how many occupiers would stand firm?

The telephone shrilled before he had time to speculate on his own posible reaction.

'Edward?' It was Sylvia and he eased his hip on to a side table.

'No. This is the Russian Embassy. Is that a beautiful spy?'

She was not in the mood for games. 'Listen, Edward, I'm on my way to Slough. Yes, precisely. Anyway, I may be late tonight, and I'll have to come back here to file my copy, so let's scrap the arrangements and I'll come over to you when I can, by cab.'

He put down the phone and thought about tonight. She would be tired, definitely, and irritable, probably. They would wind up in bed and make love because not to do so would be unthinkable. Imagining it now, he felt aroused, but the reality tonight might be less than satisfying. He wanted her so much and most of the time his need was more than reciprocated, but Sylvia was ambitious and there were times when their lovemaking took second place.

Would it be better if they married? Sylvia was not keen

on children, as she had made abundantly clear, and if there were to be no children was there any purpose in marriage?

He looked at his watch. His mother would be napping now, no point in phoning. Instead he picked up a cylindrical mug he had found in the back shop, which was certainly silver and might be Hester Bateman, and reached for his cleaning kit.


Helen had never made a conscious decision to go back to the church. She had walked down into town as usual, to catch the bus to Belgate, and then had turned at the corner and made for the doorway. She didn't want help or advice; she shrank from the idea of pouring out her troubles to anyone. But the cool darkness of the church promised refuge, a womb into which she could retreat and think through her problem for herself.

It was inevitable that the priest would come to her, and in the event she didn't mind. He moved into the pew beside her and she hitched obligingly along to make room. He reached for her hand and held it in a warm, firm grip while he leaned his head on his other hand. She saw his lips move, and then he straightened up and turned to her. 'Tell me what is causing you pain, my child.'

It was the easiest thing in the world to say it: 'I'm going to have a baby, father.' She watched his face for a wince, a tightening of the lips, but there were only the calm blue eyes, shot through with the yellow veins of age, expectant on hers. 'I'm not married, father, and I know it's wrong.'

He was smiling now. 'It's wrong but it does not cut you off from the love of God. Never think that. God loves the sinner and hates the sin. Do you love the father of your child?'

That was easy to answer but hard to admit. 'No. I did love him but I realize now that he didn't love me.'

The priest was nodding as though he had heard it before. 'Will he marry you? Will he support the child?'

Helen shook her head. 'He can't. He . . .' She wondered if she should explain about Alistair, and decided against it.

'He won't, father. And I don't want him to . . . it would be a mistake.'

'What about your family, do you have a loving family?'

Her mother would kill her when she found out, and if she didn't, her father would. They had forgiven Lilian when she married; they would never forgive her when she was deserted. 'They're very good, father, but they would never forgive me for this. I don't know what I'm going to do.'

Something in her voice alarmed him. 'You must not contemplate murdering your child. That is *not* an alternative. I will help you, as I have helped many other girls, but such murder would imperil your immortal soul.'

A woman had entered the church and was making obeisance to the altar. She sat down without glancing at the priest and the girl, and then fell to her knees, the rosary moving between her fingers.

'My child, you have a chance to do good. See yourself as a handmaiden of Our Lord. Bear your child, and give it to someone who longs for a child and has been denied. That is the ultimate affection, to give up your child for its greater good.'

These were words he was giving her, simply words. There was no baby yet, no creature of arms and legs and brain: how could she give up what did not yet exist?

He was patting her hand again. 'You're confused. Believe only this, that I can and I *will* help you. We can keep this secret from your friends and family. We can arrange for you to keep the child, or to give it into loving hands. We can organize everything for you, help you in every way, if only you will give up any idea of abortion.' His voice shuddered on the word as though he could not bear to utter such an obscenity.

'But how would I manage, father?'

He had her now and the knowledge showed in his face. 'Listen to me, my child, and you'll see how simple it is to take God's way and do what is good and right.'

It was going to be all right. She had found someone at last. Tears came into her eyes and brimmed over on to her

cheek, and he was there with a handkerchief, voluminous
and silky, so that she could wipe them away.


'Get a chair,' Lilian said. 'Take one from that bed there.
They've got two. Ooh, bananas, just what I could fancy.
Pull your chair in, I've got heaps to tell you.' She waited
until her mother had settled herself and then began her
tale.

'Well, you know I palled up with the doctor's wife. As
soon as I knew she was our doctor's wife I made meself
known. "Am I glad to see you," she said straight away.
White with pain, she was, you could see she'd been
through the mill. "Come in," she said, "I could do with
some company." Anyway, I got it all: how she gave up a
good job to marry him. How her sister-in-law's nice but
very strait-laced. She's a solicitor's wife, looks Jewish, but
Diana says she's Catholic. Anyroad, she wanted me in
there with her all the time. "Give her a bit of peace," the
Sister said, but I soon put her right. "We're friends," I told
her.'

Her mother leaned forward. 'Which one is the Sister?
They all look like bairns to me.' The nurses were clustered
around the desk at the end of the ward.

'Her in the dark blue, the fat one. Fancies herself no end.
Anyroad, I was telling you . . . when Diana . . . that's her
name . . . when she was leaving she said, "Keep in touch,"
and she gave the bairn two pound. Two pound! It's there
on the locker. She was looking in the crib and ooh, I felt for
her, mam. I mean, you could kill the little sods, but you
don't like the thought of losing them. Still, she's young
enough . . . and he'll know all the treatments and everything. Anyroad, to cut a long story short, I've decided to
call the bairn after her, and I'm going to ask her to be
godmother.'

She sat back to watch the effects of her news.

'What did Billy say?' her mother asked. She had clamped
her lips together and Lilian could see there was trouble
brewing.

'He thought it was all right. What should he think?' And

77

then, when her mother sniffed and shrugged her shoulders, 'Come on, mam, spit it out. I can see you're getting your back up, so you might as well say so.'

Her mother shrugged again. 'I'm not saying a thing. I mean, it's no business of mine. But I would've thought your own sister might've been considered, if you were thinking about godmothers. Still, you've never liked her – even when she was a bairn you were always carping.'

Lilian waited, her face impassive, until her mother was silent. 'Have you finished? I knew it would be that, your little white hen! I'll admit I cannat stand her sometimes, but she is family. Girls have two godmothers, in case you've forgotten, and I've already decided to ask our Hel.'

She savoured her mother's deflation for a moment and then reached for a banana. 'We'll have to have a do for the christening. Especially with Diana and the doctor coming. You can see she's used to having things nice.'

They were discussing the fine details of the christening feast when Helen appeared. 'There now, there's your niece. What d'you think of her?'

While Helen admired the baby, unloaded gifts for mother and child, and found herself a chair, Lilian's eyes followed her.

'Everything all right?'

Helen looked up and met her sister's gaze. 'Yeah, everything's fine. We've been a bit pushed at work but apart from that . . .'

'You can hold her, if you like,' Lilian said generously, and watched as Helen at first demurred and then consented to lift the baby from the crib and hold it in her arms. 'By, it's well to be seen you've had no experience.' For once Lilian was in a superior position and she meant to exploit it. 'You're holding that bairn like it was a time-bomb. The worst it'll do is wee on you. Give it to me mam if you're scared. They don't bite, you know – not at this stage.' She put a reflective hand to her breast. 'Mind, our Karen was a little devil for biting when she was feeding. I used to beg for mercy.'

She watched as the baby passed from aunt to grandmother, thinking that for once everything was going according to plan. She had a beautiful baby, she had put Billy straight about getting some protection, and she had made a new and influential friend. It had all been worth it after all.

Diana did not cry until she pushed open the nursery door and saw what they had done. Everything was boxed and crated, dust sheets hung over furniture that could not be hidden in any other way. The mobile was gone from the ceiling and the light shade with its pattern of chicks and bunnies had been replaced by a plain blue one. She had wanted to clear the room herself, but she had been forestalled.

She tried to keep her voice casual when she came downstairs. 'Who cleared the nursery?'

David's expression was hunted. 'We thought it might be the best thing to do. Anne gave me a hand.'

Diana nodded, her fury suddenly evaporating. They were trying to do their best in a situation none of them understood and of which they had no experience. You were supposed to give birth to life, not death.

As she walked in the garden, noticing the rampant growth that seemed to have gone on in her absence, she thought about her sister and brother-in-law. They had come to the hospital and commiserated, they had supported David, notified family and friends. Anne had packed her a bag, forgetting no tiny detail. So why didn't she like them? Or more particularly, why didn't she like Anne? They were in the same boat now, two barren women. Surely Anne must want a child, must have tried to conceive. Barren, barren, barren! She repeated the word until she made herself cry, sinking down on the stone garden step the better to accommodate her grief.

'Don't cry, darling.' David was hurrying across the lawn, kneeling to comfort her, stroking the hair from her forehead and leaning his cheek against hers. 'We'll try again, darling, as soon as it makes sense. There'll be other babies. I know how you feel, but it will pass, I promise you.

He was wrong, she thought, staring across his shoulder

at the garden, blurred now into a wish-wash of colour. He thought she wanted a baby, a substitute for the one she had lost. But there could be no substitute. She didn't want another baby or any baby, ever again. And if she didn't want children, would David still want her?

It was nine-fifteen when Edward heard Sylvia's taxi draw up in the Mews, and he was half-way down the stairs when he heard her knocking on the door. 'I'm coming!' He released the catches and stood by to let her pass.

'Oh God, I'm tired.' She was clattering up the stairs and he saw that for once the magnificent red hair was tangled and uncombed. For some reason it made him feel suddenly tender towards her, so that he made a great show of taking her coat and settling her comfortably.

'Gin or sherry?'

She groaned and sank lower in her chair. 'It ought to be brandy and sal volatile after the day I've had, working with utter bloody ineptitude. Make it G. and T., please.'

She relaxed over the drink and brightened considerably when he produced moussaka. 'God, Edward, you're a wonder. If you're not careful I might decide to marry you.'

'Seconds?' he said, lifting the serving spoon.

She shook her head and belched gently. 'No, thank you, but it was gorgeous. Where did you learn to cook like that?'

He grinned. 'I didn't learn at all. I must've watched my mother over the years, although I don't remember consciously taking note. When she was in hospital I thought, "I can't cook, I'll eat out." But I soon got tired of that, and when she came home it wasn't feasible, so I just did it. Boiled eggs at first, and then it began to be a bit more adventurous. Now . . . if the business ever goes I'll turn this into a trattoria. I can just see myself with a napkin on my arm. "A table, sir, . . . for how many?"'

Sylvia had put down her coffee cup and was stretching her arms above her head and yawning. The breasts beneath the silky blouse rose, and briefly he wondered if she was making the gesture for effect. If so, it was unnecessary – he was itching to reach for her. She let her hands drop to rest on her head and made a moue of apology. 'Sorry . . . I'm just not in the mood.'

Edward felt deflated and a little irritated. Everyone had bad days, him included, but they didn't expect the world to pay for it. 'What mood *are* you in?'

She was pushing at the heel of one shoe with the toe of another till the shoe fell to the floor and the process could be repeated on the other side. The long legs moved and writhed as she wriggled her toes. He felt desire flicker again, and die as quickly as it had arisen. She was playing games with him and that wasn't what he wanted – to be used for relief at the end of a working day. He looked at his watch. 'You need a good night's sleep. Shall I get the car out?'

For a moment she looked at him and he could see the debate going on behind her eyes. If she got up and moved towards him now they would end up in bed. On the other hand, why the hell should she? He saw her ponder, and then decide. 'Don't bother,' she said. 'I'll pick up a cab in the High Street.'

He walked with her to the corner and stood until a cruising cab drew to a halt beside them. 'I'll call you,' he said and she nodded.

'Lovely meal. Thanks. See you.'

He turned away as the cab moved off and walked into the silent mews, feeling flat and empty now that she was gone. He should have handled it better. If he had done, they would be in bed now. He let himself into the silent shop, finding no satisfaction in the fact that once more he had his kingdom to himself.


They had talked in Luigi's, in a back booth in an almost empty coffee bar. Helen had told him of her decision and Alistair had argued against it, looking ill and strained and sometimes beating his fist on the marble-topped table in emphasis. 'You're crazy, Helen. And unfair. How do you think I'll feel, knowing I have a child somewhere . . . growing up in God knows what circumstances. You know what Catholics are like, they'll say anything to make you

81

go through with it. I just wish you'd think straight. It's not a baby at this stage, it's an embryo. Microscopic. It wouldn't take a minute to sort everything out, and we could go back to normal again and be happy.'

Helen listened without argument. There was no need for argument now: she had made up her mind. She was going to Northumberland, to a house run by nuns, as soon as her eighteenth birthday was over in four weeks' time. She would hand in her notice at the hospital and tell her family she was going to work in the south. If necessary, Father Connor would provide her with letters to back up her story. 'Everything will be done, my child. Put your trust in God, and leave these things to me.'

She had promised to be a good girl, to live a healthy life and produce a beautiful baby for someone else to love, and she had realized what good sense it all made. She would indeed be a handmaiden. Once it was over she would be free to make a new life somewhere – even that would be arranged for her. She would not have to face the hospital, and there would be no triumph for Lilian, no rubbing of salt in the wound. There would be no wound; just a task to perform to the best of her ability.

She looked across at Alistair, noticing the faint dandruff on his collar, the tiny bubble of foam at the corner of his lips. How blind love was, that she had never before noticed these things. And his hands were mean, the nails bluish and thin, like the nails of a dead man. She shivered a little and began to fasten her jacket.

'Well, there's just one thing,' he said as they stood up to go. 'Don't come running to me when it all goes wrong and it's too late to do anything about it. I won't be made responsible, I'll tell you that now. I'll deny it's mine, and there are ways of proving it could be someone else's.'

He had the grace to hang his head when their eyes met, and when he looked up again she saw that he was ashamed. 'I'm sorry, Helen, but you won't appreciate what this could do to me. I have to protect myself. I want to help . . . I honestly want to stand by you . . . but what you're suggesting is going to cause trouble for both of us.'

They were out in the street now, walking towards his

car. She would have preferred to get the bus but that would make her late home and she couldn't face a row. He got into the car and reached across to open her door and she smiled to herself at the withdrawal of courtesy. When he had wanted her he had folded her into the car as tenderly as a bride folding her wedding dress. Now she was allowed to fend for herself.

She waited until they were out on the Belgate road before she spoke. 'Alistair, I promise you now that I will never bother you again, that you will never see me or hear of me, or of the baby – if you will do just one thing for me.'

He was staring straight ahead but she knew she had his full attention.

'I want you to inform Sandy, and anyone else you might have told, that it was a false alarm. That there is no problem now. I want you to behave for the moment as though everything was normal. We'll go out together just like we did, and we'll both put a good face on it. In five or six weeks I'll be gone, and you'll be free, but till then I want you to do everything you can to back me up.'

He drove on in silence for a while, and then she saw his head incline in a nod. 'OK, if that's what you want . . . but I meant what I said, Helen. There'll be no going back.'

'I know,' she said and sat, composed, for the rest of the journey.

He got out to open the door for her and stood awkwardly by as she climbed out. 'I'm sorry for the mess, Helen . . .'

She was already moving away. 'Just do what I ask, Alistair. That's all I want from you.'

6

Down below in the garden her father was inspecting his asters, purple and pink and white, an exotic blaze of colour among the vegetables. The rows of leeks and onions were depleted now, the pea stalks withered, the potatoes lifted and eaten. Helen stood for a moment watching him,

83

wearing the trousers of his one good suit, his white shirt dazzling under the chequered braces. In a moment he would put on his jacket, and it would be time for them to go to the church.

She ought to finish dressing and go down but she couldn't tear herself away from the familiar sight. Soon she would leave this bedroom for the last time, kiss her parents, and go. She would come back some time, but it would never be the same again. Childhood and safety and the certainty of being loved would be gone forever.

They did love her, she knew that – although neither father nor mother had ever told her so. She half-smiled, hiding her face in the folds of the curtain, as she imagined making a formal statement of affection. They would never find the words.

Affection . . . the priest had used that word. *An ultimate affection*. He had tried to console her these last few weeks, tried to make up for the sacrifice he obviously thought she was making. In fact, she felt no sense of loss; all she felt was a mounting impatience, a desire to correct a foolish, almost disastrous mistake and get back on course. At times she wondered if there was a wickedness in her, that she could be so coldly determined. At other times she felt strangely grown-up and in command for the first time in her life.

'Helen!'

When she peered over the banister her mother was in the hall, looking up, face flushed beneath her petalled hat. 'Will you come down and fetch your father in? He's trying to drive me mad. He knows the time full well . . . . and will he come? If he shows me up in front of Billy's side, I'll never forgive him.'

Helen picked up jacket and bag and made her way downstairs. 'Get a move on, dad,' she called. 'We'll be late.' They both knew he would have to make his return to the house a leisurely one – manly pride demanded it.

'Do I look all right?'

Helen looked her mother up and down. 'Lovely. Very smart. Blue's your colour.'

Her mother compressed her lips to hide her satisfaction

84

and picked up her husband's jacket, ready to enfold him. 'You should've invited the doctor . . . Alistair. He'd've been welcome, and our Lilian's got everything laid on. He could've talked to Dr Whittington.'

Now was the time for Helen to broach the subject!

'I won't be seeing Alistair again, mam. It didn't work out. We can't talk about it now, but I'll tell you all about it tonight.' It was done!

She listened while her mother talked about better fish in the sea, the fickleness of the medical profession in general and hospital doctors in particular, until her father's shadow crossed the threshold and it was time for them all to depart.


'I didn't exactly say "Yes", David. Not outright. She sort of assumed I'd do it.'

David was backing out of the drive, twisting his head from side to side to check the road. 'Well, I think it was bloody insensitive in the circumstances . . . and I hope we're not going to stay long. Socializing with patients is not my idea of huge fun.'

Diana made soothing noises and crossed her hands over the christening present, gift-wrapped on her lap. She didn't feel too bad about her role as godmother. It was all part of the strange world she now inhabited, in which she went through the motions of living without really taking part. She had realized the necessity of consoling everyone else very early on. David first, making him think everything was all right. Her mother, distracted by the distance between them, wanting to come north but unwilling to make the journey. 'I'm fine, mummy. Honestly. I'm sad; well, I would be, wouldn't I? But it'll pass. And everyone here is being so kind, it's quite overwhelming. So you mustn't worry. . . .'

With Anne and Howard the need had been to show she was not going to make scenes. Howard had never actually said, 'Brace up,' but the words had hovered around his lips. Anne had been gentle and considerate – yes, she *had*! Diana told herself she must come to terms with her phobia about Anne, who was a good woman. Being religious was not a crime. The fault was in her, that she allowed her sister-in-law's faith to make her uneasy.

'What did you buy?' David said now, glancing down at the box on her knee.

'A hairbrush. It's pink with little lambs on it, and a silver edge. Lilian will love it.'

David snorted and changed gear to take the Belgate turn. 'She'll never be off our backs. Don't say I didn't warn you! You know what they call her at the surgery: News of the World. "Here comes News of the World," they'll say. They've probably got her filed under N.'

Diana pulled a face to show she thought him mean. Lilian was warm-hearted and well-meaning. She would not have chosen her for a friend in normal times, but they had come together at a moment of crisis, when there had been no time to weigh the pros and cons of friendship. Now there was a christening, a formality to be gone through. She would hold the baby that bore her name, and make her promises, and keep them as far as she could. Perhaps it had all been meant to turn out like this. A baby by proxy! A child at second hand, to watch growing and developing, a child to like and take an interest in, with none of the pain and terror that accompanied a child that was your own.

Lilian had risen at half-past six to bake and butter and rinse salad vegetables in salted water. She had used Billy as a scullion until he had rebelled and locked himself in the outside toilet with a mug of tea and the *Sunday Sun*. 'Five minutes, Billy. Five minutes and I've got you timed.' In the event, she had lost herself in icing the butterfly cakes and scattering them with hundreds and thousands, so Billy got a good half-hour's grace and emerged a happier man.

'Wash your hands, move the bowl. And scrub your nails. They look like you've been clawing the coal out, never mind hewing it. Oh my God, there's the bairn. Run up and fetch her before she wakes Karen. And get a move on, Billy. It's all very well you saying, "Have a big christening!" It's me that gets the backwash. Well, go on . . . before she wakes the street!'

When the table was laid Lilian contemplated it with satisfaction. Ham, tongue, pickles, pease pudding, salad, buns and salad dressing. Sausage rolls, sandwiches. Two big cakes, small cakes, trifles in waxed paper cups that looked like waterlilies and would have to be saved and put away for the next big occasion. Beetroot . . . she had forgotten the beetroot. She tipped it from jar to bowl, arching her body away from the draining-board in case of splashes. Borrowed knives and forks to supplement her own, plates . . . a pity they didn't match, but you couldn't do everything . . . paper serviettes with silver babies and bells on them, glasses for sherry and beer, and tea-cups stacked in three tiers on the sideboard. There now, that was everything.

Panic flickered. What if the men made pigs of themselves? She would speak to Billy about his side; hers knew how to behave, and if anyone showed her up in front of the doctor there would be hell on! The christening cake stood proud of the rest, white-iced and covered in favours, on a borrowed glass cake-stand. She would make sure Diana got the silver cradle, for a lucky omen. They would surely be at it every night, mad for a new bairn. More fools them!

When Billy came down, the baby asleep on his shoulder, she came straight to the point. 'Now, Billy, let's get one thing straight. Tell your lot it's F H B. Family Hold Back, before you ask. F H bloody B. After the doctor and Diana have helped themselves, they can – but tell them it's a buffet, not a pie-eating contest. I haven't got over your Ken at the wedding, scooping everyone's left-overs on to his plate. "Don't let good food waste," he said. Me mam was mortified!'

The sickly sweet smell of baby faeces assailed their nostrils. 'I think she's papped,' Billy said, holding his daughter away from him with huge, blue-flecked coal-hewer's hands.

'I expect she has,' Lilian said complacently. 'You'll have to change her nappy, won't you?'

For a moment Billy contemplated defiance then he sighed. 'Where are they, then?'

But Lilian was swooping on her precious baby. 'You don't think I'd let you loose on a month-old baby? Go and do something useful while I get on with it. And I've got that Double Maxim counted, Billy, so don't get any ideas. You can take the baby when she's dressed, and give our Karen her cornflakes while I get ready. And Billy . . . giv'us a kiss and cheer up. There's worse things happen at sea.'

They sang 'All things bright and beautiful' and gathered at the font for the ceremony. Diana held the baby and smiled at everyone, noticing and accepting Lilian's pride, Billy's wobbling Adam's apple, and the softening of David's hitherto solemn face. It had been right to come. She handed the baby, now Diana Helen Elizabeth, back to its mother and walked out into the sunlight, duty done.

She sat where she was told, in the place of honour, when they got back to Lilian's house, and posed with the baby for Billy's sister, who had a camera with flash. At first she watched David anxiously, knowing he was a reluctant guest, but as the meal proceeded and the other guests relaxed, she saw him unwind and then join in. He looked at the baby with a professional eye and poked it gently with a forefinger. 'She's a little beauty,' he said, and try as she might she could detect no note of envy in his voice.

By one o'clock the table was emptied and the baby's grandfather on her father's side was singing a song called 'My Brother Sylvest', which seemed to require a lot of chest-beating. Diana disentangled a line or two, and followed a beat behind. David was singing with gusto and even Lilian's parents, disapproving at first, began to beat time to the singing. '*He's got an arm it's like a leg. He's got a row of forty medals on his chest . . . big chest!*'

At half-past one the men melted away. 'To catch the last half-hour at the pub,' David whispered, and they rose to begin their own goodbyes.

'Come down any time,' Lilian offered at the car door.

'And you must come to tea,' Diana said. It was difficult to say anything else when the least remark made Lilian's face glow with pleasure.

'They're the salt of the earth, you know,' David said, as they drove towards Darlasden. 'The Durham miner . . . good British stock . . . like the DLI.'

She raised an eyebrow and waited till he looked sideways. 'DLI,' he said. 'Durham Light Infantry. The backbone of the British army.'

'I've never heard you be so sentimental before,' Diana said. 'How much is native patriotism and how much beer?'

David was grinning. 'Fifty-fifty . . . but they're a grand lot. Even Fenwick. He must have the heart of a lion to put up with Lilian. She slapped his hand when he reached for the last sandwich – actually slapped it, and he just took it in his stride.'

'What would you have done if I'd done that?' Diana asked. They were coming to a halt in front of their door.

'I'd have put you across my knee, my darling; so if you and Lilian are going to have this beautiful friendship don't let it give you ideas.'

They turned in the hall and faced one another. 'You were brave today,' he said.

She reached to kiss his cheek. 'And you went out of your way to be nice. I'm grateful.'

His arms were round her. 'How grateful?'

She shrugged and considered. 'We – ll. Fairly grateful.' It was two days since her period and she was unlikely to conceive. She let him guide her towards the stairs and up into the quiet bedroom.


Edward ate his Sunday lunch in a small restaurant opposite Hyde Park. Most of the tables were unoccupied and the street outside was strangely quiet. A woman came in, gaunt and dark-eyed and oddly familiar. She sat in a corner and ordered, and he saw that the hand that held the menu was trembling and the wrist was circled by a plastic hospital name-tag bracelet.

He tried to concentrate on his food but the woman's face haunted him. He had seen her somewhere. And then, as she smiled up at the waiter, he recognized her. She was an actress, frequently on television, alone now, shabby and ill in a modest London bistro. In a strange way it cheered him. He was not the only person alone in London after all.

When he left she was staring into space, her pudding untouched in front of her. He wondered how old she was. Fifty, sixty maybe? She played character parts on screen, and on Sundays she ate alone and probably went back to an empty flat, just as he did. He walked to the park, seeing the first leaves fall, winnowing down from the trees, still green and alive. By tomorrow they would have started to curl and wither.

He sat down and watched the passers-by, couples with pushchairs, young girls with huge dogs on leads, elderly men with clothes that suddenly looked a size too big. He had not heard from Sylvia since she had walked out the other night, and he felt lonely. And frustrated too, which was probably the reason for today's low spirits. But there was another cause for his malady.

His mother's illness had brought him to a crossroads, and he couldn't decide which fork to take. He had spent the last few months simply marking time. Sylvia was not the only woman in the world. He had met her through a friend he had made in his Oxford days; he could look Neville up again and see if there were other ravishing females on tap. Except that Sylvia *had* been special, and he wasn't in the mood to go hunting. At his feet a sparrow pecked hopefully at grit. He felt in his pockets for something edible but there was nothing, and the sparrow flew away.

Edward walked back to the Mews, hands in pockets, thinking of the coming winter. At Christmas he would close the shop for two whole weeks and go north. He could afford it; business had picked up. In the meantime he must start to look further afield for stock. He had meant to look at Darlasden that first trip to Berwick – perhaps he would make it next time? And there were all the Yorkshire villages and towns, veritable Aladdin's caves.

By the time he got back to the shop he felt more cheerful. The Lancashire oak chest he had bought yesterday was half-way across the foot of the stairs. He would have to move it tomorrow. The torchères still guarded the opening, and he patted one gilded head as he passed. At least he had Mark and Antony for company.

It was not enough, though. Safe in the flat he picked up the phone and dialled Sylvia's number.

Helen waited until the ceremonial clothes had been cast off with exclamations of relief, and the tea was brewing in the pot.

'Mam . . . . dad. I have to talk to you. It's important.' She saw her mother's mouth tense but she didn't hasten to reassure. She knew what her mother would be fearing. Let her fear the worst so that the apparent facts, when they came, would seem pleasant by comparison.

'Well, then, what is it?' Her mother's tone was sharp with anxiety.

'You're sugaring that tea twice,' Helen warned and settled herself on a chair. Her story was pat inside her head, well rehearsed and with its back-up all in place.

'I'm finished with Alistair, I told you that earlier.'

Her mother nodded but her father shook his head. 'You never said owt to me. Nobody tells me anything.'

For once her mother didn't respond. 'Go on, then, our Helen.'

'Well, like I said, it's over. You needn't worry, I don't care. But it's made things awkward at work and I don't want to stay there.'

Her father put down his mug. 'You can't give a good job up on account of a lad.'

'I'm not giving up a good job, dad. I'm going to a better one. There's a doctor comes to the Infirmary sometimes, a very high specialist. Anyway, he comes from London. All the top surgeons are there. His name's Mr O'Hara.'

'I thought you said he was a doctor,' her father said suspiciously but her mother shushed them.

'She told us how surgeons are called "Mr", Tom. I wish you'd listen sometimes. What about this doctor?'

'Well, he wants a secretary for six months while his own one's on a course. It'll be good pay, better than I'm getting here. I'll be able to send something home every week, I expect. The important thing is, I'll be getting experience so that I can better meself later on.' She was gaining in confidence now, secure in the knowledge that there was a Mr O'Hara who would back up her story if necessary, and that something to send home each week would be forthcoming.

'Well, I don't know . . .' her mother said, doubtfully. 'What do you think, dad?'

Helen didn't wait for him to reply. 'I'm going, mam. I'd rather go with your blessing, but I'm going anyway.'

---

'By, it's bonny, isn't it? Too good to use. I'll put it away for her.' Lilian held the pink enamel brush with its soft bristles and silver trimming at arm's length. 'I mean, it's not what it cost, Billy, you know I'm not like that. It's just her bothering with our bairn that chuffs me.'

'Aye,' Billy said, reaching to the side of his chair for his can of beer. 'He's a nice bloke, mind. Down to earth. Talks to you man to man. He thought our Kenny was a right turn . . . and did you see him singing?'

'Don't bring that up, Billy, you know it's a sore point. They have to bring everything down to their level, your family. Still, it didn't go off too badly, all things considered. I don't like to think what it cost, mind.'

Billy reached out to squeeze his wife's shoulder. 'Don't fret about that, pet. I'll get a few SatSuns in, we'll soon make it up. You put a grand do on, everybody said so, even me . . .' Too late he realized his mistake.

'Go on then, Billy,' Lilian said in silken tones. 'Even your what?' She had had more than twelve hours of sweetness and light, and the chance of a rumpus was too good to miss. '*Even your mam*? I might've known she'd be carping about something. What was it this time, the food or the china? Two Christmases ago she didn't like the Airwick in the netty! I've worked and slaved for that christening and me hardly over the birth, and she complains . . .'

'But Lilian pet, I never said . . .'

Lilian's voice dropped an octave. 'Be quiet, Billy Fenwick, and let me have my say for once.'

He reached once more for his can and tried to compose his face into an expression that could not be classed as anything other than neutral.

# 7

Helen had been at Stella Maris for fourteen weeks now but it was still difficult to feel at home there. She had come in Father Connor's large and elderly car, her cases piled on the back seat. Her father had put her on the London train in Darlasden station, she had alighted at York and caught the train back to Newcastle. The priest had been there waiting, his black Homburg in his hand, his black limousine outside. 'He's enjoying this,' she had thought as he enquired about her getaway. It was a kind of game to him, a spy story with an end product.

He had driven her into the wilds of Northumberland and left her in the care of the Sisters, their habits covered by white aprons, their long skirts pinned to lift them from the floor. 'I shall pray for you daily, my child, and visit you from time to time,' he had said, holding her hand. 'If you need anything, the good Sisters will let me know. Remember to write to your parents each week and give the letters to Reverend Mother. I'll see that they bear suitable postmarks when they reach their destination.'

Everything had been taken care of, down to the last detail. She had given her parents a London telephone number. If they used it, they would be told she was out and would ring them later. She would make the call from the convent, and everyone would be happy.

A gliding Sister, seeming to run on castors, had showed her to the room she would share with three other girls. 'We hope you'll be happy here, Helen. I shall make a special novena to St Teresa, and you must pray too.'

Helen looked around at the girls, each of them in various stages of pregnancy. 'This is Helen, who's come to join us. Helen, this is Terry, Brenda and Mary, your room-mates.

Please help Helen, girls. You remember what it was like to come away from home for the first time.'

When she had gone, the girl with the largest bump gestured towards a bed in the corner. 'That's empty. You'll have to share a wardrobe with Terry, so I hope you don't mind lops.'

The girl on the bed by the window took aim with a pillow, and the speaker ducked.

'Cigarette?' said the third girl. Helen was surprised: there had been no-smoking signs everywhere as she mounted the stairs.

'I thought we weren't allowed to smoke?'

Brenda groaned. 'You're not going to be like that, are you? You're not allowed to breathe here, according to the penguins.' She dropped into a fair imitation of Sister Colomba: 'Don't imperil your immortal soul, children. Don't cause grief to Holy Mother.'

Since then, Helen had become equally uncaring of the rules. There were too many of them and they were too petty to obey them all. So, like the rest of the girls, she obeyed as few as possible. When she was free of chores she walked in the countryside around the convent. It was winter now, the fields bare, burned black in places, yellow with stubble in others, here and there a field green with a winter crop.

It was the first time she had really taken notice of the countryside. She realized how little she knew of her native heath. Trees, hedgerows, meadows, all were foreign to her. The birds and small creatures that inhabited them were strangers too. One day, when she had time, she would learn more. In the meantime she gathered sprays of blood-red hips and fronds of browning fern to fashion into autumn displays for her bedside table, and dreamed of the coming year when she would be free.

There were still Christmas shoppers thronging the High Street, penetrating the Mews with bulging purses, but Edward had no qualms about closing for two weeks. On his last trip to Berwick his mother had looked suddenly fragile, smaller than he remembered, her hair a baby-like fluff around a pink head, her shoulders, when he touched them, like coat-hangers under the clothes. To hell with the shop, he had thought, and decided then and there to make it a good Christmas.

If he and Sylvia had been together, it might have been different. It would certainly have been harder to leave but he would probably have gone just the same.

Mrs Stepinska had been enthusiastic. 'It's good you should be with mama for the holy festival. You are her best present of all, nothing like the child to the mama. Ever.' Her usually bright face had clouded and he had wondered if her words had a personal meaning, but the next moment she was rattling on about Christmas presents and what she would send for his mother. As far as he could make out it would be a box of delights, gifts within gifts, and would be ready in time. He glanced at the bracket clock on the shelf. She had four hours to deliver, and then he was off.

The shop bell jangled and he looked up to find Sylvia standing in the doorway. 'Is it safe to come in?' She was dressed in red, her hair swept up on to the top of her head. She looked stunning and they both knew it.

'Of course. Long time no see.' Edward was glad to see her, and he feared it might show on his face.

She moved to the counter and put black gloved hands on the glass top. 'I've been meaning to ring for weeks to return your call, but life's been so hectic . . . and then . . . Well, it is the season of goodwill, and I was shopping in the area, so I thought, why not look up Edward?'

He had meant to stay open through the lunch hour but now he threw caution to the winds. 'I was just about to go out for some food. Why not join me and we can catch up on one another's news?'

She was close to him as he shrugged into an overcoat and set the door locks. It was a different perfume this time, heady and evocative . . . or perhaps he was so sex-starved that the scent of carbolic soap would have roused him?

A few flakes of snow had fallen, wetting the uneven pavement and giving him an excuse to take her arm.

'Where shall we go?' she said, as they emerged on to the High Street.

He raised his arm at the sight of a cab. 'Somewhere special,' he said. 'Let's celebrate.'


Lilian lifted the heavy fruit loaf to her nose and sniffed. The bugger had a good right to reek of spirits. Every Friday night for the last month Billy had brought home a miniature rum, and they had anointed it together. It was a ceremony she enjoyed, except it gave Billy ideas.

She smiled, thinking of his face when he opened his stocking. 'Don't bother with much. See to the bairns,' he had said, and she had nodded. But his pile in the box beneath her bed was as big as Karen's. She would wrap them well in advance and leave them under the bed till Christmas morning. Karen would come in and climb in between them at the crack of dawn, as she always did, and Billy would fetch her stocking from the foot of her cot. And then, when Karen had torn off paper and string to reveal her presents, she, Lilian, would say, 'See what Santy's left for your dad.' He would say, 'You shouldn't have, Lily,' but he would be pleased.

He would have something for her, still in the bag in which he had bought it. It would be nice if he did it up in Christmas paper and silver ribbon, but he wouldn't know how. And nicer still if he bought something for her and labelled it 'From the bairns'. But it would never cross his mind, because he was a man and men's minds didn't work like that. It was women who had loving ideas. Those only came to men if they were prodded into it.

She had the marzipan rolled out now but it kept crumbling at the edges, so she drew edges to middle and rolled again. This time it cracked but her patience was gone. She lifted it on to the cake in pieces and nipped them together with her fingers. She had lowered the cake into its tin when Billy came through the door.

'Something smells nice.' He was taking his boots off at the door and padding towards his chair. 'I saw your dad round the bookies – he says your Helen has decided not to come home from London for Christmas.'

Lilian's face twisted as she moved to fill the kettle. 'We won't be good enough for her, I expect. What a thing to do to me mam! Did me dad say how she was taking it?'

Billy had subsided into his chair and was toasting his feet on the fender. 'He didn't seem to think it mattered one way or another. I don't blame her, meself. You're only young once. If she's got the chance to enjoy herself, I don't see why she shouldn't.'

Lilian felt a sudden and inexplicable hurt. 'Don't we have enjoyable Christmases here?' She was silently begging him to be tactful because she had too much on for a row.

'Why, of course we do, pet . . . but you can't compare Belgate and London. I mean, it stands to reason.'

She began to put his sausage and bacon into the pan, determined not to betray her pique, but inside she seethed . . . at Billy, at life, and especially at Helen. Little bitch, always wanting something else – and getting it half the time. No Woolworths for her at fifteen, no marriage to a miner and two kids before you could turn round, no Christmas built painstakingly over the months and paid for agonizingly afterwards.

As the sausages split in the pan and curled outwards, she made no attempt to salvage them. It was just like Billy to come in and upset her. He was bloody lucky to be getting fed at all, never mind anything else.


Dembry's was a seething mass of gift-seekers. As they came down the escalator Diana clutched David's arm in case they became separated. 'How much more?' he said.

Diana looked at her list and then at her watch. 'We could have some tea, and then start again.'

The store had three café-restaurants. They chose the Austrian tea-room and ordered toasted teacakes and tea. Around them the citizens of Darlasden laughed and twittered their way towards Christmas. 'There must be a lot of money around,' David said, glancing at the other tables.

'Mmm,' Diana was looking at her list again. 'We can get

something for Diana Two next, and then go down to the china department for Howard and Anne.'

They had taken to calling Lilian's baby Diana Two, to avoid confusion and were used to its frequent visits. At first David had resented Lilian popping up here and there, but he seemed resigned to it now and his interest in the baby was obvious. 'Let's look at you, then,' he would say, holding out his fingers to the baby's tenacious grip. Diana Two was a strong child, rosy-cheeked like her mother but, as David had observed, more pleasant than Lilian would ever be.

'She doesn't mean to go on,' Diana had answered, feeling she must stick up for her new friend even if that friend had come upon her rather like the old man from the sea, to be carried around forever. Now she drained her tea-cup, crumpled her napkin, and reached for lipstick and mirror. She would buy something for Lilian, a luxury . . . nothing expensive, just a token. That would be a minor pleasure. The choosing of the baby's gift would be an ordeal. Each time she saw her god-child, she remembered the horror of that day when all she had hoped for had been wrenched painfully away from her. David was ready, even eager to try again. She herself was not so sure.

They walked together into the fairyland of toys and tiny life-like models, to sift through hooded coats, and dressing-gowns with ladybird buttons, and fluffy rabbit slippers for infant feet. It would be wonderful to buy for her own child, but dare she risk it again?

She looked at David, his face alight as he held up tiny garments. She loved him so much. If she wanted to keep him, perhaps she had no choice.


'Oh God, I wish we had a telly.' Brenda was looking out on the darkening garden for want of something better to do. 'If I was at home now we'd be having a real good time. Me mam always lays a good Christmas on . . . even if she has to pinch it.'

In the last few weeks Helen had grown used to Brenda's tales of skulduggery but the girl from Whitehaven, who had only come yesterday, was round-eyed. 'What d'you mean?'

Brenda turned, scenting fun at the newcomer's expense. 'Well, round about the end of November we all say what we want, and then she goes out and nicks it. It usually works . . . but there was one year she was in Durham. We didn't have much fun then.'

It was time to call a halt. 'Don't believe a word of it,' Helen said. 'Her mother's a very nice woman who comes to visit her sometimes. It's a pity her daughter's a born liar.'

'It's this place,' Brenda said, lowering herself into a chair. 'There's more excitement in a mortuary. I used to believe all sorts about nuns – you know, orgies and everything. Living it up with the priests and the communion wine . . . But all they do is work. Work and pray.'

'Do you ever think about them?' Terry said. 'Really think, I mean? They're just girls like us, some of them. What brought them here?'

'Same thing as brought us here,' Brenda said. 'Men, probably. They're running away from things like we are.' She looked at Helen. 'Why are you here, Hel? You could've kept your baby, you with a good job, an' all. I'd keep mine if I could . . . still, no use thinking about that.' Her brow had clouded and she bit her lip. 'For God's sake, let's cheer up. Tell you what, we can play some poker . . .'

'The sisters won't like that,' the new girl said, alarmed. She needn't have worried. A search of the games room and the office revealed no set of cards, only a pack of Beetle cards and a Ludo set without a dice.

'Tell you what,' Brenda said, 'I'll tell your fortunes.' She seized upon Helen's hand and held it firmly. 'What do I see here? I see two men, one dark, one fair. They're fighting over you, Hel. And I see water, an ocean, and I see . . .'

They were never to hear the rest of the revelations. 'Oh Brenda,' Sister Dymphna said, 'I'm surprised at you! There is nothing to be gained from trying to see the future . . . it's in the hands of God.'

'And a bloody mess he's likely to make of it,' Brenda said defiantly.

Sister Dymphna's eyes rolled in mock-agony. 'Oh sure, there go my poor ears . . . popping again so I can't hear a blessed word. What was that you were saying, Brenda?' She moved to the door without waiting for an answer. 'Sister Mary Margaret is making gingerbread for tea, not that anyone here will be interested.'

She quit the room to a smacking of lips, and Brenda fished in her smock-pocket for a cigarette. 'Better make the best of the ginger cake, kids. We're in here for the foreseeable future, whether we like it or not.' She choked on the last word and then began to hum, under her breath: '*Have yourself a merry little Christmas, make the Yuletide gay . . .*'

'Shut up, Brenda,' Helen said, feeling her heart would break.


Edward's lunch with Sylvia lasted for an hour and a half. It was prickly at first, after she discovered that he was going to Berwick that day, but osso bucco and lemon mousse cheered her considerably, and over coffee and Cointreau she told him what she had been doing since they parted company in the summer.

'Well, there was a man, as you might expect. No, nothing to do with publishing, he's an architect. We had something going for a while . . . well, I was on the rebound from you, you bastard . . . but it went. Who knows why these things happen? And then I thought of you, and all your winning ways . . . so I decided I had urgent business in Kensington, and here I am.'

He reached for her hand and covered it with his own. 'I'm glad. I'll be in Berwick for two weeks but when I get back we can see a lot of each other. I've missed you. A couple of times I almost picked up the phone again . . .'

Sylvia pouted. 'But you didn't. You're so self-contained, Edward. I know you like me, but you'll never really go overboard, will you? There's just that something there . . .'

He wasn't sure what she was talking about, but he might as well capitalize on it. 'Perhaps that's the secret of my fatal charm. Anyway, let's not have post-mortems. We're together now, that's the important thing.' He was glad she was back in his life. Bloody glad. The thought that sooner or later they would wind up in bed was already making it difficult to concentrate on anything else.

They took a cab back to the shop and Sylvia rinsed his breakfast dishes and tidied the kitchen as he finished his packing. While he was looking round to make sure nothing had been forgotten, he heard Mrs Stepinska below.

The promised gift was huge, contained in a brown paper carrier. It would be hell to transport to Berwick, but was sure to evoke delight when he got there. He kissed the rouged cheek and promised to convey love to his mother, and then presented Mrs Stepinska with the small gift-wrapped parcel that contained her favourite 4711 cologne.

She gripped his lapel with her red talons and whispered in his ear. 'She's back then, the red-head! Plenty of fire there, mebbe too much for a boy-chick like you. Still, it's good to get fingers burned a little.'

He was smiling as he opened the display case and palmed one of its contents. In the cab, he held it out to Sylvia. 'Sorry, it's not wrapped. If I'd known you were coming . . . it's a Liberty necklace, circa 1910. Amethyst and pearl . . . it'll suit you.'

She held it up by its delicate gold chain. 'It's beautiful, Edward . . . but I can't accept it, it's too much.'

He took it from her and fastened it around her neck, his finger ends jumping when they touched her cool skin. Her hair was a silken weight on his hands as he fiddled with the clasp. 'It's not worth a fortune, but it will be one day. All Liberty's stuff will appreciate.'

She opened her coat to let the necklace lie on her red jumper. Her hand lay on her breast, following its curve, and he knew he wanted her. Now. Perhaps he could stay in London one more day? Her eyes were on him and he knew she had read his thoughts, but in that instant he remembered how his mother's face would light up at the sight of him. 'I'll be back before you know I've gone,' he said, and reached for the door as the cab drew up at King's Cross.

* * *

When the children had gone to bed and Karen had cried on the landing for the statutory ten minutes, they got out the tree. It looked somehow dejected, its paper needles crushed from a year in the cupboard under the stairs.

'What d'you think?' Lilian said.

Billy shrugged. 'It'll do. Once you get it decorated, it'll look smashing.'

Lilian was still dubious. Another artificial tree, or even a real one, would strain her pocket, but she never worried about money at Christmas. If you did that you were finished. You got for your family; you didn't go mad, but you saw them all right and worried about it afterwards. If it had to be a new tree she would do it somehow.

'Let's try it,' Billy said, coaxingly. 'Let's get the toys on, and the lights, and see what it looks like.'

Lilian pursed her lips to consider. 'All right then, but if they've all got to come off again you can do it, Billy Fenwick.'

She put the best toys up herself and altered his to a different branch, just to show who was boss. It was as though the tree perked up with ornamentation, and then Billy draped the lights around the branches and plugged them in.

'Switch off the light,' she said and shivered with pleasure when the tree came alive in the darkened room. 'It'll do,' she said. It was going to be a good Christmas, she could feel it in her bones. To hell with Helen and her fancy men. There was nothing in London you couldn't get better in Belgate. A huge fire glowed in the grate, her children were healthy and asleep in their own beds, she had cupboards full of everything, enough for twenty Christmases – and a £20 'club' still to spend. She was a very lucky woman. The sudden knowledge amazed her.

'There now, our lass. Are you satisfied?' Billy's arms were coming round her from behind, rising to cup her breasts. His breath was warm on her ear. 'Do you feel like it, Lily?'

She snorted 'No, but I bet you do.' She smiled in the darkness at the thought of his embarrassed face. 'I'm not half-done, Billy. I can't go up yet.'

'Who said anything about going up?' He was urging her gently to the fireside rug, his lips as gentle and sweet on her as they had been that first time. He was a canny lad, really. She put up a hand to help his fumbling fingers. 'I hope you've got something, mind, Billy, because if I fall wrong you'll never see another Christmas.'

They had chosen a Minton vase for Howard and Anne, trails of autumn leaves and gold rims. 'They're difficult to buy for, aren't they?' Diana said, leaning back against David's chair to look doubtfully at the gift.

'Not for me,' David said cheerfully, seizing the vase and putting it back in its box. 'Pass the paper, and let's get it wrapped. They're damned lucky to be getting anything, so let's not waffle about it.'

'No,' Diana said, passing paper and sticky tape. 'We've got too much to do . . . I get goose-bumps thinking about Christmas Day. Just thinking about it.' They were having Howard and Anne and David's parents on Christmas Day. She was pleased about it, and terrified too.

'You'll be all right.' He wasn't being properly reassuring, he was just saying it didn't really matter, that it was only one day and would pass like other days. But it wasn't any other day, it was her first Christmas as David's wife and it must go well!

When the gifts were wrapped and put aside, they went out to the garage to get the tree. Its scent had filled the place, so that it assailed them as they opened the door from the kitchen. 'Ooh, isn't it lovely?' Diana said. 'You can't beat a real tree.'

David seized the trunk and manoeuvred it towards the door. 'I hope you'll still say that when the needles are all over the carpet, and it keeps keeling over in the bucket, and the baubles get smashed. Quite apart from the fact that this brute is going to fill the whole place, leaving no room for anyone who isn't prepared to roost on the branches.'

'Shut up and pull,' Diana said, trying to fold the branches through the doorway.

When at last the tree was in the sitting-room there was a

trail of havoc in its wake, things swept from one surface or another, a jug of milk, a chair overturned, even the carpet pulled up in the doorway to the dining-room. 'I hope you're satisfied,' David said angrily, and then, catching her eye, he started to laugh. 'The joys of family life,' he said, wiping a tear of merriment from his eye.

They were suddenly sobered, each knowing what the other was thinking.

'Are we a family?' Diana asked.

He moved to her, holding her gently. 'Of course we are, idiot. One unit, indivisible. I love you.'

She put her face against his shoulder. 'I'm scared, David. I'm scared of getting into it again and having it all go wrong. Of letting you down by heaping another massive disappointment on you.'

He was tutting and shaking his head, gripping her wrists and drawing her down beside him in a fireside chair. 'But you didn't, Diana. Don't talk as though it was something you did alone. It was my baby too and, God help me, I loved it as much as you did. It couldn't make the journey so we lost it. *We* lost it, darling. You were carrying it because that's something only a woman can do, but it was *our* baby – so if it was failure it was *our* failure. And if we try again we'll do it together. We'll decide it together, we'll plan it together and we'll see it through together . . . only this time, God willing, it'll be a happy ending.'

There were spangled baubles in a box on the table, waiting to trim the tree. Seen through her tears they dissolved now into a jewelled mass. 'Oh, David, it's going to be a lovely, lovely Christmas,' she said. 'As long as I can produce a meal that Anne won't despise.'

His hand was on her breast so surely he must feel her heart trying to break through her chest. 'Damn Anne,' he said. 'You cook like Mrs Beeton.'


They had all been in bed for an hour or more but still Helen felt wide awake. Sister Dymphna had peeped in once and gone away satisfied, and someone from another room had gone to the toilet. There was a moon tonight and it stole between the cracks in the curtains, touching the white cotton bedcovers with silver, falling on the feet of the Virgin in the far corner. It still fascinated her, this faith that was strong as a rock, more devious than the Mafia, a thing of idols and incantations, and yet a comfort to those who held it.

There was no pressure from the Sisters, not even an air of loving regret that most of their charges had not entered into the joy and safety of Catholicism. One of the girls had converted and was now more fervent in her prayers than Reverend Mother, but Helen felt no such urge. She was a spectator here, pausing briefly to observe and then passing on. Under the bedclothes she ran her hands over her swollen belly as the baby kicked. It was a strong baby and she was glad. She had eaten eagerly, even food she didn't like, in an effort to do her best for the child. Soon her part would be over, and she longed for that moment – but she feared it too, because it meant going out into the unknown.

She could not go back to Belgate, not for a long time, if ever. She had changed in the last few months. Motherhood showed not only in her swollen figure but in her face. She must keep away from her mother, and especially from Lilian, until she had had time to forget.

She was pondering how long forgetting would take when the whisper came from the opposite bed. 'Is anyone awake?' It was Brenda.

'Yes, I am . . . Helen.'

There was a small moan from the speaker and then, 'I think I've started, Hel. Oh God, I feel awful.'

Helen swung her feet to the cold lino and reached for dressing-gown and slippers. 'I'm coming over. Try not to wake the others.' She found Brenda's hand and knew from the frantic grip that something important was happening. 'I'll get Dymphna . . . lucky for you it's her and not Mary Boniface.'

Helen had seen several girls go into labour in the last few months. They were always taken beyond the green baize door at the end of the top corridor, to emerge two days later, white-faced but smiling. Unless they had changed their minds and wanted to keep their babies. Then they would spend a morning with Reverend Mother, and if they stuck to their guns they would move with their baby to the cottage in the grounds, and from there into limbo.

*'They don't let them back with us in case the rot sets in,'* Terry had said once, and Helen had smiled, secure in the knowledge that nothing could change *her* mind.

Sister Dymphna was in the kitchen, feet on a chair in a most un-nun-like fashion, an open tube of mints in her hand. The sight of Helen brought her legs to the ground and set the crucifix that hung from her waist in motion. 'Is it Brenda? I thought it would be soon . . .'

She took the dimly lit stairs two at a time and was at Brenda's side when Helen reached the bedroom door.

'There now, there's my good girl. It's your time, that's all. Nothing to be afraid of . . . I'll be with you, and our Blessed Mother will share your pain.'

Terry slept on oblivious, but Mary sat up in the bed, suddenly anxious. 'What is it? What's going on?'

'It's nothing, child.' Sister Dymphna's arms were around Brenda, helping her to her feet. 'You be a darling girl, now, and get back to sleep. Brenda will be all right with me . . . Helen will just help me as far as the infirmary and then she'll be . . .'

Her words petered out as Brenda moaned and bent almost double. 'There now, there now. We'll soon have you comfortable.'

She looked at Helen. 'Can you take her arm? We'll walk her along if we can.' Brenda's flower-sprigged nightgown had come open to reveal huge blue-veined breasts and Helen felt a shudder of revulsion. Was this what they had come to, all of them, to be swollen and distended and moan like cattle in an abattoir?

As if she read Helen's mind, Sister Dymphna reached to pat her arm. 'Come on, now, you're my good, sensible girl. Brace up and help Brenda. I can't do it alone.' She was smiling but her eyes were anxious. 'She's not much more than a girl herself,' Helen thought and it lent her new strength.

'Come on, Bren,' she said, seizing her friend's arm. 'You'll soon be out of it all, lucky thing.'

They moved slowly along the landing and then Sister Dymphna was pushing the door open with one strong, square-fingered, incredibly clean hand. 'Thank you, Helen . . . now get what sleep you can. There'll be no news for an hour or so. I'll come and tell you as soon as there is.'

Brenda's eyes were fixed on Helen's face, imploring her to stay but there was nothing else to do but return to her room.

'Is she OK?' Mary's voice was tearful and Helen made an effort to display a cheeriness she did not feel.

'Yes, she's as right as rain. It won't be long, according to Dymphna. Now let's go to sleep.'

Terry groaned from the other bed and raised herself on her elbow. 'Yes, why don't you . . . then we can *all* get some kip.' Suddenly she noticed the empty bed. 'Is she . . .?'

'Yes,' Helen said, and put out the light before her own tears of uncertainty were plain for all to see.

## 8

The view from the bedroom window was of a concrete yard and slate-roofed outhouses. Beyond lay beautiful Northumberland and in the distance the Cheviot hills, but all Helen could see was the yard and the occasional Sister flitting back and forth, shawl-wrapped against the cold. It was Christmas Eve, and Belgate would be all a-twitter with last-minute preparations. Thre was a Christmas tree in the convent hall downstairs, and a few streamers in the dining-room but Christmas to the Sisters seemed to mean an excess of devotion and little more.

Helen had bought gifts for her family and written cards. Father Connor had collected them two weeks ago and promised they would be dispatched from London in plenty of time. She had bought small gifts for the girls in her room, and for Sister Dymphna. They were wrapped and hidden in her locker and now she had nothing to do. The sky was too leaden for walking, and besides she was clumsy now, top heavy and unsteady on her feet. She put her hands under her swollen abdomen, fingertips meeting. This was her burden, but she had no sense of its being a child. She wished it well with all her heart but there was no feeling of motherhood. Perhaps she was that exception, an unmaternal woman.

She heard a noise below and looked down. Two of the girls were walking across the yard. Comparative newcomers, they were well wrapped against the cold, their bodies still girlish. From the way they walked they seemed to be little more than children and she felt pity rise up in her for their plight. In time they would feel as she did, weary and uncomfortable. Beside herself! That was a favourite phrase of her mother's when she was harassed: 'I'm beside meself.' Helen felt her eyes prick and then fill. She leaned her forehead against the icy glass and tried not to think of home but it was useless. 'Oh mam,' she said aloud. 'Oh mammy!'

If she went on like this she would break down and it wouldn't be good for the baby. She fished for a hanky in the pocket of her flowered overall and blew her nose. Only ten more days and then, if she wanted, she could howl her eyes out. She thought suddenly of Lilian in the last weeks of her pregnancy – she hadn't sympathized enough with her, thinking that Lilian laid it on. Now she knew better. And Lilian had been right about Alistair, although thank God she would never know it.

Helen tried to remember Alistair, seeking to evoke some redeeming feature. Why had she loved him, if she ever had? Perhaps it had only been the glamour of the white coat, the stethoscope ever so casually dangling from the pocket. Or perhaps she had fallen for the concept of love without looking too closely at the object of her affection.

Ice was forming inside the bottom panes and she shivered at the sight of it. Winter, winter. At least by spring she would be free.

\* \* \*

Diana carried the tray to the living-room and set it on the coffee table. Anne was standing in the bay window looking out on the winter garden but she turned at Diana's entry. 'It's a grim time of year, isn't it?'

Privately Diana was enjoying the run-up to Christmas, but it wouldn't do to say so. 'Mmm,' she said and began to pour.

Making a fuss of cups and handing biscuits was a temporary relief, and she racked her brains for topics of conversation. She was beginning to despair of her relationship with her sister-in-law. They had nothing in common, but she could have overcome that if she had sensed a desire for friendship in Anne. It was not there. Her sister-in-law gave her the impression of total self-sufficiency, of needing and wanting no one, no kind of human intercourse. If you praised Anne, her lips smiled but her eyes said 'Why the fuss?' If you contradicted her, she simply let it go – and there was seldom anything to contradict because she was not given to definite statements.

Diana watched Anne over her coffee-cup, envying her immaculate grooming and at the same time repelled by it. She wore pastel colours, beiges and blues and sometimes pale greens. On anyone else they wouldn't have lasted an hour. On Anne they remained spotless. 'You're jealous,' Diana thought wryly and then dismissed the idea. She did not envy Anne; she almost pitied her.

'Are you ready for Christmas?' Anne's eyes were golden almonds under the heavy lids as she spoke.

'Almost,' Diana said. 'Well – a quick dash to the shops when David gets in should do it. And I'm going to stuff the turkey tonight and prepare most of the vegetables. I hope Ma Whittington's prepared to make allowances.'

If Anne had been anyone else they could have had a cosy discussion about their mutual in-laws, but she was not anyone else. Diana tried to reminisce about Christmases past, but Anne contributed little. Getting desperate, she decided to try religion.

'Are your services very different to ours? I know you always go to Midnight Mass.'

For the first time Anne's face took on a touch of animation, but her words were brief. 'I can't really compare, I've never been to any church other than my own. Christmas is certainly a very holy time in the Catholic church.' So even religion was a non-runner, Dian thought. She tried again.

'It's really a time for children.' She spoke ruefully, thinking of herself but probing a little, too.

'Of course,' Anne said, leaning forward to put her cup on the tray. 'And now I must go, Diana, if you'll excuse me. I still have things to do. We'll see you tomorrow, and do ring me if there's anything I can do to help.'

When Anne had driven off in her blue Anglia, Diana gathered up the cups and carried them back to the kitchen. Thank heaven the need to make conversation was over. It was sad that there could not be a bond between them, but, if she was honest, she was happier with Lilian whose background was so very different from her own. They were going over to Belgate this afternoon to leave gifts for the children. David would laugh and play with the kids, and Lilian would glow with pride. Diana found her lips were curving at the thought. He deserved children of his own, and she really felt incredibly well: perhaps she would talk to him over Christmas.

She was standing with her hands in the suds, thinking of the future, when caution overcame her, 'Steady on, Diana,' she said aloud. 'Get tomorrow over first. If you can survive cooking four courses for seven people, you can survive anything.'

On the kitchen table the newly delivered turkey looked like a mountain. A range of mountains. 'Ye gods,' she said and fled upstairs to dress for town.


Edward had bought all the items on Dorothy's list; now he was free to look for himself. He wandered from shop to shop, enjoying the close feeling of the ancient town of Berwick, the lack of haste in his fellow shoppers. In London the pavements would be boiling with frantic men and women, ready to push and pull to get ahead. In Berwick everyone seemed to know everyone else, and they smiled at him, a stranger. Or perhaps the fact that it was Christmas Eve was making him sentimental.

He turned into a side street and halted outside an antique shop. There were items there to make his mouth water. An ivory bust of a grotesque that looked sixteenth century – not exactly his field, but he would love a closer look. And some nice walnut chairs, Edwardian probably. If it was a complete set, they would be a find. He was always intending to specialize but it wasn't easy. He pushed open the door and went inside.

When he emerged an hour and a half later he had spent £1,600 and would take delivery on 8 January, his first day back in the shop. The dealer had been anxious to do business and drop his prices for a fellow professional. Carriage had been arranged and paid for, and they had parted on good terms, with promises to do business again in future.

Edward walked down the main street in search of a phone box. He had spoken to Sylvia several times from his aunt's home, but it was difficult to have an uninhibited conversation when he knew both mother and aunt were eager to hear what he said and know that all was well with his love life.

A box appeared, and he pulled open the door. He rang the magazine first, but Sylvia was not there. There was no answer from her flat either, and he felt suddenly crestfallen. He came out into the darkening street, wondering what he really felt for Sylvia. Was it love? By this time next year would he be a married man with a home and perhaps a child on the way? Sylvia might have something to say about that! She wanted him but she wanted him on her terms.

'Spare something for the hungry, sir?' The Oxfam collector was shaking a hopeful tin, and he fed it his loose change, adding a pound note for good measure. 'Have a good Christmas,' the collector said, moving away. In a shop window a clockwork Santa Claus drove clockwork reindeer through clouds of make-believe snow. 'Merry Christmas,' a man said to no one in particular.

'Merry Christmas,' Edward replied, feeling suddenly

cheered. He hoisted his parcels higher in his arms and headed for home.


Lilian parked the pram by the back door and lifted the baby into her arms. 'Get inside Karen. Go and see your nanna.' She felt the pleasure she always felt at going back into her parents' home. Her mam would sit her down, relieve her of the bairns, make her a cup of tea, and generally fuss over her. On days when she was off-colour her mother would produce the ideal remedy for whatever ailed her, and stroke her forehead till she felt better.

Today, though, she felt well, except that she was worn to a frazzle. 'Let me get in, mam. I'm nearly down to me stumps. Give your nanna a kiss, Karen, and then find something to play with.'

The baby succumbed to the warmth of the room and lolled in her arms, dark lashes on pink cheeks, mouth pouted as though to receive the teat.

Her mother put the kettle on and came across to admire. 'By, she's a bonny bairn, our Lilian. A bonny bairn . . .' And then, for fear of jealousy, 'And so's our Karen. What a little picture!'

They sipped their tea and compared notes about their Christmas preparations. Lilian and her family would come home tomorrow for Christmas dinner, bringing the contents of the stockings to be strewn about the grandparents' floor. None of them would have it any other way.

'It won't be the same without our Helen,' her mother said at last, dipping her digestive biscuit in her tea and lifting it hastily to her mouth before it dropped. 'The first Christmas we haven't been a proper family.' She shook her head sadly and dunked her biscuit again.

'You've got us,' Lilian said, 'and you've got our Diana, now.' She looked down at the sleeping baby, a flicker of unease occurring at the thought that one day this baby might strike out on its own and leave her. Such a thing was unthinkable. 'Any road, I think our Helen'll live to regret. She'll need us before we need her, you can depend on that.'

Privately she suspected Helen was up to no good. Why else would she stay away from home at Christmas? What if she had gone right to the bad and was part of some terrible white slave set-up? If the papers found out it would all get back to Belgate. The thought of Billy's family waving copies of the *People* or the *News of the World* in her face was terrifying.

'She's a good girl, our Helen,' her mother said firmly. 'I won't have a word said against her. She's always been clever, that's part of the trouble, and she's got to spread her wings. But she won't like being away from us now, Lily.'

Lilian's tea had gone cold and she pushed it away. It had always been the same: she did her best to be the good daughter, but it was Helen who got the credit every time. She swung her daughter to her shoulder and rose to her feet. 'Well, I'm not living it up in London, I'm slogging it out in Belgate being a poor miner's wife, so I'll have to get on. We can't all be clever.'

She turned at the door for a parting shot, holding Karen's protesting arm in a vice-like grip. 'Any road, we'll be round tomorrow at half-past twelve. I know I'm not clever, but at least I'm here.'


Stella Maris was more cheerful once the curtains were drawn against the evening chill and the girls gathered in the sitting-room for their five o'clocks. This afternoon one or two were tearful, thinking of past Christmases at home. Some were discontented, thinking of the excitement tonight in the towns and cities they had left behind. Helen was trying not to think about Belgate, about the flurry in her mother's kitchen or the last-minute thrill of the Darlasden shops. Last Christmas Eve had been her first as an earner, and she had bought good presents for everyone. If only she had kept her head . . . but 'if onlys' were dangerous on a night like this!

There was a sudden flurry of excitement as Brenda appeared in the doorway. 'Hallo everyone!' She sounded defiant and there was a sudden lull as the girls tried to think of the appropriate thing to say. Should they congratulate or commiserate? They were dying to question her, to wring out the last drop of information, but no one was prepared to make the first move.

'You look thin,' Terry said at last, and then Mary, her smile returning, offered, 'Have one of Dymphna's butties . . . that'll put a stone on you.' It was easier after that to talk about Brenda's rediscovered waistline, to offer to set her hair, or relay the latest gossip about Mary Boniface's row with Sister Teresa. No one mentioned the baby, and Brenda's determined air gradually vanished to be replaced by a look of washed-out sadness that made Helen long even more fiercely to be home once more. To leave the green baize door unopened and flee back to safety and the sage-and-onion kitchen of home. The radio was crackling in the background, something about America ransoming the Bay of Pigs prisoners for 53 million dollars. For a second Helen remembered the day of the invasion, walking down into town to meet Lilian, free as a bird. No point in thinking about that now.

She was making room for Brenda beside her on the settee when the first pain came, a sudden and not unpleasant thrill across and through her abdomen. She knew at once that it was something different, but she sat quietly sipping her tea, making jokes, joining in the effort of welcoming Brenda back to the fold. And then it came again . . . a tuning-fork striking the very centre of her, reverberating until she caught her breath.

'OK?' Brenda was looking down at her, concerned.

'Yeah, I think so. I'm not due for ten days but something's going on.'

Brenda's eyes had suddenly grown liquid. 'You'll be all right, kid. It's not as bad as it's cracked up to be . . .'

And then Mary Boniface was bearing down on her, and the laughter was dying away as the green baize door opened to swallow her.


'David . . .' He was sitting opposite her, relaxed in his chair, watching the flames take the apple logs they had placed on the fire. She had his attention but it wasn't easy to begin. 'I've been thinking.'

He cocked an eyebrow. 'I should be careful . . . unaccustomed exercise is dangerous stuff.'

'Shut up, I'm serious.' She got up and crossed the hearthrug to sit pressed up against his legs. 'I've been thinking about the best Christmas gift I could give you . . .' She felt a sudden tremor of his knees and then his hand was on her head, stroking into the nape of her neck and lingering there.

'Go on.'

'I think I'm ready to try again. At first I thought I would never ever lay myself open to such pain again. And it wasn't just the loss of the baby, David . . .' He was letting her talk and she was grateful. 'It was the feeling that I was in a situation I couldn't control. People were doing things to me . . . things were happening . . . and it was as though I didn't matter at all. Something inexorable was rolling over me and I thought if I ever got out of that situation I'd never willingly enter it again. But I've had time to think now and I realize how much is at stake. So, unless the idea appals you, I'd quite like you to make love to me – properly. And we'll see what happens.'

He was coming out of his chair, kneeling to face her, taking her face in his hands. 'I love you, Diana One. You'll never know how much.'

Thinking of how he had held Diana Two this afternoon, of the look on his face that should be for a child of his own, she smiled at him, and said: 'How much?'

He shrugged. 'An inch or two or several million.'

'If this were Hollywood,' Diana thought, 'we'd start writhing on the floor or else he'd carry me up to bed . . . But this is real life, which is so much more satisfying. So we'll sit here together, watching the fire, making love without touching or speaking, until it's time to mount the stairs.' Anyway, why should they hurry when they had all the rest of their lives?

* * *

115

They were filling the pillowcases: oranges and apples first, then nuts and mesh bags of gold-covered chocolate coins. It didn't matter that the baby would know nothing of the meaning of such things, she must have her share. Pointless to worry that Karen would discard orange and nuts, take one bite from the apple, and then gorge on the gold coins. That was as it should be.

When all the glorious etceteras had been inserted it was time for the real gifts, boxed and wrapped. Karen's doll, and nurse's set, her make-up kit with lipsticks and rouges that tasted of strawberry and were guaranteed not to harm. Some leatherette boots with miniature high heels that were grown-up enough to ensure delight. Toy cigarettes, pink tipped, in a cellophane packet. Two boxed games, and a selection box with snakes and ladders on the back. 'Is it enough?' Lilian asked, suddenly afraid. It had seemed so much; now it looked puny.

'Why aye, man,' Billy said, disconcerted at his wife's crestfallen face.

Lilian's eyes had filled with tears. 'I wish we could give them more, Billy.'

He looked left and right in the hope of divine intervention but none was forthcoming. It was up to him.

'Listen, Lily. There's no bairns in Belgate got a better mam than my bairns. And I'll defy anyone to say different. You're a grand little provider, Lily. I worry about the tick sometimes, but you always make the money go round. Our Karen'll be over the moon in the morning, and so she should be.'

He had run out of steam and they both knew it. 'Well that was a speech and a half,' Lilian said, trying to hide her pleasure. 'I know what you're up to, mind – you're angling for an hour down the club. Anytime you talk fancy, drink's at the bottom of it.'

Billy was looking undeservedly sheepish, and she felt her lips twitch. 'If you give me a hand with our Diana's stocking you can have half an hour. But watch yourself, the bairns'll be up at the crack, and I'm not doing it all meself.' She thought once more of how glorious Christmas morning would be and fell to packing her baby's gifts while Billy held open the pillowcase.

When he had placed his gifts beneath the tree Edward switched off the television, banked up the fire and closed the grate for the night. In the morning they would let in the air and it would blaze away, or that was the theory. He was alone now in the downstairs part of the house; the two old ladies had retired an hour ago and he had not heard a sound from them for the last half-hour. He felt a sense of peace that he was here with them, now, to help them celebrate Christmas. And Sylvia would be waiting for him on his return. Ten more days: he yearned to see her.

He had bought his mother an antique shawl, its black cotton ground embroidered in blue and purple, fringed with gold; and a pair of serviceable suede slippers, fleecy-lined. But the *pièce de résistance* was a gold-mounted tortoiseshell stick, a delicate but sturdy aid to walking. She would like it, he knew, and it would be of service to her. For his aunt there was an Otterburn rug, bought earlier that day, and a small German figure of a hare, silver but unmarked, to add to her collection of animals.

Mrs Stepinska's gift to his mother was there too, bulky and mysterious. It had rattled faintly when he put it down, and he had prayed that nothing had come adrift on his journey. He thought of the Mews, quiet at the day's end, with only the odd home-goer to disturb its peace. It was good to visit his mother, but his heart was in London.

Perhaps, if he and Sylvia got together, he might be able to bring his mother home again? Even as the thought occurred, he dismissed it. His mother would try to make it work, and Sylvia too, to be fair, but it would be a disaster. Sylvia was a free spirit and any man who married her would have to remember that.

He moved to the door, taking one last look round before he put out the light. The guard was at the fire, papers moved away, all plugs pulled from sockets – just as his aunt had requested. When his eyes became accustomed to the dark he looked at the bulk of the tree and the glitter of parcels beneath.

Behind him a clock began to chime midnight. Another Christmas was beginning. Somewhere, now, someone was giving up their last breath, and a baby was coming into the world, as the Christchild had done – its life fresh and unmarked before it. Whoever and wherever it was, he wished it well, as he turned and felt his way up the darkened stairs.

Helen had lain in the narrow side-ward for what seemed like hours now, the pains taking her and carrying her further and further up the shore, leaving a tidal mark of agony as they ebbed. 'Oh God . . .' she cried out once, and saw God's messenger, Sister Mary Boniface, unmoved at the foot of the bed. In the intervals she thought of the baby, fighting for freedom within her, both moving forward towards their mutual goal, to be rid one of the other.

Sometimes other Sisters came and went, and then the doctor appeared. 'Two fingers dilation, doctor.'

'That's good, Sister . . . not long now.'

Once Sister Dymphna came and stroked her brow. 'There's a good girl. Not long now, my dear. Jesus and Mary are with you.'

In the more lucid moments, when they had ceased to poke and pull at the very centre of her, when she did not yearn to vomit or pass water, when she was not in the grip of fear, she felt a marvellous sense of unreality. It was none of it true. She had never lain with Alistair, allowed him that first painful entry and then the freedom of her body. Never looked into his face, and seen the boy who had masqueraded as a man and was now rejecting her. A phrase popped into her mind, one she had heard her mother use, and Lilian too: '*He may be a boy but he has a man's tool.*'

She was laughing, then, and startled faces were gathered round and above her like the petals of a flower. 'Hold on, Helen. Don't push! Hold on now, do as you're told.' And then the last painful slither and it was done, and they were

118

holding it aloft, a red creature with a face like thunder. 'It's a boy, Sister.'

'You have a son, Helen. God has been good,' Sister Mary Boniface said, her face creased with effort and satisfaction.

Helen was smiling and nodding with the sheer relief of the separation. She had done it. She had served God as his handmaiden, and it was over, and she was free. They were holding the baby out to her now, shawl-wrapped.

'Is it all right?'

'He's a beautiful boy. Look for yourself.'

But she was turning away, from Sister Boniface's suddenly disapproving face, from the harsh light on the ceiling, from the pain of the past, and from a baby who had been her penance and was now nothing to do with her at all.

## 9

The euphoria of Christmas and the glad New Year had ebbed away. Edward could see it in shop windows, now a rag, tag and bobtail of sale goods; in the preoccupied faces of passers-by; and then, when he had boarded the train, in the gloomy faces of his fellow passengers.

His mother had borne up well at their parting. He had promised to come back very soon and to phone constantly, to keep her up to date about Sylvia and the goings-on in the Mews, and to take care of himself.

'I love you, Edward,' she had said, urgently. 'I've loved you every day of your life. Never forget that.'

He had not passed it off with a joke: it had been too important for that. He had simply said, 'I know,' and had hugged her close.

Now he was going away to take up his business and his life again, and to be happy if he could, because that was his mother's wish. She could have held him to her with one word, but her love transcended that.

He opened his *Guardian* as the train pulled out, but put

it away as the countryside unfolded and he saw the sea appearing and disappearing. It was mid-morning and he had been up since six o'clock. He closed his eyes and dozed a little, and then came awake with a start as the train rattled over points. He would be in London by teatime and would settle back in tonight. Tomorrow he would open the shop and get ready for delivery of the goods he had bought over Christmas. He would need to go further afield to look for stock if he was to boost the business, but that would mean getting help in the shop. No one in the Mews could help; they were all taken up with their own affairs. And the trouble with strangers was the necessity to trust them. There were valuable things in the shop if you knew where to offer them for sale, and too many by far for him to make an inventory. If he chose the wrong person, he could be cleaned out.

He decided to postpone uncomfortable thoughts and concentrate on his paper. The Cuban missile crisis was still rumbling, but there were other new worries now. The last year had been a bad year, not just for him but for the country. The Vassal scandal came easily to mind and there had been others. But there had been Telstar, and the space-flights, too. The world was opening up, and all in all he felt a certain optimism about the next twelve months, an anticipation of something about to happen that would ultimately be for the good. He put the paper aside and closed his eyes, thinking of how it would be to hold Sylvia again.

Helen had packed her bags and said goodbye to the girls and the Sisters. Now she sat on the edge of her stripped bed and waited for Reverend Mother's summons.

The minutes ticked by and she began to wonder if she had been forgotten. She had to catch her train in an hour and there was still the journey to the station. She stood up and moved to the landing, peering down into the hall for signs of a messenger. Reverend Mother's door was open and she could hear voices . . . a man's voice and a woman's, murmuring.

Behind her the green baize door swung open and Sister Dymphna emerged, a baby cradled in one arm, a carrier bag dangling from her other hand. She seemed taken aback at the sight of Helen and hesitated, her face flushing. 'Is it mine?'

There was no chance of dissembling. 'Yes, Helen, this is your baby.'

'Is he going now?'

The nun's head bobbed. 'Yes. They're waiting downstairs.'

If she was expecting an outcry it did not come. Helen put out a hand and touched the child gently but she did not try to see his face. 'God bless,' she said and then again, 'God bless you.'

Sister Dymphna paused on the top step, her big black shoe poised to descend. 'They are good people, Helen. Good Catholics. But there is still time to change your mind. Reverend Mother will help you keep your baby if that is what you wish to do.'

'I know,' Helen said. 'She's told me that. But I'm quite sure, Sister, I really am.'

The nun nodded and gathered the baby closer. 'Well, your child will have everything, Helen. And you have made a family complete.'

As she watched the retreating figure, Helen remembered the church on that first day. What had the priest said then? *'That is the ultimate affection; to give your child to someone who needs it.'* She returned to her room, and sat down once more to wait.

She heard the great front door of the convent swing open, and went to the window. A long maroon car was in the drive and a man's fair head, gleaming in the winter sun. Then the woman, with smooth black hair, stooping over the baby in her arms.

She turned round at the sound of Sister Mary Boniface's voice. 'Helen . . . come away from the window. Reverend Mother is waiting for you. Hurry along, now, or you'll be late!

Her bags weighed heavy as she moved along the landing and down the carved oak stairs. Behind her, the room that had been a prison for so long was suddenly a haven, the most desirable place in the world. She put her bags down on the tiled floor and knocked on the dark door.

'Come in, my child. Sit down.' The old face was a rosy apple under the white headband. 'You're going to London, Sister tells me?' Helen nodded. She tried to think of her reasons for going there but suddenly there were none. To her relief the nun was not disposed to argue.

'Well, you must not lose touch with us. You have three months to change your mind about giving up your baby. You know that, of course?'

'Yes, Mother. They told me when I signed the papers.' She was remembering the interview with the Welfare Department here in this same room with its oak panelling, its saint-filled niches, the Pope smiling benignly from above the mantel. 'Yes, everything was explained.'

The hands folded on the desk were old and wrinkled, the broad wedding ring scratched and worn. Brides of Christ, that was what they called them, but they were married to work and hardship and caring for people like her who had ruined their own lives. 'I'm really grateful, Mother. You've all been kind.'

The old woman was coming round the desk, lifting her hand to smooth Helen's hair. 'Bless you, child. You've been a great help while you were here, and we're sorry to lose you. Your baby has gone to its adoptive parents, good people who will give your son love and a Christian upbringing. But it is your privilege to change your mind, and if you do you must come to me and tell me. I will do all that is necessary to restore your baby to you and help you. You will be helped, whatever you decide. Now . . .' Suddenly her eye was on the clock, her tone brisker. 'This folder contains your travel ticket, and ten pounds, and the address of our Mother House in London. There you will find friendship and help with rebuilding your life. We shall pray for you here, as we pray for all our girls, and their children, and the good people who have taken them to their hearts. Go with God, my child, and remember we are always here if you need us.'

When she was out on the drive, half running over the

gravel for fear of missing her train, Helen felt hot tears come, but whether they were tears of anger or tears of relief, she could not be sure. Thank God, it was all over!

Guilt tugged at her: Sister Dymphna had been kind, and they *had* given her a way out of her terrible dilemma. 'God bless them all, and forgive me for my ingratitude.' She was hurrying for the station when she realized that her legs were not as strong as she had believed. She slowed to a walk, her cases bumping her thighs, and at a more sedate pace made for the train that would take her to freedom.

Lilian parked the pram at the door and adjusted the covers up and around the sleeping baby's face. If she lifted her now they would get no peace, but she couldn't leave her outside long on a day like this. Karen was sucking on a stick of barley sugar, and when Lilian took her hand she felt their palms adhere. 'Tsk, Karen . . . you're all clagged up. Get in and ask your nanna to wash your hands. And keep that barley sugar off your duffle-coat.'

Her mother's kitchen was warm and smelled of proving bread. 'Sit down, pet. I'm just masting the tea. There's some stotty there, if you want a bit.'

Lilian sliced the still-warm bread cake and spread it thickly with butter. She thought her mother was mad to keep on baking bread when the Co-op was almost giving it away – but there was no comparison between this mouth-watering concoction and a sliced loaf, and you had to admit it.

'I've heard from our Helen.' There was an air of smugness in her mother's words and the bread turned to ashes in Lilian's mouth.

'Oh, she's condescended to write, has she? Well, mind, that's nice of her with her big, important life.' This morning she had faced the clubwoman and told her there could be no payment till next week, and the woman's contemptuous, threatening words still rankled.

'She's had a lovely Christmas . . . five-course meals and everything, and the doctor treating her just like one of the family. She got her parcel, and she thanks everyone very much . . . well, you can read it for yourself.'

Lilian scanned the lines of neat handwriting, picking out phrases like *'marvellous time'* and *'everything laid on'*. It was thick blue paper that felt almost like cloth. Trust their Helen to land on her feet.

'Very nice,' she said at last, laying the letter aside. 'Still, I can't sit here wittering on about our Helen. I only popped in to see how you were getting on, and the bairn can't stay out in that yard.' She brushed aside her mother's suggestion of bringing the pram indoors. 'No, I'd never get it through the doors without scratching the paint. You don't want your house bashed up on account of my bairns. You want to keep it nice for our Helen coming home . . . if she can find the time.'

And then, when her mother's face changed from coaxing to implacable: 'It's always been the same, mam, admit it! I've had our Helen pushed down me throat day and night since the day she was born. We all know she's clever, mam. You don't need to show off about it.'

Karen was looking from one to another, eyes round. 'Come on, pet. We'll go down your Nanna Fenwick's and see if we're wanted there.' To throw Billy's mother in her own mother's face was the ultimate insult, and even as Lilian used it she regretted it. There would be no overtures of peace now . . . well, not before hell froze over . . .and it was all Helen's fault.


Helen had a mortal fear of losing her ticket. She handed it over at the barrier, and when it was clipped and returned she clutched it in her hand. 'Is this the London train?' Even when the porter had said yes, she wasn't sure. She tried to remember the names of villages either side so she would know if she was going in the right direction. If they came to Newcastle it would be all right.

She looked along the train for an open door. Her cases were pulling on her arms and she felt distinctly unwell. 'It's only fear,' she told herself. 'It's only fear.' But it was more than that. It was eleven days since she had given birth, and she wasn't up to all this effort.

For a moment she contemplated retreat. She could go back to the convent . . . they would take her in. They had not wanted her to leave so soon; it was she who had been mad keen to get out into the world again – and now she was out, she couldn't cope.

A man had opened a door and was swinging it back on its hinges. 'Do you need a hand?'

Helen nodded, feeling tension ebb from her as he hoisted up her bags, and then extended a hand. 'Mind the step. That's right. Where do you want to sit?'

She sat down opposite him, subsiding into the seat, feeling the fabric of the upholstery tickle cheek and legs. With her head leaning against the side of the carriage, she felt a little better. She was aboard now, with a five-hour journey in which to gather herself together.

As the train pulled out she eyed the man opposite. He was reading, and she saw that the book was called *Anatomy of Britain* by someone called Sampson. He wore quite expensive clothes, but they were a bit shabby and his shoes were well-scuffed suede. She pondered his age. Thirty, maybe, or thirty-five? He looked up suddenly and smiled, and she revised her estimate. Twenty-five maybe, or roundabouts.

'Are you going to London?' he asked, and Helen nodded. He smiled again and returned to his book; and she opened her bag and put her ticket, damp and crumpled now from her hand, into an inside pocket. She checked her ten-pound note and the money in her purse. She had £7 16s saved from her pocket money at Stella Maris, and another five-pound note she had brought with her all those months before. £22 16s, nearly £23. More money than she had had at one time in her life before. How long would it last in London? Unless she went to the Mother House it probably wouldn't last a week. She looked at the address Reverend Mother had given her. She would have to go there, but she didn't want to. She wanted to forget.

She felt tears come and closed her eyes to squeeze them out of existence. Her head rested on the back of the seat

125

and she wondered if you could get nits from upholstery. No use worrying about that now. She was tired, terribly, terribly tired. If she slept a little she might be able to work everything out. The train was thrumming along, and she folded her hands in her lap and gave way to the lullaby.

David was pressing to know Anne's reasons for calling off the lunch they were all to have had together. 'I don't know why, darling, but never look a gift-horse in the mouth,' said Diana, blithely. 'She simply said something had come up and she couldn't make it, and I said, "Oh dear, what a pity!" So can you take me to lunch or can't you?' They arranged to meet in the Swan and Diana ran upstairs to get ready, feeling like a child suddenly excused lessons with the grimmest of teachers.

'*I'm going to see you today, all's well with my world*': She sang the Joyce Grenfell song as she hurried round the bedroom. For Anne she would have worn a suit and her beaver lamb. For David she would wear her red cashmere coat with the black astrakhan hat and tie he said made her look like a Tsarina. She put on black patent court shoes with three-inch heels, which were manifestly unsuitable for January pavements – but who cared? She loved him. A whole year married, and she loved him more every day. Poor Anne, who hardly seemed to love Howard at all.

As Diana went to get out the car, teetering on the icy concrete, she wondered again what had happened to make Anne cancel lunch. Anne was always so well organized that the idea of something going wrong for her was almost inconceivable. She slipped a little as she closed the garage doors, and then gave in: stilettos were idiocy on a day like this. She clung to the wall as she made her way back to the front door, unlocked it, and ran upstairs for her boots. David would still love her, even if she turned up in a brown paper bag. All the same, the sight of herself in the bedroom mirror, red and black and sparkling-eyed, brought a smile to her lips. She was feeling well, and with luck she would soon have the bloom of pregnancy. It was going to be all right this time, she just knew it. As she came back downstairs, she thought once more of Anne: she would have to ring her tonight and make discreet enquiries. If there was something wrong they would have to help. Anne was family, like it or lump it.

A flake of snow hit her nose as she got into the car, but it was a solitary one. The sky was grey and probably snow-filled, but soon she would be snug in the Swan with a log fire crackling and her most favourite person in the world opposite her for one whole hour. As she waited for a break in the traffic she looked once more at the lowering sky. 'Snow if you like,' she said, 'and see if I care!'


From behind his book Edward watched the newly boarded passenger. She hardly looked old enough to be travelling on her own, but even with her eyes shut there was a steely determination about the chin and the hands clasped reso-lutely in her lap. She might have been pretty but for the curious blueness of her skin and the too-thin nose that looked sharp enough to cut paper. Her legs were long and gangling and her clothes hung loosely on her, as though they belonged to a big sister. He saw her eyelids quiver and dropped his own gaze. Mustn't get involved: the first rule of English travellers.

At Darlasden he noticed she seemed to shrink in her seat, only relaxing when the train pulled out and they were still alone in the compartment. He stood up to go in search of coffee, but his conscience smote him at the sight of her, bony knees clamped together, hand moving occasionally to check that her bag was still beside her. If he was any judge, this was her first time away from home.

'Can I get you a cup of coffee?' He saw pleasure in her eyes and then caution, followed by fear.

'No thank you, I'm all right.'

He pulled open the door of the carriage, and then stood his ground. 'Look here, you look as though you could do with a hot drink and it's a long way to London. It's just as easy to bring two as one.'

The girl smiled a little and began to scrabble in her purse. He held up a hand. 'I'll take the money when I come back.'

He bought two cups of coffee and a round of ham and tomato sandwiches. Back in the carriage he solemnly accepted the price of the coffee, and then proffered his sandwiches. 'I can only eat one. Please accept the other. I'll only have to throw it away if you don't.'

She ate uneasily at first, and then eagerly, and the coffee seemed to bring colour back into her cheeks.

'My name's Edward Portillo,' he said when the coffee was done, holding out his hand, 'and I'm on my way home to London. I've been spending Christmas in Berwick with my mother, who is elderly.'

She smiled, the first genuine smile he had seen from her. 'I see. I'm going to London to work.'

It was his turn to nod. 'The big city . . . well, there are lots of openings. Or perhaps you have a job lined up?'

'No. I just decided to go down, and this seemed a good time. I'm going to start looking as soon as I get there. Tomorrow.'

She sounded so childlike, so convinced that it would all fall into place, that Edward felt alarmed. London had a habit of eating girls just like this one. 'But you've got somewhere to stay?'

She frowned slightly, and he knew he had touched her on a sore spot. 'I've got an address . . . but I'd rather not use it, if I can help it. I thought I'd get a room for a few days, in a boarding-house. I can always move on once I'm working. There's plenty of boarding-houses, isn't there?'

'Quite a few,' he said, 'but you'll need to be careful.' Her hands were positively scrawny, the nails bitten so that their otherwise perfect ovals were blurred, and her dark hair was looped back and caught with a kirby grip. She looked pathetic, and Edward lost the last vestige of his former reserve.

'I'll tell you what . . . why not come home with me when we get to King's Cross? I'll ring around one or two places, fix you up somewhere decent, and then you can go over by cab. You can't just walk around London streets *looking*; the place is too vast. And if you ask for a cabbie, he'll take you wherever he gets a rake-off. You have to be careful about districts in London, especially when you're on your own.'

She was looking so dubious that he tried to make a joke: 'I don't live alone, I have two blokes sharing with me, Mark and Antony.' If anything, this news seemed to alarm her even more. 'I'm pulling your leg. They're torchères . . . figures for holding lamps. I called them Mark and Antony when I was a youngster, and it's stuck.'

Edward had to restrain a smile at the emotions chasing themselves across her face – varied emotions, but fear of the white slave trade appeared to be paramount. 'Thank you very much,' she said at last, 'but I couldn't bother you.'

Edward smiled and shrugged. He would have like to help, but he wasn't prepared to cajole her. Hundreds of girls like her came to London every week: if she got into deep water, she would simply be one more.

'Well, the offer still stands,' he said. 'See how you feel when we get there.'


Billy came in at six-thirty, eyes black-rimmed in an otherwise clean face. Lilian lifted his mince and dumplings from the oven and served them to him on a tray. He had taken off his boots and was toasting his socked feet on the fender. 'By it's nice to be home, Lilian. Bairns all right?' He was lifting a dumpling to his mouth on the blade of his knife when their eyes met and he thought better of it. Robbed of the opportunity to tell him off about his table manners, Lilian sought for another excuse.

'Get your feet out of the hearth, Billy. It's bad enough eating off your knee without that. And you'll have to make the tea. I'll dish your pudding up, but that's me finished.'

'Had a hard day, Lily?' He was trying to get on her good side and it irritated her.

'Don't make out it matters to you, Billy Fenwick. I could be worn down to the bone, and as long as your meal was put out for you you wouldn't give a damn. I've seen the light lately, I really have. If you want to be appreciated, be selfish: that's the thing. Think about Number One, like our Helen.'

He was scraping the plate with his knife, making neat furrows side by side. 'Leave the pattern on the plate, Billy. There's sago in the oven, you won't starve. Like I was saying, it doesn't pay you to stay loyal in this life. I could've gone off, too; I could've gone down Coventry when Evelyn Andrews did. I could've gone chamber-maiding down south. But me, mugsy, I stayed – and am I better thought of? I am not!'

'Come on, Lily. We love you, me and the bairns.'

For a moment she wondered whether to be mollified or not. Being narky wore you out if you kept it up too long. But his eyes had strayed to the oven and the sago: that was how much he cared! 'I would like to believe you, Billy but I don't. And for the hundredth time my name's not Lily . . . it's Lili-an!'


David came in from evening surgery at half-past five. 'I hope you haven't cooked anything elaborate?'

At first she thought he was making fun. 'Just *filet de boeuf* Whittington *avec pommes de terre et petits pois*, followed by *crêpes Suzette*.'

David shook his head. 'No, I'm serious. We've been summoned to Howard's for dinner. Half-past eight. He says they've got a surprise for us.'

Diana pulled a face. 'Nice surprise or nasty surprise?'

'Your guess is as good as mine. He didn't sound frantic, so it can't be calamity. But you know that legal manner of his. I asked a couple of questions but he just countered them. "I'd prefer to leave it till tonight," he said, and that was that. What *were* you making?'

'I was going to do steaks, so they'll keep. I wonder what it can be? Do you think they're going to separate . . . they've never seemed really together, have they?'

'Not a chance. Anne is too much of a religious fanatic even to contemplate it, and Howard would weigh the legal pros and cons forever and then decide to stay put. No, whatever it is, it won't be that.'

'Perhaps they're going to move?'

David shook his head. 'Why have a special dinner for that? And it's nothing to do with the parents, because I rang dad and sounded him out. They're going over to lunch tomorrow: Anne rang and invited them earlier today. So *something's* up. But what?'

They went upstairs to get ready, each carrying a glass of gin and Italian. 'I wish we didn't have to go out,' Diana said, slipping out of her dress and reaching for a wrap. David had loosened cuffs and collar and was pulling his shirt over his head. 'Undo it,' she said. 'I hate unbuttoning things for the wash.'

'Slave-driver,' he countered, obeying her command. When he had dropped it in the linen basket he moved towards her. 'I don't want to go out, either, but we do have forty-five glorious minutes before we have to leave.'

She wrinkled her nose. 'That's not long enough for anything constructive.'

His mouth turned down at the corners. 'Pity.'

Diana frowned. 'You could try chasing me round the bed. That's quick . . . if I let you catch me, that is.'

He stepped back. 'As usual, you've solved it. I'll give you a count of three . . .'


He had been a perfect gentleman all the way down, bringing her tea at Doncaster and a packet of ginger biscuits. All the same, she was not going back to his flat with him! She was not as green as she was cabbage-looking, so if he had any funny ideas he'd be disappointed. She had decided what to do. She had once known a Belgate girl who had lived for a while in Earl's Court with her divorced father, and she had talked about it as though it was all flats and rooms to let. Anyway, it would be as good a place as any to make a start. She would walk out of the station and look for a bus that went to Earl's Court. Once there she would walk up and down until she saw somewhere suitable, and even if it cost a fortune it need only be for one night. Tomorrow she would find a YMCA or the Sally Army, and ask for advice.

'We're coming in to London now,' Edward said, closing his book and standing to get his bag from the rack. He turned back to her. 'Have you thought about my offer? No strings, I promise you. By tonight I'll see you safe in a decent guest-house.'

Helen trusted him, but she still wasn't going to risk it. He was posh – everything about him said that, and he had a very intelligent face. All the same, it wasn't worth it. You heard terrible tales about London. 'Thanks very much, but I'd rather manage on my own.'

She was standing now and all of a sudden she didn't feel too good. She saw his lips twist with exasperation. 'Well, at least let me help with your bags. You look as though you're going to flake out.'

He commandeered a porter when they reached the platform, and took her arm, and she could tell from his grip that he thought she was being an idiot. They were through the barrier when she saw an elderly lady peer suddenly over her rimless glasses. 'Edward . . . is it you?'

Edward was holding out his hand and Helen saw he was pleased. 'Miss Francis, how nice to see you. Are you going north?'

They chatted about his mother as the station seethed about them. So this was London, Helen thought, resisting the urge to cover her ears against the clatter. There were pigeons walking between people's legs, as cheeky as you please. Suddenly she became conscious of the old lady's none-too-well disguised curiosity about her.

'This is . . .' Edward said at last, and she finished it for him.

'Helen . . . Helen Clark.'

When he had kissed the old lady and made his goodbyes, Edward took Helen's arm again. Her legs were threatening to fold and the huge echoing station seemed like a noisy cauldron bubbling and buzzing around her. 'Are you all right?' he was saying and she nodded.

'I'm OK. Just a bit faint.' Her voice did not sound like her own and her ears were buzzing. If he left her now, she would drop. Men who knew respectable old ladies couldn't be real villains. Besides, if he murdered her now, at least one person would know it was him. 'I will come back for a little while,' she said, 'if you still mean it. Just for long enough to get turned round.'

He was smiling at her tolerantly. 'Now you're talking sense.'

They moved to a barrier and shuffled in a queue towards a taxi. 'Inkerman Mews,' he said, heaving their bags in beside the driver, and then sitting down beside her, keeping well away. For a moment Helen wondered if she had been foolish, but it was done now. She tried to relax and steady her uneven breathing as the taxi sped through streets that looked suspiciously like Darlasden and not grand and imposing at all.

At last they reached their destination, a funny little street tucked away from the traffic. Edward unloaded the bags, opened a door and ushered her in. 'Go straight up. I'll pay off the taxi and follow with the cases.'

Helen made her way gingerly through a darkened shop, peering sideways at what looked like looming furniture, until lights sprang on and she heard the shop door close behind her with a ping. In front of her were two little black boys made of pottery, chipped here and there, and holding lamps in their hands like the Statue of Liberty.

'Mark and Antony,' Edward said, patting one of the crinkly pot heads. 'And now, let's get the kettle on.'

He had installed her in an easy chair and was filling the kettle when the phone rang. Helen knew at once, from the intent way he listened, that something was wrong. 'I see. Yes, of course . . . I'll catch the next train . . . Give her my love, and tell her I'm on my way.' As he put down the phone he looked terrible, like an old man.

'Is it your mam?' Helen said.

He nodded. 'She's had some sort of cerebral attack. I'll have to go back to Berwick.' He looked suddenly confused and she rose to he feet.

'Look, I'm going to make you some tea, and then I'll get out of your way.' She moved to the kettle, and he sat silent, thinking, as she tried to locate teapot and caddy without bothering him.

'Thanks,' he said at last, as she put the tray in front of

him. He had a railway timetable in his hand, which he had been studying, and now he put it down. 'There's a train in an hour that I can probably catch. And I've been thinking. We could do one another a favour. I've got deliveries arranged for tomorrow, and there are sure to be phone calls from people expecting me back. You've got nowhere to stay. Would you like to stay here and, well, take care of things for me? Answer the calls, take in deliveries? It would be an enormous relief to me to know you were here. My girlfriend will be around, and I have an elderly friend across the Mews who'll look out for you.'

Helen's heart was leaping at the very thought of not having to move on just yet, but she had to remonstrate with him. 'You don't know me. I mean, I could make off with some of your good things as soon as your back was turned!'

His eyes were anxious but he smiled a little. 'If you could see yourself, I think you'd know why I'm not too worried about that. You don't look as though you could make the corner of the street, never mind a get-away. So will you stay until I get back?'

Helen hesitated for only a second. 'All right, then, I will.'


# 10


It had rained for three days but Helen had not minded. To be here in this safe little eyrie, above a shop full of enchantment, was a kind of Heaven, its only flaw being the knowledge that Edward would come back eventually and she would have to leave.

On that first day he had made a series of phone calls, interspersed with staccato instructions to her about where she would find towels and coffee and iron rations if she ran out of food. He had given her a sheaf of papers relating to the shipment of antiques, and a phone number where he could be contacted in Berwick if the need arose. This had taken forty hectic minutes. He had then rushed out and reappeared with a small grey-haired woman called Mrs Stepinska who would, he announced, help out in any emergency. All this time Helen had expected him to take sudden fright and announce that he couldn't possibly leave his home in the hands of a stranger, but he had kissed Mrs Stepinska, his eyes suddenly filling with tears, had picked up his unopened bags, nodded to Helen, and roared off in a black taxi-cab.

Mrs Stepinska had spent the next hour singing the praises of Edward and his mother in heavily accented English, only half of which Helen had understood. But she had gathered enough to know that she was safe, for the time being at least. She had declined Mrs Stepinska's invitation to supper on the grounds that she was exhausted, but had accepted some fresh bread and milk and a piece of mysterious and highly spiced sausage.

At first she had been uneasy, afraid to touch another's possessions, unable to relax because she felt like an intruder, terrified of the unseen metropolis outside the door. Now she had been in London for four days and was brave enough to venture out for her own bread. Today would be her last day in the haven of Edward's home: his mother had died the night of his return to Berwick. Today she would be buried, and he was catching an early evening train back to London.

Helen picked her way through the shop, crowded now with the newly delivered stock, and opened the jangling door. It was not yet nine o'clock and the Mews was still quiet. Further down, the joiner was opening up, and a duster was being shaken from one upstairs window, but apart from a visiting pigeon there was no other sign of life. 'I like it here,' Helen thought. 'It is the safest place in the world.' She stepped out on to the glistening pavement and locked the door behind her. When Edward came back he must find his cupboards replenished and a list of likely residences that he would approve and she could afford. He had been kind and she must not be a burden, especially now when he was so sad.

'They had a great love, one for the other,' Mrs Stepinska had told her. 'Not often does the boychild love the mama like that, above rubies. Or if he does, it is not a good love because it comes out of weakness. This Edward is a strong man, but still he loves the mama. He will be sad today.'

As Helen turned into the busy High Street she thought about Sylvia, who had phoned twice to ask if everything was OK. She had sounded very capable, and very close to Edward: perhaps they would marry and that would help heal his wounds? The bread shop loomed up, smelling like paradise, and she stepped inside.

David and Diana had talked of little else but the baby ever since they had arrived at Howard's to find it installed in a nursery complete even to tiny white wardrobe and nursing chair, with frilled lemon cushions to match the curtains.

'I *still* don't know how she could have kept it quiet,' Diana said, elbows on the breakfast table, coffee cup held in her cupped hands. 'I mean, we talked babies, quite a lot . . . Diana Two, and her cousin's baby. I even mentioned that we were thinking about it again. And all that time she was planning it, going through all the necessary channels, dealing with the priest, decorating a nursery. How on earth did Howard keep it from you? You're brothers!'

David reached for the marmalade. 'Being brothers doesn't make you bosom buddies, you know. I don't think we exchanged many confidences when we were kids. When I was at University we were quite close . . . but then we only saw one another at intervals.' He bit his toast and chewed for a moment. 'Anyway, if I'm any judge, Anne set it up and then told him it was happening.'

'*Could* she do that?' Diana asked.

'Not completely. At some stage he'd have had to consent, but if it was almost a *fait accompli* by then, he wouldn't have had much choice, would he? Anyway, can you imagine him standing up to her? She'd just need to give him one of those looks of hers . . . like a stoat and a rabbit . . . and he'd sign anything.'

Diana washed up the breakfast dishes while David got ready for his morning surgery, and then walked with him to the car, pausing to look at the ice-bound garden in the hope of seeing some breaking bulbs. It had been a desperately cold winter, the worst for years. She shivered and tucked her hand into the crook of David's arm.

'What you said about Anne, about the stoat and the rabbit . . . it was pretty savage,' she said.

David nodded. 'I know.'

'You don't like her do you?'

He was unlocking the car door. 'Not much.' He climbed into the seat and wound down the window for a goodbye kiss.

'If you're right,' Diana said, 'it doesn't say much for the baby's chances.'

David turned on the engine and let it idle for a moment before he replied: 'At least it'll have a wonderful auntie.'

Diana bent to kiss him and then stood waving until the chill bit through her sweater and sent her scampering back into the warm.


There were more people in the tiny church than Edward had expected and wreaths in abundance, including one from *'Stephan and Maria Stepinski with gratitude for true friendship'*. There were no flowers from Sylvia. She had written a sympathetic letter and promised to send a donation to Oxfam.

They sang the hymn his mother had requested long ago, 'O love that will not let me go,' and Edward felt a sudden joy within him. She was safe now, and moreover she was freed from the limitations of earthly living. She could be with him now wherever he might go. He felt faintly surprised at this thought: he had never believed in an afterlife, but now he was acknowledging a continuation of sorts. Beside him his aunt was quietly sobbing, and he abandoned philosophical thought to give comfort.

In the crematorium they sat while music rolled as though from heavenly choirs, and he tried not to hear the whir of machinery that meant there was no longer a hand to touch, a cheek to kiss, not even a cold and still one. 'I loved you, mother,' he thought, 'and you know I did.' And then he saw her quite clearly in his mind, nodding agreement, and he understood that he was going to be all right.

Back at his aunt's home he handed tea-cups and sausage rolls, and made conversation with people who had barely known his mother but who wanted to be kind just the same. When they had all gone home, he went upstairs to collect those things of his mother's he wished to keep. 'I want you to have these,' he said, handing Dorothy the embroidered shawl and the slippers, still in their box; but he kept the stick for himself because he knew his mother had prized it.

There was another hour to his train. 'Mother left a will, Aunt Dorothy; I don't know the terms but I know you were mentioned in it. As soon as I have details I'll be in touch. And I want you to know how grateful I am for everything you did . . . for us both.' He kissed her, and then set about amusing her as best he could until it was time to say goodbye.


However Lilian did her sums there was one inescapable conclusion. You couldn't get a quart out of a pint pot and that was all there was to it. 'Bugger Christmas,' she said aloud and then, remembering small ears, 'sugar Christmas. Sugar, sugar.' Well, the clubwoman would have to take less for a while; she would get it all in the end, every penny. Lilian decided to start a savings campaign and raked out a jar to hold sixpences. Last time she had done that she had got it half-filled and then had had to cash them in for a second-hand washer to replace the third-hand one with which she had started married life. This time she would go on to fill the jar, no matter what demands came along.

Once she got past nappies she wouldn't care about a washer. She could take the odd load round to her mam's and rinse the others through in the sink. In the corner the lidded nappy bucket stood, reeking of Milton and shit. Lilian hated the daily ritual until they were out on the line, blowing in the wind, white and fresh enough to bury your face in them and breathe in Omo and warm wet cotton.

She put aside pen and pencil and put on the kettle. There were compensations to motherhood: there was satisfaction if your bairns thrived and were a credit to you; and the Family Allowance; and the right to put the kettle on whenever you felt like it. You didn't get that with a nine-to-five job.

All the same, she had had her last bairn. There was a new lady doctor at the practice and by all accounts she was sympathetic. Maybe she would arrange a sterilization. Men doctors never would, they liked to keep you breeding in case you got above yourself. But a woman, now, she might talk sense.

In the corner Karen was humming quietly as she dressed and undressed her doll, alternately threatening to thrash it or kiss it to death. In its carrycot the baby slept the sleep of angels. The tea in Lilian's hand was warm and sweet. She pulled up another chair to take her feet, and had a sip. If only life could always be like this.


'Hello?' Helen had heard the shop bell ring and came out on to the landing, but the woman was already half-way up the stairs.

'Hello again. I'm Sylvia, we spoke on the phone.' She moved past Helen and led the way into the sitting-room, looking right and left. 'So Edward's coming home today. It was sad about his mother, wasn't it?'

Helen sensed that she was not expecting an answer. Every word, every gesture was staking a claim . . . to the flat and to Edward's life. Well, she needn't worry, Helen thought, tomorrow I'll be gone and she can have her precious Edward. 'Would you like some coffee?' she asked aloud, and Sylvia nodded, unfastening the huge scarf that swathed her shoulders.

'Yes, please. Edward tells me this is your first time in London? We spoke on the phone last night, and I said I'd look in on you.'

Helen was assembling cups and saucers, and her hands were shaking so that the crockery rattled. Why did she feel scared, as though Sylvia knew everything about her, knew and disapproved? 'Yes. I've never been here before, but I've always wanted to come.'

Sylvia was accepting a cup with slim scarlet-tipped fingers. 'Thank you. No sugar. Where are you going to live?'

Helen felt flustered. Should she say, 'Well, I don't expect to live here so you needn't worry?' Should she tell a fib and talk about a job and a place to live as though they already existed? Looking at Sylvia's slightly elevated eyebrows and the suede-booted leg swinging gently to and fro from crossed knees she had an urge to say, 'What the hell has it got to do with you?'

But this was Edward's home and Sylvia was his girl and deserved courtesy. 'I've got a list from an agency, and I'm going to go over it with Edward when he gets back. I'm moving out tomorrow, anyway, even if it's got to be a hostel.'

A spasm of annoyance crossed Sylvia's face. 'So you'll be here tonight?'

Helen nodded. 'Yes, Edward asked if I'd stay. He doesn't know what time he'll be back . . .'

The leg was positively gyrating now. 'He needn't have worried, I could have come round. Still, if that's it . . . Well, I must go. Tell Edward I'll phone him tomorrow.' She was flinging the multi-coloured shawl around her neck again and pinning it with a silver brooch. When it was fixed she ran fingers through her wonderful hair and picked up her bag. 'In case we don't meet again, good luck. London can be wonderful.' She sounded doubtful that it would be wonderful for Helen but as she went down the stairs Helen kept a dutiful smile clamped on her face.

'And good riddance,' she said, as the door clanged shut. All the same, she was an inconvenience here, all right, and would have to get out tomorrow, wherever she went. She gathered up the cups and rinsed them, and then set about tidying the flat to welcome Edward home.

Diana rang the bell and turned to look at the garden. Anne was the gardener and you could see her hand in the clipped hedges, the formal plots, the neat metal edging to the borders. She turned as the door opened. 'Hallo . . . I haven't come at a bad time, have I? We wanted you to have this . . .' She held out the prettily wrapped baby gift, and Anne took it from her.

'Come in. How kind of you.' She closed the door and put the present on the monk's bench in the hall.

'She's not curious,' Diana thought, surprised. 'If that had been me, I'd have been ripping off the paper by now.' She laid her coat on the hall chair and followed Anne through to the morning-room. 'Is Michael sleeping?' she asked, seeing no sign of the baby.

Anne nodded. 'He was fed at eight, so he's not due again until twelve.'

They sat in the morning-room to drink coffee, while Diana itched to see the new baby. 'Do you feel confident about handling him?' she asked. 'I know I'll feel terribly nervous when the time comes.'

Anne leaned forward to offer biscuits. 'No. It's a completely new situation, of course, but I've had guidance and I'm reasonably sure I'll manage.'

Around them the room was as tidy as ever, no evidence of a new baby anywhere. 'There should be something,' Diana thought – playthings, perhaps, or a clothes-horse full of drying nappies . . . anything to signal a new arrival. If she had had a baby, she would have wanted it to show everywhere. But then, she would not have been brave enough to take a strange baby – so who was she to criticize? She turned her attention back to Anne and listened to a long discourse about preserving beech leaves in glycerine.

'I can't leave without a peep at the baby,' she said firmly when it was time to go.

Anne smiled briefly and led the way upstairs. 'He's a good baby,' she said as they entered the lemon-and-white nursery. 'He likes his routine.'

The baby lay, awake, in an immaculate cot, the blue unfocused eyes looking rather sad and worldly wise in the tiny puckered face. Surely Anne would pick him up and cuddle him? But the baby remained in the crib, as Diana hung over him and cooed at him, and eventually they left the room and made their way downstairs, through the totally silent house to the icy garden beyond.

'If I'd had any sense I'd have picked the little thing up myself,' Diana said to David, over lunch. 'Except that I'd never have dared.'

David smiled. 'Well, she won't be able to have things all her own way. Babies are individuals you know. It may bring out her mother instinct eventually.'

Diana pushed away her plate, suddenly full. 'I wouldn't take bets on it,' she said.


Billy brought her cocoa to bed and Lilian cupped her hands around the mug for warmth. 'This bedroom's like an icebox,' she said, thinking of Helen warm and snug in centrally heated luxury. Billy was hastily pulling on his pyjamas, shivering as the cold air of the bedroom struck his bare flesh. 'By God,' he said, diving between the flannelette sheets, 'it'd freeze the balls off a brass monkey.'

She let him lie long enough to get cosy before she delivered the bad news. 'The light, Billy . . . it won't put itself off.'

He groaned and turned on his side, pulling the bed-clothes around his ears. 'I left it on for you, Lily, so you could drink your cocoa.' The warmth of the mug had permeated her cold hands and she was comfy now, ready to enjoy the game.

'Don't put it on to me! I never asked you to leave it, I could've drunk up in the dark. Anyroad, never mind whose fault it is, get up and fix it and let's get some sleep.'

Billy's answer was a mock snore, ending in air expelled from between vibrating lips, and Lilian couldn't help laughing.

'I'm not kidding, Billy. I said up, and I meant up!' He pulled the sheets and blankets tighter around his neck. 'I won't go.'

She contemplated tickling him, a certain way of bringing him to his knees, but if she did that the covers might be disarranged and they'd both freeze. She was about to offer a kiss by way of payment when she thought of what kissing could lead to and changed her mind.

'All right, Billy, I'll get up. I'm dead tired and me legs feel like lumps of lead after standing on that concrete floor all day, washing. But I'll go . . .' He was half-way across the room before she could finish and they were plunged into darkness.

He was shivering when he got back and she put her arms around him to warm him up. 'You've got a tongue on you like a razor, Lily, but I love you.'

'I know you do . . . and so you should.' His body was bulky and strong and Lilian felt a sense of pride that he was hers. Her fingers could feel the fragility of the cotton pyjamas, his only pair, worn thin by washing and drying on the fireguard, and in the darkness her eyes filled with tears. He didn't get much and he never asked for anything. When their ship came in she would buy for him till they didn't have cupboard space to hold it.

He was growing heavy in her arms and she knew he was going to sleep. She wouldn't have minded now if he had wanted it – but better be safe than sorry.

As she composed herself for sleep she tried to remind herself of the unfairness of life and how lucky . . . . unfairly lucky . . .Helen had always been. But at that moment it was difficult to feel deprived: she was warm, with her man in her arms and her bairns asleep for the next seven hours, given luck. She hitched him closer to her, moved her mouth free of his hair and gave herself up to sleep.


There were vast tracts of darkness outside the train windows and when lights sprang up and the train rattled through stations it went too swiftly for Edward to identify where they were. He guessed they were north of Peterborough now, which meant he would be in London by eleven o'clock. The funny little girl would be there, probably hatpin in hand to defend her honour if he turned out to be a villain. He smiled into the window, remembering the stringy legs and the saucer eyes. Given a few square meals and some decent clothes, she would probably be quite attractive but she was certainly safe from him.

He probed gently at his emotions, anxious to see how in command of himself he was. He felt a great sadness, certainly, but a sense of peace was also there. For a moment he wondered whether his mother's determination to go to Berwick had been deliberate: if she had stayed in Inkerman Mews and died there, his sense of bereftness would have been so much greater. He had learned to live without her, while still having the knowledge of her presence, and so the blow of losing her had been slightly lessened. She had been wise, and all she had wanted was his happiness. He must try not to disappoint her.

Perhaps his future lay with Sylvia? She would be an asset as a hostess and he sensed she would take an interest in the business once she was his wife. He stopped there, pondering his choice of words: Not 'if' she was his wife, but 'once' – as though his decision had already been made. It made him feel elated, but slightly uneasy, and he changed the direction of his thoughts. Tomorrow he must fix up his waif with a decent place to stay and make sure she had the wherewithal to live until she got a job. She had appeared in his life at just the right moment, and the valuable stock from Berwick had been delivered safely, thanks to her. The least he could do was give her a helping hand.

He still wondered what she had been doing on the train, but it wouldn't do to try and probe. Firstly because she would undoubtedly tell him to mind his own business, and secondly because he mustn't get involved. She might be a runaway for all he knew, or the flotsam of a broken home. The last thing he needed was irate parents knocking on his door. He resolved to be kind but firm, and above all speedy, then he dismissed Helen from his mind, thought briefly and enjoyably of Sylvia, and settled down to make business plans for the rest of the journey.

# 11

They breakfasted in the kitchen of the flat, each a little uneasy at having such an intimate meal with a stranger. Last night they had exchanged only pleasantries. This morning there was talking to be done.

'Now,' Edward said, when his toast was finished and he could put elbows on the table and get down to business. 'I need to know a bit about you if I'm going to help you. No . . .' He held up his hand as she flinched at his suggestion. 'I'm not asking for details of your personal circumstances. Frankly, I don't want to know all your business. What I do need to know is how much you can afford to pay for accommodation, where you want to work, what skills you have . . . that sort of thing.'

She too was pushing aside her plate and folding her arms on the table, and he could see she was screwing up her courage. 'At this present moment . . . right now . . . I can't afford anything. Well, the YMCA or something like that. But when I get work . . .'

He was interrupting. 'You mean you came down to London without any money, without friends, without a job?'

She shook her head. 'No, that's not strictly true. I came down here because I needed to get away from home, and I had an address, somewhere I could get accommodation and my keep until I found my feet. For reasons of my own I don't want to take advantage of that particular place, so I'm going to the YW today, if they'll have me. Then I have a list of places – quite cheap places – to check out. I got them while you were away. If I get a job at once . . . .'

He was smiling now: '. . . and of course London is just teeming with vacancies?'

'Something like that,' she said defiantly. 'Well, it is, isn't it?'

He poured himself another coffee and held up the jug.

'More? Pass your cup. Yes, there are openings, but only if you have the right skills.'

'I'll do anything,' Helen said firmly. 'In the beginning, I'll do anything.'

'What did you do in the north?' Edward saw her hesitate, as though she was wondering how much it was safe to tell. What *was* the child up to?

'I worked in a hospital,' she said at last. 'I was a medical secretary. I've got O levels, I can type and do shorthand: I had a Saturday job in my last year at school: I worked in a cake shop, so I know about serving and cashing up, and things like that.'

She was watching to see if he was impressed, and Edward decided to oblige. 'Well, it sounds as though you'll be OK. What do we do with you in the meantime, though?' He thought for a moment and then made up his mind. 'At lunch-time we'll check out some of the rooms on your list. If we find somewhere decent I'll lend you the money for the first week or two, and you'll probably need to put down a deposit. Don't worry, I'll get it back from you. I'm going to be pretty busy during the next few weeks, with my mother's affairs to square up and her things to go through. I'll give you a job for a week or two, as a sort of general dogsbody. Sometimes you'll be in the shop, some-times up here tidying up – whatever crops up. I might send you on the occasional errand, if we're sure you won't get lost. I'll pay you . . . oh, £12 a week, and you can start paying me back the rent when you feel you're solvent. I can't employ you forever, so keep your eye open for a permanent job. Well, that's the package. What do you say?'

He had expected, if not effusive acceptance, at least a degree of gratitude, but Helen was frowning. 'Are you sure you really need someone? I mean, I can manage . . . I don't need you to invent a kind of job just to help me out.'

Edward was annoyed. 'My dear child,' he said, 'You're not important enough for me to *invent* anything! Now, do you want it or don't you?'

Her chin came up and she started to gather up the breakfast dishes. 'Yes, I want it if you really mean it. Thank you very much.' She moved to the kitchen door and turned. 'But I'm not a child. I'm eighteen.'

Lilian sat down opposite David and loosened her coat. She had asked after Diana and he had enquired about the baby, left now with her mother. It was time to get down to business. 'Well, it's like this, doctor. You know I wanted me tubes tied when I had the bairn?'

David nodded. 'Yes, and I know you were disappointed when they said no. But it really isn't a good idea to do something like that at the time of birth unless there are sound medical reasons for doing it. Lots of women, most women, are fed up at the end of nine months of pregnancy. They think, "I never want to go through that again," but when they've recovered from the birth they often feel quite differently.'

Lilian was nodding vehemently. 'Well, I have recovered, doctor, and I still feel the same, only more so. We've got as much as we can manage. Another bairn would be a disaster.'

'How does Billy feel about this?'

Lilian raised her eyes skywards. 'If you knew Billy better, doctor, you'd know thinking's not his strong point. He's any way for an easy life. He won't kick up a fuss, if that's what you mean. He doesn't want more bairns, any more than I do. In fact, he'll be pleased.' She paused, trying to think of a delicate way to put things. 'It makes it awkward, you see . . . you know what I mean. If we can stop worrying, it'll make it all a lot easier.' She grinned. 'He'll be like a dog with two tails, if you want the truth.'

David smiled. 'I know what you mean.' He was looking at her notes. 'How old are you, Lilian . . . twenty-three? I still think that's a bit young for such an irrevocable decision. Let's make a hypothetical case. Suppose you and Billy split up, and you want to remarry. Your new husband quite naturally wants a child of his own, but you've been sterilized. How would you feel then?'

Lilian forced a patient smile to her face. Trust a man to miss the point. 'I'd feel relieved, doctor. I don't want any more bairns, no matter who's the father. And I won't be splitting up with Billy – if I left him, he wouldn't last two minutes. So there's no snag there.'

'OK, let's compromise. I'll give you the pill . . . which is a very, very safe form of contraceptive if you use it properly. And you postpone the sterilization for a year or two. How's that?'

Thank God, she was getting somewhere at last. She had heard about the new birth pill and the peace of mind it could bring.

'I think that sounds fine, doctor. Whatever you say. If you say take the pill, I'll do it.' She would eat horse muck off the street if it meant she could stop worrying every time. She took off her coat and rolled up her sleeve, while David set about his examination.

'But how do they get it like that?' Helen was looking at the Galle cameo glass vase Edward held, her brows knitted in puzzlement.

'You know how they make cameos, don't you?' he asked and when she shook her head he crossed to the jewellery display case and took out a cameo carved in classic style. 'Well, look . . . this is a piece of layered stone. They cut away the top layer to a specified pattern so that the under-layer shows through and forms a picture. In this case it's a classic head, but it can take several forms. With glass it's the same process but there they've formed the layers themselves, overlaying one layer of glass with a kind of skin of coloured glass . . . even several skins, on a good piece. Once they've done that they can remove some of the top layer . . . or layers . . . to produce a pattern, just as they do for jewellery.'

'How do they remove it?' she asked, her eyes round now with interest.

'Well, they can etch it away with acid . . . they use bitumen of Judea to preserve what they want to keep . . . or they may carve it away with a tool. On cheaper pieces they simply stencil a pattern on top to resemble a cameo, but this is the real thing.' He turned it over to show her the cameo signature *'Galle'* preceded by a star. 'He was a master. Very collectable now, and destined to get more and more desirable.'

'Is that Galle?' She was pointing at a grey glass vase cameo'd in amethyst and amber.

'Yes,' he said and grinned at her triumph. 'You're learning,' he conceded. 'Now run upstairs and make coffee.'

'How's the bedsit working out?' he asked her, as they drank. Helen was trying to mask her enthusiasm, and he felt a glow of pleasure. She was happy. Plumper now and less like a stray. She had had her hair cut and although she was still shabby there were little touches of style about her dress, like the broad belt around the waist of her black sweater and the red neckerchief she wore.

'It's lovely,' she said. 'Well, I know it's not much but it's really cosy and the other tenants are nice. They keep themselves to themselves, but you can tell they're friendly.' She pulled a little face. 'I'm really grateful to you, you know. You've been very kind, getting me on my feet, and there was no call for you to do anything for me.'

'You've been a help to *me*,' he said. 'That night, when I heard about my mother, I don't know what I'd have done if you hadn't been here. I'd still have gone north, but my mind would have been a whirl. As it was, I was able to just take off, knowing you were here to take care of things. And it's funny, but I had complete faith in you . . . in spite of the fact that you looked like a refugee.'

He was sorry the moment he'd said it. He saw her struggling with herself, wondering how much to tell. 'Anyway,' he said firmly, 'that's all in the past.'

She nodded, smiling again. 'Well, anyway, like I said I'm grateful. And I'm not forgetting that I can't go on working here forever. I've got me name down at a few agencies, so there should be something soon.'

'No hurry,' Edward said and was surprised at how much he meant what he said.

Diana watched as Anne laid out the bathtime paraphernalia, towels, powder, cottonwool swabs, soap, baby lotion

. . . every possible aid was there, laid out like an operating theatre. 'There,' Anne said, using her elbow to test the water. 'Just right.'

Diana was nursing the baby; now she surrendered him to Anne and watched as Anne laid him on her knee and began to undress him. 'She's good at it,' Diana thought, surprised. Anne was indeed amazingly competent, handling the baby's tiny limbs in a way that Diana would never have dared to do.

'Have you had much experience with babies, Anne?'

Her sister-in-law shook her head. 'No, not really. We did some baby-care in Hygiene at school, and later I helped at a home for children . . . but nothing since then. It's a matter of common sense, isn't it? And I've read up the latest steps in child management.'

She had picked up the naked baby, one hand splayed at the back of his neck, the other holding the tiny ankles as she lowered him into the water. 'There now,' Diana said, falling on to her knees to get nearer to the bath. 'Is that nice?' The baby's eyes turned in the direction of her voice. 'Who's a good boy, then? Who's having a lovely bath?'

It should be Anne saying all this, she thought at last. But Anne was going through the steps of the ritual, face serene and unmoved by the baby's obvious appreciation of the water.

Diana was filled with a sudden terrible urge to get home to David, and it was a relief when Howard came into the nursery. The baby was dry now, laid on a thick towel to be creamed and powdered. Howard leaned over and clicked tongue against teeth in an effort to amuse his son. 'He's trying,' Diana thought; 'at least he's making an effort.'

Anne picked the baby up and held him to her shoulder. 'There now,' she said. 'A nice, clean boy.' She might have been speaking of any domestic chore well done, as she laid him back in his crib.

Diana looked at her watch. 'Good gracious, it's nearly six o'clock. David will think I've deserted him.' She stood up and looked down at the baby. 'Michael's beautiful, Anne. A perfect little boy. I envy you.' And then, unable to restrain herself . . . 'Are you very happy?'

Anne was screwing the top back on a jar. 'Of course I am. A son, that's what every woman wants, isn't it?'

Diana went down the stairs, Howard accompanying her. She turned in the door and for the first time felt a warmth for her brother-in-law that was part affection and part compassion. 'Congratulations, Howard. I hope you'll all be very happy.' His face softened and for the first time she saw a resemblance in him to David. 'I hope so,' he said, and stood waving as she started the car and drove off into the evening traffic.

Mrs Stepinska had come into the shop at closing time and stayed to chat as Helen cleared away the Sheffield plate she had been polishing with a soft cloth. 'Edward's out with Sylvia,' she confided, and grinned as Mrs Stepinska's mouth formed an O beneath her rolling eyes.

'I think we have wedding bells . . . . only natural now the mama is gone.'

Helen nodded. 'He loved his mother, didn't he? Was she nice?'

Mrs Stepinska settled herself on a ladderback chair and launched into her subject. 'She was a lovely woman, very handsome, tall like her son. Always the silk blouses, the gold chains. Nice dress, clean, you know . . .' She sought for a word and found it. 'Elegant! She was elegant. Not pretty – *jolie laide*, like the French say. Now Edward, there is a pretty man . . .'

Helen knew what she meant. Edward did have good features, but his hair was a little too long for Helen's taste and his clothes were very classy but a bit fancy. She smiled, thinking what they would have called him in Belgate. 'Poncy' or 'arty-farty'.

The older woman was leaning forward, eyes alight. 'You're smiling . . . tell me what makes you smile. I like the secrets.' She sighed. 'No secrets any more, no naughty little flirts. It's terrible to get old and good. When I was a girl . . .'

'She's off,' Helen thought, and found herself a shelf to

tidy rather than break the old woman's reminiscence by showing her the door.

Mrs Stepinska was still in full flow when Edward arrived, alone. 'Sorry I'm late.' He gestured to the half-tidied shelf. 'You shouldn't still be working, Helen. Come on, leave it until tomorrow.' The cold had brought colour to his cheeks and the reddish-brown hair had curled in the damp air. Yes, he was goodlooking in a way. Obviously Sylvia thought so.

'Do you want some tea?' Helen asked, and when his face brightened at the prospect she scurried upstairs, leaving Edward to see Mrs Stepinska out of the shop and across the now-silent Mews.

Lilian had planned it all out and so far everything was going like clockwork. The bairns had gone down like lambs, and she had had a blissful hot bath, up to her ears in soapy water. It was now seven o'clock and Billy would be coming through the door any moment. She patted some of her precious Coty L'Aimant behind her ears and then, daringly, between her breasts.

It was exhilarating to feel like this, sexy and safe. She had started on the pill, the magic pill that was going to solve all their problems, as soon as she got back from the chemist's. Whether or not it had some extra ingredient, the plain fact was that she had been able to think of nothing else but getting Billy into bed ever since she'd taken it. She had rehearsed it over and over in her mind. He would come in and find her, pink from the bath, scented, hair brushed and combed, and guaranteed to have him panting. He would expect to be rebuffed but this time there would be no sharp dig in the ribs, no turning away of her face or rush to check the calendar. This time she would draw him to her, guide his lips from cheek to throat, down between breasts, down . . .! She found she was standing in the centre of the kitchen, clutching the teapot to her and murmuring endearments. 'There's no need to go mad, Lilian Fenwick,' she told herself sternly, and went on with making the fry-up he always liked when he was on back-shift.

She turned the liver and bacon and spare ribs in the pan, lifting each piece as it was done and adding it to the potato and beans already on the plate. As he came through the door she put it on the table and lifted the kettle back on to the fire so that it would come to the boil. When she had filled his huge mug with tea, and sugared and stirred it, she sat down opposite, letting her dressing-gown gape open at the neck in true Hollywood fashion.

'Bairns all right?' Billy asked, not taking his eyes from his plate.

'The bairns are fine, went out like lights.' Even her voice sounded different, low and seductive, almost throbbing.

'Nice liver, Lily.'

She itched to say 'Lili*an* . . . my name is Lilian,' but she kept it back. Not tonight. Tonight was made for love.

When he asked for something sweet she made him a lemon curd sandwich, cutting off the crusts to make it a real treat. She looked at the clock: twenty to eight. Ten minutes to digest his meal, five minutes to get washed. They could be in bed by eight o'clock, and all the night before them.

Billy sat in his chair, placing his refilled mug on the hob beside him. Lilian leaned across him to get his slippers, hovering for a moment so that he got a good blast of L'Aimant. Any moment now it would begin, and tonight he would meet his match! She had put his slippers ready for his socked feet, and was just about to suggest bed when she heard a gentle zizz.

She jumped to her feet and stood over him, looking at the face of a baby with a lock of hair drooped across the brow. 'Billy . . . Billy Fenwick, don't you dare go to sleep. Billy!'

But there was no response, only a gentle reverberation of his lips.

Lilian shifted her dressing-gown across her chest and tightened her belt. Pill! She would give him pill when he woke up. She contemplated throwing the plastic package into the heart of the fire, but reason prevailed. She banked up the fire, got out her back numbers of *Woman's Weekly* and went in search of some real romance.

'Good, wasn't it?' David said, as they moved to the aisle. He had insisted on standing for the whole of the National Anthem and the cinema was almost empty. 'Yes,' Diana said. 'Very exciting.' The film had been *Dr No*, made from one of Ian Fleming's James Bond novels of which David was a devotee. 'Sean Connery's very handsome but I can't understand all he says sometimes.'

They made their way out into the night air, shivering after the warmth of the interior.

'We've got time for a drink,' David said, looking at his watch. They dived into the nearest pub and sipped Whisky Macs as the late-night crowd hummed around them. 'That Ursula Andress . . . now there is a woman,' David said, shaking his head in wonder. 'When she walked out of the water I felt my socks quiver.'

'Watch it, mate,' Diana said. 'You're a married man.'

He smacked his lips. 'That wouldn't stop me.' He was teasing and she liked it.

'Well, I may not be built like a Sherman tank, but what I lack in quantity I make up in quality.

He pursed his lips and nodded sagely. 'You could be right . . . but I'd need proof.'

Diana drained her glass. 'I'll give you proof, all right. I just hope you'll know what to do with it.'

He stood back and waved her ahead. 'Leave that to me, my dear.' He twirled an imaginary and villainous moustache. 'I don't think I'll disappoint you.'

She took his arm as the pub door closed behind them. The sky was a pattern of stars above them, cold and clear. 'I like winter skies,' she said, taking one last look before climbing into the car.

David grinned. 'Glimpsed through glass, preferably double, with a roaring fire behind, I'm inclined to agree with you. Out there in the open, they leave me cold.'

The car coughed and spluttered and then sprang to life.

'How was Anne today?' His voice was casual but Diana knew he wasn't just making conversation.

'How is Anne ever?' she answered. 'She was calm, competent and with not a hair out of place. She has taken to motherhood like a duck to water, which is what we might have expected.'

'Don't sound so depressed,' he said, glancing sideways at her woebegone face. 'So will you, when the time comes. And you'll be a damn sight better at it than Anne.' It was there again, that note of pure dislike in his voice.

'I've been meaning to ask you, David: why did Howard and Anne adopt? Is she unable to have children?'

David's voice, when he answered, was too careful to be telling the whole truth. 'As things stand, yes.'

She persisted. 'What do you mean?'

He accelerated as the limits of Darlasden came up and the speed limit was lifted. 'I think we should drop the subject, darling. They haven't had children . . . they've got one now, and I wish them joy of it.'

He sounded as though he meant what he said, so Diana let it go. 'Anyway, Howard is really trying with that baby. He's not like you . . . it doesn't come naturally to him. But he's really trying to be a loving father. I watched him today, just making little efforts to communicate with the baby. It was quite touching.'

In the darkness of the unlit road, David's voice sounded sombre. 'I hope you're right. A baby needs love . . . as much as it can get.'


Helen had never been out so late in her life, not in a restaurant, anyway. It was eleven o'clock and people were still coming in, as though it were mid-afternoon. Her amazement showed on her face and Edward was hard put to it not to smile. He had ordered for her, Tandoori chicken and a green salad with nan bread, guaranteed not to scorch her palate. Sylvia had ordered for herself, to show him she was still cross. Edward ate his King Prawn Bhuna, and admitted to himself that the evening wasn't turning out as he had intended.

Helen had still been in the flat earlier in the evening when Sylvia arrived, and he had seen the nervous glance she had given the older girl. It was silly that she should fear Sylvia and he found it oddly upsetting. On the spur of the moment he had decided to get them better acquainted. 'We're eating out, Helen – why don't you come with us? We can put you in a cab for the journey home.'

Helen's eyes had flicked to Sylvia's face, and to Sylvia's credit she had tried to sound welcoming. 'Yes, of course. Why don't you come?'

Since they got into the restaurant, however, it had been a different story. Sylvia had showed her displeasure in every conceivable way. Now she was drumming her long fingernails on the red cloth, her food almost untouched in front of her.

'Is there a ladies' room?' Helen was looking anxious and Edward pushed back his chair. 'Yes. Over there, in the corner.'

When Helen had left the table Sylvia put her elbows on the cloth and laced her fingers together. 'She doesn't have much conversation, does she?'

Edward was tempted to point out that Helen's silence was probably because Sylvia had made her feel awkward, but he decided against it. 'She's quite a chatterbox in the shop. Perhaps she's tired. It must be an upheaval, coming down here to no proper home or job.'

'Have you ever asked her why?' Sylvia said, curious.

'It's none of my business. She'll tell me if she wants to. Actually, I hope she doesn't; I don't want to get involved any further than I already am.'

'And how far is that?' Sylvia's eyes were challenging . . . and also very attractive, heavily shadowed tonight, the dark lashes curling outwards. She must have them tinted, or perhaps it was mascara.

In the distance Edward could see Helen emerging from the ladies' room. He would have to be quick. 'Look, Sylvia, in half an hour you and I will be alone, and I'm looking forward to it. In the mean time, can you try to be nicer to Helen? She's very green, and she's a long way from home.

156

Also, I don't know, but I think she's had trouble of some sort. So give the kid a break.'

Sylvia looked at him for a moment. 'Will I get good conduct marks?'

He grinned and touched her wrist with his fingers. 'All you want, and more.'

She looked up as Helen approached. 'Come and sit down, Helen. We were just saying how nice it is to have you here.'

# 12

There had been snow in the night. Helen could see it through the thin curtains, piled like a fur collar on the windowsill. She was happy here in her one room. It was cosy and clean, and from the window, on a clear day, she could see across what seemed like half the rooftops of London. It still amazed her that she was here, that the events of the past year had taken place at all. It seemed yesterday that she had walked into town to meet Lilian, that April day when Dembry's had opened. Since then she had been loved and rejected, had borne a child, given it up, journeyed to the far end of the country, found a new home and started a new job. No wonder it seemed incredible.

Thinking of the past made her think, for once, of the baby: she hoped he was happy. She never usually thought of Alistair, but now she forced herself to summon him to mind. If he was still at the Royal Infirmary he would be romancing some nurse or clerk, as foolish as she had been. She felt no animosity towards him; the fault had been in her, that she had been so gullible, so determined to believe what she wanted to believe.

But thinking like this was a waste of time. She leaped out of bed and reached for the coat that doubled for dressing-gown. By next winter she would have a thick dressing-gown with slippers to match: it was there in her plan, complete now to the tiniest detail. She washed in the basin on the dresser, heating the water in the electric kettle. She used the shared bathroom for bathing, but the rest of the time she liked to keep herself to herself. She had seen most of the other tenants, young people like her and quite approachable, but they seemed taken up with their own affairs and that suited her.

When she was dressed she put on a pan and poached her Sunday eggs, adding salt and vinegar to the water and serving them separate from the toast to avoid sogginess. After breakfast she would wrap up and go exploring, adding to her knowledge of London. She carried the last bit of toast to the window and threw it to the waiting sparrows. The teeming city looked strangely deserted on Sunday morning, a place of windows and balconies, flat roofs and ornamented peaks. 'I know I'm going to like it here,' she said to herself and went in search of her boots.


David and Diana, as non-Catholics, had no part to play in Michael's christening. 'We're heathens,' David said, 'so we can't be godparents. Well, that'll save us a bob or two.' In the event, they enjoyed the service. The baby was baptized Michael Anthony and was quiet throughout the ceremony. Howard held a candle and a white cloth to symbolize the beginning of a new life with God, and the baby was anointed with holy water and oil while everyone stood round, joining in. 'I feel involved,' Diana thought and looked up to see that David, too, was absorbed.

She looked across at Anne, hoping to see some sign of pleasure, of emotion, even sentimentality . . . but there was nothing visible on her face except a serene acceptance of all that was taking place. 'It's a lucky baby, really,' Diana thought. 'It will never want for anything. It will have a good education, and mix with all the right people.' The priest made the sign of the cross over the baby and she squeezed tight her eyes. 'Please God, bless the baby and keep him safe. And make him happy, God. Every baby has a right to be happy.'

Back at the house Diana tried to make herself useful,

handing round canapés and drumsticks, filling glasses to toast a baby that was nowhere to be seen. 'It's his snooze time,' Anne had said, when someone demanded the baby's presence, and no one dared to argue.

'Well, she can't just jettison his routine,' Diana said when David pulled a face.

'Why not?' he said. 'Rules are made to be broken, daft rules anyway.'

Diana felt an odd sympathy with Anne now that she had admitted to herself that she could never adopt. She could never be unkind to someone else's baby, but nor could she love it – she had realized that with Diana Two. She liked her god-daughter, would do anything for her, but she could never be a mother to her; acknowledging that fact had made her more understanding of the task Anne faced.

'I could never take someone else's child,' she thought again, 'but perhaps I won't need to even contemplate it.' It was there, under her heart, a tiny cell that would one day be a baby. She was three days overdue and this time she knew it was no false alarm.


The park was beautiful under its mantle of snow, Edward thought, broken here and there by patches of green where grass poked defiantly through. The letter lay close to his heart in the inside pocket of his jacket. He had found it this morning, after Sylvia had left and he had set himself to go through some of his mother's things.

It was there, in her desk, inscribed simply 'Edward'. He had opened it and read it while the kettle steamed in the kitchen and the Sunday sounds of London filtered through the window. Read it and absorbed it, so that he could remember it now, unseen. It was dated 1959 and written in the bold hand he knew so well.

'My dear son, I hope it will be a long time before you read this but it will give me comfort to know that it is done, waiting for you to read one day when I am no longer at your side. I have loved you, Edward, each moment of your life. You have given me more joy than I can hope to describe or than anyone who does not know you could ever comprehend. You have made my life a joy. Before you were born I used to dream of how you would be, but the reality has been so much better than the dream.

I have had one fear always, the fear of the moment when you and I must part. Lately, I have come to realize there is no separation where love exists, so I have you forever, my darling, and you have me.'

He had cried then and walked to the kitchen to make coffee before he could read further.

'I am proud of my son, of the way he looks, the way he behaves and most of all, proud of the way he thinks. I want you to be happy, my darling, and I hope you will give me this one last gift: that you will never think of the past except to celebrate its contribution to the future. Go forward bravely, but never be afraid of standing still, if that is what you choose to do. And now no more than any good-night. God bless. I love you.'

Edward was almost at the park gates when he saw the broken ground, the pale green shoots of bulbs pressing upwards to light and air. He smiled and walked on, sensing that winter would soon be over.

Helen had walked in the park, and had peered in the windows of closed and darkened shops. She had bought a pint of milk in a corner shop and was going home to a lunch of fried corned beef and boiled potatoes. In Belgate, now, her mother would be basting the joint, peeping at puddings blown up light as air, chopping cabbage ready to drop into boiling water ten minutes before dishing up. If it was beef there would be horseradish from the garden, if it was lamb, mint. For pork it would be onion gravy.

As she let herself into the house she found she was salivating, wrinkling her nose as though the smells of Sunday at home were assailing her nostrils. But this was

London, not Belgate, and corned beef was woefully short on aroma.

She was on the landing and fumbling for her key when the next door opened. The boy was about her own age, dressed in a bright red sweater, but it was his shoes that caught her eye, black and white with thick rubber soles. She had never seen anything like them and it showed in her face. He pulled his own door to and tested it, grinning at her discomfiture.

'Hello,' he said. 'Just moved in?' And then, gesturing towards his feet, 'I'm going to the Princess . . . the Princess Bowl, up Dagenham.' He lifted his hand and she saw that the leather case he held contained two bowls. 'It's a bowling alley, twenty-four lanes. Do you bowl?' He had moved towards her and was looking down at her.

'No, I don't know anything about it,' said Helen, 'except it's the new craze.' He was making no move to go, and she fitted her key in the lock.

'You're not from round here, are you? Let me guess . . . you're not Yorkshire, not a Scouse. Say something else?' He put up a hand and cupped it round his ear.

'Like what?' she said defensively.

He clicked his fingers. 'A Geordie. You're a Geordie.'

She shook her head, and her door suddenly gave. 'No, I'm not, I wouldn't be seen dead in Newcastle. I'm a Wearsider, from County Durham.' She was inside her room and closing the door, but he put up a hand and held it open.

'I thought everyone from up there was a Geordie; just shows my ignorance. I'm from Northampton myself. We're all a bit thick up there. I'm called Alan . . . Alan Bates.'

'Helen Clark,' she said reluctantly. 'Well, I mustn't keep you.'

He was not to be deterred. 'How about coming out for a drink one night? Or the flicks? Then you can explain the essential differences between Newcastle and Durham. I'm quite house-trained and I don't bite.'

When Helen had turned him down and closed the door she realized her heart was pounding as though she had been running in a race. She put down the milk and sank into an upright chair. It was daft to go on like this, especially when he had been quite nice. But her eyes were pricking and she knew she was going to cry. Her room, which had been such a haven this morning, was suddenly bleak and shabby, a used place that did not belong to her at all. Worst of all, she felt cheap within herself. 'I never want to speak to a boy again,' she thought. 'Or go out with one, or let one use me and then treat me like rubbish.'

She got up and put on the kettle, but not even tea had any appeal. In the end she sat down at the table, put her head on her arms and cried until she could cry no more.


When supper was cleared away David put the Mendelssohn Violin Concerto on the radiogram and Diana curled on the settee beside him, her head on his chest, his arm heavy and protective around her. She waited until the last notes of his favourite piece had died away and the machine had clicked off. 'David,' she said then, 'I think perhaps I'm pregnant.'

He said nothing for a while but she had felt him wince at her news. 'If it's true, is it what you want?' he said at last.

'It's what you want,' she countered. 'I've seen you with Diana Two . . . and with Michael. You love children, so I want to give you some.'

He laughed to ease the tension. 'Some? One will do to be going on with.'

She nudged him with her shoulder in mock-rebuke. 'You know what I mean.'

'Yes, I know. And I would like a child because it would be part of you. But I know how unhappy you were when . . . well, I couldn't say all I wanted to say then, because we were never encouraged to wear our hearts on our sleeves at home and I'm too old to learn now. I know you were heart-broken though . . . I know you cried in the night, quietly, into your pillow . . . I know you felt cut-off from us all and alienated from the whole idea of childbearing. I just want to be sure you're ready to face all that again . . . if need be.'

She thought carefully before she replied. 'Yes, I think I

162

am. You're right, I was devastated and I did feel isolated . . . but part of that was because I was still a kid.'

He leaned to kiss her temple. 'So you're an old woman now?'

'Be serious, David. I meant I still had a childlike view of things. I thought every good thing was mine by right. I loved you, you loved me; a healthy baby was the logical outcome. But life isn't always logical, I know that now. And happiness is a privilege, not a right. I may have this baby safely, I may not. I won't assume it'll all go well. I'll hope it does, but I won't take it for granted. Also – I hadn't had time to settle in here, I knew no one . . . I barely knew you, my darling. I was still learning about you. But I've grown up in these last few weeks – you can smile, but it's true. And I know Durham now; I've found my way around, and I've made some friends.'

'Not the News of the World,' he said, in a mock-horror, and she knew he was joking to cover his fear.

'The News of the World, among others,' she said firmly. 'Lilian has a good heart beneath it all, and I do count her a friend. Apart from the fact that I might one day have to sue her daughter for alienation of affection . . .'

He kissed her then, holding her close to tell her how much he loved and needed her. 'Let's not think about it, Di, until we know for sure. If it's true, fair enough. If not, I'll simply love you more.' But Diana knew, in her heart, that the coming baby meant more to her husband than even she could imagine.

Edward sat beside Sylvia who was intent on the Mahler, but his mind ranged here and there, coming back always to the letter. At first he had wondered why it had not reduced him to paroxysms of grief, but he was coming to see that his mother had given him a peace that transcended grief. He missed her, but that he had had her for twenty-seven years was both a wonder and a strength.

They had always been partners, the two of them against the world. Certainly against his father. Remembering the drunken rages, the raised voices in the night, the sound of

163

breaking glass, he realized that when he had run to her, as a child, as an outraged adolescent, as a young man determined to protect, she had imparted calm to him, a certainty that together they were safe. And yet she had taught him to love the world, to welcome it into his life, to go out and seek whatever it might have to offer him.

As though she sensed something, Sylvia chose that moment to reach out and take his hand. He felt a sudden tenderness towards her, a tenderness that lasted through their taxi-ride to the silent Mews, through the solemn ceremony of undressing and taking her into his bed. He wanted to be a good lover, to give as well as to receive. He touched her gently until her back arched and she reached for him, guiding him into her hastily as though there was not a moment to be lost.

# 13

The early morning sun was shining in, showing up dust on polished wood. Today they would clean the shop, springclean it. Edward drew back the bolts on the shop door and stepped out into the Mews. It had the glow of an April morning, that indefinable something that sets the blood astir.

'Good morning, Edward.' Mrs Stepinska was peering into her window-box and beckoning with an imperious hand. 'See . . . the little darlings!' The daffodils were just opening their trumpets, towering above the grape hyacinths and crocuses that had been the first heralds of spring.

'Wonderful,' Edward said. 'You've got a green thumb.'

He had thought to fox her, but she was smiling. 'This is the green finger you talk about, but it's not in the hands, it's in the love I give them. All through the winter I whisper, "I know you are there my babies. Lie still and grow strong." Then the sun comes and *pfft* . . . they grow.'

She looked at him, weighing the wisdom of what she wanted to say. He smiled reassuringly, knowing what would come and welcoming it. 'Your mama, she loved the spring. "I'm going to the park, Maria, to see the crocus." Off she would go, always the nice coat, nice hat, even for the park. And when she came back, oh the joy of her face. I tell you she cheered me always with that smile.'

Edward patted the old woman's arm. 'She was fond of you, Mrs S. You were a good friend.' He was remembering that last Christmas gift, the carved wooden box giving way to a silk scarf, old silk but still beautiful, and inside that the tiny gold cross. 'She loved your Christmas gift. I put the crucifix on her watch strap, and I know it gave her comfort.'

When he got back into the flat he picked up the phone and ordered spring flowers to be sent to Mrs S. Stepinska, 5, Inkerman Mews, and to his Aunt Dorothy at Sea Winds, High Chare, Berwick. It was three months since his mother's death. Time to pay tribute.

For Sylvia, he ordered roses, a dozen, dark red and sent with his love.


'So it will be a Guy Fawkes baby,' Chris Milhill said, when they had checked dates. He turned to David, who was trying to look poker-faced but only succeeding in looking like a pools winner. 'You can celebrate with fireworks.'

Diana felt strange and slightly irritated by talk of celebration at this stage. While the obstetrician had examined her she had felt a terrible calm. Now it was beginning to crack, and she wanted to be outside before the storm broke. But first there were things to be settled.

'I want you to tell me honestly what the chances are this time,' she said. 'Of things going wrong, I mean.'

Chris's eyes flicked to David and then back to meet hers. 'No doctor, no honest and competent doctor, will ever say "Never". All I can tell you is that the circumstances of your miscarriage have absolutely no bearing on this pregnancy. If there was a hereditory factor, I would tell you. If there was some physical defect, something in your anatomy, that made it probable – or even possible – that you would miscarry again, I would tell you. You're an intelligent woman, you have a right to know . . . quite apart from the fact that your husband is a colleague.

'There are many well-documented causes for miscarriage, but the majority remain inexplicable. Sometimes there's an abnormality in the foetus and nature decides to go no further . . . or there may be some kind of problem in the immune system. We're still uncertain. In some women, the hormones which maintain pregnancy are inadequate, or the cervix can't keep the foetus in place. That's not so in your case.

'As far as I'm concerned, you are embarking on a normal pregnancy with every chance of a healthy baby. Such risk as exists is the risk that faces every young woman embarking on giving birth. Don't drink, don't smoke, don't overdo exercise . . . or anything else for that matter. Sleep well, eat well and, above all, don't worry too much.'

'It's true, darling,' David said as they got into the car. 'What Chris said is absolutely true. There's no reason why you should worry. You will, and so will I – but we've got to keep it in proportion. And now I am going to take you out to the most slap-up lunch that Darlasden can provide. Name your pleasure!'

'There's just one thing, David.' He nodded and waited for her to speak again. 'I don't want any preparation this time . . . no shopping, no nursery, no toys. When the baby is safely in the world, you can rush and buy up Dembry's . . . but till then, nothing. And make sure that everyone else knows that's the way it has to be.'


'Well, I think it's lovely,' Helen said defiantly.

Edward flicked the vase with his finger. 'Cheap, mass-produced rubbish.' The vase was green and ornate with pink and white cabbage roses and gilt edges.

'Why did you buy it, then?' Helen asked. Edward grinned. 'Good question . . . because I'm a sucker for elderly ladies with pinched expressions and anxious eyes. Now put it in the back shop and we'll trade it down.'

Helen felt a small glow of satisfaction. She knew what

'trading down' meant. A while ago it would have sounded like Double Dutch; today she knew it meant selling to another dealer whose standards were less high than your own. It was a pity this job couldn't last, but there wasn't really work for a second pair of hands and she was not skilled enough to stand in for Edward, freeing him to search for more stock.

'I'm going to get my hair cut,' he said, looking at his watch. 'I'm taking Sylvia to some ritzy place tonight . . . have to look the part. Can you cope?'

Helen nodded. 'Is it somewhere nice?'

'It's a dinner-jacket job, that's all I know – so I can't go looking like a street musician.' His hair wasn't really long, Helen thought as he waved goodbye. Compared with Alan's hair, it was positively cropped. Of course, there was a difference in their ages – she wasn't sure how old Edward was, but he must be nearly thirty. She brought her coffee downstairs so she could carry on with her shelf-cleaning, but first she ate her cheese and Ryvita and took a second look at Lilian's letter.

'*Dear Helen,*' it said. '*As you don't seem to have time to write to us I suppose I'll have to write to you. We are all in our usual although I am run off my feet. You knew what you were doing when you chose a job first. You make a big sacrifice when you have bairns but of course someone has to do it.*' Helen smiled at the implied rebuke, but there was a sadness, too, that she could never again be truthful with Lilian, never speak of shared experiences. Lucky Lilian, really, with a husband she loved and who was such a canny lad. And two children she could watch grow up to adulthood.

She probed gently at her own feelings but there was no pain, just a kind of satisfaction. She should never have got into such a situation, but she had done her best to make it right, and that was a good feeling. She put the letter aside and thought about her date with Alan. In seven hours she would go out with a man again. Would it work? Would it bring back memories? Would Alan be like Alistair, out for what he could get? Well, if he did, he would get his head in his hands to play with. She tidied away the crumbs of her lunch and went back to work, half-fearful of the evening ahead, half-excited about what life had in store.

Lilian parked the pram in Diana's doorway and lifted the baby into her arms. 'There now, come and see your Auntie Diana. Bring her teddy, Karen, and remember what I told you about asking for a wee.'

She rang the bell and waited, peering through the stained-glass porch windows at the interior. It was posh, but then a doctor had to put a good face on things. It was only right.

'Lilian!' Diana sounded genuinely pleased to see her and a small glow of pleasure blossomed in Lilian's chest.

'I hope it's not a bad time . . . but I thought you'd like to see the bairn.' There was a statue on the hall table just like something out of a museum, and a hall floor that gleamed like an advert. 'By you've got a nice house,' she said, following Diana through to another room.

There was a woman sitting there, with a baby in a carrycot beside her. 'Lilian, may I introduce my sister-in-law, Anne Whittington, and her son Michael. He's four months old.'

Lilian looked into the carrycot and cooed. The baby's blue eyes were staring up at her from a solemn face. 'He's been here before,' Lilian thought, noting the lace-edged pillow and coverlet – 'all white, like the trimmings of a coffin,' she said to herself. But aloud she commented: 'A proper little lad, isn't he? I wish I had a boy. Not that I'd part with our Karen or our Diana, but you always hanker after a lad, don't you?'

Karen had put out her hand, and the baby seized her finger. 'Ooh, look,' Lilian said, 'he's got a grip, and no mistake.'

Anne was leaning across, smiling at Karen but detaching her finger nevertheless. 'I don't think we should disturb Michael. He's still very small. He needs his rest.'

Inside Lilian, hostility rose. 'Come off, Karen, if the lady says so.'

Diana was holding out her arms for Lilian's baby, her

namesake. 'Let me take Diana . . . you take your coat off and sit down. It's lovely to see you. There's tea there, it's quite fresh, and there's a spare cup. I thought David might have popped in but he hasn't.' She was rocking the baby from side to side, her face alight with pleasure as the little girl put exploratory fingers on her godmother's nose and cheeks. 'She looks a picture, Lilian. Pink is definitely her colour.'

Lilian took a covert look at the sister-in-law as she sugared her tea. Very classy, but as sweet as a battleship, she decided, and clutched Karen to her knee. She might have known she wouldn't get a chance to chat to Diana, to hear all the latest news and strengthen the ties of their friendship. Some bugger always spoiled things. All the same, she might as well make an effort.

'Is he your first?' she enquired sweetly, nodding towards the cot.

Anne smiled. 'Yes, my one and only.'

This was more like it, Lilian thought, and released her clutch on Karen's kilt. 'Did you have a bad time? I almost had to have a piesiotomy. By, I suffered. I told them a thing or two, mind, when I got me breath back.' She looked expectantly at Anne, seeing Diana's slightly anxious expression but intent on getting an answer to her question.

'Michael was a gift of God,' Anne said, smiling slightly. 'A chosen child.'

Lilian struggled to sift through the two phrases. All children were gifts of God, unless they were slip-ups, in which case you could say they came from the other place. Chosen? Perhaps she meant it had been a planned pregnancy, but that made sod-all difference at the end.

'He was adopted,' Diana explained, 'so he's very much wanted and loved.' She was cradling Diana Two to her cheek and beaming at her nephew, but there was something funny about what she had said. Lilian couldn't quite put her finger on it, but there was a rabbit away somewhere. She looked at the sister-in-law, expecting to see her nodding agreement, but she was sipping her tea and replacing the cup in the saucer as though nothing special had been said.

Lilian would have pushed the matter further, but Anne was standing up, murmuring goodbyes, gathering up the carrycot handles and moving towards the door. Her bum was no bigger than a Pyrex dish, Lilian thought enviously as she shifted her weight on the chair. Of course, anyone could keep their figure if they could live on steak and prawns and fruit – it was poverty that gave you a backside like a house-end, poverty and pregnancy. Anne might not look so classy when she'd had two bairns, only her sort never did do it the hard way. Lilian tried to take comfort in her own fertility, but there was none to be had. 'Come off that cabinet, Karen,' she said instead, and aimed a blow at her first-born's head.

'There now,' said Diana when she came back from seeing Anne to her car. 'Now we can talk.'

Lilian held out her cup for a refill. This was more like it, a chance to chat with Diana. 'She seems nice,' she said, hoping God would forgive the lie.

'Yes,' said Diana carefully . . . and then, in a burst of confidence that gladdened Lilian's heart . . . 'but I'm glad she's gone. Now, tell me all your news.'


Edward had bought a harewood display table in Berwick, late Victorian, more delicate than the rule and beautifully bonded in satin wood. As he polished it gently, he saw wood and glass take on their proper gleam. He had meant to sell it, but now he wondered. If the shop were to prosper and expand he would have to specialize. The days of the Aladdin's cave were numbered. If he concentrated on Georgian and Victorian furniture, smaller pieces that would be in demand by those who wanted to live in graceful surroundings, he could speed his turnover and increase his profit.

But that would mean doing away with bric-à-brac, treen, miscellaneous silver, even jewellery. Mark and Antony would have to go. He was a young man taking over an old business – perhaps it was time for change? And then he remembered his mother's letter: *'never be afraid of standing still . . .'* He found he was whistling the 'Marseillaise' and laughed aloud at the absurdity as he opened the display table and started to lay small *objets d'art* on its velvet inner surface.

He had finished and was just about to lock up the shop and get ready for his date with Sylvia, when the phone rang.

'Edward, it's me, Sylvia. Look, I know this is short notice and I'm truly sorry . . . but I've got a chance to interview Brenda Lee!'

Edward moved the receiver to his other ear. 'Who?'

Sylvia's voice was impatient. 'Brenda Lee! The singer . . . you know, "Sweet Nothin's"? You *must* know Brenda Lee, she's never out of the Top Ten.'

'That explains why I've never heard of her then.' He did know the little girl singer with a voice like a powerhouse, but he was peeved at Sylvia's crying off, and not disposed to be co-operative. 'How long is this going to take you?'

'I don't know . . . all night I suppose. I'll have to hang around till she's free. You don't seem to realize how lucky I am to get near her.' As usual, Sylvia was annoyed that he didn't give her career its proper reverence.

'So tonight's off altogether? Oh, well, I suppose I'll survive. Ring me tomorrow.'

As Edward went upstairs to search out something to eat, he acknowledged that he had handled the phone call less than well and would be made to suffer for it. And he would miss Sylvia tonight, the excitement of being seen with such a striking woman . . . more eye-catching than ever now that she had cropped her hair in the Quant fashion and had shortened her skirts. And would miss her in his bed . . . or her bed. Perhaps he loved her after all, and should do something about it? He opened the cupboard door and pondered the choice between Scotch broth and macaroni cheese.

'Well, I wouldn't like to meet her on a dark night, put it like that.' Lilian added emphasis to her words by knocking the spoon sharply on Billy's plate so that the mashed potato it held fell in a huge white blob into the gravy. 'More?' He nodded and she obliged with another gooey spoonful.

'So who is she, then?' Billy said, forking mince into his mouth.

'She's Dr Whittington's brother's wife, Diana's sister-in-law. She's got a bairn – adopted, but it's all right. It makes you wonder how people can give up bairns. He had a canny little face. Anyroad, our Karen was that canny with him, holding his little hand, and everything. "Don't do that," she says, "keep your dirty hands off him."'

'What did you say?' Billy asked apprehensively.

'I ignored her,' Lilian said grandly. 'Well, I wasn't going to make a scene and upset Diana, was I? She was taken up with our Diana or she'd have said something herself. You could see she was mad, but she daresn't say anything.'

Behind them, on the hearthrug, Diana Two was lying free of her nappy, legs in air in the warm glow of the fire. Karen sat cross-legged beside her, experimenting with an old lipstick, lips at first, then nose, then eyelids. 'Never mind,' Lilian said complacently. 'She's going in the bath.'

'What was her bairn like?' Billy said, looking proudly at his own offspring.

'Well, it didn't look English to me,' Lilian said. 'It was dark, you know . . . sallow. A bit like, well . . . coloured.'

'Black?' Billy suggested helpfully.

Lilian realized she had gone a bit too far. 'No, not black . . . just different. I mean, you never know where they come from, bairns like that – you have to take what you can get. I just hope it doesn't come to that for Diana. She only wants bairns of her own, she told me that. She wouldn't let on about it to anyone, but she told me. You wouldn't believe some of the things she told me, Billy. Not that I would ever tell anyone, not even you. I'm like the grave when it comes to a confidence.'

She would have liked Billy to give emphatic agreement to this, but he was too busy eating and it didn't really matter. On a night like this, with her man and her bairns beside her and everything going right except money, she felt like a second cousin to the Queen.

* * *

Diana had paid dear for the early salad, but tossed now in a glass bowl it looked worth every penny. 'It's a lovely change, isn't it?' she said, looking down at her plate. 'It makes you realize it really is spring.' They ate cold chicken and salad, and then a chocolate mousse, and she had half a glass of Chablis and bravely refused a refill.

'What a good girl you are,' David said, when they were safely installed on the sofa, coffee on a tray and the television set burbling gently in the background.

'Yes, I am,' she said complacently, and then – 'but how good a mother will I be?'

'Ah, well, now that's a question,' he said teasingly.

'No, I'm serious, David, so don't fool around. It was watching Lilian and Anne today that made me think. We say "motherhood", and we have this vision of a sort of Virgin Mary figure cradling her child. But we don't all fit that mould. Does that mean that there are good mothers and bad mothers, and that giving birth is no guarantee that you're up to the job?'

David shifted her weight on his arm and put down his cup. 'Well, of course there are different degrees of motherhood. There are women, often extremely fertile women, who never give their kids a kind word. There are other women who never give birth and yet are utterly maternal.'

They both realized they were on dangerous ground now. David fell silent, and Diana changed direction.

'Rule out extremes, the cruel and violent mother, the woman who just isn't intelligent enough to fill the role . . . take only ordinary women like Lilian and Anne. Lilian is a bit sloppy, good-hearted, probably unhygienic. She's never heard of nutrition, and she'll have her kids out of school at the first opportunity. She'll box their ears, but she'll also cuddle them till they're black and blue.

'Anne, on the other hand, will never raise her hand to her child, and probably not even her voice. Michael will have all his injections at the optimum time, and get every vitamin known to man. He'll go to a good school and probably wind up a judge. But she makes no move to pick him up unless it's for a good, efficient reason like nappy-changing. So who's the better mother?'

David kissed her brow fondly. 'Don't worry your head about Anne's kid, or Lilian's. My old boss used to say, "Trust Nature", and the longer I'm in practice the more I understand what he meant. We're all products of our genes and our environment, but there's also an X-factor, that something in us that drives us forward and helps us survive. There's a tendency nowadays to discount that, to put everything down to "circumstance". Anne's son will survive . . . he's got a wonderful aunt and uncle, and his father's not a bad old stick, really. And Lilian and Billy are true salt of the earth. Their daughters may grow up to surprise you.'

As she relaxed against him, Diana gave thanks for a husband who was a comfort and could put even the knottiest problem into its proper perspective.


Edward had switched television channels and found nothing to amuse him. He wasn't in the mood for radio and even his precious collection of LPs failed to please tonight. If it had been Saturday he could have relaxed with 'That was the week that was', but it was Friday and there was nothing on TV to hold him. He wanted to go out! There were men friends he could ring, but ten to one they would have dates, which would further demoralize him, or they would ask probing questions about Sylvia. He could go out for a drink, but London pubs were the most chilling places on God's earth unless you were in company. All the same, it was better than nothing. He reached for his jacket and went downstairs and out into the April night.

Damn Sylvia, he thought, as he marched along. He had been looking forward to a gala evening, a big night out. And if he was honest, he had wanted to make love to her. Wanted it very much. He paused at a jeweller's window looking at gems twinkling behind a wire grille. If he proposed, there would have to be a ring. A ring of Sylvia's choice. It would be modern – diamonds certainly – and expensive. He could afford it but he would have preferred something more romantic. He had seen a beautiful Theodor Fahrner opal ring in Kensington Church Street, and his mother had left him several rings, rubies and sapphires and an unusual oval turquoise cabochon, set with pearls and small turquoises. But Sylvia would opt for something contemporary, and perhaps she was right. If you didn't support craftsmen of your own generation there would be nothing to pass on to the future.

Edward drank tepid beer in a poorly lit and slightly grimy pub, whose only point of interest was the official vandalism that had stripped it of every redeeming original feature. At quarter to ten he said good-night to the barman and walked, unanswered, back out into the night.

He was crossing the street in the direction of the Mews when he changed his mind. Helen's attic room was only two streets away and he had been promising to visit it and approve the changes she had made. Visiting most girls at ten at night might be misconstrued, but Helen had treated him as a totally asexual being ever since her first suspicions on the train south. His spirits began to rise as he made for her door. They would drink something . . . cocoa probably . . . and talk, and inspect her precious abode, and then he would go home and sleep like a baby. It was rather nice to have a female friend who was not . . . he sought for a word. Helen was certainly attractive, particularly now that she had gained some weight and lost the hunted look, but he had never felt anything except fatherly towards her, and it made a change. Soon she would find a job and they might lose touch, which would be a pity – so if tonight's visit cemented their friendship, all the better.

The outer door gave to Edward's touch and he mounted the stairs to her door. It was conspicuously cleaner than when he had helped her move in, and a neat card was pinned to the door, with her name on it in capital letters. He knocked and waited, then knocked again.

It was quite a few minutes before he accepted that Helen was not there, and he felt suddenly angry. The one time he had time to call on her, she was out! He was half-way down the stairs when he saw her coming up towards him, a blond kid who needed a haircut behind her and half-supporting her.

'Edward!' She was flushed and her words were slightly slurred. She was drunk!

'Where've you been?' He meant the question to be even but it came out clipped, and he saw the boy bristle. Well, let him. Someone had got her like this and should be ashamed of themselves.

'We've been to a dance-hall. I can twist, Edward. Alan showed me.' She tried to do a twisting movement on the stairs and almost over-balanced.

'Whoops,' Alan said, and caught her, his hand around her midriff underneath her breast.

'I think it's time you had some coffee, Helen, and pulled yourself together,' Edward said coldly.

The boy tightened his grip. 'She's all right. I'll take care of her.'

'I bet you will,' Edward thought and felt his fists ball in his pockets. The boy was trying to push past him.

'It's OK, I'm her neighbour.'

Edward reached for Helen's shoulder bag and took out her key. 'And I', he said, tugging at her arm, 'am her employer. Now if you'll excuse us . . .' If it came to a clash of wills the boy would win: Edward had no rights whatsoever. If it came to fisticuffs, he thought he could put the boy flat on his back quite easily, but it wasn't a prospect he relished. On the other hand, if he just walked off and left Helen and Alan together . . . which he would do if he had any sense . . . he knew precisely what would happen. Helen had been brought home early and tipsy for only one reason.

As if she suddenly realized what he was thinking, Helen straightened up, lifted her bag back on to her shoulder and turned to the boy. 'I've got to go now, Alan. I've had a smashing time, honestly. But I've got an early start in the morning.' Her words were slurred but she was smiling at the boy, and Edward seethed. It was inevitable that Helen would have men eventually, but surely she could do better than this.

He opened her door and ushered her inside, licking his lips in search of the right words – stern enough, but not preachy . . . He was still forming a sentence when she put a hand to her mouth and ran for the door. He followed her along the landing to the lavatory and stood outside, his back to the wall, till the sounds of retching ceased.

'Come on then, let's get you sorted out.' In her room he soaped a face-cloth at the basin and washed her face, lifting back wet wisps of black hair with a fore-finger. 'I'm sorry,' Helen said, still looking decidedly green. And then . . . 'What are you doing here? There's nothing wrong is there?'

Edward shook his head. 'I was out for a walk and I thought I'd look in. I'm glad I did.'

'I've been stupid,' she said.

He nodded. 'You've got that bit right. What were you drinking?'

'Only barley wine,' she said. 'It was horrible, but Alan said it was mild.'

Edward picked up her unresistant hands with their slightly nibbled fingernails, and washed them back and front. 'I wouldn't believe everything that young man says. I'm not a connoisseur but I think "barley wine" is a rather potent beer. You, my dear, were set up. I thought you had more sense.'

For some reason she looked suddenly stricken and he felt pity for her. She was just a kid and utterly naïve, however competent she might try to appear.

'I'll make some coffee,' he said, moving to the gas-ring.

She was standing up, stepping out of her high heels, shivering now. 'I've been an awful idiot. I'm sorry, Edward, I've let you down.' She was still drunk enough to be maudlin.

'Yes,' he said, spooning instant coffee into cups, 'you certainly have. Here I was all ready to offer you a permanent job . . .' Even as he said it he couldn't believe his ears, but it was done now. 'Here I was, ready to say, "Will you work for me full-time?" and I find you like this.'

He paused till he couldn't stand her stricken expression one moment more. 'Well, if you want the job you'll have to pull your socks up . . .'

'If I want? *If I want!*' Helen was shrieking with glee and reaching up to twine her arms round his neck like a boa constrictor.

'Steady on,' he said, pulling back his head to look down at her face. 'I can't pay much and you'll have to work like a slave.' He felt like a father and it was a nice sensation. He patted her arm and detached her. 'Now let's get that coffee down you. You won't be much good to anyone in the morning.'

# BOOK TWO
*1967*

# 14

## *October 1967*

'It's very nice,' Edward said admiringly. 'In fact, it's super.'
The green Mini was not new but its bodywork gleamed
and the chrome was spotless. 'How much?'

Helen grimaced. '£280 – I could just afford it. Still, it'll be
really useful. I'll go off and find all sorts of treasures and
you can mind the shop.'

'Nothing I'd like better,' Edward said. 'I'd love to stay in
a cosy shop surrounded by *objets d'art* instead of combing
rural England. Anyway, stop making demands and I might
take you out to lunch. Strictly teetotal, remember, or the
dreaded breathalyser will get you.' Barbara Castle had
finally brought in her drink-driving law and the word was
on everyone's lips; TV screens were full of hapless motor-
ists blowing for all they were worth.

'Just my luck,' Helen said. 'I get my first car and someone
spoils the fun.' She was stroking the dashboard of her new
acquisition and Edward leaned on the car door, watching
her. She had changed in the last five years. She seemed
taller and heavier . . . well rounded, a woman instead of a
girl. The dark hair still curled, cut fashionably short now.
She had never gone in for those terrible beehives, thank
God, and her clothes had a certain *élan* that was all her
own. And now she was a car owner!

He had given her a bisque doll on her first birthday in
London, a Jules Steiner kicker-cryer, somewhat battered
but still in its original clothes. He had meant it as a joke,
but Helen had been enchanted with the gift and spent
some time reading about dolls in general and Jules Steiner
in particular. Eventually Edward had suggested she handle

any dolls they were offered; then, when the dolls appeared to be making inroads, he had handed over to her the stock, waiting for payment until she had sold on.

Eventually Helen had moved into profit, and now her name was beginning to mean dolls in the trade. She could look at a doll, however battered, and pronounce it a Lanternier or a Steiner or a Tête Jumeau, and give the approximate date of its manufacture. She had done more than become an expert on dolls: she became knowledgeable enough in general to set him free to look for stock instead of waiting for it to come to him. They had had a good year last year, and this would probably be a better one. If things went on like this he ought to make her a partner . . . except that she might change to fit her new status and become as boring as Sylvia had, now that she was the wife of a barrister and lived in Hampstead. Better leave well alone.

'So,' he said, 'are you coming to lunch or not?'

Helen gave the steering wheel a final pat and stepped out beside him. 'Yes, I'm coming,' she said, 'but I'll have to be back by two. I've got someone coming in with what might just be a Bru.' Edward raised disbelieving eyebrows and she grinned. 'Yes, I know, I live in hopes – but I can dream, can't I? If it is a Bru I can trade this in for a Cortina.'

He wrinkled his nose. 'Common.'

She pushed him playfully towards the shop. 'Lock up, and stop being élitist.' She waited while he turned the key and then fell into step beside him as they walked towards the mouth of the Mews.


Christopher Milhill was turning from the handbasin, drying his hands, as Diana emerged from behind the screen, buttoning her blouse and shrugging into her jacket. 'Sit down, Diana.' They were on Christian name terms now, no longer doctor and patient but partners in what was becoming a desperate struggle to produce a live baby.

She sat opposite him as he studied her case notes, knowing he was seeking an acceptable form of words. He knew her details by heart: first pregnancy 1962, aborting at five months; second pregnancy 1963, ending after four months; third pregnancy 1966, ending at five months and one week.

'Well,' he said at last, 'you're perfectly fit and healthy. No complications. No reason why things should automatically go wrong in any future pregnancy.'

The obstetrician put his fingertips with their clean, square-cut nails together and then put his hands palm downwards on his desk. 'If you embark on another pregnancy, Diana . . . and the decision is yours . . . I can't promise anything, except that I'll watch you like a hawk. I'd like to take you in at two months and keep you in more or less continuously until the birth.'

Behind him, on the peach-painted wall, there was a photograph of his children. Three of them, all smiling, all alive. She forced herself to meet his eyes. 'I know you can't say, Chris, not for sure, but what about an educated guess at my chances?'

He shook his head, and she nodded. 'I know. I'm being unfair. Well, I'll think about it.' She rose to her feet. 'You've been very kind, Chris. As usual.' The phrase only served as a reminder of all the fruitless vigils they had shared and she saw that he, too, was remembering.

'Talk to David,' he said. 'Don't shut him out. It's his problem too.'

As Diana went out to the car she tried to school her face. No point in worrying David. She must resolve this in her own mind – this gamble, for that was what it was. A gamble, with the odds now stacked against winning.

David was waiting in the car, his face tense.

'I'm fine,' Diana said. 'Everything in order.'

He smiled. 'Good,' he said. 'Now where do you want to go?'

'You choose,' she said and he nodded.

'OK, we'll go to the Swan. I don't want to be late back, I've got to do a call . . . it's Diana Two actually. Lilian says she's running a temperature of over 100. But you know Lilian – nothing by halves. I'll drop you at home after lunch, and then pop in and see her.'

Diana settled into her seat, and checked her hair and make-up in the mirror that backed the sun visor. Lilian's

Diana was lively, tractable, loving and bright – and David adored her! If *only* she could give him a child of his own. She thought of the obstetrician's parting words: '*It could go well next time, Diana. I'd do everything I could to make it so . . . but it would be wrong of me to give false reassurance.*'

'Oh God,' she said aloud, 'I'd like something nice to happen. Something, anything, as long as it's nice.'

David glanced sideways at her. 'Like what?' His mouth smiled but his eyes were unhappy, and her conscience smote her.

'Well, best of all I'd like a man, about 5 foot 11, fair, professional status, mole on right buttock . . . to take me out to lunch and seduce me. Oh, and I'd like him to be rich and deck me in diamonds.'

'I don't know anyone who fits that bill,' David said, changing gear, 'but I know a man who loves you. Will he do?'


The old lady was still rambling on about her will, and Howard Whittington nodded gravely without listening. Someone would have to take down the details carefully, so there was no point in trying to memorize them now. In the shelter of his desk he turned his wrist to check on the time. Twelve noon. He was meeting Anne in the Swan at twelve-thirty. He tried to hurry the client along but the old lady was not to be rushed, so he resumed that 'I have all the time in the world face' of the family solicitor and let his thoughts wander.

There was a photograph of the children on his desk and he shifted a little so he could see it better. They were growing up so well. Michael was almost five now, and Susan four. Neither of them was flesh of his flesh, but they were precious to him just the same. He was better off than David – how long would he and Diana go on trying, when their efforts always ended in disaster? In a way their plight was worse than his own had been.

He remembered David coming down from medical school, talking about doing paediatrics and then settling for general practice. He had always loved kids. Neither of them had ever imagined their marriages would be barren. He tried to remember if they had thought of the future at all. If they had, he couldn't bring it to mind. They had simply assumed they would be happy because that was how it always was, for everyone. You larked about with your friends, watching them drop off one by one . . . he had been best man three times and groomsman twice . . . and then you settled for the right woman, had at least two children and not more than four. Four was slightly feckless. You prospered, and put them through good schools, grew old alongside your wife and merited a paragraph in the *Darlasden Echo* when you died.

That had been the pattern for his father and his father before him, but this generation was not conforming to it. He had started it: '*A Catholic girl*,' his mother had said in tones of doom when first he spoke of Anne. And then David had brought Diana from the south and made her pregnant inside a month. 'Made her pregnant': it was a familiar phrase but odd all the same. '*Made her*', as though it were a simple matter of force.

A picture of Anne, serene in the honeymoon bed, her black hair about her shoulders, rose up to torment him. If only he had been able to confide in David . . . but there were things you couldn't tell. Not even to a brother.


They ate spaghetti at a window table, looking out on the High Street. 'Fashion's gone mad,' Edward said, gloomily. 'If skirts get any shorter they'll be redundant altogether.' He was watching a girl with endless legs disappearing along the pavement.

'It's the age of anything goes,' Helen said. She had never taken to the worst excesses of the mini-skirt, preferring the elegance of almost-covered knees. 'Anyway, it's not just women, there are dozens of men's boutiques in Carnaby Street . . . and to say they're "way-out" is an understatement.'

Edward was smiling. 'Don't look now,' he said, 'but there's a girl sitting at the table behind you. Now that *is* "way-out"!'

185

As soon as she dared, Helen sneaked a look. The girl behind her had the long straight hair and fashionably pale lips that were *de rigueur* but the whitened face was painted with here a heart and there a flower. A bird flew free on her forehead and thick black lashes were painted on her cheeks. She looked surreal until she lifted a forkful of pasta to the colourless mouth and tried to catch the drips.

'I wonder if any of those girls have to work?' she said, grinning as she turned back to Edward. 'That look is fine for Twiggy, but can you imagine me turning up at nine-thirty on a winter morning looking like a painted firescreen?'

'I think it'd suit you,' Edward said. 'A little sprinkling of violets just below your left nostril . . . very choice.'

She pulled a face at him. 'Idiot! Anyway, finish your wine. We've got to get back for my client.'

Edward reached for the bill but she grabbed it. 'My turn.'

Out in the street they walked in step, giving way to people in a hurry. 'This is nice,' Helen thought. What would the last few years have been like without Edward? She was brought back to earth by his hand on her arm. 'Don't look now,' he was saying, 'but someone's dumped an old banger outside the shop. I'll have to ring the breakdown gang.'

They were laughing as they walked down the Mews and opened the shop door, and Helen felt happiness welling up inside her. She liked her boss, she loved her job, she had a new car, and by three o'clock she might own a precious Bébé Bru.

The phone rang and she moved towards it. 'I'll take it, Edward.' As the voice at the other end rattled on, Helen listened and felt the joy of the afternoon melting away. At last she collected herself. 'Thank you for letting me know. Of course I'll come . . . as soon as I can.'

'Bad news?' Edward's eyes were on hers, calm and sympathetic.

'It's my niece . . . my sister's little girl, Diana. She's got meningitis. They think I should come home.'

Edward was picking up her bag and gloves, and reaching for her arm. 'I'll run you home in the Mini and check with

British Rail while you pack. Leave everything to me . . .
let's just get you on the train.'


Diana knew from David's face that something was wrong.
She had been glued to the television since she got home,
still enraptured by flowers more real than real, of faces that
blushed, of the sheer joy of pictures in glowing colours that
only now and then went hectic green and red and had to
be adjusted. She switched the television off. 'What is it,
David?' He was putting down his bag and scrip pad, his
actions slow and deliberate.

'You're frightening me,' she said. 'What is it? What's
wrong?'

'I'm sorry,' he said, moving towards her. 'It's Diana Two
. . . I told you Lilian had asked for a house call. I wasn't
alarmed – she asks about every second week. This time,
though, it was serious. Diana has meningitis . . . it's not
confirmed yet, but I'm sure . . . and she's in the Infirmary.
I've just come from there.'

'Oh David,' she said, 'I'm so sorry. You've always loved
that little girl.' She had watched him for five years, playing
with the child that might so easily have been his own. She
crossed to the sideboard and poured him a drink. 'I know
it's early, but have this. Do you want to eat yet?'

He shook his head. 'No, not at the moment. We're going
to lose her, Di. It's not just that I'm fond of the kid . . .
although I admit I am . . . it's just that the death of young
life is – an obscenity. I ought to be able to do something.
She was begging me to give her a swing four days ago.
"Higher, higher," she was shouting. She always was a little
devil.'

'You're talking as though she was already dead,' Diana
said. 'Surely there's some hope? The Royal Infirmary pae-
diatric intensive care's among the best in the country.'

'I know,' he said dully. 'But I have this feeling. She has
severe malaise, neck stiffness, the rash. It's bacterial meningitis, all right. She was drowsy and confused . . . so
unlike herself.'

Diana couldn't think of anything comforting to say, not

in the face of his despair. 'Come here,' she said and drew him down beside her on the settee.

'Is someone seeing to our Karen?' Lilian could hear someone murmuring reassurance, but she asked again: 'What about our Karen?'

Billy was squeezing her hand, and she knew it but she couldn't feel it. 'She's with your mam, pet. You've no need to worry.'

They were sitting in a tiny waiting-room, white-painted, with Snow White and the Seven Dwarfs marching round the walls. 'Happy, Dopey, Grumpy, Doc . . . that was four. Happy, Dopey, Grumpy, Doc . . .' she sought in the recesses of her mind for the missing names. She had taken the girls to see the Walt Disney, so she ought to know. Happy, Dopey, Grumpy, Doc, Sneezy . . .

'Oh God,' she said aloud. 'Please God, let her be all right.'

A nurse appeared, bright as a button. 'Anyone like a nice cup of tea?' She wanted to smash her fist into the girl's face. She had earrings in, gold sleepers: that would never have been allowed by Matron in the old days.

'Can I see her?' she asked desperately, and, when the nurse shook a regretful head . . . 'I'm going to see her. Don't give me that . . . that's *my bairn* in there. Tell her, Billy . . . that's my baby.' She was pleading now. 'Please, just a little look. She's always been a mammy's girl . . . she'll be upset if I'm not there. It'll set her back no end. I won't speak, I won't do anything . . . please, oh please God, let me see her for a minute!'

The nurse's perkiness had vanished and disapproval had taken its place. 'I'm afraid your daughter's unconscious, Mrs Fenwick. She wouldn't even know you were there. She's getting the best of attention.'

Lilian was crying now and inside her head the knowledge grew that she must make a scene. They would take no notice of her otherwise. It had always been like that . . . if you were nobody you got nowhere, unless you made them sit up. 'I want a second opinion,' she said firmly. 'I want to see her, or I want another doctor brought. I mean it, so don't look like that. Tell them, Billy – tell them I know my rights.'

If her baby had been drowning she would have thrown herself into the water, but these buggers wouldn't even let her near Diana because she was nobody.

'Hush, Lily, pet.' Billy was tugging at her arm and she threw off his hand.

'Get off, you. You don't care. You've never cared!' He was looking stricken and she was sorry, but this was life and death. 'I want to see my little girl! If I don't get in I'm sending for Dr Whittington. She's his wife's god-daughter, so you want to watch what you're doing. He'll sort you lot.'

'I'll see sister,' the nurse said to Billy. 'Perhaps we can give her something to calm her down.'

She had lost. They had taken her daughter away and she would never see her again, never hear her say, 'Come on, mammy, I want you. Hurry up!' Always a little bossy-boots, ever since she was born.

Lilian sat down on the seat and folded her hands. 'It's all right, pet,' she said to Billy and put up a finger to wipe his cheek.


It was already dusk when Howard switched on the desk light to clear away his papers. 'Will you be wanting anything else, Mr Whittington?' Mrs Fraser, his secretary, was there in the doorway, a pile of mail ready for posting in her arms.

'No, thank you, I'm done for today. Has Judith finished the Jenkinson will?'

Mrs Fraser turned in the doorway and spoke to someone in the outer office. The next moment Judith was pushing past her in the doorway, the will form in her hand. 'Good-night Mrs Fraser.' He took the typescript from Judith and locked it in the drawer of his desk. 'I'll check it tomorrow.'

Judith was young, seventeen, but she had the face and figure of a woman of twenty-five. She looked up at him now, and he saw that her eyes had curious black flecks in the green pupils. 'Well done, Judith. It was involved, wasn't it?'

She nodded and smiled. 'Interesting though.' The disposal of Mrs Jenkinson's bric-à-brac had run to three pages.

She was half-way to the door when he called after her. 'Do you want a lift? You go my way, don't you?'

Judith paused in the doorway. 'Thanks a lot, sir, but I'm meeting someone.'

As he left the office Howard saw a light in the female cloakroom. She would be primping and powdering for some Darlasden youth, no doubt. On the drive home he kept thinking about Judith. She was bright, no doubt about it. He was very fortunate: Elizabeth Fraser was competent and had a charming manner with clients; his junior was streets above the other typists who worked for his partners. If Judith continued to show promise, he would talk to her about obtaining some qualifications.

He left the car in the drive and let himself in at the kitchen door. The cooker 'On' light glowed, and a pan bubbled gently. He heard the click of heels on the floor of the utility room and Anne appeared, a basket of newly ironed clothes in her hands. 'You're early.' She was looking at him with that half-smile that had once so intrigued him. Watching her now, he remembered the first time he had seen her, a green watered silk evening coat buttoned to her neck, her dark hair centre parted and coiled at the nape, silk-gloved hands holding a beaded evening bag. If anything, she had grown more elegant in the seven years since that first meeting. And more remote.

He followed her to the dining-room, bending to fondle his labrador's golden head as he rose to greet his master. 'Good boy, Jack.' The dog moved to paw at its master's knee, and Anne gave a small 'tsk' of disapproval. Howard raised interrogatory eyebrows in order to gain time, but he knew what she meant. When they had married and set up home, he had assumed his dog would go with him but she had never cared for Jack. The dog was old now, lumbering and smelly, but for what remained of his life he had a home here, whatever Anne might say about the children's safety. It was the one point on which he would not be moved – and besides, the children adored the dog.

Anne said nothing about Jack as she set the table for dinner, but Howard felt impelled to justify himself. 'He does no harm, Anne. He's old; that's not a crime.'

She smiled again. 'Of course not. And I suppose the children will survive. Now tell me about your day.'

As usual she had made him feel guilty, but he had long since ceased trying to analyse how she did it. It was simply there, in every line of her body – in the neat, rounded breasts, the trim waist, the knees discreetly together beneath the softly draped skirt. It was there in the hands, the curiously white and competent hands that held cutlery and napkins and had never once, in all the years, held him as a woman should sometimes hold a man.

'It was an average day,' he said. 'Old Mrs Jenkinson remade her will . . . again, and the Whitehouse place on the Belgate road is up for sale. Where are the children?'

'Upstairs,' she replied. 'We'll go up later.' She stood back to check the table. 'Do you think the nights are cutting in now?' she asked politely. They might have been strangers on a train.


Helen's father was waiting at the station, mufflered against the chill, coming forward to take her case. 'This is a bad do, lass, but it's nice to see you all the same. You've been away too long.' Helen had been home three times in five years: it was not enough. Now she was coming home to tragedy.

'Where's mam?' He was waving for a taxi and it gave her a shock. She had never seen her father in a taxi in her life. If anything was needed to make her realize the gravity of the situation, this was it.

'Your mam's looking after Karen. Billy's with Lilian at the Infirmary.'

She had wanted never to see or hear of the Infirmary again, but this was not a time to be squeamish. 'I think I'll go straight there, dad. Lilian might need me. Explain to mam. I'll come home when I can.'

She left her bags in the taxi with her father and waved as it pulled away. He looked years older than she had remembered. She turned and looked at the grim portals of the Infirmary. It was five and a half years since she had walked from them for the last time, but she had come a long way since then. She tilted her chin and went in search of her sister.

Lilian and Billy were in a waiting-room, holding hands quietly as a clock ticked on the wall above them. Their resignation shocked her. 'Hallo, Lilian. I came as soon as I could. How is she?'

It was Billy who answered; Lilian simply put out a hand and patted Helen's arm. 'She's trying to comfort me,' Helen thought, and was amazed.

'The bairn's not conscious,' Billy said. 'The last we heard, she was holding her own. They come in every now and then to tell us how she is.' Helen noticed that there were white hairs at his temples. He was only twenty-nine or thirty, but today he looked an old man.

'How are you, Billy?' she said. 'I haven't seen you for a long time.'

'I'm bearing up, you know, Helen. I'm bearing up. I'll be all right when the little girl's out of the wood . . .' His voice cracked then and he turned away.

'I think I'll go and make some enquiries,' Helen said, rising to her feet. 'Can I get you some tea or something? Perhaps one of you could go home for a break while I'm here.' They both shook their heads and she left them sitting together and went off to find the sister. Would she recognize a former colleague? Would she herself be recognized? She moved past trolleys and oxygen cylinders, and tapped on the windowed door.

'It's not good,' the sister said, when she had checked Helen's identity. 'The child's very weak. There's always a chance, but . . .' She shrugged, and then wrinkled her brow. 'Haven't I seen you somewhere?'

Here it was! 'Yes,' Helen said, 'I used to work here. Five or six years ago. I was a medical secretary in ENT.'

'Oh yes,' the sister said vaguely, 'I knew I'd seen you somewhere.' She doesn't remember, Helen thought and felt a sense of relief. No one remembered her, or her affair with Alistair. It had vanished without a ripple and that was how she wanted it to be.

'There's no real news,' she said to Lilian when she got back to the waiting-room, 'but that's not a bad thing. The longer she hangs on, the better chance they have to help her.' She remembered that from her own hospital days . . . if accident victims lived for twenty-four hours they usually survived. Surely it would be the same for sick five-year-olds?

She sat in the waiting-room, not speaking except to ask if she could fetch tea or coffee. A nurse came and drew the curtains against the night. A storm blew up, and rain rattled at the window-panes. And still the clock ticked, wheels squealed on rubber in the corridor outside, nurses joked with one another, and she saw Billy's disgust that they could be so light-hearted in the face of death.

'It has to be like that,' she wanted to explain. 'If they took it all to heart, Billy, they couldn't go on.' Had she laughed, those years ago, while people had suffered and been afraid? She tried to remember but it was a blur, as though she had never been there at all. She was Helen Clark who dealt in antique dolls and worked with Edward Portillo in Inkerman Mews. That was real.

'She was tall for her age,' Lilian said, suddenly. 'I always had a job with her clothes. She was long in the leg. You mind that, don't you Billy?'

He was nodding agreement, half-smiling, when the doctor appeared in the doorway, looking from one to another. 'Mr and Mrs Fenwick. We've tried very hard with your little girl but . . . I'm afraid we're not succeeding. If you want to be with her . . .' He turned to Helen. 'Only the parents, I'm afraid. I'm sorry.'

When she was left alone Helen walked to the window and drew back the curtains on the night sky. The rain had ceased. Stars winked above, and there was a crescent moon. 'Please let me be better to Lilian,' she said, not caring whether it was God or Fate who heard her as long as she was helped to keep her vow.

# 15

It was very quiet in the bedroom. Beside her Billy slept at last, and Lilian turned to pull the blankets up around his shoulders. At least it was a sunny day she thought, and was glad. No one would get wet! She was concerned for them all in their grief and confusion, but she herself felt nothing, nothing at all.

She sat up carefully and swung her legs to the floor. Let Billy sleep as long as he could – while he slept he didn't feel the pain that racked him by day. Poor Billy. She looked down at him and adjusted the blankets once more before she turned to the window.

In the browning garden the swing that Diana had given them at Christmas swayed gently, empty now. She thought of her daughter, legs sticking out of the seat, looking up at the window: *'Watch me, mammy. Watch me!'* And then to her father, *'Higher, daddy, higher!'* It was nice to think of it. She ran and reran the scene in her mind, smiling. This was real, not the little coffin in the next room, set up on the drawers because it had no need of trestles.

She felt wise this morning, wise and strong. She would help them all, because they couldn't cope if she didn't. At the side of the house she heard the milk-cart. Eight pints he would leave today, six more than usual because they were having a funeral. Soon her neighbours would come with plates, their best baking covered with clean tea-towels. 'Leave it to us, Lily. We'll see you right.' They had all flitted in and out of her house this week, round-eyed in horror at the loss of a child. Any child, every child. 'It goes against nature,' one of them had said. 'It goes against nature.' Lilian looked down at the garden, seeing the approach of winter. She had never really looked at it before because it had held no interest for her. But it was nature too.

She knew that something was wrong with her, that her

194

thoughts at this moment were not her own. It was as though what had happened had cracked her mind, letting out thoughts and feelings she had not been aware of before. Perhaps she was more like Helen than anyone had guessed. Perhaps she had brains after all . . . but it wasn't worth the loss of a bairn to find out. Below her the swing creaked suddenly in the wind. Lilian laid her cheek against the cold glass and cried quietly for a while, careful not to wake Billy before the moment came when he would have to face the day.

Helen felt better when at last she had something to do. She answered the door bell, collected wreaths and showed them to Lilian, all the while marvelling at her sister's composure and fearing it. This wasn't Lilian, this dry-eyed creature with a kind word for everyone. For years she had feared the lash of her sister's tongue; now she would have given anything to feel it once more.

Edward's flowers arrived at ten-thirty – 'With sympathy, Edward Portillo'. A small wreath, tiny pink chrysanthemums and stephanotis. Helen held it in her hands for a moment, feeling comforted, then she took it to Lilian. 'It's from my boss, Lil. He's really sorry. He asked me to tell you that when we spoke on the phone.' But Lilian was looking past her to the doorway, to Dr and Mrs Whittington. Helen, busying herself with the chairs, realized that Diana's presence meant more to her sister at the moment than any comfort she could bring. 'It's good of you to come, Dr Whittington,' she said and saw that his eyes, too, were bright with emotion.

After that it was as though the day changed gear. She went into the kitchen to find it a hive of industry, with Belgate women moving smoothly from table to stove. They smiled and one or two said, 'Hello, Helen', but she knew she was no longer one of them. They were a unit now, united in grief. They would cook and bake for Lilian, and dust and sweep if necessary, until she was mended and then they would go back to the rough and tumble of village life and give her a mouthful if she crossed them.

Helen climbed into the second car when the time came, beside Billy's parents, his mother black-clad and weeping at the loss of a grandchild, her husband tugging at an unaccustomed collar but dry-eyed, as befitted one who had seen death in the pit several times in his life.

In the church she caught her breath at the sight of so many people, heads downbent, eyes flicking to the tiny coffin and away, singing 'The Lord's my Shepherd', uneasily at first and then as though they meant it. They were all there, her family, the people she loved. Mother and father, Billy and Lilian, her aunts and uncles on both sides, and cousins she hardly knew. Only Karen was missing, safe somewhere on the other side of Belgate, until she could come home to a house that was no longer a place of death.

'We are here today to give thanks for the too-brief life of Diana Helen Fenwick. She was only five years old . . .' Helen bowed her head as the vicar requested prayer, but a new and unwelcome thought had entered her mind. Her family was *not* all here: somewhere she had a son. She had hardly thought of him for five years, except occasionally when something reminded her and she paused to wish him well. She had wondered, sometimes, if she was unmaternal. It had been easy to consider him someone else's baby, to think of him, warm and safe, growing up secure. But Diana had been secure, and now she was dead. They all rose from their knees and turned obediently to Hymn 452: 'There's a friend for little children, above the bright blue sky'. Was it true? Did Someone care for children, all children, even those who were given away?

She was walking in procession down the aisle, hearing weeping but herself dry-eyed, when she saw Edward in a side-pew. She might have known he would come. He smiled at her and nodded when she gestured that he should stay, and then they were out in the glaring sunlight, moving towards the churchyard and she could hear her mother sobbing as though her heart would break.

She would have gone to comfort her but Lilian was already there, somehow splendid now as she supported her mother and laid her other hand upon her husband's arm in an attempt to still his tears. 'There, there, Billy,' she said. 'There, there.'

Helen felt her own eyes fill with tears. 'I mustn't break down,' she thought and turned to scan the faces until she found Edward's and knew that she would manage after all.

In the church Diana reached for David's hand and held it through the hymns. He hated to lose a patient, any patient. But little Diana had been more than a patient, she had been a surrogate child, and he was grieving. She grieved too, but her chief emotion was disbelief. It had been hard enough to accept the death of her own baby, a child she had never seen. To accept that Diana – naughty, boisterous Diana who could charm her way out of any situation – to accept that she was in that locked coffin so soon to be lowered into the cold ground, was impossible. She stood at the graveside, looking at Helen, solemn and cried-out, and she wondered if it was worse to have and lose a child than to never give birth to one at all.

When the committal was over Diana waited, knowing somehow that Lilian would turn to her. 'Come on, Lilian. I'm here. I understand,' she said, taking Lilian's hand, feeling once more the bond that had tied them so firmly that night in the hospital room.

'Are you coming back for some tea?' Lilian asked. They were at the leading car, and must separate now.

'Of course we are. And I'll stay as long as you want me to.'

'Poor News of the World,' David said, when they were back in their car. 'She doesn't know what's hit her yet. I'll drop in on them tomorrow and give her something to help her out.'

Diana put her hand on his knee and patted it. 'You're a good doctor. You care.'

His voice, when he replied, was bitter. 'I care, all right, but I'm not terribly efficient, am I? Letting a child slip through my fingers?'

'You did everything you could, David. A doctor, any doctor, is only human.' She tried to change the subject.

'Lilian's sister . . . I don't know much about her except that she lives in London. Was she your patient too?'

He nodded. 'She's a bright girl, academically bright. She was university material, if she'd had encouragement. She worked at the Infirmary as a medical secretary, then all of a sudden she upped and went off to London round about the time that Diana Two was christened. Remember, she was also a godmother? She went off very suddenly – boyfriend trouble, probably. She looked distressed today.'

'So she's never married?' Diana asked.

'Not as far as I know – and, knowing Lilian, we would've heard if it had happened.'

'Will this change Lilian?' Diana asked as David manoeuvred the car alongside the kerb near Lilian's terraced house.

'Perhaps,' he said, switching off the engine. 'But she's a lot stronger than she seems. All Belgate women are. She'll survive, and she'll make sure Billy survives.'

'You like him, don't you?'

David was handing her out and locking the car door. 'I'm sorry for him. Living with Lilian can't be all joy . . . and he loved his daughter. Still, he'll come through.'

'This is very kind of you, Mr Whittington.' Howard held the car door for Mrs Fraser as she climbed out.

'Not at all. I'm happy to help.'

The house was a pleasant semi-detached, probably built in the 'Thirties with a pocket-hanky garden at the front and a glimpse of greenery behind. 'How much did you say they were asking?' She earned £18 a week as his secretary, and on that she could support a mortgage of about £1,500.

'About £3,200, but I'll get about £4,000 for Glebe Crescent.' Howard had forgotten that she owned her own home in a pleasant part of Darlasden. 'So you'd have some change once you'd paid removal costs and that sort of thing?'

'Yes, but that isn't why I'm moving. My husband left me reasonably well provided for, and I have my salary from the firm. I want to get away from the old house, from memories, if I'm truthful. Since Tom died it hasn't been the same, and I know the children feel it, too. So a fresh start will be good for all of us.'

'Were you very happy?' He had never before asked her a personal question, but Mrs Fraser seemed not to mind.

'Yes, very happy indeed. Tom was a nice man . . . very jolly. I think you would have liked him.'

He turned the key in the lock and they stepped into the echoing hall. There had been a fervour in her voice when she spoke of her dead husband. Had he ever been happy with Anne? Perhaps before they married . . . and since the children came things had certainly been easier. But there had been a real warmth in Mrs Fraser's voice when she spoke of her marriage, which he envied.

As they moved through the empty rooms, Howard thought of his wife, dark hair flowing over the rose silk peignoir, face rapt as she knelt at the prie-dieu in their bedroom, her lips moving silently, her fingers threading the beads of her rosary. If he were dead, would she speak of him as Mrs Fraser had spoken of her Tom? He doubted it. And if she died . . . guilt rose up in him and he moved closer to inspect the cracking woodwork in the hall.

'There's something amiss here. I think you ought to have a survey first, if you feel you want to make an offer. I can speak to Cartwright for you.'

Mrs Fraser's eyes were on his, and there was gratitude in them and admiration. She was a good-looking woman, left alone with two children to support. He would have to do what he could to help her.


Helen and Edward caught the train from Durham at five o'clock. 'Are you sure you don't want me to stay?' she had asked Lilian again and again, and had received the same answer: 'There's nothing you can do, pet. You get back to your job.' She wanted to get away, not because she was shirking the atmosphere of grief but because she needed to think. Since that moment in the church when she had remembered her son, her thoughts had scattered around her mind like mice in a granary, nibbling away at any peace of mind she might have had. She was glad that Edward was there to share the journey.

'I haven't thanked you for coming,' she said as the train pulled away and the magnificence of castle and cathedral came into view. 'It meant a lot to me that you were there. It was a long way to travel.'

They gazed at the glory that was Durham for a moment, and then he smiled at her. 'I wanted to be with you. And it was nice to meet your family after all the years of knowing them at second hand. I liked your father; he's a man of few words but he has a nice dry wit. And your mother and Lilian are just as I imagined them.'

'You haven't really seen Lilian,' Helen said. 'She's so unlike herself, it almost frightens me.'

Outside the train windows the autumn countryside rolled east to the sea and west to the Pennines. 'Durham is beautiful, isn't it? I think I've never realized until now how beautiful it is . . . and how much I care about it. Perhaps I'm changing as I get older.'

Edward was smiling at her. 'You're wearing well . . . for your age! But I know what you mean. We often take our native heath for granted. Be glad that you've realized it while you have time to value it.'

'Do you think they'll be all right, Lilian and Billy?' she asked suddenly. 'Perhaps I should have stayed?' He was shaking his head but she carried on. 'I feel very confused . . . today brought back so many memories . . . things I thought I'd buried long ago.'

'Well, I'm here to talk if you want to discuss things. I've done some thinking, too and realized I know very little about you. You erupted into my life, and I've never really liked to question you about any of it. Still, we can talk when we get home if that's what you want to do. In the meantime, let me fill you in on the news of Inkerman Mews. The joiner has skipped the coop . . . and with rent owing. That's caused a flurry in the dovecote! And I think Maria is coming round to the idea of selling her place. She'd be far better off in some sort of sheltered accommodation, now that she's without Stephan – but you know how independent she is. She asked me to make some enquiries about the property . . . what she'd get if she sold . . . I was staggered, I promise you. I thought my premises were worth about £40,000. She could pick up £70,000 for her building. *Seventy thousand*! I could hardly believe it.'

'But *you'd* never sell?' Helen sounded so shocked that Edward threw back his head and laughed.

'I might. I never like to say never! But it won't be this week, I promise you that.'

They were silent then, each looking from the window at the landscape, darkening now, with lights springing up here and there, and a ghostly moon above them in the sky. She wondered what he was thinking. Of his mother, perhaps, or Mrs Stepinska, who had so much filled the space created by his mother's death? Perhaps this day had opened wounds for him, too.

'I really am grateful to you, Edward,' she said suddenly. 'I don't know what I'd have done without you in the last few years.' She didn't add that she might need his help in the future, but she knew that she would have to be honest with him before long – because he was the only person she could turn to now.

Lilian wiped round the washing-up bowl and then draped the dishcloth over the taps. Through the kitchen window she could see the swing. *'We'll take it down, Lily, love. Just for the time being . . .'* Billy had said, but she had put her foot down. It was Karen's swing, too. Besides, it wouldn't make any difference. She missed the bairn every day, and would go on missing her, swing or no swing.

The food left over from the funeral was piled on the bench, enough for a week or more. They had all been so kind . . . good neighbours . . . but she could see in their faces the relief that it was not their bairn. There was pity there, and sympathy, and a desire to do good – but most of all there was relief.

The gate at the bottom of the garden creaked open as Billy came through, holding Karen by the hand. The house was returning to normal, bit by bit, the outsiders gone, now Karen coming back to where she belonged. But it could never be the same again. 'I took everything for granted,' she thought. 'I thought I had a right to a home and a man and bairns. Now I know different.'

'There now, pet, there's your mammy. She's been on about it all the way home, Lily, wanting to see her mam.' Billy was trying to remind her that she had had two children.

She held out her arms. 'Where's my big girl, then? Come and tell me what you did at Sadie's. Did she make a nice big dinner? And did you play with their Christopher's toys?'

Karen's eyes stared up at her, round and apprehensive. 'Speak to your mam, Karen.' Billy's voice was sharp with anxiety.

'It's all right, Billy, she's tired. Come and take your coat off, pet, and we'll have a nice cup of tea. Your daddy'll put the kettle on.'

She pulled Karen's unresisting arms from her coat and drew her to her knee. 'There now, you're back with your mam.' It was her little girl, but the thin limbs, the curling hair, only reminded her of what she had lost. 'There is no comfort there,' she thought. 'There is no comfort anywhere.'

At her knee Karen stirred and then pulled away, keeping her eyes on the glove puppet she had picked up from the cracket. 'Where's our Diana?' she said . . . and then again, more aggressively this time, 'Where's our Diana?'

They looked from one to another, mother and father, each hoping the other would find words.

In the end it was Lilian who lifted her daughter on to her knee. 'Our Diana's gone to Heaven, Karen. She's gone to be with Jesus.'

Karen was nodding angrily, as though she had had her suspicions confirmed. 'Can I have some bread and jam?' she said, slipping from her mother's knee. She ate at the table, making faces at the puppet that covered her left hand, talking to it in hostile tones, while in the fireside chairs her parents looked into the flames and wondered how they were going to manage.

\* \* \*

'There now, out you come.' Howard lifted his son from the bath and swaddled him in a white bath towel. The boy's face was rosy, the dark hair wet and wispy against the broad forehead. 'Could we play ludo after, daddy?'

Howard longed to say 'Yes', just as he longed to cuddle his son, to lift him high in the air and kiss him, but rules were rules.

'It's too late, old chap,' he said, beginning to dry the sturdy little boy. 'Give you a game tomorrow, though. It's Saturday, remember? We have all day.'

When Michael was pyjama-clad and into his blue dressing-gown they walked along the landing to the master bedroom. Anne was already there with little Susan, kneeling at the prie-dieu, hands clasped, ready for family prayers. Michael took his place beside his sister and Howard sank to his knees beside the bed. A candle burned in the niche that held the statuette of the Virgin; it flared and flickered alternately and there was a smell of smoke in the bedroom.

Howard remembered all the times of his humiliation, the smell of smoke mingling with the scent of failure in his nostrils. Looking up, he found Anne's eyes on him, reproachful. He searched in his pocket for his rosary beads and watched the children's fingers fumbling with theirs as they joined in the words: *Holy Mary, Mother of God, Pray for us sinners now and at the hour of our death.*

He was allowed to kiss each child once, when prayers were over, and then they were shepherded to their own rooms. He went downstairs and picked up the evening paper. The British Lawn Tennis Association was proposing to abolish the distinction between amateurs and professionals. An open Wimbldeon? He could hardly comprehend it. There were pictures of Prince Charles, looking uncertain, getting ready to begin his course at Trinity College. And Attlee, Attlee of the social revolution, was dead.

Over dinner Howard made polite conversation, talking of his day and mentioning the news. 'I wonder what history will say of Clement Attlee?' he said, more to himself than Anne.

'I expect it will deify him,' she said. 'That's what usually happens to dead politicians, isn't it?'

Howard had rather liked the unassuming little man who had ended the Indian Raj but he knew better than to display enthusiasm for a socialist in front of his wife. 'You're probably right,' he said, and followed Anne through to the living-room, carrying coffee on a tray.

'Do you want to play tonight?' Anne asked. They often played chess in the evenings, and the board was set out, waiting. He stood up and moved to collect it. 'We might as well.' He would have agreed to anything as long as it postponed the moment when he must ascend the stairs with Anne, go into their room, and close the door behind them.

'Will you come back with me?' Helen asked as she and Edward queued for a taxi in the cold night air, at King's Cross. 'I know it's late, but I'd really like to talk.'

Edward nodded. 'Of course I will, if that's what you want. But if you come back to the Mews you can stay overnight, which means we can talk as long as you want to.'

She thought for a moment. 'OK,' she said at last. 'That makes sense.'

Satisfaction suffused him. They would drink coffee and brandy, and talk into the night. He felt a sudden prickle of fear – Helen was becoming indispensable, and it wouldn't do. One day she must leave and make a life of her own, and then he would have to manage without her. He noticed she was smiling to herself. 'Penny for them?'

'I was thinking about Maria. If she sees us go in together, what will she think?'

It was his turn to grin now. 'The worst,' he said, 'and she'll love it.'

The familiar smell of the shop greeted them. 'Go on up,' he said, 'and light the fire. I'll see to this.' When he had paid off the taxi, collected the mail and papers and locked the shop door, he could already smell coffee. He carried the bags up into a room already redolent of comfort. 'Now,' he said, when they were settled opposite one another, 'what's on your mind?'

'When I came to London, the day you met me on the train, I told you some story about trouble at home, but that wasn't the truth.'

'I guessed that.' Edward could see that she was struggling to find words.

'I hadn't come from home, I'd come from "a Home", a Catholic home called Stella Maris . . . Our Lady, Star of the Sea. I had a baby there, Edward . . .'

Suddenly he thought he understood. 'That wasn't *your* baby today?'

She was shaking her head. 'Oh no, that was Lilian's baby all right. But I did give my baby away . . . for adoption. I don't know who took it. I signed all the papers, and that was that. No one knew, no one at home. Only a priest who helped me, and the Sisters . . . and . . .'

'And the father?' he finished for her.

'Yes,' she said. 'Although he really had very little to do with it. With the adoption, that is. Anyway, I did what I thought was best and I can honestly say that I've hardly thought about it since . . . about my baby, since. It was a boy. And then, today, in the church I suddenly thought . . . Diana was five and she's dead. And he is five, and I don't know whether or not he's alive. I've got to find out, Edward. I've got to know he's all right. I won't interfere, or tell him I'm his mother, I won't even speak to him . . . but I've got to know.'

She was looking at him defiantly, as though she expected him to be disapproving. Edward got up and walked to the sideboard, took out a bottle of Courvoisier and poured two generous measures. 'I think we need a drink.' He turned back. 'I suppose I really knew all along. Well, I knew it was something important. You looked completely drained and washed-out that day on the train – that's why I spoke to you.'

She smiled suddenly and he realized how beautiful she had become. 'So if I'd been fit as a flea, and glamorous to boot, you'd've shunned me?' It was a return to the usual Helen, and it cheered him.

'Something like that. Anyway, down the hatch.'

They drank for a while, both silent. 'She's wondering what I'm going to say,' he thought. Time to put her out of her misery.

'You'll have to look for him, of course,' he said. 'Accept the fact that it may not be possible to find him, but you'll have to try . . . because you'll have no peace now until you do.'

# 16

Helen turned carefully in the narrow bed that had belonged to the infant Diana. On the other side of the room Karen slept soundly, one plait unravelled on the pillow, the other clutched in her hand. Helen looked at her watch: six-thirty. Whatever she did, she mustn't wake the child. She slid her legs from under the blankets and got to her feet, shivering in the November air. She pulled on her dressing-gown, slid her feet into slippers and made her way carefully across to the window.

It was still dark outside but orange light outlined roofs and treetops. In the deserted garden the swing was at a standstill. She closed her eyes, imagining her niece on the slotted seat, swinging backwards and forwards. Somewhere her child, her son, would be sleeping now. Would he wake to a loving home, a garden with a swing? Edward had told her adoptive parents were parents by choice and therefore inclined to be loving, but you could never be sure.

She pondered her feelings. Was this the awakening of mother-love, or simply a long-delayed sense of responsibility? Was she suffering from guilt at the way she had walked away from her child all those years before? The sun was radiant on walls and garden, outlining her Mini parked outside the gate, before Helen abandoned speculation and got down to making plans, collecting pad and pencil from her handbag to make notes.

What did she have to go on? The baby must have gone to a Catholic home, for Father Connor would not have gone to so much trouble if he had not intended her son to grow up in the true faith. She wrote down *'Catholic'* and underlined it. Would he have handed the baby to some central agency, or handled the adoption himself? She had been counselled by a social worker before she had signed the preliminary papers and again afterwards. But who had picked the adoptive parents?

The sun was over the rim of the opposite roof and Karen yawning awake when Helen remembered what the priest had said: *'I know these people,'* had been his words; *'they're good people . . . good Christian people'*. Did that mean they were his parishioners? If so, she had a place to start. Good Catholics were always at Mass on Sundays. She could sit unobtrusively in the congregation and mark down all the five-year-olds . . . she might even recognize something about him and know she had found her child.

She wrote down *'St Mary Madgalene's'*, then detached the paper and shredded it safe from Lilian's eyes. She had no need of notes. She would simply go to church on Sunday and begin her quest.


'That's right, up you get.' Howard eased his daughter on to his shoulders and straightened up. Her small hands clutched his forehead as he set off down the stairs. Below, Michael was standing by the door, his case at his feet, the satchel containing his books slung across his chest. Howard felt his throat contract. There was something pathetic in the small figure, correctly dressed in his school uniform, his face grave and determined. If only the boy had the courage, the spirit, of his sister. She was nearly five years old too, and already the signs of rebellion were there. Whenever she stood up to Anne, he was torn between admiration and fear of the consequences. She must not be hurt; neither of them must suffer.

He lowered himself to the bottom stair and let her clamber down. 'Look what you've done . . . my hair's all higgledy-piggledy.'

She grinned at the strange word and repeated it. 'Higgledy-piggledy!'

He straightened his hair and she reached out to ruffle it. He pulled a face and straightened it again, and she put out a hand to disturb it once more. Her face was positively pretty when it was animated. 'You're a monster,' he said, and grinned as she began to grimace and threaten him again.

'Susan!' Anne was above them on the landing, her arms full of coats and extra woollens. 'Don't do that. Go and get in the car.'

Susan's eyes met his and Howard saw the question: '*Do I have to?*' He reached out and patted her arm. 'Run along, there's a good girl. I'll come and say goodbye in a moment.'

He stood while Anne checked the bags. 'Have you got your missal, Michael?'

The child opened his satchel to check. 'Yes. I've got Susan's too. Will we be coming home for Mass?'

Anne was moving him towards the door, her face gentle as it always was with her son. 'No, Michael, we'll be staying in Yorkshire for two weeks. We'll go to Mass there.' His face clouded, as though this alteration to the pattern of his life perturbed him, but he moved on obediently enough.

Howard carried the cases out to his wife's car and loaded them into the boot. 'I'll say goodbye then . . . until a week on Saturday.' He bent to brush his lips against his wife's cheek, recoiling a little at its peach-like texture. He kissed Susan and turned to his son. 'Goodbye, Michael, be a good boy. Take care of mummy and Susan.'

'He's too grave,' he thought, as his son's anxious face looked from the window of the departing car. 'He's too serious for a child of five. And there is nothing I can do about it.'


Somewhere in the Mews someone's radio was playing the ubiquitous 'Don't cry for me, Argentina'. Edward found himself whistling it as he crossed the road and let himself into Mrs Stepinska's hallway. 'It's me,' he called, repocketing the key with one hand and clutching the Pyrex casserole with the other. 'It's me,' she warbled from above, in imitation. He grinned to himself as he mounted the stairs. She was housebound now, but as perky as ever.

'Chops and barley,' he said, putting the casserole on the crowded dresser-top. She lived in one room now, the diameter of her existence narrowing day by day. Sometimes he suspected that she sat in her chair all night rather than traverse the room to her bed in the corner, but he forbore to question her.

'You heard from your Helen?' Mrs Stepinska said, when she had ticked him off for bringing her food, salivating at the same time at the thought of the meal to come.

He nodded, pushing a reluctant cat from a chair so he could sit facing the old lady. 'Yes, she's with her sister in Durham. I don't know when she'll be back. It can't be too soon for me.'

She leaned forward to stir the fire, and he noticed that her hands were becoming deformed, the knuckles huge and red-chapped, but the face, when she looked up at him, was still the face of the coquette. 'We have a drink, you and I? Benedictine. Big glasses.'

He poured as she directed, and held his glass aloft. 'Your health!'

She acknowledged the toast and then said. 'To my poor England.'

'Poor England? What's the matter with her now?' She was more informed about the fortunes and politics of her adopted country than many native-born Englishmen or women.

'Today they devalue the pound with the beautiful Queen's head on it. And *your* Mr Callaghan . . .' she had long since decided Edward had left-wing views and was solely responsible for the entire Socialist movement, 'your Mr Callaghan, he says it is a bad thing but he does it just the same.'

Edward listened patiently while she advocated hanging for anyone left of Disraeli, then he got down to the business in hand. 'What about this letter?' he said. It was behind the clock, in a thick white envelope, and it offered £100,000 for Mrs Stepinska's house.

Edward whistled softly. 'Well, well. It's going up.'

'Is this the right sum?' she asked eagerly. 'Is it the fair play?'

He shook his head. 'I'm not sure. It seems a huge amount, but property prices in London are rising. Let me make some enquiries and then we'll talk again.'

She leaned towards him, clutching his hand in her own. He noticed that her hand was damp, almost wet, and then he saw her glistening cheeks and realized she had been crying. 'Pouf,' she said, noticing his gaze. 'I'm foolish, foolish, old woman. It's time to go for me but . . .' She put both sets of fingertips to her lips and pressed for a moment.

'When we come to England I am frightened. You believe that? I am one frightened lady. It was no good to be a Jew in my country. My Stephan was not Jewish, you know that, but he say we should go. He leave everything for me and I think we will be nothing here. We sweep the roads, we wait on tables . . . all this I think. And then we come here for such a small rent and we prosper. We work, but at our own trade and then we buy. We are citizens. And now . . .' She was smiling, her eyes glittering like jet. 'Pouf! I am rich woman . . . fill up the glasses and tell me what I do with this great sum of money they want to give me.'


'Sit down there, Lily, and take the weight off your feet.'

Normally, Lilian liked her mother to make a fuss of her but today she couldn't be bothered. She wanted a bit of peace. 'Ta,' she said, accepting the over-sized mug of tea and the statutory custard-cream.

'Has she said anything yet?' Her mother's eyes were bright with curiosity and it nettled Lilian.

'Has who said?'

Her mother tried to hide her exasperation. 'Our Helen, you know who I mean. Has she said owt?'

'She's said she's fed-up of London. She's said she misses home. She's said she wants to spend time with me and our Karen. She's said it's funny weather for the time of year. If

210

you mean has she said what she's up to, the answer is no. I have no more idea of why she's come than you have. Mebbe it's right what she says – that the bairn dying made her think.'

Her voice broke then and her mother rose to comfort her. 'Don't take on, Lily, I know how you feel. I know how *I* feel, never mind you, and she was only my grandbairn.'

They sat for a while, brooding on their troubles, until the fire began to drop in the grate. 'Eeh well,' Lilian said, getting to her feet. 'I better be getting back.' She didn't make for the door. She was no more desirous of going home than she was of staying there. '*I don't care,*' she thought, '*I just don't care.*'

It was as though her spring had been overwound and snapped. Everything was an effort now, even getting out of bed, getting washed, making meals and sweeping up – things she used to enjoy once. She even felt apathetic about Karen, and that she couldn't understand. It didn't make sense. If you lost one bairn, you should have double the love for another. But it didn't work like that. She didn't seem to have love for anyone anymore. 'Not now,' she had said to Billy last night. '*Not now and not ever,*' she had thought, and had known as she thought it that she was being unfair. She had made the excuse of Helen sleeping in the next room, but he had known it for what it was.

'Have a fresh cup before you go,' her mother said persuasively, and Lilian sank back into her chair. She must make an effort; if she didn't, she would become a zombie.

'Well, I reckon it's a man,' she said, suddenly. 'Our Helen's had some fancy chap down there, and they've fell out – that's what it'll be. She's come up here to play hard to get, but as soon as he gets in touch she'll be off again. She's never had a real feeling for home, mam. Not like me.' The tea was hot and sweet, and her mother was soothing her brow. Lilian sipped her tea and surrendered herself to comfort.


'That was good,' David said, putting his napkin to his mouth. 'I almost didn't marry you, you know. Well, I thought someone so beautiful was bound to be useless in the home. But I was wrong.'

'Thank you,' said Diana meekly and then flicked him with the tea-towel she had used to carry in the tureen.

'I'll make the coffee,' David said magnanimously and led her through to the sofa. She switched on the television but it was boring news about unions, so she switched it off again. 'We'll talk instead,' she said, making room for him and accepting a cup. 'How's Lilian? You were seeing her today, weren't you?'

'She's OK. A bit apathetic still . . . inclined to weep if you show sympathy. But she'll be OK. At the moment Billy is treating her like a shell-shock victim, and it's beginning to irritate her. If she can have one good row she'll be well on her way to recovery.'

'You're becoming cynical,' Diana said, and then kissed his cheek to soften the words. 'How are you, while we're on the subject? Have you got over it?' She wondered if this was the time to tell him of her suspicions, but decided against it. She would wait for Chris Milhill to confirm things. After all, David didn't yet know she had stopped taking the pill.

'I'm OK. I still miss the little beggar, though. She'd come in and take the surgery by storm, and if she wanted to do something you couldn't restrain her. Tough as old boots, she was. I think that's what hurts – so much life, and then it's just snuffed out.'

Diana knew what he meant. There was life in the womb, pulsing, throbbing, kicking against you . . . and then it was over suddenly, drained away and everyone telling you it was just one of those things and better luck next time.

'Her sister's there,' David said, as though to break her mood.

'Helen? I thought she went back to London straight after the funeral?'

He nodded. 'She did, but she's back now, staying with Lilian.'

Diana held out her cup for a refill. 'That's strange, I thought she was a dedicated career woman. They're so

different aren't they . . . in looks, in personality, in aspira-
tions . . . and yet she's come back when her sister's in
trouble. I like that.'

'She may have come back for reasons of her own. She's
been in London quite a while . . . perhaps it's losing its
pull.'

'Or she may have had an unhappy love affair . . . maybe
a vengeful lover will come charging up the A1 to drag her
back . . .'

'. . . by the hair?' David suggested.

'Ooh, yes . . . by the hair. Then Billy can set out to save
her and preserve the family honour . . .'

'I think Lilian should be the rescuer,' David said, grinning. 'She'd be worth two of Billy in a scrap.'


'I've enjoyed that immensely. Thank you so much.' Across
the table Howard saw his secretary's face glow with
pleasure. When she had invited him to share her supper,
he'd been on the brink of saying no until he thought of the
silent house without the children, and had accepted.

'I'll just get coffee. Would you like some cheese?'

Howard pulled a face to indicate that he was replete and
then, as she left the room, he looked around. Good
furniture, family stuff probably, one or two nice water-
colours, a picture of her with her husband and children.
The husband had been dead for seven years now, and the
colours in the photograph were fading. He wondered how
old she was? Thirty-five, probably, but he could be wrong.
She was in his own age-group, anyway.

He looked at his watch: five minutes to eight. He couldn't
take his leave straight from the table, but with luck he'd be
home by nine. In the kitchen the percolator was going
plop-plop-plop, sounding as though it was on its last legs.
He could buy her a new one as her Christmas gift.

Christmas. Only eight weeks away . . . or was it seven?
In Yorkshire now the children would be sound asleep in
their grandparents' retirement home, dreaming of Christmas. His face softened as he remembered his own childhood dreams of Christmas. As soon as the leaves began to

fall he and David would talk about presents, impossibly wonderful gifts which might just come their way. Susan would be like that, with unreal but marvellous expectations. Michael would most probably equate Christmas with the Advent wreath, the crib and the incense-perfumed church. Poor Michael. Guilt nibbled at the edges of Howard's mind and he was almost engulfed by the hopelessness of it all when Mrs Fraser came back with the coffee.

'Shall we sit somewhere more comfortable?' She was looking anxious and Howard felt his lips twitch. With any other woman, he might have suspected seduction but not with Mrs Fraser. She might hanker after him a little – in fact he knew she did – but she was as upright as an English oak.

He settled in a comfy old club armchair and sipped his coffee. It was proper coffee and he felt himself relax. As long as he was away by ten, it would be all right. 'How are your boys?' he asked. He knew they were both away at a good school, sponsored by their dead father's fellow masons.

When Mrs Fraser's face lit up like that she was quite pretty, he decided, as he settled back to enjoy some polite conversation.


He had hoped it would be Helen on the line, and it was. 'How are you?' Edward said and then, glancing at the pad beside the phone . . . 'I've got several hundred messages for you, most of them from men! Still, first things first; how is it going?'

He listened as she outlined the progress she had made. 'So you're going to the church on Sunday . . . well, that makes sense. They all go to church some time on a Sunday, and if they have children it's almost certain to be in the morning.'

Helen sounded so excited that he felt fearful for her. She was looking for a needle in a haystack. In a novel or a television play the child would bear a striking resemblance to mother or father, and there would be instant recognition. In real life it wouldn't be so simple.

'Where are you ringing from?' he asked at last, and when she told him it was a call-box, 'I hope it's on a main road. It's ten o'clock; you shouldn't be out on your own.' She was reminding him that she was in law-abiding Belgate when he glanced at the pad again. 'Stuart has rung four times. He says will you ring him? Peter Moore rang to say he's got a Kammer and Reinhardt bisque-head character doll but he thinks it may be out of your price-range, and Jenny Stanness wants you to go to her leaving party. It's on the 12th.'

He waited while she scribbled a note of her calls and then asked the question he had been longing to ask. 'When do you think you'll be coming back?' He missed her, he missed the jokes, the comradeship, the occasional craziness . . . he missed the sight of her moving around, addressing Mark and Antony with total seriousness as though they were her old friends, too.

Helen was finishing her explanations and he changed the receiver to his other ear. 'No, there's no hurry. You know I can cope . . . indefinitely. I just wondered.'

He listened as she told him once more what a good friend he was and how much she relied on him. 'What are you doing tonight?' she asked at last, and he looked towards the clock. It was seven-fifteen and he would have to hurry.

'I have a date,' he said into the phone. 'Not being the type who lets opportunity slip, I chatted up Jenny when she rang, and I'm seeing her at eight. I've always fancied voluptuous redheads . . . remember Sylvia?'

'I'll stand by to be bridesmaid,' she said, and then, 'Put your grey suit on . . . the one with the wide lapels. It makes you look interesting.'

In the gilt-gesso mirror on the opposite wall his reflection stared gravely back at him. He did look a bit fuddy-duddy. 'Perhaps I should wear denim?' he said. 'Or grow a Zapata moustache . . . Sexy?'

'Ticklish,' she said. 'I'll have to go now. Enjoy tonight, and give me chapter and verse next time I ring.'

He put down the phone and made for the bathroom. Jenny had always appealed to him and it had been a while since . . . well, since. He realized he was grinning at himself in the bathroom mirror. 'You lecher, Portillo,' he said aloud, and turned on the tap.

# 17

The church was dark except where candles glittered at the feet of the saints. Rain pattered on the stained-glass windows, dull now in the absence of sun. The congregation was asking forgiveness for its sins and Helen tried to join in, but her plea for mercy turned into a plea for help: 'Please God, let me find him. Let me see he's all right, that's all. I don't want anything else, I know I have no right. All I want to know . . . that he's safe, that he's well. That they're kind. Please God, let them be kind.' She prayed, repeating her plea like a rosary, as the Mass went on around her. Then, as the priest began to speak, she settled to the serious business of checking out the congregation.

There were dozens of children, but most of them could be eliminated on account of age or sex. By the time the Mass had ended and the priest had given his blessing, she had narrowed it down to three small boys, all in the clutches of loving families.

She slipped from the church as soon as she could and took up her stand among the laurels, where they would all have to pass her by. Suddenly, what had seemed so easy was impossible. Three children, three families, three different directions. Which one should she follow? At least it had stopped raining, that was one small mercy. She slipped the scarf from her head and ran her fingers through her hair.

The first child emerged from the doorway, a book clutched in his hand. Behind him, in the porch, his parents were chatting to a priest. The boy moved a few steps forward and turned back. His chubby legs were encased in red cord trews topped with a navy duffel coat. His hair was brown, even reddish. Alistair's hair had been red. She struggled to remember Alistair but the face wouldn't come, only the hair and a memory of freckles. Other people were coming out now and Helen felt afraid. They would spill out and go left, right and centre, and she would lose them. Another whole week to wait.

The tiny fingers holding the Jesus book must have slackened their grip. The book fell to the ground and without thinking, Helen moved forward. 'Is this yours?' she said gravely, bending to hand it to the child. He nodded, solemn blue eyes unblinking. 'What's your name?' she said. Any moment now his parents would loom above them and snatch him away.

'Thomas,' he answered and then, 'I'm four and a half.'

Four and a half. She wanted to do fiendishly efficient sums, but they wouldn't come. 'When's your birthday?' she said, but her voice was suddenly rough and the child's eyes grew wary.

'Thomas?' The mother was there now, hovering defensively over her young.

'His book fell,' Helen said, straightening up. 'I picked it up for him . . . and he was telling me he's four and a half.'

The mother smiled proudly at her son. 'Five at Easter, aren't you, Tommy?' Relief made Helen grin like an idiot. One down, two to go.

The other two were emerging together, the mothers chatting, the two little boys side by side. If they went the same way she might manage . . . but one of the fathers was going off, obviously to collect a car.

Helen walked boldly up to them and looked at the woman on the right. 'I'm sure I know you . . . did we meet at the Poly? Let me think, was it Edmundson and you lived in Varley?'

The woman was shaking her head. 'Sorry, I didn't go to the Poly and I'm Cheshire, Mary Cheshire. I used to be Malloy.' No word of where she lived . . . still, it was an unusual name.

'I'm sorry,' Helen said, and backed away.

'Are you new here?' the woman was saying pleasantly but she pretended not to hear. She melted into the crowd and fixed her eyes on the remaining mother. She couldn't use the name trick again. If she had picked the wrong one, and it was this one who went off in a car, she was lost.

She wanted to pray but there was no real faith to back it up. In church it was different, you were carried along by mutual fervour. Out here, in the street, telling lies to total strangers, it seemed indecent to pray.

A car drew in at the kerb and the group on the path broke up. The woman called Cheshire walked towards the car and Helen let her breath out in relief. Something had gone right! She waited until the other couple had gathered up their three children, and then she began to walk behind them, trying to work out their brood, weighing the possibility that they were all adopted and the small boy in the middle might be her own son.

Even after eight years Howard still felt an interloper in St Mary Magdelene's. Today, without Anne and the children beside him, he tried to join in the service and at the same time work out why he had come. Was it fear of Anne, of her asking whether or not he had been to Mass? He could lie. It was unlikely she would check up on him, and even if she did, what could happen? What was he afraid of? Not of Anne, but of something within himself that Anne was aware of and despised. Not the obvious . . . although that was cause enough for contempt. He was an impotent man, a man who could not make love to his own wife.

The congregation was falling to its knees and he followed suit, glad of the opportunity to hide his face in his hands. He must not think about that, not now. He tried to think of mundane things, November winds and the approach of Christmas, his meal with Mrs Fraser and other such pleasant occasions to come. But thinking of his secretary brought other thoughts to mind – Judith, the junior! Judith of the plump thighs, the knees dimpled behind with puppy-fat, the white midriff showing when she lifted her arms to the shelves, the breasts, round and bursting with juice. Plums. Plums in a pie. Little Jack Horner sat in a corner. If there was a God at all let Him cleanse these thoughts. Father forgive me . . . mea culpa, mea culpa, mea maxima culpa.

When Judith turned her head there was a bracelet around her neck, a crease in the young flesh. He knew how her body would be, white with a ruddy V at the throat and burnished forearms. For a moment he was puzzled at the depth of his own knowledge. He had never seen a naked woman, not in the flesh, so where had the image come from, to haunt him now?

There was a shuffling as the worshippers resumed their seats for the sermon, and Howard tried to compose his face as he lifted it to the priest. But Anne was there in his head now, Anne on their wedding night, holding her clothes against her when he entered the room so that his eagerness drained from him.

There had been other girls before Anne, fumbled encounters in darkened corners, but she had been different. He had respected her, wanted her to be his wife. That first night he had been ready to worship her. He had felt holy at the prospect of their love. And then, as she moaned softly in pain, it had come to him that the woman beneath him was not a lover but a martyr. When it was over she had moved away and he had heard her in the bathroom, washing herself to remove his presence. She had not enjoyed his lovemaking, she had endured it.

After that it had been she who moved toward him, but he had known why. She wanted a child, a child for God, and he was an instrument, nothing more. With that knowledge came an impotence that had never left him.

Howard thought of her now, on her knees in some Yorkshire church, exultant in prayer. He had wanted to enjoy his marriage but there was no joy to be had of his wife. Perhaps, with someone like Judith, he could try again? He wrestled with the rag-bag of his mind, trying to shift the more disreputable bits out of sight, reaching at last for his beads and fingering them for calm, as he whispered the Hail Mary. He took out his hanky and blew his nose gently in the shelter of the final hymn.

* * *

Lilian drained the potatoes and added milk and margarine, mashing with a fork until there was a pale yellow purée in the pan. It was half-past twelve and Helen nowhere in sight. There was a rabbit away somewhere and no mistake.

'Billy!' He was stretched out under the *Sunday Post* and she had to shout again to bring him to life. 'Check that oven and see if the beef's done. Don't let in the draught or you'll spoil the pudding. Call the bairn and, Billy . . . do not sit down at my table with your belt undone. That's not the way I was brought up.'

While Billy carried out those tasks he could remember, Lilian drained the sprouts, mashed the turnip, put the plates to warm, and opened the tinned peaches and Carnation milk.

'There's something up,' she said, when they were seated at the table and still no sign of Helen. 'As soon as she mentioned "Catholic church", I knew she was up to something. She's never got religion, not living in London, and if she did it wouldn't be with the Micks. Unless it's a man . . . it's amazing what some women'll do for a man. Look what I gave up for you!'

Billy held out his plate for Yorkshire puddings and tried to look grateful, or as grateful as he could look with the belt of his 34-inch trousers eating into his 38-inch waist. 'You'd think she'd've said if it was a man,' he said, pouring gravy into the centre of each Yorkshire pudding with the precision of a bomb-aimer. When each cavity was full he swirled the jug over his plate in a satisfying criss-cross and put it down on the clean cloth.

'You're never finished?' Lilian said in amazement. 'I thought you were going in for painting, like that Andy Warhol. He throws everything everywhere, doesn't he? I mean, I don't want to seem greedy, Billy, but you've drained that jug.'

'You make lovely gravy, Lily,' he said, apologetically looking down at his plate, then, 'I could lift some off with me knife, if you want?'

She rose to the cooker and refilled the jug, setting it down with a bang in front of her daughter. 'There you are, pet. Your mammy sees to you. It's a good job somebody does.'

She ate in silence for a few moments until it dawned on her that for the first time since Diana's death she felt mildly happy. Guilt flickered, and then retreated as she looked at the clock and wondered what her sister was doing now.

Helen had followed them through a maze of streets to the corner semi that was their home. Now they were safe inside and she was standing under a dripping sycamore in Acacia Avenue, not sure of what to do next.

Behind her a door opened and an elderly lady peered out. 'Mitzi? Mitzi . . . come to mummy, Mitzi?' She sounded worried, and sympathy stirred in Helen's breast. The old lady was bending to peer round the doorway and the top of her head showed pink and vulnerable through the thinning hair.

'Have you lost something . . . can I help?' It was a poodle who had gone missing, let out to obey the call of nature and not yet returned. 'Go back inside, I'll find her for you.'

She discovered Mitzi, eyes cold in a white face, caught by her collar on a broken railing. Once freed she could well have trotted home alone, but Helen had other ideas. 'Come on, Mitzi,' she said, hoisting up the dog, 'you look just like a passport to me.'

Safe in the old lady's warm kitchen Helen loosened her coat and accepted a cup of tea by way of thanks, while Mitzi glowered ungratefully from her basket, occasionally emitting a high-pitched bark of disapproval.

First, she must explain her presence in the neighbourhood. 'You'll think I'm crazy,' she began. 'Well, I am and that's a fact. But it's my little boy. He's got mumps. He's over it now but still at the weepy stage. You know what they're like at four . . . well, nearly five.

'Anyway, he has this friend who goes to his school . . . we're Catholics . . . and he knows he lives in Acacia Avenue. Tommy, that's my son, loaned him his Action Man, and today he suddenly decided he had to have it back. *Had* to! Nothing would pacify him, and if he cries it gets on his chest, so here I am walking the streets looking for a five-year-old with a borrowed Action Man!'

The lies had rolled effortlessly off her tongue and looking at the innocent blue eyes opposite Helen felt ashamed. Still, it was in a good cause! The old lady was pursing her lips. 'I know most of the little ones around her . . . what's his name?'

'Well, that's just it . . .' Helen said. 'I only know he's called Stephen . . . no surname.'

The old lady shook her head. 'Stephen? There's no Stephen round here. There's Anthony in Number 2 . . . he's a Catholic but he's a big boy, nine or ten. Then there's the Cahills in the corner house, they have a boy about five. I'll tell you what, let me top your cup up and then you can pop and ask her. She'll know, she's a big Catholic. She'll know just who you want.'

'Well,' Helen said doubtfully, 'if you think she won't mind . . . ?'

The old lady's nod was emphatic. 'Not Maureen. What a nice girl she was, and she hasn't changed. She's gone through a lot to have a family. Caesareans, every one . . . still it's their religion, isn't it? They've got to keep going.'

So the little boy with the slight knock knees had been delivered by Caesarean section and not by Father Connor! 'You've been so kind,' Helen said. 'I'm glad we got Mitzi back, but I mustn't keep you.'

She waved until she was out of sight, and then sped on to the phone box at the end of the street. There were three Cheshires in the tattered directory, and she copied the addresses into her diary before she dialled a taxi and started in pursuit of the third and last child.


Edward had carried Mrs Stepinska lamb and tinned new potatoes and mint sauce from a jar. Now he ate his own at the kitchen table and wished away the hours till it was time to meet Jenny. When Helen was here, it was different. If they did not have dates they ate together on Sundays, sharing the chores and arguing over who got which Sunday paper. She would have a fit if she knew he was eating

222

tinned potatoes, the ultimate culinary obscenity but rather nice if you dipped them in gravy.

For the first time Edward allowed himself to think properly about what she had told him after Diana's funeral. Until now he had concentrated on the practicalities of sending her north and operating the business single-handed, but he could not avoid it any longer. She had a child. He tried that on for size, and found he didn't mind too much. A boy, and five years old. Not an immaculate conception – before there had been a baby there had been a lover, and he minded that all right! He minded it very much indeed. In fact, if he let himself, he could be sick with rage about it. She had been no more than a child, eighteen, and some bastard had taken advantage of her.

Edward tried to reason with himself. She had men in her life now, and it was hardly likely that they were all platonic relationships. He was not celibate himself – who was, in 1967? But there were limits. He tried to remember the age of his own youngest partner and gave up when shame threatened.

He got up from the table and rinsed his plate free of gravy before he put it in the washing-up bowl. 'You're a hypocrite,' he said aloud to the little plastic mirror above the sink that his mother had nailed there years before. 'You're a bloody hypocrite,' he said, squirting washing-up liquid in a green tide. But his disapproval of Helen's seducer still rose up in his throat like bile.

When she found the child, what about the lover? If she reappeared with the villain in tow he would smash every damned thing in the shop and go on until he had to be forcibly restrained. But in his heart he knew he would do none of those things. He would wish her well and shake the lover by the hand: such was the way of a civilized society.

He grinned as he turned on the tap and plunged his hands into the foam. Tonight Helen would ring as she always did, and afterwards he would probably make comprehensive love to Jenny, who seemed not to know what an inhibition was and would soon be flying off to her new job in Paris. When he had finished washing up he put on his coat and went for a walk in the park before the light died.

Howard had carried the tray of tea and rich tea biscuits through to his study when the phone rang. It was five-thirty, so it would be Anne. He hastily poured a cup and carried it into the hall, stirring in the sugar before he lifted the receiver.

'Darlasden 54913.' He made moist thumb prints on the mahogany surface of the hall table while they exchanged small talk. The journey had been uneventful, the children were enjoying Yorkshire, the weather was bracing but fine, she said. He was coping with his meals, Mrs Bickerstaffe was keeping to her usual routine and in addition was peeling his vegetables, nothing of note had happened at the office, and he had been to Mass.

He knew they would come, the carnal thoughts so wicked in the church, but more sinful still in this cold hall with its iconed alcoves, so redolent of their mistress. Anne was *here*, watching him, knowing his innermost thoughts, drawing aside the hem of her garment for fear of contamination. He forced himself to concentrate.

'So you're coming back on Monday? A week on Monday. No, of course not. As long as they're enjoying themselves.' Useless to say that he wanted his children back, needed them back, two human spirits for him to embrace, two small bodies with arms that clung about his neck, protecting him from all the blackness in his soul. 'I'll speak to you during the week, then,' he said to his wife, and waited for his son to come to the phone.

'Hallo Michael, how goes it? You did?' He listened to a small boy's enthusiasm for rural life, and then commiserated with a small girl who was not allowed to do all that her brother, the elder by six months, was allowed. 'Wait till you come home,' he promised. 'We'll see what we can do together, you and I.'

In the silent study he topped up his cup with hot tea and reflected on the bleakness of his landscape, struggling to control his mind and keep it within Sabbath parameters.

224

He took down a well-thumbed copy of Cervantes and tried to read, but all he could think of was the warmth of a young thigh next to his beneath a desk, the potent smell of cheap perfume, and the touch of skin on skin when their hands brushed across the documents with their scarlet ribbons. 'Father, forgive me . . . for I wish to sin. I want it with all my heart.'

Karen had come down twice and been taken back to bed, first by her father and then by her mother. 'Now, you can less it, our Karen. I'm not coming up again, so be warned. You've got school tomorrow, so get some sleep. And it's no good shouting of your dad, it's not him you're dealing with now, it's me – and you can't pick the soft out of me like you do out of him!'

There was one last despairing wail and then peace, and they settled on either side of the settee, the television opposite. Lilian felt guilty about television at first, as though to watch it was to betray her grief. But you couldn't deprive the bairn, and at the end of a day down the pit Billy deserved his relaxation. She had tried to ignore it, to mourn quietly as though impervious to music and laughter, but that hadn't worked either, and in the end she had simply given in.

A comedian was on now, his brow furrowed, his eyes anxious, but his words cocky. Billy was laughing and she felt a tremor of disapproval. Diana had been his bairn too, but men never felt like women. At once she remembered his tears, the bleakness in his eyes at the graveside. 'Don't be a bitch, Lilian Fenwick,' she thought, and satisified herself with remarking that the comedian's jokes had been old when Adam was a boy.

There was a click as the back door latch went down, and Helen appeared through the scullery. She looked cold and pinched in spite of her posh coat, and Lilian leaned forward to stir the fire. 'You look half-starved. How was me mam and dad?' Helen unzipped her boots and pulled them off, standing them neatly side by side under the dresser. 'OK.

He's a bit chesty. We had a nice crack, though. They don't change.'

Lilian was dying to ask about the morning, about the trip to the Catholic church that was supposed to be just idle curiosity but was obviously much more – but there was something in Helen's face, some depth of misery, that stayed her words.

'Do you want some supper?' Billy came suddenly alert beside her at the mention of food. 'Not you, Billy, you've hardly got your tea down. But there's bubble and squeak if you want it, our Hel? It won't take me a minute.' She wanted suddenly to do something for the little sister that had been such a pain in the arse but now looked ready to drop.

'It's all right, Lil. I might have a cup of tea, but then I've got to make a phone call. I could do a fry-up for you and Billy when I get back, if that's what you'd like?'

They sat on for a while, arguing gently about who would cook what for who, until Billy's snores threatened to drown out Shirley Bassey on the box, and both sisters remonstrated with him to stop.


Edward let himself into the shop and slid home the bolts. He felt along the wall for the switches, and lights sprang up, making the contents glitter and gleam in a way that always pleased him. As a child he had seen the shop as an Aladdin's cave, and it was still a treasure trove, the hub of his universe. For a moment, while he moved to the stairs, he thought about Mrs Stepinska's offer from the property developers. Presumably he could do as well if he offered his premises for sale on the open market? One hundred thousand pounds was enough for a lifetime, enough to get right away from Kensington, from Britain even. If it came to it, he might pull up stakes and join Jenny in Paris.

The phone started shrilling in the flat upstairs and he hesitated. He could switch on the shop extension? In the end he sprinted up the stairs, convinced it would not be Helen ringing this early but hoping against hope that it was.

'Hallo . . . Edward Portillo.' As he heard her voice he reached behind him to feel the chair and subsided into its depths. 'Helen! How did it go?' He already knew from her voice that as yet there had been no successful conclusion to her quest. 'I see . . . so it still could be them?'

She had tracked down several families named Cheshire, two of whom might fit the bill, but darkness had cut short her endeavours. 'I went to mum and dad's for an alibi, Edward. Lilian smells a rat . . . she'd like to ask outright, but she just doesn't dare. Am I really that intimidating?'

They laughed then, while he stressed her ogre-like qualities. She asked about Mrs Stepinska and he about little Karen.

'I've missed you,' he said, when the formalities were over. 'No one to nag me, no one to spill coffee on my desk, no one hogging the phone to talk about dolls and shoving the damned things up my nose. I got that Bru for you, by the way. I was feeling flush, and it's absolutely original – mint isn't in it.' The doll was sitting on the chair opposite him, small eyes glittering above the pursed mouth and faded ivory silk of its dress. 'I've called it Cassiopeia Pocohontas Portillo and I don't think we'll trade it on. It has class.'

Helen was laughing, so he had achieved his objective.

'What happens tomorrow?' He listened while she outlined her plans to beard the Cheshires in their den. 'And if that doesn't work out?'

'I know the answer's there, Edward. In that congregation. In that church.'

Privately Edward thought she was indulging in wishful thinking, but he couldn't bring himself to tell her so. 'What about the priest?'

'Father Connor? He left a while ago . . . retired, I think. But he'd never tell me, Edward. Not in a hundred years would that old man betray a confidence.'

There was despair in her voice and he cast around for cheer. 'When you come back we'll make plans. The Mews is changing, I can feel it. Perhaps it's time for us to expand?'

# 18

'Well, you know how nice she is – you've met her.' There was a light in Lilian's eyes at the thought of their visit to Diana Whittington's. She cherished her friendship with 'the doctor's wife'. To be able to take her sister, her swanky sister from London, along to observe how close she and Diana were, would be truly pleasurable. They would collect Karen at school at half-past three and walk to the detached house in the leafy road where all the posh people lived. Lilian felt no jealousy of Diana; it was only right that a doctor was a bit above the rest, with all those years at college. But Helen was different, no better than anyone else.

'What time are we going?' Helen asked. She didn't sound at all excited at the prospect, and Lilian bridled.

'Well, you don't need to come if you don't want!'

Helen stood up and started to carry the breakfast dishes to the sink. 'I want to come . . . I just wondered what time, that's all.'

They settled the fine details as one washed and one dried, and then Helen took down her coat from the door. 'I think I'll go for a walk. I haven't really looked at Belgate since I got back. Can you still get up around the cricket club?'

She walked quickly until the houses of Belgate petered out. She felt like a stranger now. Sometimes people looked at her as though wondering whether or not they knew her. More often their faces were blank, without any sign of recognition, as blank as her own face, for it seemed she knew no one.

It was a relief to be out on the hill above the neat turf of the cricket ground. The fields were striped brown and black, the hedges withered and pale except where hips and haws still glowed red. Beyond, the sea was turquoise, a dark band on the horizon separating it from grey sky. Wind caught at her hair, whipping it across her face and making her lips sting. She wore her hair longer now, unfashionably long by London standards, and she tucked it behind her ears.

She acknowledged again how beautiful Durham was, its colours as gentle as its contours. She drank in the view, permitting her eyes to moisten and her throat to tighten at the sight. But she was not crying for the landscape, she was crying for failure. Two weeks had passed since that first hope-filled visit to the church. She had followed up all three Cheshires, posing as a market-researcher at two houses to elicit details, but it had been in vain.

Last week she had stood outside the church and watched again, hoping to see a new face, a small figure that would be worth following. But she had known then that it was a wild-goose chase. Whoever had taken the baby might have moved away, or become a backslider. There were a thousand possibilities. She could stay here forever and never find the right one.

The thought that her son might have died in infancy reared its head, and was firmly repressed. That could not be. The only concept that was bearable was that he was alive somewhere, thriving and happy. The wind howled behind her, as though in commiseration, and Helen began to pick her way down towards the path again.

'It's wild out there,' she said when she was safely back in Lilian's warm kitchen.

'Serves you right for going,' Lilian said warmly, lifting a floured hand to rub her nose. She rolled the pastry, folded it, turned it and rolled it again. 'They don't call it Windy Nook for nothing, you know.'

'I got a good view of Belgate,' Helen said. 'It hasn't changed much. I think it's about time for me to go back to London. I'll go on Monday, probably. So I just fancied a look at the old place.'

Lilian was looking sympathetic. 'Why don't you pack it in and come back here? You could get a good job here with your experience.'

'Doing what?' Helen said. 'There's not a big market for antique dolls in the Durham coalfield.'

Lilian let the question go and turned to something more interesting. 'Is it that friend of yours, the one you work for, Edward? I wondered . . . well, you going to the Catholic church and all that . . . and he's got a funny name. Billy said he might be an Eyetie?'

Helen felt a sudden lift of her spirits at the mention of Edward, but Lilian was on the wrong track. 'He's my boss, Lilian, and about the nicest guy I've ever met, but there's no romance. Sorry to disappoint you and all that, but Edward and I could be on a desert island together for twenty years and it wouldn't occur to either of us. And he's not Catholic or Italian, he's as English as they come.'

'Oh, well,' Lilian said, giving the pastry a vicious slap on the board, 'you can't blame a body for wondering, can you?'


David put down the telephone receiver and turned back to the breakfast table. 'I'll have to bolt this and get out, everyone seems to be wanting visits. I sometimes think I'll close the surgery and buy a helicopter.' He scooped grape-fruit into his mouth with one hand, sugaring his tea with the other.

'Only one spoon,' Diana said sternly. 'You told me to remind you.'

'Not today,' he said, 'definitely not today, my darling. I need the energy. I'm off now . . . don't forget it's Round Table . . . oh, and of course, you've got Lilian and that sister of hers for tea. Well, give them all my kind regards and tell Lilian to keep healthy.' He collected his bag and stethoscope from the hall table, and kissed her heartily on the cheek. 'I love you. See you tonight.'

When she had waved him off Diana went back to the morning-room and sat down to finish her tea and brown toast. She felt excited, and it frightened her. There was no point in thinking about it yet, much less celebrating. But she would have to tell David soon, and she would have to watch herself with Lilian this afternoon – or Lilian would be rushing in to David and congratulate him before he knew what she was talking about.

It would be a strange afternoon altogether. Lilian's sister was a very different type, so they couldn't just rabbit on about the house and husbands and the price of food. Helen looked . . . if not trendy, certainly arty. Perhaps it would be world events or Jean-Paul Sartre? As she stacked the dishwasher Diana started to giggle at the combination of Lilian Fenwick and Jean-Paul Sartre, and for a moment quite forgot to speculate about whether or not she had definitely conceived.

'And you're certain the goods were not in your basket when you picked it up at home?' Howard said.

The sobbing woman opposite shook her head vehemently. 'No, I know they weren't . . . but I don't know how they did get there. I never took them.'

Her husband sat beside her, white-faced with fury. 'It's ridiculous to accuse my wife . . . *my* wife . . . of shoplifting. I give her everything she could possibly want. But I intend to sue. I want you to put the matter in train . . .'

The woman's knuckles glowed white as she twisted her hands together. Her eyes were stark with terror. 'She did it,' Howard thought and sympathy surged through him. He would have to restrain the husband from making matters worse.

'I can understand how upset you are, but I think we should all calm down. I think you should talk to my partner, Mr Cotton. He's our expert on these matters, and I'm sure he'll be able to help.'

When he had transferred them to the waiting-room and briefed Bill Cotton, he walked to his window and looked down on the seething pavements. Women were flooding into Dembry's, some of them with hunched shoulders and anxious faces like the woman he had just seen. She had taken the goods, he was sure about that – and no wonder, with a hectoring bully for a husband. Now her life was in ruins. The wages of sin . . .

A shiver ran through Howard. How thin was the dividing line between good and evil, safety and outer darkness. He closed his eyes as Judith came into his mind. Judith

smiling, Judith compliant, Judith's lips parting, opening
. . . he put a hand to his mouth and drew in his breath.

Behind him the door opened after a discreet knock and
he turned round, glad of the interruption. 'I thought you
might like a cup of tea. Mr Cotton asked me to make some
for his client, and I thought you could probably do with a
cup.'

Howard smiled at Mrs Fraser gratefully. 'What would I
do without you, Mrs Fraser? Yes, I could do with a cup,
thank you.'

She was placing it on his desk when the phone rang and
she lifted the receiver. 'Mr Whittington's office. Oh yes, of
course . . .' She handed him the receiver. 'It's your wife.'
She was making to leave the room but he held up a hand
to detain her. 'Anne . . . nothing wrong, is there? You're
coming home tomorrow. I see. About one-thirty. I'll let
Mrs Bickerstaffe know. See you tomorrow, then.'

He was about to put down the phone when he caught
sight of Mrs Fraser's reflection in the mirror. There was
utter dejection on her face, and it took him by surprise.
Why was she so cast down to hear that Anne was returning? 'My wife's coming home,' he said, trying to gain time.
'I've missed the children. It'll be good to have them back.'
He had not said he would be glad to have Anne back, and
he thought he detected a flicker of pleasure in Mrs Fraser's
eyes at the omission. He had known she was fond of him,
had even liked that idea – but it wasn't fair to her to let her
go on like this. 'You've been very kind while Anne was
away,' he said. 'You can stop worrying about me now.'

It was crude surgery but it worked. She turned away,
once more the perfect secretary. 'Do tell me if you'd like
another cup. In the meantime, I've nearly finished the
Remington lease.'


Edward brought the car to a halt in the Mews and climbed
out to open the passenger door. 'Come on then, Maria, my
girl.' It took time and patience to get her out of the car, and
once or twice she winced with pain. 'We'll have tea when
we get upstairs.'

'Tea?' she said, putting out a blue-veined hand to the doorpost. 'Pouf to tea. I want something with a kick, something to put life into me.'

He feigned horror. 'You're not talking about alcohol, I hope? Not at twelve-thirty in the morning?' He made the mistake deliberately, knowing she would seize on it. Her pleasure in correcting him on the time of day carried her up the narrow stairs and into her chair.

'Right,' he said, fetching her favourite Benedictine and two glasses. 'Fill those, and I'll get the eats.' He had brought sandwiches from Berman's when he came to collect her to go out. Now he removed the cellophane and arranged them on a plate. 'Smoked salmon, your favourite, cream cheese and shallot, and the shaggy one with the mustard trim is mine.'

'This is good,' she said and then, raising her glass, 'Here's to my new abode . . . and to our continuing friendship, my Edward. No, don't put on that face of yours, you have been good boy, first to your mama, then to me. I'm grateful. Now let us get down to real business. What did you think, today?'

He considered for a moment. 'I thought the Home wasn't bad, actually. Oh, the matron is a little fussy, but I thought she was good-hearted. It was warm and clean; you'd have your own room and your own possessions around you; it's near enough for me to see you often . . . I think you could do worse. However, it's pricey – can you afford it? I could help a little . . . and there's what you'll get when you sell this place.' He hesitated. 'I don't know if you own it outright?'

'You mean mortgage?' she said, grinning. 'No, no mortgage. Free and clean.'

It was his turn to pounce. 'Free and clean – your English is slipping again.'

He was saved from her retaliation by the pounding of feet on the stairs. 'It's only me!' Edward had met the nurse before, and liked her. She was tall and mousey-haired, with an engaging chubby face and capable short-fingered hands. 'Are you two drinking again?' she said. 'Honestly,

233

a bad influence and a geriatric delinquent, what a combination!'

'Can I get you a glass?' Edward asked as she slipped out of her navy coat and began rolling up the sleeves of her dress.

'Not alcohol . . . but I'd kill for a cup of tea.'

He went off to the kitchen while she administered Mrs Stepinska's weekly injection, and then returned with tea on a tray. When the girl smiled she looked about sixteen. He felt Mrs Stepinska's eyes on him and caught her nodding enthusiastically, urging him on.

'Do you ever drink?' he asked, as he poured the tea.

'Yes, sometimes,' she said, 'but not while I'm on duty. You'd be amazed how often it's offered. If I said yes every time, I'd be reeling by mid-afternoon.'

'You must come out for a drink some time,' he said. 'Then I can give you the lowdown on our friend here. It'll curl your hair.'

'I can hardly wait,' the nurse said, scooping up bandages and paper wrappers. 'What about tonight? And my name's Celia.'


They all had tea in a pleasant room at the side of the Whittingtons' house. Karen on the hearth-rug with a jigsaw puzzle Diana had bought for her. 'Oh, this is nice,' Lilian said, sinking back in her chair.

'More cake?' Diana asked, handing the plate first to Lilian and then to Helen. They had both taken a piece and were holding their cups for refills when the phone rang.

'Excuse me,' Diana said, and vanished into the hall.

'It was Howard, my brother-in-law,' she said, when she came back. 'His wife's been in Yorkshire for a couple of weeks, visiting her parents. He just rang to say she's coming home tomorrow, and he's like a dog with two tails. He does love his children.'

'And they're not his own bairns, are they?' Lilian said, round-eyed. She turned to Helen. 'They're both adopted – they couldn't have their own. It just shows you! Them as can't have them values them, and those that drops them like a hen lays eggs don't give a damn for them.'

'How many children have they adopted?' Helen asked.

'Two,' Diana said, 'a boy and a girl. The children aren't related, they were separate adoptions. It was all arranged through the local priest, my sister-in-law being a devout Catholic. Of course, Howard converted when they married.'

Helen tried to sit still and keep her cup from rattling in the saucer. 'How old are the children?'

The boy was five in December, the girl a little younger. 'Michael's just started school,' Diana said. 'He's very bright. So is Susan, but she's rather a handful. And my sister-in-law is . . .' She stopped suddenly and looked at Lilian. 'Oh Lilian, I'm sorry. We're talking non-stop about children, and I never thought about how it might affect you. I've been thoughtless . . .'

Lilian was shaking her head and suddenly, even in the midst of her own confusion, Helen felt proud of her sister.

'You can't make better of it, whether you talk or not. I miss our Diana every day. I always will, I expect. But the world keeps turning. You can't ask folks to watch their tongues all the time on account of your feelings. You have to get on with it. And, besides . . .' she looked down at her daughter, full length now on the rug, pondering the puzzle, 'I've got our Karen, haven't I?'

She looked first at Diana and then at her sister, and Helen realized there was pity in Lilian's eyes for their childless state. She listened as they talked then of mundane matters, television and supper dishes and the optimum length of skirts. She struggled to look interested, or at least calmly disinterested, but inside her emotions were threatening to implode. Michael, they called him Michael. Her son's name was Michael . . . for this baby was her son, she knew that with every fibre of her being.


'*The world keeps turning*' – the phrase re-echoed in Lilian's mind on the walk home. Helen seemed edgy and preoccupied, which Lilian put down to jealousy of Diana's nice home and the handsome husband who had appeared as they were leaving and had put himself out to be pleasant.

'*The world keeps turning.*' She thought about it as she chipped potatoes for Billy's tea and fried the thick Cumberland sausage that was his Friday treat. He had never made a single demand of her since the bairn died – well, only that once, and that had been more to comfort her than anything else. She had waited for his hand in the night, ready to repulse him, but it had never come. And he liked his little bit, he would be missing it. Many another man would have said so.

Lilian thought about sex as she shook the chip basket and turned the sausage. It was a funny thing, at once a nuisance and a comfort. In the aftermath of the bairn's death she had thought she would never have sex again, not ever. But that had been selfish. The world did keep turning, and that was a fact. She felt her eyes fill. Perhaps it shouldn't keep on turning – she had lost a child, flesh of her flesh. It was hard to give birth . . . labour was a bloody good word for it. And she had loved the little monkey.

A sob rose in her but she quelled it. Not with Karen and Helen in the house. She would cry in her own time, and one day she would remember Diana without pain. 'I loved her every minute of her life,' she thought, smiling, pitying children who were only born to be given away.

'Get that down you,' she said, when Billy, newly washed, sat down at the table. Upstairs she could hear Karen chattering excitedly to her aunt. 'What was your shift like?'

He shrugged. 'Lovely sausage, Lily.'

'Lilian, Billy. Lily-*ann*. If I've told you once, I've told you fifty times. We had a nice time at the doctor's, in case you're interested. He offered us a run home but I said no thank you.'

'It's a canny walk from their place,' Billy said, scooping up his food.

'Not with your knife, Billy,' she said. 'Not with your knife. There's bread-and-butter pudding if you've got room after that lot.'

'With extra raisins?' he asked, eyes shining.

'Wait and see,' she said tartly, a little alarmed that he had suddenly put down his knife and fork and was coming round the table.

'I want you to know, Lily . . . Lilian . . . that you're a bloody good wife . . . and mother. And I'd cut my right arm off if we could have that bairn back.'

His voice broke and she made her own voice rough, in case she too gave way to tears. 'I know that, Billy, I never doubted it. Now for God's sake eat your tea.'

She would suggest an early night and she would take him in her arms and make up to him for all he had to put up with. It was easier to love in the dark. And easier to cry.


Edward was combing his hair when he heard the phone. 'Helen? I'm glad it's you. I'll be out later on and I didn't want to miss you. Tell Lilian she should get a phone installed.'

Helen's euphoria was evident, even at a distance of 265 miles. 'Steady on. It does sound hopeful, but try to keep it in perspective.'

'But don't you see, Edward, I was right! I knew he'd be there in the church . . . but they were away, so that's why I missed them. As soon as Diana said the priest arranged it, I knew. I don't know how I sat still . . .'

Edward looked at the clock. He was meeting Celia, the nurse, at eight but this was important. 'I don't want to pour cold water on it, Helen, but I've got to point out that this priest probably made a habit of that sort of thing. You wouldn't be the only kid who'd turned to him for help, and they wouldn't be the only childless family . . .'

He might as well have tried to stop a tidal bore.

'I know it's him, Edward, don't ask me why, but I know. The right age, even the right month for his birthday! It all adds up. I'm going round there tomorrow. She's never seen me but I'll be careful, I'll think of something plausible . . . but I've got to see him. And then, once I know he's there – don't you see? – I'll be free. Diana – that's the doctor's wife, you met her at the funeral, remember? – she says her brother-in-law worships the children. There's a

237

girl as well, the same age, but don't suggest they're twins because they're not. She was adopted when she was two, and Diana says she's a bit of a rebel. Anyway, it's a wonderful home. If I'd chosen it myself I couldn't have done better. And you don't know how I'm longing for London and the shop . . . and even you, you old misery. You said you were going out – I hope I'm not keeping you if it's a woman?'

'It's a woman and you are keeping me. She's very nice, she's a sexy nurse, very pulchritudinous and I shall probably wind up proposing . . . if I ever get there, that is.'

'Don't do anything irrevocable till I get back and give her the once-over. How did you meet her? I hope you didn't pick her up in one of those dives you frequent?'

She approved when he said Celia was Maria's nurse. 'How is Maria? You took her to look at the home today, didn't you?'

They talked of Mrs Stepinska until the pips sounded for the umpteenth time. 'I've no more change, Edward. Have a good time with your nurse and don't forget . . .'

Edward was not to know what he was supposed to remember. He put down the phone and went to finish dressing, elated that he would not have to manage on his own for much longer. Helen was coming home.

# 19

The sun was shining but it was icily cold in the park and Helen shivered inside her buttoned coat. Across the deserted bowling-green, Anne Whittington walked between her children, talking intently to the little boy, halting occasionally to hurry up the little girl, who had to keep pausing to pull up her knee-socks.

Helen had found their address in the telephone directory and had waited for two hours. When they emerged she had followed them, moving from cover to cover in case of discovery. She needn't have feared, for they never looked back. They moved briskly on what was obviously a familiar course, across the main road, past the shops and into the park. Now they were circling the bowling-green and if she stayed where she was, or moved in an anti-clockwise direction, she would meet them face to face.

In the distance she could hear the traffic. Somewhere a child laughed out loud and a bicycle bell rang, but Helen felt strangely isolated in both place and time. It was as though she were suspended in space and there they were, two hundred yards away, in a similar state of inanimation. They could stay here like this forever, slowly circling the green. She need never look into his face and find the truth, never feel his mother's hostile eyes upon her, never have to walk past him, wondering what to do.

And then she was moving forward and they were moving too, and the distance between them was dwindling. It was him. She knew it even before his eyes lifted shyly to hers and then flicked way. He was talking to his mother about an airline crash, and Helen vaguely remembered a headline in that morning's paper; a Spanish airliner had crashed near London with thirty or forty feared dead.

He was thin but tall for his age, several inches above his sister. There was a strange composure about him, a serenity almost, that was entirely absent in the little girl, who skipped and chattered, pausing now and again as something caught her eye. Helen halted once she was past them, and turned to stare, drinking in details. His hair curled, in spite of being cut short; he had beautiful ears set close to his head; and his eyes were dark blue and ringed with dark lashes.

She closed her eyes and tried to bring back his face. God, please God, one more look! She moved to a bench and sat down, watching the tall woman in the tweed coat shepherd her children out of the gate.

He was with his mother and that was as it should be. He was safe, he was well, he was obviously bright and in the right place to achieve his true potential. She had nothing to worry about.

How had she known this was the child? For a moment she considered the possibility that she was, in fact, fooling herself. She had run out of leads, and he was her last chance. Was she telling herself it was so, because she needed a bearable conclusion? Could you look on a strange child and in one instant know that he was flesh of your flesh?

When she got to her feet, she had resolved her doubts. There was circumstantial evidence, the priest, the age, the birthdate . . . that was it, the birthdate! If that child had been born on 24 December, he was her son. She turned towards the gate and went in search of proof.

They were there in the phone book, Cotton, Whittington and Grey, Solicitors and Commissioners for Oaths. She dialled with her right forefinger, crossing left fore- and third fingers as she did so. If they put her through to Howard Whittington himself, she would have to ring off; she wasn't that good a liar.

'Can I speak to Mr Whittington? Oh, I see . . . well, perhaps his secretary. Thank you.'

There was a pause and then a calm voice. 'This is Mrs Fraser, Mr Whittington's secretary. Can I help you?'

Helen began to babble, about ringing Mr Whittington's home in vain and needing to know now. 'I must fix my son's birthday party and he says . . . well, Michael is his friend and Jonathan, that's my son, he says Michael's birthday is the same day as his . . . Christmas Eve . . . but he's only four so he could be wrong . . .'

'If you'll just hold on I'll check. I know it's near Christmas . . . it may be in Mr Whittington's diary.' Helen put her hand against the glass side of the phone box and pushed. Would it, would it, would it be . . . the final piece?

'Yes, it's there in the diary. It is the 24th, I'm afraid . . . but perhaps you should try to contact Mrs Whittington. I don't recall Michael ever having a formal birthday party.'

Helen sought for words, but relief had robbed her of speech.

'I think it's kept more as a family occasion,' the secretary was saying. 'Mrs Whittington . . .' There was a pause. 'Mrs Whittington likes to emphasize the spiritual side of these occasions . . . which, of course, is right. And of course, Christmas is a religious festival.'

So Michael's mother was religious, Helen thought, as she replaced the receiver. Well, that was no crime. In fact it was a bonus in an increasingly faithless world. The main thing was that now she knew: it had all worked out as she had intended. Her son was safe and she was free.

Edward let out his breath in a low whistle. 'When did you accumulate this lot?' The netsuke were jumbled together in a large hat box, each inside a rolled lisle stocking. 'That's a *karashi-shi,*' he said, holding a round piece of ivory between thumb and forefinger. 'Unsigned, probably late eighteenth-century. And this brute is a wolf, ivory of course, eighteenth-century or very early nineteenth, and probably a Tomotada. Yes, there's a signature; that makes it worth a packet. And God, here's a *babu,* nineteenth-century, beautifully patinated . . . have you any idea what this lot is worth? There must be a couple of dozen. Netsuke are still underpriced but even so . . . we're talking thousands, I should think.'

They were beginning the long labour of dismantling the Stepinska flat, choosing what would go with her to The Haven and what would be sold or given away. Mrs Stepinska pulled out another hat box and lifted the lid. 'My Stephan collected the ivory. We were mad to own things again, you know, so it was all acquire, acquire, build, build . . . to say, "I am no longer a refugee with all I own in my pockets." We were foolish but that's how it was. For him the ivory, for me . . .'

He was lifting them from the box and unwrapping the tissue paper, grey now with age and devoid of crackle.

'Vesta cases . . . beauties! Look at this one!' It was a tiny gold portmanteau with a hinged lid, two inches long but perfect in every detail. 'The vestas . . . the matches went here. This little end compartment would be for pills. It's English, I think, mid-nineteenth century . . . and this one is Russian. Champlire enamel, marked Moscow 1877. How many have you?'

There were thirteen of the small boxes to hold wax matches, and a tiny toothpick box in cloisonné with silver

mounts. 'Not as intrinsically valuable as the netsuke . . .
not in the long term . . . but you, my dear Maria Stepinska,
are sitting on a small gold mine. I should have known you
were a magpie.'

'Do you remember when you were a small boy and you
used to come for honey cake? You couldn't work out why
it was Stepinski for Stephan and Stepinska for me. You
were so polite a little boy, you wanted to get it right.
Stepinski/Stepinska. Round and round we went. Your
mama, she was kind. She made a gift of you to my Stephan
for talking.'

He felt he dared ask a question. 'You never had
children?'

She shook her head. 'No, no children. We were both
agreed no children. I was thirty-three when we married.
No chicken, boychick. Poland was a bad place then, for
Jews. And then Europe was a bad place for everybody.
Even here, we thought, they will come eventually. Even to
England. No one can stop them. And then, when we were
a little bit safe again, we tried but I was old then. Old for
babies. And when it didn't happen, I think we thought
that is good. No risks. And we had each other and we had
all this, this . . . home . . . can you imagine? We had a
home again, a place.

'Anyway, enough of old boxes and lifting lids. We put
the lids back on the boxes for now and the lid on the
memories for ever, and we have a drink and you tell me
about Celia. I still like to hear about love you know, even if
I'm too old to enjoy it for myself. And you are bad boy
with girls. Sexy eyes, sexy mouth. Always greedy for love.
What a bad boy but a *mensch*, just the same!'

He kissed her brow then, where the hair was thin and
caught up with a tortoiseshell comb, and spun his evening
with Celia into the most romantic concoction that could be
imagined.

'Chris?' Diana heard the obstetrician on the other end of
the line and relaxed. 'I'm really sorry to ring you at the
hospital . . . I haven't pulled you away from anything vital,

I hope? . . . but David is here in the evenings and I don't want him to know just yet.'

She had grown to like Christopher Milhill tremendously since that first terrible night when she had lost the baby. With each subsequent loss they had grown closer, and he had become keener to present her with a live baby one day. 'I'm only a couple of weeks overdue but the suspense is killing me. How soon can I have a test, and do I have to come to you or just bring a specimen?'

She answered his questions as truthfully as she could, calmed by his matter-of-fact tones. 'Yes, I know it's early days and I'm not building up my hopes – but remember how we talked last time, about my coming in right at the beginning and staying under observation? Well, I thought the sooner we knew, the better.'

When she rang off she felt good. They would check and David would know nothing until there was something positive to tell him. She knew how much he still wanted children, although he never talked of it now, studiously avoiding any subject that might cause her pain. 'I love him so much,' she thought. 'I have to do this for him, get it right.'

She wandered from room to room, looking for something to do, but there was nothing. In the end she settled in the window seat and looked out on the winter garden. Birds sat hopefully in winter trees; in a moment she would go in search of cheese and crumbs, and feed them. In the mean time she wanted to hug her secret to herself and enjoy it.

She had hated her inability to produce a living child. In a way it seemed worse to be fertile but unproductive, than to be barren like Anne. Perhaps if she had been able to say, 'I can never have a child of my own,' she could have come to terms with adoption? But the idea of mothering someone else's child still repelled her, even though she liked other people's children, and she had loved Diana Two. If a child were dropped on her now she would cope, but it wouldn't be the same. There would be a barrier. She would be kind and fair, and she would try to be loving, but it would have to be worked at and love that was not spontaneous was not really love at all.

She thought uneasily of Michael and Susan. They were cared for, but were they loved? Howard showed them affection but in a very dignified solicitor-ish kind of way. And Anne . . . Diana comforted herself with the thought that Anne was as loving to her adopted children as she would have been to children of her own, as she was to Howard, or her parents, or anyone else but God and the saints. Which was not very loving at all.

It felt a little blasphemous to begrudge God and his saints their due reverence. Diana put philosophical thoughts aside and went in to get the birdfood.

Helen and Lilian had moved from one department to another, looking rather than buying. 'I could do with a sit down,' Lilian said. 'Shall we have a cup of tea?' They sat in a window table in Dembry's Austrian tea-rooms, eating wickedly creamy cakes and drinking tea from individual pots. At a nearby table a baby kicked its legs in a high chair, and Helen saw Lilian's eyes go to it more than once.

'I'm going back to London soon, Lil. Will you be all right?'

Lilian turned her back on the high chair and gave her sister her full attention. ''Course I will. Nobody needs to bother about me.' Even to her own ears it must have sounded false. She smiled ruefully and put out a hand to touch Helen's arm. 'Take no notice of me, I can't help going on. I'll be all right eventually. I'm all right now, in a way. It's just that sometimes it catches you . . .' Her eyes filled with tears and she stuck her tongue into her cheek as she struggled to keep her composure.

'You know, you see a bairn and you remember . . . the way they felt in your arms, the little arms and legs, the way they always trusted you . . . it's hard, our Hel, but let's get one thing straight. You mustn't let any of this put you off having bairns. I know what they say – if you have none to make you laugh, you'll have none to make you cry. But I still say there's nothing beats a bairn of your own, nothing on God's earth.'

For a moment, a single moment, Helen was tempted. It

would be nice to confide in Lilian now, to lean forward and say: 'I know what you mean, Lilian. I've had a bairn, I know how it feels.' But it wouldn't do. In the long run it wouldn't help anyone, not her, not Lilian. If she knew where Michael was, so close to her and the family, she would never be able to leave it be. It would end in disaster for everyone.

Instead she said: 'I will have kids one day, if I meet the right man. You need a man, you know – you can't do it on your own!'

A trace of the old Lilian flickered out of her sister's drawn face. 'Get away! And here was me thinking you only needed a gooseberry bush. Don't teach your granny to suck eggs, our young'un. And pass that teapot. If I've paid for it, I'm drinking it. Down to the last drop.'


Howard signed the last letter and handed it to Mrs Fraser. 'Anything else?'

She shook her head. 'I don't think so, sir. There was a call from Graham Dix and Son about the McMurray conveyancing, but I've seen to that . . . and someone rang up about Michael's birthday.'

'Michael? My Michael?'

She was opening the door to leave. 'Yes. Some question of clashing birthday parties. It was in your diary, so I was able to sort it out. Apart from that, it's been a quiet day.'

He put his finger to his lips. 'Ssh! Don't let anyone hear you say that, or all sorts of trouble will ensue.'

Mrs Fraser smiled and began to close the door behind her. 'Oh, and see if Judith's finished that affidavit, will you? I'll take it with me tonight and check it at home.'

He was packing his briefcase when there was a knock and Judith entered, the typed pages in her hands. 'It's done, Mr Whittington.' She laid it on the desk and then walked round to stand beside him while he gave the typescript a cursory glance.

'It looks all right. I'll check it tonight. The client's due back tomorrow, isn't he?' He could feel the warmth of her

245

body against his arm although they were not quite touching. His hands began to shake slightly and he made a great show of knocking the sheets of paper into line against the desk. If he turned to her she would be ready: he knew that, had known it for a long time. She wanted him. It was there now, the faintest touch against his side, her breath panting slightly at his right ear.

'Right, that's fine, thank you Judith.'

Did she hesitate for a moment before she moved to the door. Or did he imagine it?

He snapped the locks on his briefcase and turned to get down his coat. His hand was still shaking, and he went back to the desk to make a note on his memo pad. He would speak to Mrs Fraser on Monday: Judith would have to go.


Helen got off the bus at the corner and walked down the darkened street. It had been a crazy impulse, but one she couldn't resist. In the beginning she had intended to walk right into the garden under the cover of darkness, up to the window to peep between the curtains and see them together as a family. One last look! But on the bus her courage had deserted her . . . or reason had reasserted itself. Anyway, she was going to walk along the street and look at the house. If there was anything to see, she would stand and gaze. If not, she would go on her way.

The houses were large and prestigious, set back from the road and surrounded by gardens. She paused at the Whittingtons' gate. The house was called Holly Lodge. Michael Whittington of Holly Lodge. In the darkness Helen smiled. It had all worked out so well.

A car came round the corner, its headlights arcing through the darkness towards the gate where she stood. She moved on as the car paused on the centre line and signalled left. As it turned into the gates of Holly Lodge she saw Howard Whittington's figure behind the wheel, and heard the crunch of tyres on gravel. She watched, clinging to the iron railings, as the car drew up outside the double garage and the driver got out. A moment later the garage door swung up and the car disappeared inside.

She watched as the garage door was closed and the light went out. A moment later a light sprang up in a room at the side of the house and she saw Howard Whittington struggling out of his coat. When his arms were free he bent to pick up a child. Helen craned her neck to see. It was the girl. And then he leaned down and she saw the dark head of his son, and saw the father nod gravely as he listened to some childish confidence.

It looked right. It looked all Helen could have hoped for. She closed her eyes for a moment, giving thanks for all of it – the seeking, and the finding, and the contentment she felt now at the knowledge of her son. 'Their son,' she said aloud. 'Their son!'

The next moment Howard had moved to the window to draw the curtains, blotting out the light and leaving her in darkness.


Edward smiled as he entered the darkened Mews. It had been good to make love to a woman again, a woman as nice as Celia. They had eaten in a small Italian restaurant near her flat and half-way through each of them had known what the other wanted, so that they ate faster and faster, anxious to get up and leave.

She had turned in her door and reached for him but there had been nothing brazen about her, just a simple acceptance of pleasure. They had loved and laughed, and then huddled together for warmth until he remembered she had an early start and he ought to let her sleep. He left her lying in a cocoon of blankets, her face slack with contentment. 'I'll ring you,' he said and she smiled.

'If you don't, I'll set my big brother on you!'

He had laughed then. 'How big?'

She pursed her lips. 'Huge.'

Edward had put two fingers to his lips and thrown her a kiss, and then left.

Now, as he walked down the quiet Mews, the taxi moving off behind him, he couldn't help grinning, which was ridiculous. The relief of sexual tension, that's all it was. Or else too much Chianti. He fitted the key in the shop doorway and let himself in, smiling again at the lovely familiar odours. He had just shot home the bolts when the phone began to ring. This late, it could only be Helen.

'I'm coming home, Edward! It's worked out wonderfully, and I couldn't sleep until I told someone.'

Edward listened while Helen told him of the day's events, details spilling out of her as she repeated things over and over. 'I feel so good about it all. I don't want to interfere, I just needed to know. I'm going to come back here, Edward, once a year, at Christmas or Easter . . . some time I can find them in church. No one will notice me there, and I can see how he develops, what he makes of himself.'

At last she paused. 'Oh, God, I forgot to ask you. How was your date?'

He played dumb. 'Date? What date?'

'The sexy nurse . . . last night.'

She sounded genuinely interested and embarrassment stirred. It wouldn't do to tell her everything. Celia was quite . . . something! 'It went well. I saw her again tonight . . . and I'll probably see her tomorrow. So there.'

When she had rung off Edward went to fill the kettle. Helen was coming home: that was the word she had used. He smiled and began to whistle gently as he poured out the whisky for a nightcap.

# BOOK THREE

*1977*

# 20

## *Easter 1977*

When Helen woke there was enough light in the room to make out the shape of Patrick's head on the pillow beside her. She raised herself on her elbow to see the clock: four forty-five. In fifteen minutes the alarm would go off, if she didn't stop it. She leaned across to depress the switch and then eased herself out of bed as gently as she could. No point in waking Pat. He would try to persuade her to come back to bed and there wasn't time.

In the bathroom she closed the door and switched on the light, crossing to the mirror to peer at her face with its lines of sleep and traces of yesterday's make-up. It had been a mistake to let Patrick stay: she should have kept him at arm's length last night and gone to bed early, like a sensible woman of thirty-three. But that would have been out of character. Sensible women of thirty-three did not have out-of-work-actor boyfriends of twenty-three. They had husbands and children and lived in converted rectories in the Home Counties.

She felt better after a shower – wide awake and even eager. She always felt like that on this day, her day of pilgrimage. She put out the light and tiptoed cautiously back into the bedroom, not drawing breath until she was safely armoured in the clothes she had selected yesterday. She stood at the dressing-table to wipe the red polish from her fingernails and then went back to the bathroom to wash the pink traces from her fingers.

She had put on her coat and was looking for pen and paper to leave a note, when the figure in the bed came to life. 'Helen, where are you?'

'I'm here, Patrick. I'm off now. Remember I told you yesterday – about going up north?' She sat on the edge of the bed while he groaned his disapproval of her leaving him. 'It's only for a few hours. I'll be back tonight. Lock up here when you leave, and ring me this evening.'

She bent to kiss his damp forehead, smelling his lingering odours of sleep and love, smiling slightly at the memory of last night. 'Oh God, Helen. Helen . . .' And then the rolling away, the pause, the turning back . . . 'I do love you, Helen.'

He was lifting himself in the bed now. 'Look in the cupboard . . . there's a plastic bag. Put the light on.' He cut short her protests about time, and about doing it tonight instead. 'Look now, or else you'll spoil the fun!'

The Easter egg was huge in its cellophane-fronted box. 'Pat loves Helen' it announced in pink fondant swirls.

'You are an idiot,' Helen said, and kissed him again. 'I haven't had an Easter egg for years, and never one as beautiful as this. See you tonight.' And then she was away before he could notice the dark green coat, the absence of make-up, the subdued accessories. She was not in the mood for explanations.


Howard made tea in the kitchen and carried it upstairs on a tray. Anne was already at the prie-dieu, her beads threading through her fingers, her black lashes fanned on pale cheeks. She was still beautiful. They had been married for eighteen years and yet she had changed very little. A slight sallowness of complexion, a wing of white at the temple that was not unattractive – that was all.

The pink silk nightdress she wore, ornamented with lace and covered by a matching négligé, reminded him of that first night in the hotel, when his desire had ebbed with the realization that she was stone. The lingerie had been white then, just as beautiful, designed – he had thought – to attract, to give pleasure to the onlooker. He would have liked to have joy from looking at her, from slipping the silk from her shoulders, kissing the bone, the blade, the hollow of the spine, the cleft between the buttocks . . . God! It was starting again, the evil in his mind.

His cup clattered into its saucer and he froze for a second, but Anne prayed on, serene.

When he came back from dressing she was sitting by the window, drinking her tea. 'Wake the children, will you, Howard? We don't want to be late for Mass. And remind them we're lunching with Diana so we won't be back here until later.'

He crossed the landing, noticing that Michael's door was already open. He must be in the bathroom. He knocked on Susan's door and then, getting no reply, knocked again and peeped inside. There was an inert lump beneath the bedclothes and he smiled, shaking his head ruefully at the sight.

'Susan . . . time to get up for church!'

There was a pause and then a muffled voice. 'I've died. If you want me in church you'll need a hearse. And I want a Requiem Mass with all the trimmings.'

Howard laughed out loud and started to back away. 'Come on . . . let's have a quick resurrection, please.'

When he turned Anne was crossing the landing and he felt a shiver of apprehension in case she had heard his flippant remark. 'They're both up,' he said hastily, closing Susan's door behind him and despising himself for the lie.


Helen was glad when the newspaper had been perused and put to one side. Horror in Idi Amin's Uganda, industrial unrest everywhere at home, the young Foreign Secretary, David Owen, looking debonair but scared of his new office – the only hint of brightness was talk of the Queen's coming Jubilee.

She looked out at the landscape, fields green with spring wheat, hedges taking on the colours of spring. Was this really her tenth pilgrimage? She closed her eyes, counting the years. Easter '68, '69, '70 . . . yes. Michael was fifteen years old now. She had watched him grow, and almost felt she knew him. Once she had nearly exchanged a few words with him as they were jostled by parishioners on the church pathway. But the moment had passed and afterwards she had been glad.

They were approaching Darlasden now. She put her ticket in the outer pocket of her bag, ready to show at the gate, and rose to her feet. She had so much to be thankful for: her own flat, a partnership in the business. None of it would have been possible without Edward. He was coming to lunch tomorrow, and she must make a special effort. The train shuddered to a halt and Helen stepped on to the platform.

The sun was shining and she looked at her watch as she came through the barrier. There was time to walk. She crossed into the High Street and walked past Dembry's. The town hall clock was slow, as usual, and sweet wrappers were eddying in the bowl of the fountain. How many more years would she make this journey? Soon Michael would go away, to university perhaps. Fleetingly she thought of Alistair, who had fathered him . . . he had been clever enough academically, but in a way Helen hoped that he had bequeathed little or nothing to his son.

The darkness of the church yawned suddenly before her, and she paused to bend her knee to the altar, more out of a desire to be inconspicuous than reverence. And then, kneeling, she whispered the prayer she always made: 'Please let him come, God. Let him look happy.'


'Forgive me, God. Forgive me and help me.' The fear was on Howard now, the battle commencing as it always did in this holy place. Why did it affect him here, where he so desired to be good? He glanced along at his wife and children, their eyes fixed on the priest. Susan's lip was trembling still from the encounter with Anne before church. Howard winced, remembering the tension in the hall as Susan had stood her ground, the pink rouge standing out on her cheeks, the black pencil stark around her eyes.

'Very well,' Anne had said at last, coldly. 'If you will not remove that make-up, none of us will go to Mass.'

Michael's eyes had flared dismay, and Howard saw the

sister look to the brother and then acknowledge defeat. She would never hurt Michael, and Anne knew that. Susan had clumped upstairs, rebellion still in every line, to wash her face while they had waited for her in the spring sunshine. Howard had never once seen Anne raise her hand or her voice, and yet she held complete sway over the children. Over them all!

'*Bitch*!' He felt as though he had shouted it aloud and looked guiltily from side to side. If he had, no one had noticed. 'God forgive me for my blasphemy, forgive me for what I am about to do in your holy place . . . give me absolution.' He let them come, then, the girls with their breasts and thighs, trooping through his mind as they had trooped through his office over the years. Judith, Angela, Deirdre of the yard-long legs, and Yvonne, big-breasted Yvonne who would smile at him for sixpence and more, much more, for half a crown. He could have taken any one of them, had them . . . they had wanted it, wanted him . . . wanted, needed, yearned for it. And Mrs Fraser's eyes on him: 'Yes, of course, Mr Whittington. If you think the girl is not up to standard, she must go.' She knew, she must know, now. Her watchful eyes were on Yvonne all the time. But she couldn't know all of it, the utter wickedness of it all. That was for him and Yvonne alone.

Helen refused to think about it until she was in the train and moving out of the station. Only then did she allow herself to recall the scene in the churchyard, the bleak words, the girl's face. Had she imagined it, that black despair? Michael had looked . . . pensive – but then, he had always taken church seriously, down all the years. 'Some things just have to be borne': what kind of remark was that for a fifteen-year-old to make?

Thoughts were milling around in her mind. That day she had walked into town, the day the Americans had invaded Cuba. The clown outside brand-new Dembry's, and Lilian, heavy with the child that would be Diana. The fear, the terrible fear that became certainty and Alistair's running away. Suddenly she was back in Stella Maris, feeling the pains, electric in her pelvis, the tearing, the bearing down. And Sister Mary Boniface seeming to glory in the pain. She had cried for Sister Dymphna then. Dymphna, who had carried her baby away.

It was strange to remember, so clearly, things she had thought forgotten. She had put it from her mind, or thought she had put it from her when, in reality, she had simply shelved it until now. She had not wanted the baby, not ever . . . even in that moment on the landing when Dymphna would have put him into her arms if she had asked. Why had she rejected him? And if she could summon up a valid reason for so doing then, why the pangs of guilt and regret that were racking her now?

If she had come and found that all was well she would have returned to London, rejoicing – shelving Michael once more as soon as the train neared King's Cross. But all was not well. Something was wrong and it mattered desperately, far more than she would have thought possible.

As the train passed from Cleveland into Yorkshire she tried to analyse her alarm. What had she seen? A family group, calm, reverent . . . as they had been all those other Easters. But then the girl's eyes, desperate and sad. Had they been desperate? Or was it some perfectly harmless occurrence, period pains or a broken love affair, a tiff with a brother or the loss of a dearly loved pet, that Helen was magnifying out of all proportion? And was she doing it because she wanted an excuse to become involved with them? *'Some things just have to be borne'*. Some things? *What* things?

Helen got up to go to the restaurant car eventually, her mind still in turmoil. Edward would know what to do, he would help her. But if it turned out that Michael needed her, she would have to go to him. Did that mean she loved him with a proper maternal love? She speculated while the dining-car stewards fussed with silverware and glass, and gave up eventually because she could come to no satisfactory conclusion.

\* \* \*

'Come in . . . lovely to see you. I must dash back to the joint. Take their coats, darling.'

Diana escaped to the kitchen to baste the lamb and mix mint with sugar and vinegar. David came through to her after a while, with a glass of wine in his hand. 'For the cook. I've settled them all with drinks. The kids are drooling over the pooch as usual.'

'I don't know how Anne can bear it,' Diana said as she tested the potatoes. 'She knows the kids want another dog, she sees how much they love Lupi . . . and it doesn't move her an inch.'

David shrugged. 'You can't simply blame Anne. You know where I rate her as a humanitarian – a little short of zero – but Howard is responsible, too. He should put his foot down, and get them one.'

'Is that what you'd do?' Diana teased.

He leaned across to steal a sprout. 'I should put you across my knee, my girl, and don't you forget it.'

'Well, there's precious little chance of Howard laying hands on Anne. Perhaps we should give them a puppy, and force her into it? She could hardly say no. You are their uncle, after all.'

'Have you forgotten that Howard's dog got the chop in the end? I wouldn't like to see it happen to a puppy. Anyway, I'll get back to them, if there's nothing I can do here! Sue has a face a yard long, so I'll try and cheer her up.'

When he had left, his words rang on in Diana's head. He loved Michael and Susan, and he still hankered for children of his own, even though it was nearly ten years since she had lost the last, the final baby. She had become resigned to her barren state in these last few years, but she knew David still yearned. Was she a selfish bitch to say no to adoption? Even Anne had accepted it. *Even* Anne – perhaps she had adopted because she wanted a son to give to God, like all good Catholic women? Perhaps Susan had been brought in simply to complete the equation? If so, it showed.

On paper Anne was the perfect mother. But something was amiss – Diana knew it without being able to advance a single piece of evidence. She racked her brains for one remembered clue but there was nothing . . . except the way the children stuck together! That was unnatural. Most children fought . . . David had a pamphlet on sibling rivalry . . . but Michael and Susan were always together, always in agreement, as though they had united against a common threat. And when Susan threatened rebellion, Michael's eyes grew anxious, as though he could hardly bear it.

Suddenly she smelt a whiff of something unpleasant: the parsnips had boiled dry and were stuck to the pan. So much for day-dreaming in the middle of a lunch party. She began to pick out the good bits with a fork and then ran cold water into a pan that hissed and steamed as though possessed.


The train was less than five minutes late into King's Cross and Helen raced along the platform to the telephone. 'Edward? Yes, I'm back. Are you doing anything special? OK, I'll be with you in ten minutes.' She had to queue for a cab, but the streets were quiet and she settled back in her seat as they sped towards Kensington.

Thank God for Edward. She couldn't go to her own flat now. In all probability Patrick would still be there; he would know something was wrong, there would be questions, and she couldn't face those at the moment. He was a good lover, he was fun, but that was all. He would never give her the feeling of security that she craved, and not just because he was a fairly penniless and usually-out-of-work actor. She was earning more than enough for herself now, and the money she had made last year from the dolls had stunned her. But she wanted something else from a man that Patrick could never give her. She sought for a word and could only think of 'gravitas' which wasn't quite right, but would have to do.

She paid off the cab and was looking for her key when she saw through the glass door panels that Edward was descending the stairs. 'Come in . . .' and then, when he saw her face, 'I prescribe two stiff drinks. Come on, up you

258

go. I don't know what's upset you, but it can't be anything we can't cope with between us.'

'Oh Edward,' Helen said, when she was safe in the flat with a glass of Courvoisier in one hand and her other held out to the fire. 'It's so good to get here and talk to someone who knows. I'm not sure, but I have this terrible feeling that it's all going wrong.'

'Tell you what, how about you and me going up to London for a day?' Diana stood with her hands in the washing-up bowl, looking at her niece as she dried the plates from the lunch table. Susan shrugged, her face still sullen. Diana took a breath and tried again. 'We could see Vic, my brother. You remember him? We could do some shopping, and then Vic could take us out for a slap-up meal. What do you say?'

'She won't let me go,' Susan said flatly.

Diana tried not to sound exasperated. 'Of course she will. She knows you'll be safe with me, darling.'

Susan was smiling now, her heavy dark eyebrows rising in triumph. 'It's not my *safety* she's worried about, Auntie Di. Nothing simple like that! She won't let me go because I might enjoy it . . . and enjoyment, as we all know, is not character-building.'

'My God, she's bitter,' Diana thought, lost now for words. Susan was big for her age, hefty in fact, with none of her brother's grace or delicacy of feature, and the expensive paisley wool dress with its self-belt and Peter Pan collar did nothing for her. 'She needs some acne treatment and a good hairdo, an eyebrow shape and some teenage clothes,' Diana thought. 'She'll never be pretty but she could be striking one day.'

'I'll tell you what,' she said aloud. 'We'll wait until she's in a good mood . . .' Susan's snort was a masterpiece, and Diana grinned. 'OK, well, perhaps we won't wait that long. But I'll ask her next week and we'll see what she says. We'll go to all the good boutiques . . . I owe you a birthday present soon.'

Susan's face brightened. 'I've been dying for some court shoes . . . or one of those big, sloppy sweaters.'

By the time they were ready to leave the kitchen Susan was much happier.

'Anything left to do?' It was Howard, peering round the kitchen door.

'Daddy,' Susan said admiringly, 'your sense of timing is immaculate. You've come as we've just put the last tea-spoon away.'

Her father smiled. 'I learned at law school that there is always an optimum moment!'

When Susan had gone in search of the dog, Howard turned to Diana. 'You seem to have cheered her up. Thank you.'

Diana, lifting plates into the cupboard, tried to sound casual. 'What was wrong?'

There was silence and eventually she turned around. Howard was looking abashed. 'Oh, the usual thing. I think Anne has difficulty in accepting that the children are growing up . . . well, that Susan is growing up. Michael is another matter. I sometimes think . . .'

He fell silent and Diana reached out to touch his arm. 'You love those children, don't you, Howard?'

He nodded. 'More than I can easily say. They've meant everything to me. I sometimes think what my life would have been like without them . . . and it frightens me.'

Diana couldn't resist one more question, one she had been longing to ask him. 'Does it make a difference that they're not your children, Howard? Well, you know what I mean – they are yours, they adore you. But . . .'

'I didn't play a part in their conception?' He shook his head. 'At the beginning, for a few days, perhaps it made a difference. But it really is supremely unimportant, that single moment of conception. What matters is mutual need, one for the other. And we have that.'

When he had gone Diana stayed on in the silent kitchen, listening to the murmurs from the living-room and ponder-ing Howard's words.

* * *

There was subdued lighting in the restaurant and some-where, far off, faint music. 'Am I being silly?' Helen asked, for the third or fourth time. Hitherto Edward had replied with further questions. Now he appeared to have made up his mind, but he waited until the waiter had refilled their glasses and moved out of direct earshot.

'I think you're probably alarming yourself needlessly. This is a teenage girl we're talking about. They tend to dramatize a bit, and, let's face it, church is an emotional place. Ten to one she was perfectly OK once she got outside. And what Michael said *could* mean something – or nothing. However, the damage is done now. You're not going to rest until you know more. So I think you should ring Lilian.'

She looked at him in surprise. 'Why Lilian?'

Edward finished his syllabub and put down the spoon. 'Because, my dear girl, your sister is still intoxicated with her newly installed phone and inclined to be loquacious if anyone rings her on it. She's very thick with the doctor's wife, who is the aunt of your Michael. All you have to do is steer the conversation around to the Whittingtons in general, your Whittingtons in particular, and Lilian will give you chapter and verse.'

'And after that?' Helen asked.

Edward shrugged. 'It depends on what emerges. If Lilian tells you all is well, I think you should accept it. If not, you'll have to go up there and see what you can do.'

There was a pause while Edward ordered coffee and brandy, and then returned to the topic that increasingly intrigued him. 'Michael's real father. You've never talked about him, and I've never asked . . . never been interested before. Now, though, it occurs to me, that if he is still there, on the spot, he might be able to put you out of your misery?'

Helen shook her head. 'He didn't belong to Darlaston. He was a Scotsman. Remember I worked at the Infirmary? He was a houseman, a junior doctor. I suppose I fell for the white coat and the stethoscope . . . the young ones always carried the statutory stethoscope in case anyone mistook them for ancillary staff.'

'Did you love him?' Edward tried to sound off-hand, but to his own ears he failed.

'It's difficult to say. I thought I did for a while . . . but I didn't *know* him. I thought he was strong; he was weak. I thought he was kind; he was unfeeling. I thought he was handsome; now, when I remember him, he comes across as an awful drip. What does annoy me is that he's got off scot-free. All these years.'

'Did he offer to marry you?'

Helen laughed, but Edward knew her well enough to hear how brittle the laughter was. 'No. He said his daddy wouldn't like it. He wanted me to have an abortion; he even had a friend poised to do the dirty deed. So I suppose I'm being unfair. I decided what was going to happen, and I'm the one who must pay the bill.'

Edward lifted his glass. 'Well, here's to a speedy solution . . . and remember, you've always got me if things get sticky.'

There were shadows beneath her eyes and her mouth, usually upturned in laughter, was sad. He frowned and reached to pat her hand. 'Come on . . . it's not like you to be down. We'll sort it out in the end.'


David moved ahead to open the field gate and Diana followed, the dog weaving around her legs. 'It doesn't feel like spring,' David said as they breasted the rise of the hill. The sky above was grey, and there was a clean edge to the landscape that betokened a storm. Diana reached for his hand and then slipped their linked hands into the pocket of his anorak. 'David?'

'Uh hum?'

His hand was large and warm in her hand, and she squeezed it until she felt an answering pressure. 'I'm thirty-seven years old.'

He whistled softly, his breath shooting out into the air like a wraith. 'Thirty-seven! Perhaps we should turn back – you might not last the half-mile.'

Inside his pocket she struck against his hip. 'Shut up, I'm serious. I'm thirty-seven and I've been thinking. I talked to Howard today, in the kitchen. He was upset about Sue . . . about Anne riding her too hard. Anyway, he was speaking about the kids, and what he said made me think.'

'OK, I've accepted that you've been thinking. You've said it three times. Now for God's sake, tell me what about?'

She took a breath and plunged. 'Well, you know I've always said I couldn't adopt? I always felt awful about that, because I knew you wanted to, but I was so against it that I had to say no. It wouldn't have been fair to go ahead when I felt like that. Now, though I've been thinking . . . sorry, I've said it again. But I have . . .'

Inside his pocket he was gripping her hand until her rings cut into her flesh. 'It's not just because of what Howard said, is it? Because, frankly, that won't be enough.'

'I know that and no, it's not that – although I do think it tipped the scale. I think the truth is that I've finally accepted I'll *never* have a child of my own. You accepted that long ago, the third or fourth time. I just went on hoping – even after the last time I still felt I had it in me to have a full-term baby. Now, I know I won't, and in a way that realization has been like a door opening, rather than one closing. I'm still not sure I can do it, David, but if you agree I'd like to make some enquiries, at least.'

He had stopped in the darkening field and was reaching for her. 'My darling, I've loved you since the first moment I saw you in that silly bistro. And whatever happens . . . whatever you decide . . . that won't change.'


'Billy, have you seen that clock? It's quarter to eleven, Billy, and our Karen's not in yet.'

Billy lowered his head to see over his glasses. 'It's only twenty-five to, pet.'

'Don't quibble, Billy. I said she should be in by half-past ten. She's far too fond of bending the rules.'

'Well, she is seventeen, Lilian.' There was a note of defiance in his voice and Lilian had to suppress a smile. He would do anything for his beloved daughter, even stand up to his wife! 'That's as may be, Billy Fenwick, but that's still too young to be a dirty little stop-out.'

As if on cue, the yard door banged shut. 'Is that you, our Karen? What time do you think this is?' Lilian could hear the pride in her voice, the pride she could never suppress when she looked at her daughter, as tall and straight and bonny as any lass that ever walked a Belgate street.

'I've been to Linda's, mam, listening to her Leo Sayer records. I've been where I said I was going, but my mother can't help being suspicious . . .'

'Get off me, now,' Lilian said as her daughter's arms came round her neck. 'You might be able to sweet-talk your dad, but you can't budge me.'

'Bets?' Karen said, nuzzling her mother's cheek.

Billy was grinning from the other side of the hearth and Lilian felt her face cracking. She was saved from defeat by the ringing of the telephone that stood on the occasional table.

'It'll be for me,' Karen said, untwining herself, but it was not. She spoke for a few moments and then handed it to her mother. 'It's for you. Auntie Helen.'

'Hallo, Lilian here.' Lilian was still self-conscious on the phone but it was good to hear Helen, so far away and yet so clear. They chatted for a while about life in general and Belgate in particular. 'Helen sends her love,' Lilian said to the fireside chair and then conveyed Billy's smile of appreciation down the line.

'The Whittingtons? They're fine. No, and I don't think she'll try again. Not at her age . . . Yes, her sister-in-law did adopt . . . Well, yes, I suppose it has worked. In a way. It depends what you mean . . . She's a funny woman, very stuck-up. And religious . . . you wouldn't believe some of the stories . . . Diana feels sorry for the kids. She watches what she says to me – I mean, she's a lady to her fingertips – but I can read between the lines, we're that close . . . Why is she sorry for them? Well, I think she thinks they have a hard time. And *he's* soft – not like the doctor. You'd never think they were brothers in a million years. A bit like you and me, really . . . Still, how are you? It's time you came up. Me mam was only saying that . . . you are? Well,

264

you know you're welcome. Now that mam and dad have the cottage they can't do with company but we've got room. And Billy's always pleased to see you . . . So when are you coming?'

The lights had burned late in the building opposite Edward's – tradesmen were working on a conversion, eager to complete it and move to the next well-paid job. Only three of the original owners were left in the Mews now, and of those the Chastons were going in the autumn. He watched the workmen emerge from the door below and troop towards their van, then he pulled shut the curtains and turned back to the gas fire. By now Helen would have rung Lilian, and the die might be cast. What would he do if she went north?

He would miss her expertise, but it was more than just that. He would miss her welcoming him back from buying trips, telling him about her latest boyfriend, or chattering excitedly about one of her dolls. She had become quite a name in the business now, especially for Jumeaux and Jules Steiner.

Edward poured himself a whisky and settled in his chair. The Kashan rug was becoming worn at his feet, worn by his sitting there over the years. For some reason the sight frightened him. Was he really in such a rut that he was wearing grooves in the carpets?

Perhaps it was fate, all this business with the child? Perhaps it was time to upsticks and go? He could get £150,000 now; more if he sold the shop as a going concern – £80,000 at least for the stock. On top of that he had enough invested to make a quarter of a million. It was funny how money crept up on you. He didn't feel rich, he didn't even feel secure, and by today's standards he wasn't wealthy. If he were to set up somewhere else, it would take all he had, and more.

If he sold up, where would he go? It couldn't be far from London because of Maria Stepinska. He wasn't sure that she knew him now when he visited her: The light had gone out in the old eyes and sometimes she called him by other names. But she was always pleased to see him, and while he kept guard no one could harm her.

Edward refilled his glass and turned on the television. A singer, in the spotlight, was giving his all. *'Don't give up on us, baby . . .'* Where did they get the words from for these pop songs. *'Don't give up on us, baby . . . we can still come through.'* That was what he needed, a woman in his life again. There had been several women since Sylvia, but none of them had stayed the course. Inside him the hunting instinct stirred, arousing longings that would not be quelled.

# 21

Helen looked around her bedroom in case anything had been left behind, then she lifted her case from the bed and carried it though to the living-room. All day she had been filled with doubts. Everything was going so well here: she loved this flat, the shop was heaven, she and Patrick had had good times together, and would have had more . . . Helen smiled ruefully, remembering his face when she had told him she was going north 'on family business'. He had taken it well, too well to be entirely complimentary. That was his generation – easy come, easy go. Edward was more disturbed by her going, anxious to keep their partnership alive. She picked up the Bru doll from her desk and gazed into its superior, slightly sinister face. No more dolls . . . for a while at least.

The buzzer sounded and she flicked the switch to the intercom at the front door. 'It's me, Patrick. I've got the cab . . . are you ready?'

He was waiting on the step, hair tousled above the open shirt and the black leather jacket, taking the two suitcases and hefting them into the front of the taxi. 'King's Cross,' he said and settled beside her in the seat.

'How did the reading go?' she asked, although the grin on his face told her the answer.

'Brilliant,' he said. 'I was brilliant . . . I am going to be a gas. You must come up and see it – we start in Manchester. You could make that from . . . wherever this God-forsaken place is you're going to, couldn't you?'

She promised to come to *Godspell* and see him wow his audiences, and he held her hand and squeezed it until the cab drew up at the station.

'Love me?' he said when it was time to part and Helen nodded.

'Of course I do. Now, go and be famous.' Waving to him as the train pulled out, she reflected that it was true: she had loved him, still did a little . . . but, perish the thought, in an almost maternal way. 'You're getting old, Helen,' she said to herself as she made her way to her sleeping compartment.

When the steward had left her she settled on the narrow bunk, thinking of Edward. He would be anxious now and alone. She should have let him come to see her off, as he had suggested but she had wanted to do right by Patrick. Her discarded lover! She laughed aloud at the melodramatic description. He was probably already in bed with a nubile fellow artist while she sped through the night to Newcastle and then, on a morning train, to Aberdeen.

Helen had decided to talk to Alistair at three o'clock one morning, after two hours of walking the floor. He was Michael's father, after all, and perhaps, just perhaps, he might have matured enough to help her now. She had gone to the library the following morning and looked him up in the Medical Directory: Alistair McKinnie MBBS, The Hirsel, Bucksburn, Aberdeen. She had rung Directory Enquiries and obtained his number, and had then sat with the phone in her hand, too scared to dial. That was when she had decided to go and see him face to face, and to decide then whether or not to ask for help. It had seemed such a good idea then – now she was not so sure.

She switched her thoughts to tomorrow, when Aberdeen would be behind her. She was going to Belgate to stay with Lilian while she considered the possibility of moving back to the north-east: that was the story she had given her sister. Whether or not Lilian had swallowed it was another thing. Helen grimaced, thinking of all the questions she would have to face tomorrow, and then began to get ready for the bumpy night ahead.

'Sugar?' The social worker offered the bowl to Diana and then sank back into her chair. 'Now, Mrs Whittington, I want to outline the way it works, and then we'll get down to detail. The old days, when you put in your order for a blue-eyed male baby, are over, I'm afraid. Well, you know that. The Pill, and new attitudes to single mothers, have meant that babies are in extremely short supply, and on the whole your age and your husband's would suggest that we think in terms of an older child, or children. Your husband did mention that you might consider taking a family.'

'Where do they come from, these ready-made families?' Diana asked, her heart sinking at the prospect of a group of mutinous, united little faces.

The social worker sipped her coffee and replaced the cup in the saucer. 'Bereavement . . . you'd be amazed how many kids lose both parents. Sometimes they've been dumped as infants . . . the parents intend to come back and don't. Others are taken from their parents for various reasons. One thing you can be sure of is that the children concerned will have been through the mill before we put them in contact with you. And that can be a drawback.'

Diana raised her brows and the social worker smiled.

'I was watching your face when I said they'd had a hard time, and your reaction was fairly typical: concern, pity, a desire to heal their wounds. But the last thing these kids need is someone making emotional decisions about their future. They want to be wanted, not helped. Of course you'll help them if you take them, but if it's for the wrong motives you won't be able to keep it up. They'll know how you really feel . . . and – well, it can get rough sometimes. I don't want to put you off, but I have to be honest. How do you feel about what I've said so far?'

'Honestly?' Diana asked. The other woman nodded.

'Well, then, scared is the word, I suppose. I'm not sure

enough of my own abilities as a mother. Even if it were straightforward I'd be scared. But when there are all these added complications . . .' Her voice tailed away, but to her surprise the other woman was smiling.

'Good, I'm glad you're scared. If you'd waved all my comments aside I'd have known you weren't cut out for adoption. As it is, you're displaying a healthy caution . . . I like that.'

'And I like you,' Diana thought, 'but I'm not scared – I'm petrified.'

They agreed to meet again, this time at the house with David there, and Diana walked out into the sunshine feeling like someone who had just been through a stringent medical examination.

'I am doing this for the wrong reason,' she thought. 'I'm doing it for David, that's all. I've gone beyond motherhood. If I was to find I was pregnant now, I think I'd hate it. I've made my life around David, around friends, around Michael and Susan and Lilian's Karen. I don't need children any more . . . except to fulfil my obligation as David's wife.'

As if to confirm her argument a woman approached her, wheeling a pushchair. Once that would have sent Diana scurrying for shelter, for somewhere to wipe her tears and still her trembling limbs. Now it didn't upset her at all. 'Am I heartless as well as barren?' she thought and could find no answer to her question.


Howard rang for the Gatenby file, expecting Mrs Fraser to bring it in. Instead it was Yvonne. 'Mrs Fraser hasn't come in today, sir. She rang at quarter to nine to say she had a tummy upset. She expects to be in tomorrow. I told her not to worry – I'm sure we can cope.'

Did he imagine the suggestion in her words or was it really there? 'Are you good at coping, Yvonne?'

'I think so, Mr Whittington.'

'You'll have to prove it to me some time.'

'I'd like that, sir.' Her green eyes were on his, steady and certain, and he was smiling and nodding his head.

Around him the air seemed to shimmer, but all he could see was the heavy, yellow hair that swung down on to the full breasts straining at her blouse. Was that how it happened? As easily as that? She was holding out the file and when he put his hand on her arm she smiled, moving almost imperceptibly closer so that he thought he could detect her heartbeat.

'You live at Spennymoor, don't you? There's a crossroads near there, with a white pub.'

'The Prospect. I live quite near there.'

'I could pick you up there tonight . . . at seven-thirty?'

When Yvonne had gone Howard sat on, turning the leaves of the Gatenby file and seeing nothing. What had he done? He put out a hand to the phone to ring someone, anyone; then he thought better of it and rose to his feet. If he went out now, smiling, he could say it had all been a joke. They would laugh about it, of course, and talk it over in the staff cloakroom, but however much they speculated they would never really know if he had meant it or not.

He opened the door to the outer office. Yvonne was working at her desk, unsmiling, not gossiping with any of the others. 'Did you want something, Mr Whittington?' He shook his head and went back inside.

He couldn't go to meet her, of course. It would be an act of unimaginable folly to do it. But even as he straightened the photograph of Michael and Susan on his desk and tried to compose a get-out speech, he knew with certainty that he would be there tonight, whatever it cost him.


Edward tapped at the door of the ward office and waited for the sister's command to enter. 'Hallo. I'm just visiting Mrs Stepinska and I wondered if there was anything she needed? I've brought the usual things, orange squash and fruit.'

'She could do with some tissues, Mr Portillo. It is Mr Portillo, isn't it? And some talc. Not too highly perfumed – baby powder is best.'

He nodded, and was about to ease himself out of the room when she reached for a chart on her desk. 'I see you're down as next-of-kin, Mr Portillo. Are you a close relative?'

Her words took Edward by surprise. 'I didn't know I was listed as her next-of-kin! We're very close friends but I'm no blood relation. She hasn't got much of a family. She used to speak of a cousin or two in Scotland . . . Glasgow, I think. Her solicitor will know their whereabouts. They're her heirs. She lost most of her family in the war, but that branch of the family remained.'

The sister was pursing her lips, obviously deciding whether or not to confide in him.

'There's nothing wrong is there?'

She shook her head. 'Oh no, at least, nothing more than that she's an old lady now, and frail. It's really only a matter of time . . . and there would be arrangements . . .'

He knew she was talking sense, but he felt an unreasoning anger towards her that made him brusque. 'I wouldn't worry too much about that. I'm Maria's executor, together with her solicitor, and we would see to everything. Her relatives would be informed and in due course would receive their inheritance. They're elderly themselves. Anyway, if it's any help, her solicitors are Makim, Makim and Pease. I have their number here.'

He fished in his wallet and handed the sister the solicitors' card. She copied the number, chattering all the time about there being no need for alarm and of course *he* really was the proper person to be next-of-kin because he'd always kept faith with the patient.

'Kept faith.' Edward sat in the ward and watched Maria Stepinska sleeping, her mouth open now, the upper set of teeth dropped down until she resembled a horse. He wanted to lean forward and wake her, see her face come alive again, see her go 'pouf' at the utter, stinking, bloodiness of life. But when she did wake, it was only to ask if someone had told Stephan it was time for his tea.

Edward felt unutterably depressed as he walked down the long hospital corridor. Maria was going to die soon, and Helen had already gone north. She had not even wanted him to take her to the station, preferring a tanned moron who kept his brains in his biceps . . . or his trousers.

Edward started to smile at his own idiocy, and then turned into a barber's for a haircut, in the hope of boosting his morale. There was always Maggie, warm and eager Maggie who was such a comfort in bed and kept the friendliest pub in Chelsea!


Aberdeen station was huge and comparatively empty, with beautiful Victorian metalwork and greenery on ledges, and the distant hum of trains like roaring surf. Once it must have been grand. There was still a hint of trailing skirts and tall hats doffed to ladies. A sign said 'Telephones', and Helen hesitated, but only for a second. She had not forgotten Alistair's powers of evasion.

A freshness in the air as she emerged from the station spoke to her of the sea, and there were seabirds whirling above. She sank into the back seat of a taxi and gave the address, wondering as she did so why she had come. She was not even completely sure that Michael *had* a problem. What did she expect Alistair to do now, when he had been prepared to do so little in the beginning? She wanted to pass the buck, that was it – have someone else take the responsibility from her reluctant shoulders, tell her there was nothing at all to worry about, so that she could go home and forget.

Through the taxi windows Helen could see that it was indeed the granite city, built in an age when craftsmanship abounded and money was plentiful, with domes, balconies, towers . . . The city gave way to crowded housing-estates, and then to countryside. The cab sped up a country road, along a lane, and finally drew to a halt. 'That's it there, miss. Do you want me to drive in?'

The house was stone-washed and rambling, with bay windows here and there and a lawn running down to what looked like a beck. Two large cars and a Range Rover stood at the door. Alistair had done well for himself.

Helen paid the taxi-driver at the bottom of the drive, added a £5 note and asked him to wait. 'There's a lay-by a little way back. Could you wait there? I don't know how long I'll be, but if I'm going to be longer than half an hour I'll come and tell you.'

The drive was circular, and it seemed a long way to the front door as Helen crunched over the gravel. She had worked out what to do. She would knock and ask to speak to Dr McKinnie. If asked, she would say she was a rep from a pharmaceutical firm. Once she was face to face with Alistair, she would have to play it by ear.

But she had no need to put her plan into action. As she was lifting her hand to the bell, the door opened and the man emerging jumped at the sight of her. 'Can I help you?'

Was it Alistair? He had been thin and freckled. This man was slightly beefy and pale. 'Dr McKinnie . . . Dr Alistair McKinnie?'

'Yes? Look, I'm afraid it's out of surgery hours and . . .' Something in her face had struck a chord. *'He's trying to remember where he's seen me before,'* Helen thought, and knew it was indeed Alistair.

'It's me, Helen Clark.' And then, when he still looked uncomprehending, 'From Darlasden Infirmary.' Surely she would not have to say: 'Remember, I had your baby?'

It dawned on Alistair suddenly and unpleasantly. He moved forward, closing the door behind him, almost pushing her backwards down the steps. 'What are you doing here?' It was not hostility in his voice, it was fear. 'My wife's inside. She'll be out in a moment . . .'

'I don't want to cause trouble, if that's what you're afraid of . . . but I need some advice.'

Alistair was shaking his head. 'I told you long ago that if you went ahead, it was nothing to do with me. I would have helped you then, I wanted to . . .'

She cut through his words, trying to contain her mounting disgust. 'Don't you want to know about your child, Alistair? Your firstborn child? Whether it was boy or girl, did it live, did I keep it, is it healthy and whole and sane? Aren't you interested at all?'

She heard the sound of hoofs on gravel and saw his eyes flicker. 'Be careful. It's my daughter, watch what you say.'

The girl was small and haughty in the saddle, dressed in jodhpurs and tweed jacket, hard hat atop red plaits. 'I did jolly well, daddy. Cleared three feet. Mason was so pleased with me, he said you should have been there.' Her father was nodding and smiling and casting anxious glances at the still-closed front door. 'Very good, darling, I'll hear all about it in a moment. I'm going to give this patient a lift to the bus-stop . . . tell mummy I'll be less than five minutes.'

He was pushing Helen into the red BMW and running round to the driving-seat, sending the car off in a spurt of gravel. 'Don't go far,' she said as they went through the gates. 'I've a cab waiting, and I don't think we have much to say to one another after all.'

At her direction Alistair pulled into the lay-by behind the taxi. 'I can't stay long – Fiona will be out in a moment. We're going into town. But I *would* like to know about the child: was it a boy?'

Helen nodded, and saw a twinge of disappointment flicker over his face. 'I have three girls,' he said. 'Marvellous kids, all of them. What did you call him?'

'I didn't. I gave him up for adoption. They called him Michael, if it's any help. He's a very handsome, intelligent boy and he's had every advantage. But I'm worried about him now . . . not for any good reason, just a feeling . . .'

Alistair was reaching into his pocket for chequebook and pen. 'Look, I'll do what I can, but I'm not acknowledging any respons – '

He never finished the word. Helen had reached forward and screwed up the cheque and several of its fellows with fingers that were iron with fury.

She cried as she walked from the car to the cab, thankful for only one thing; that no one, not even Edward, her dearest friend, had been there to see her humiliation.


Diana refilled her cup and carried on with telling her tale. 'When I left, I felt a bit depressed. I mean, the social worker seemed to be emphasizing all the bad points. But when I came to think about it I realized that everything she said made sense. She's coming here on Thursday afternoon to talk to us together.'

'And after that?' David was trying to sound nonchalant and failing miserably.

'After that she puts us in touch with some children . . . informally at first. If we like them and they like us, they visit. Then they come for weekends . . . and then we see.'

'So it could take years?'

Diana couldn't repress a smile. 'It could, but it won't. She thinks about six months, so maybe by Christmas . . .'

'How many do we want?' he asked. 'I mean, we don't want a small army, but we did say having only one wouldn't be fair on the child . . .'

'Let's wait and see what turns up,' Diana said gently. 'We talked in terms of families today – children, two or three, who've lost their parents but need to stay together. Not every adoptive parent can afford to do that. We can, and I think we should.'

She didn't add that two or more children, bonded by blood, would give one another the affection that she might never be able to give them, but she thought it and it comforted her.

'I will be fair,' she promised herself as they sat later watching the news on television. 'I will be fair, and I will be kind, and I will never, ever begrudge them my time or my energy. But I will never feel for them what I could have felt for my own. No one could ask it of me.'

'I saw Howard at lunch time,' David said, peering at her from over his evening paper. 'He said they were all well, and we should come over soon. I thought he was a bit off, though. I suppose distrait is the word.'

Diana was intrigued. 'Go on,' she prompted.

He put down the paper. 'Well, you know what I mean. He went through all the motions but he wasn't himself. He was having a half of lager but he even looked guilty about that.'


There was no sign of Yvonne when he got to the cross-roads, and Howard felt a surge of relief. So she had only been joking! Tomorrow no one would mention it. It could

275

all be forgotten and Mrs Fraser would be back to make everything right again.

He was about to put the car into gear and drive off when he saw her, picking her way towards him in high-heeled shoes. 'Sorry I'm a bit late. I got held up.'

Howard shook his head, his heart pounding, uncertain of what to say. 'Where shall we go?' he offered at last, hoping she would suggest somewhere far, far away from anyone and anywhere he knew.

'You choose,' Yvonne said. Her thighs were long and chubby in dark stockings, her knees still rounded like a child's. He pointed the car towards Barnard Castle and drove fast so that no one on the road would have time to recognize his car or its occupants.

They sat in the back room of a village pub, making jokes about the other customers, eating crisps and drinking lager and something disgusting called a snowball which stayed on her upper lip, giving him an excuse to reach out and wipe her mouth with a trembling forefinger.

He didn't hurry her out to the car, even though time was ticking away. He was trying to remember what to do, what it had been like with other girls. Before Anne, before he had learned to be afraid. He must be careful not to betray his own inadequacy, his inexperience, to her. But the girl would talk. No matter what he said or did, she would talk eventually.

Beneath her fluffy sweater Yvonne's breasts were full and round, the nipples erect, tiny mountains begging to be conquered. Howard realized he was swallowing hard and tried to draw a deep breath.

'Shall we go now?'

She was looking into his face, her lower lip drooping and dimples appearing on the corners of her mouth. And then her hand was on his thigh, sliding higher and moving inwards. 'Come on,' she said, 'or we won't have any time.'


Lilian had known there was something up, had been telling Billy and Karen so ever since her sister's phone call, but even she was not prepared for the sight of Helen, white-faced and weary, with a terrible bleakness about the eyes that boded no good. 'Would you like some soup, pet?' she said, the unusual endearment slipping from her. You heard of people coming home after the doctors had told them bad news. Perhaps this was such a case?

'Take her coat, Billy, and poke that fire. Karen, turn that racket down or put it off – can't you see your Auntie Helen's worn out? I'll put a bottle in your bed, our Helen, and you can go up as soon as you've had some supper. Billy Fenwick, will you poke that fire . . . it'll be out in a minute. If I have to do it myself . . .'

Busy in the kitchen, Lilian listened to the low murmur of conversation in the living-room. Not Helen's usual style at all: she liked a good crack with Billy, but today it seemed she could hardly be bothered to answer.

'What've you been up to Aberdeen for?' Lilian asked when the minestrone was on a tray with bread-and-best-butter cut in fingers. 'I hope it wasn't for a job, because I've heard of one for you right here, working for Dr Whittington in his clinic. You know how my name stands there. It'll be yours, if you want it.'

Tears pricked her eyes as Helen smiled her appreciation. Her little sister had been brought right down, and no mistake. So much for London and the high-life. And she was her sister, after all, and blood was thicker than water.

'I'll slip up and put those bottles in,' she said, 'and then you come straight up. You look properly peely-wally.'

# 22

The medical habits had come back to her fairly easily, even after fifteen years: the professional smile, the expression of sympathy, the non-committal shake of the head. 'You'll have to ask doctor about that, Mrs Cummings.' 'Doctor will see you now, Mr Cousins.' 'Is anyone here for the ante-natal group?' The case-notes, bearing good news ('The tests proved negative'), the bad ('The prognosis is uncertain'), and sometimes the farcical ('Fracture of left humerus received in fall from beer crate. Referred to Casualty OP').

It was all a million miles away from bisque-headed dolls and Wellington chests. Helen was coping but she had been here for four weeks and still she had not encountered Michael or his sister or come any closer to knowing the details of their life, except to read and reread their medical case-notes, so that she knew each knock, each infection, each touch of pyrexia or ear-ache. Michael was a healthy boy but Susan was 'highly-strung', according to one note. All in all, it was not very satisfying reading.

She had seen the job at David Whittington's surgery as a stepping-stone to making Howard Whittington's acquaintance, but she had not bargained for the lack of contact between the brothers, the absence of warmth between their wives. Today, though, there was a break-through. 'I'm expecting David's sister-in-law,' Dr Makepeace, David's partner, said as she went to her room. 'Watch out for her, will you?'

Helen felt the room rock and then steady. At last it had come.

She was sorting case-notes from the morning's surgery and thinking of the coming confrontation when suddenly Anne Whittington was there. 'I'm Mrs Whittington, Dr Whittington's sister-in-law. Dr Makepeace is expecting me. Is she in her room?'

The dark eyes were pools of calm, the face unlined, a faint downy growth on her upper lip only emphasizing her beauty. 'She is like a Renaissance Madonna,' Helen thought, taking out the case-notes and lifting the flap of the counter to emerge into the waiting-room. But there was not the warmth of the central figure in an old master, no curving fullness of figure. 'This is Michael's mother,' Helen thought, but somehow it did not feel significant.

'I'll see if she's ready. Would you like to take a seat?'

When Helen emerged from the consulting room Anne was standing where she had left her, hands crossed on the leather handbag that hung from her arm. 'Would you go straight in?'

When she had gone into the room, Helen moved back behind the counter. There had been no spark between them, no liking, no loathing, no hostility . . . nothing. And yet they shared so much.

When at last Anne's notes were returned from the consulting room, Helen studied them, secretly, in a corner like a guilty Peeping Tom. Anne Whittington was forty-three years old and had been treated for migraine and the fracture of a carpal bone in the last year. Today she had complained of 'abdominal discomfort? gynae', but had refused internal examination or referral to a gynaecologist. '*See D. W.*' was written in the corner in Sheila Makepeace's hand.

Helen filed the card under *Whittington A.*, and then took out *Whittington, Michael* and read it for the hundredth time.

Howard had thought it would be impossibly difficult to work with Yvonne without betraying the true situation, but she had been a model of discretion, no longer provocative, seldom allowing their eyes to meet. She insisted during each outing, on making firm arrangements for the next before they parted, so that there would be no need to speak of such things during working hours. The only trouble was that he could not stop thinking about her, remembering, anticipating; revolted by the lust he felt and yet exhilarated by it. He remembered how her hands had guided him, been gentle with his inexperience, so that he had forgotten his intended front of expertise and had let her dictate. It had been . . . he was trying to find a word large enough for what he had felt, but his thoughts were swamped by the enormity of it all.

He was a professional man of forty-five, the father of two children, and Yvonne was an eighteen-year-old girl in his employ and entitled to his protection. He dropped his face into his hands, wondering whether it was worth asking forgiveness or whether there could be no expiation for such a sin, when there came a knock at his door and Mrs Fraser entered.

'I thought I would remind you about Mr and Mrs Boxall.

You wanted to read through counsel's opinion before you saw them.'

Howard nodded and smiled. 'Thank you. I'd forgotten, of course. What would I do without you?'

The woman's face glowed as she replied, 'You'd manage very well, I'm sure.'

'How's your son doing?'

Mrs Fraser told him briefly of her elder son's progress, her pride showing in her face but not in her words, and then went to the door. She was looking at him with a curious expression, half-kindness, half-exasperation, and for a moment fear of discovery chilled him.

'Is everything all right?' she said. 'I don't mean to pry, but you look a little distracted.'

Howard confessed to a headache and accepted two aspirin and a glass of water. She must have been a pretty woman once, he thought, as she closed the door quietly behind her, leaving him to thoughts that alternately thrilled and tormented him.


'Yes, I do like Helen, David. I like her enormously. All I said was that she's a bit of a mystery woman. I mean, those clothes aren't chain-store, and she's very well-groomed, which doesn't come cheap. She's knowledgeable about so many things . . . she saw that old plant-stand in the waiting room and came out with details about it being a jardinière and made in the 1870s. If it's worth anything please flog it without delay, by the way; it's hideous. So why should she come back here to work for what you yourself admit is a pittance, doing work that's beneath her, and not making any real mention of what she's left behind? I rest my case.'

They had reached the top of the rise, and David bent to touch the grass. 'It's dry. Want to sit down?' Below them the county of Durham stretched away to the sea.

'I don't think it's a mystery,' he said, lowering himself to the ground and plucking at a long blade of grass. 'I used to be able to make a whistle of these things years ago.' He held the blade to his lips, and blew and blew. 'But I've lost the knack. Anyway, as I said, there's no mystery: she's had

280

a gone-wrong love affair, that's all. Probably a married man. Painful enough to send her scuttling home, anyway. It must have been fairly traumatic if it sent her into the arms of News of the World. What does *she* make of it all, by the way?'

'Oh, Lilian suspects the worst – everything from terminal illness to pregnancy. She's torn between rubbing little sister's nose in it and feeding her up in case she's on her way out. It's a hoot, actually.'

'And Billy just sails serenely on?' David enquired and Diana nodded.

'As you once said, the salt of the earth. Anyway, I've told Helen about the flat, and whether or not she pursues it is up to her. It's near the practice, it's newly fitted-out, and the rent is reasonable. If she doesn't take it, she's a fool.'

Below them cloud-shadows dappled the fields, moving on and changing shape. 'Life's nice, isn't it?' she said, and when he reached for her she took no notice of grass or insect life because his kiss was sweet. No need today to worry about the future: adoption and all its attendant perils seemed a million miles away. They were just a boy and girl on a hill, with a dog snuffling between them and unable to understand why they were intertwined.

'Get off, daft dog,' David said pushing at the squirming fur. 'We should have called this mutt Chaperone not Lupi. He's the best passion-killer in the business.'

And so they sat on until it was nearly time for afternoon surgery and they had to run, shrieking with glee, down the steep slope of the hill.


Edward was examining a walnut étagère when the shop bell rang. He straightened up and looked at the woman, framed in the doorway. There was something familiar about the figure, the red hair, the bold tilt of the chin.

'Sylvia!' he said and came towards her.

She put up a hand to her throat and touched the chain that lay there. 'See,' she said, 'I still have it.' It was the

Liberty amethyst and pearl necklace he had given her years ago.

'It's been a long time, Sylvia,' Edward said.

She nodded. 'Fourteen years.' He had reached her now and he hesitated, wondering whether or not to kiss her cheek. She smiled and held out her arms. 'It's good to see you, Edward. It's been too long.' Inside his embrace she felt and smelled unbelievably good. 'You look terrific,' he said, and let her go.

He looked at his watch: it was nearly noon. 'Have you time for a drink . . . or better still, lunch? I want to hear all your news – but don't let me stop you if you're on your way somewhere.'

Sylvia was shaking the glorious red hair. 'No, I've got all the time in the world and I'd love lunch if you can get away. Are you on your own now? What happened to that funny little Geordie girl you took under your wing?' She made a mock grimace of embarrassment. 'You didn't marry her, did you? I wouldn't like to make a *faux pas* at our first reunion.' There was still the old challenge in her voice, the provocative note.

'Come on,' Edward said. 'Let's get out of here and then I'll tell you about Helen. She's still with me, and she's quite a name in the trade now . . . but I haven't married anyone. How could I, when I was waiting for you?'

'Shucks,' Sylvia said, smiling. 'What about your other paramour, the Czech lady?'

'Polish,' Edward said, suddenly subdued. 'She's in hospital, in a coma, I'm afraid. Still, time enough for all that . . .'

It was good to walk up the Mews with a beautiful woman hanging on his arm, and on his words. They settled in a corner table at Cesare et Franco, and ordered quickly to get it out of the way. 'Now,' he said, 'tell me.'

Sylvia put out her left hand and waggled her fingers.

'No rings?' he said, and she nodded.

'As of a month ago, I'm a free woman.'

They had to wait while the wine was brought, approved and poured. 'Want to talk about it?' he said and she flung wide her arms. He had forgotten how vigorous her reactions were.

'How long have we got? I'd need a year. Suffice it to say he was a bastard to me, I was a bitch to him, and it was a relief all round when we called it a day. No children, thank God, so no complications.'

'I'm sorry,' Edward said, trying to sound as though he meant it. In fact he was elated by Sylvia's return to his life. 'Now . . . what have I got to tell you?'


Helen was determined to take the flat Diana had mentioned if it was even barely adequate. In fact, it proved to be delightful, with living-room, a bedroom, an eating kitchen and a pocket-hanky-sized bathroom. The living-room had a bay window jutting out over the front of the chemist's shop on the ground-floor below.'What do you think?' Diana asked.

Helen lifted both hands in the air. 'I think it's wonderful! But I can't really believe it – £15 a week? Are you sure?'

Diana nodded. 'Certain. They need someone absolutely trustworthy. Think of what they've got down below . . . drugs and things. They always tell the practice if it comes up to let. I thought you'd like it; I know Lilian's been marvellous but we all need our own territory, don't we?' She looked at her watch. 'I'll have to go, I'm afraid. I'm seeing the children this afternoon, so I need to gather strength. Are you going to talk to Mr Anderson now?'

Helen moved to the window and looked out at the street. 'Yes,' she said, turning back into the room. 'I'll speak to him on the way out.'

Diana looked around. 'You could do quite a lot with it . . . it's an old building, hence all the nooks and crannies. I like that. David and I will lend a hand with the move if you like. Just shout.'

They moved towards the door. 'Are you worried about this afternoon?' Helen asked.

Diana nodded. 'Yes, if I'm truthful. I doubt my own motives, you see. I've become quite resigned to not having children, which is strange because I wanted them very much at the beginning. But you become . . . well, I suppose inured is the word. I've had five miscarriages, as Lilian's probably told you. However, David has never accepted it, though he's been wonderful over the years. He didn't want me to try again last time; he'd have adopted then. His brother has two adopted children who are marvellous, so of course David is wildly enthusiastic. But I really just want to do it for him, and I'm not sure that's enough. I feel that if "authority" finds out that's my motive, they'll turn me down . . . and then I'll feel I've failed David one more time.'

Helen tried to sound politely curious, no more. 'Your brother-in-law's children are teenagers now, aren't they?'

'Yes. Michael came to them when he was just two weeks old, and he's an absolute darling. Susan was two and had had a very bumpy passage. Anne, my sister-in-law, is very good with the boy, but less so with the girl.

'I've seen the boy, I think. He seems very studious.'

Diana was shaking her head. 'Poor Michael . . . serious would probably be a better word than studious. His mother has brought him up in a very spiritual way, and she's destined him for the priesthood. At least, it seems to us that she's been the driving force. He goes off to a seminary this autumn. David gets so cross about it . . .'

Diana was still talking but Helen had ceased to listen. The *priesthood*! For her son! She wanted to know more, to cross-question and grill, but it wouldn't do. She felt Diana's hand on her arm and looked up into the other woman's face. 'Are you all right, Helen? You've got tears in your eyes . . .'

Helen shook her head. 'It's nothing. I was thinking about you and Dr Whittington, and how much you deserve a child. I just suddenly felt sorry for you. I'll be thinking about you this afternoon, and I'm sure it'll all go well. You'll be perfect parents.'

Diana put an arm around her as they moved towards the stairs. 'I hope you'll be happy here, Helen, and that we'll be friends. I think we will be. It's funny – I've known you such a small time but I feel that in my bones.'

Helen smiled and murmured agreement, but her over-whelming desire was to get out and away from even kindly eyes. They parted on the doorstep, Diana to her car, Helen to enter the chemist's shop, find the chemist and negotiate for her new home.

Edward found it hard to concentrate throughout what remained of the afternoon. He had put Sylvia in a cab outside the restaurant and arranged to pick her up at eight o'clock to go out to dinner. They still had much talking to do. He could see that the last few difficult years had taken their toll but, if anything, she was more beautiful than before.

Now he tried to get on with his work. He had bought in the remainders of a dealer who had gone into voluntary liquidation, doing it more as a favour than because he coveted the items. But they were proving more interesting than he had imagined. If only Helen were here, to see and appreciate and give an opinion. To hear about Sylvia!

He picked up a Royal Dux female nude and kissed it firmly on its porcelain buttock. In the archway the torch-ères, Mark and Antony, regarded him with scandalized expressions. If only Maria were still awake and aware, how pleased she would be with Sylvia's return. But she was now in a half-world, hovering between life and death. He looked at the nude, serene in its world of porcelain while he was flesh and must bleed. Still, there were compensa-tions: flesh could come alive as porcelain never would.

'Jealousy gets you nowhere,' he said, putting the figure on one side and diving back into the tea-chest. More Royal Dux, not quite his style. Porcelain figural vases in typical muted enamel colours and then, glory of glories, two pieces of Doulton stoneware decorated by Florence Barlow, prop-erly marked and dated 1887.

The chest was now empty except for one last piece, a Royal Copenhagen erotic group, man and woman naked and embracing. Tonight he and Sylvia would make love. He felt desire rise in him, that surge in the pelvis that could leave you breathless if it was not controlled. It was weeks since he had had sex. Months. He must be getting old because it had not troubled him until today, across the table from Sylvia, remembering how it had been with her.

'I'm forty-two,' he thought and then said it aloud, 'forty-two.' The blackamoors looked back, unmoved. They were all of a century or more: no wonder they felt superior.

The phone rang and he put down the group and moved to answer. 'Helen! You have? Good. One bedroom . . . well, you could always get a sofa-bed. Of course I'm coming up – I want to see more of this antique-packed county you're always boasting about. As soon as you're settled . . . Me? Oh, nothing much. Maria is holding her own, no change. Nothing else . . . except, guess who walked into the shop today? Sylvia! Yes, *that* Sylvia.'


'Well, I'm sure I hope you'll be very happy,' Lilian said. 'Not that you couldn't have stopped on here. Isn't that right Billy? *Billy!*'

Billy came from behind his paper at the sound of Lilian's voice. 'What was that, pet?'

Lilian sighed heavily. 'Don't blame him, his clockwork's rusted. I said our Helen was welcome to stop as long as she wanted.'

'Oh, aye, love. Aye, Helen. There's nothing spoiling here. Lily likes company about the place.' He went back behind his paper and Lilian wondered whether or not to pursue him. Perhaps not – there was more to be got from chasing up Helen.

'You say Diana got the flat for you?'

Helen was nodding. 'Yes, wasn't it kind? She really is a lovely woman, it's such a pity about her infertility. She was saying today that she's had five miscarriages. She said . . .'

'You don't have to tell me about it, our Helen, I've lived through it with her. You know how close we are. That's why she's being so good to you, on account of you being my sister. She said to me a while ago that she didn't know how she'd've stuck Darlasden if it hadn't been for me all these years. She's a long way from her own folks and she doesn't get on with Anne – that's her that's married to the solicitor.'

'Yes,' Helen said, 'she mentioned her today. Nothing nasty, though . . . just about her having adopted two children. Have you met them?'

'Of course, many a time. He's a beautiful boy. Indian blood or something, I used to think, but he's turned much fairer. He's at a good Catholic school in Darlasden, very bright and everything. Wants to be a priest. The girl's a different kettle of fish – what a little toy! I saw her have a strunt once, at Diana's. Down on the carpet, foaming at the mouth. Anne never smacked her, but if looks could kill she'd've been laid out. Which reminds me . . . I was round me mam's today and me dad was talking very morbid. What he wanted at his funeral, who'd get his watch . . . Billy naturally, as he's the only man in the family. Anyroad, it can't be much fun for me mam with him going on like that.'

They talked family then, which made Lilian much less uncomfortable than talking about her best friend with a sister who seemed determined to worm her way in. 'It's always been the same,' Lilian thought. 'I've never had anything but what she wanted it . . . or one better.'

A gentle snore came from behind the paper and reminded her of her husband – one possession that Helen had not managed to deprive her of or to equal, in spite of her fancy clothes. The thought cheered Lilian up for at least five minutes.

The house was in darkness downstairs when Howard let himself in. He rehearsed his story while he checked carefully for tell-tale traces of the squalid hours he had spent with Yvonne. He felt the same strange mixture of emotions that he always felt now, shame and exhilaration. He wanted her so much that their love-making was never enough. Sometimes he thought the anticipation was the best, because the pleasure of it was still ahead. And then when he was doing it, getting it right, feeling her respond

. . . Howard put a hand to his mouth in the dark hall, racked with desire again just at the memory.

He glanced up the stairs to the faint light from the transom above his bedroom door. If Anne knew, if she came out and smelled it on him – sex. He could move towards her and defy her to say anything about it. He could face her down now. He would have to do it sooner or later, and he was no longer afraid. All the same . . . if he could make the bathroom without her hearing, strip off the clothes that still smelled of Yvonne, of Yvonne and him together, it would be better. He had put pyjamas and dressing-gown in the airing-cupboard before he went out. All he had to do was negotiate the stairs.

He moved forwards, feeling with his hands for banister and wall. Tonight Yvonne had giggled in his ear that he was a good lover. In the aftermath, when he had still been sick with regret that it was over, that there was no more, she had turned and laughed against his ear. He was smiling fatuously into the dark when light streamed across the landing. 'Howard?' Anne was there above him, silhouetted against the light. In her long robe she looked like a statuette. He smelled incense, suddenly, and polished wood, and felt his knees tremble beneath him.

'It's me,' he said apologetically. 'Did I wake you?'

She was moving to the landing switch, lighting the stairs, and he looked down at his flies, sure he would see them open and pathetic.

'I wasn't asleep. Did your . . . meeting . . . go well?' There was no mistaking the deliberate hesitation, and emphasis.

'Yes, it did go well . . . but it dragged on. You know these things . . .'

He was trapped there like a fly in a web, unable to advance. Sex smelled: he had never realized it until these last few weeks. Alone with Yvonne in the car, or in her narrow little room, he knew the air reeked of what they had done together. Or perhaps it was the odour of sin? '*I accuse myself of impure actions . . . mea culpa, mea culpa . . .*'

'I thought I'd have a bath before I turned in. Don't let me keep you up. No point in our both being tired.'

Anne was turning back to the bedroom, leaving the landing clear. 'That's kind of you, Howard. I've been thinking . . . you know I sleep so lightly. Perhaps if you moved into another room? It will give you more time for reading and contemplation.'

She knew!

Even when he was in the bathroom, the door locked behind him, Howard was still afraid. He had seen the pleasure in her eyes out there on the landing, the joy not in his sin, but in the wrong he had done – was doing – to her. 'She's wanted this,' he thought and sat down on the edge of the bath, sinking his face into his hands. 'She needs my sin,' he acknowledged silently, as brilliant lights sprang up behind his closed lids, 'because her own sins are not burden enough.'

## 23

The Saturday surgery was over and Helen was sorting case-notes into alphabetical order when she saw Michael. He had come into the waiting-room, white-faced, holding his right arm against his chest. She moved to the desk, her heart leaping wildly inside her ribs, and smiled.

'Had an accident?'

He grinned sheepishly and nodded. 'I was playing cricket across the way. I tried for a tricky catch and I fell. Is my Uncle David here?'

Helen lifted the flap and came round the counter. 'I expect we can find him.' Michael was definitely white now, the colour draining from his face almost before her eyes. 'Are you OK? Perhaps you should sit down.'

She put out a hand and then, as he swayed, she put her arms around him. It was the very first time she had held her son in her arms, and inside her head a voice urged her to record the moment because it would never come again.

She lowered him to a chair, still delighting in the feel of him, half-man, half-boy, as tall as she was, at once more muscular and more fragile. His face was lantern-jawed in that peculiar way of adolescence, and there was a fuzz about his face.

'He's lovely,' she thought and laid her cheek for one brief instant against the crisp dark hair. 'There now,' she said, 'sit still and I'll get some help.'

When David had taken Michael off in the car to have his humerus X-rayed for possible fracture, Helen walked behind the filing cabinets and sat down on a chair. She felt empty now that he'd gone, and fearful, knowing a Rubicon had been crossed and uncertain of how she would cope in the future. 'I love him,' she thought, throwing aside the long years of believing that she had only wanted to meet her responsibility to him. 'I love him,' she said smiling, and then leaned her head against the filed notes to cry.

As at last she wiped her eyes and went back to work she permitted herself one final picture . . . of the moment when David had been leading him away and he had turned. 'Thank you very much, Miss . . . I'm afraid I don't know your name. I'm Michael Whittington.' David had apologized then, and introduced her, and they had gone out to the car. He had probably forgotten all about her before the engine was in gear, and it was probably better if he had.


They had seemed quite small children in the Home, but here, in Diana's sitting-room, they seemed large, positively gawky – except for the little boy, who was three. The elder girl was still fiercely protective, bossing the younger girl and indulging the toddler. 'You'll have to make allowances for her,' the social worker had said. 'She's been the only mother they've had for the last two years.'

Their history was fairly disastrous. Their father had walked out when Barbara was five, Tracy three, and Gary still unborn: 'He couldn't face the responsibility of a family,' the social worker had explained, in tones that suggested it was a familiar story. 'The mother tried to cope, but she had chronic kidney trouble and had to be hospitalized every now and then. We took them into care at her request, and that's when Barbara started to become so protective. We fostered them, but none of the foster-parents could deal with her . . . she has a tongue like a rasp when she's roused. We tried to keep them in touch with the mother, but it was difficult and eventually she died in January. Barbara blames us that they weren't with their mother at Christmas – that's when she's not accusing us of bumping off her mother. So you see, they're not easy.'

Diana had found the idea of a ready-made family unit rather attractive. When she had first seen the children in the Home, washed and pressed and polished for presentation, it hadn't seemed intimidating. Now, here, with three pairs of eyes fixed on her face, she felt panic.

'Well, it is nice to see you. Sit down, take your coats off.' The little boy subsided on to the floor, the smaller girl's eyes slid to her sister for instructions. The bigger girl looked at Diana coldly. 'Which should we do first?'

Diana bit back the impulse to say 'Does it matter?', and smiled instead. 'Whichever you like . . . coats first, probably.'

'Come here, Gary. Take your jacket off, Tracy.' Barbara peeled off the little boy's thin anorak with an expertise that spoke of much practice, folded it on to a chair with the other coats and then looked back at Diana.

'Now what?' she said contemptuously.

'Well,' Diana said, playing for time, 'what would you like to do now?' It was two o'clock . . . at least two hours before David could arrive to the rescue. The child was shrugging, putting up thin fingers to fasten the pink butterfly slide that held back her straggly brown hair. 'She's plain,' Diana thought, 'and she knows it.'

'It's your house.' Barbara had shot the ball back into Diana's court. Time to box clever.

'Yes, but you're my guests, therefore I have to let you choose.'

A gleam of admiration entered the girl's gaze, and was instantly suppressed. 'One to me,' Diana thought. 'So far visitors five, home team one.'

'Could we have the telly on?' It was the little girl, Tracy, speaking. The boy's eyes were drooping with tiredness, and his thumb was half-way to his mouth.

'Of course,' Diana said, scooping him on to the settee and putting a cushion behind his head. 'There now.' She switched on the TV, smiling at the younger girl. 'Not much on yet, I'm afraid.' She turned to Barbara. 'You operate the controls, they're there on the side. I'm going to get some drinks for us all.'

In the hall she hurriedly dialled the surgery number. 'Helen . . . tell David to get here quick. If he can't, can you come? I am, not to put too fine a point on it, out of my depth. Mayday, Mayday!' At the other end of the line she heard a chuckle. 'It's not funny, Helen. The biggest one is a . . .' Diana looked guiltily at the sitting-room door . . . 'she is *terrifying*. What am I going to do with them? One of you please come to the rescue!'


Lilian panted up the stairs to Helen's flat like someone ascending the Great Wall of China. 'By, you'll be fit when you've lived here a bit.' She came into the flat's living-room, with its flowered walls and solid mahogany furniture, and firmed her lips. 'Very nice. Not what I'd have chosen, but very nice.'

Helen merely smiled and inside Lilian irritation blossomed and grew. The furniture in her view, was old and ugly, would be impossible to shift for a proper clean, and would show every finger mark. Trust Helen to make the place look like Alnwick Castle! 'Was the stuff cheap?' she enquired, and then, without waiting for an answer, moved forward into the kitchen, to comment on the lack of working-space and the proximity of cooker and fridge.

She watched critically while Helen brewed tea and put out biscuits, and then followed her sister back to the living-room. 'The carpet's a bit worn, isn't it?' Helen said something about it being Chinese and a bargain, but Lilian knew a clapped-out carpet when she saw one and she was seeing one now.

'How'd'you get on at the surgery?' She listened while

Helen enthused about her duties, and then asked one or two pointed questions about patients of her acquaintance.

'You know I can't talk about the patients, Lil,' Helen said firmly.

'Please yourself,' Lilian said, seething at the fact that Helen once more had the upper hand. 'I can see for myself Tracy Joiner's pregnant, I don't need a clerk to tell me.' She emphasized 'clerk' to underline her sister's lowly status, but Helen gave no sign of minding and Lilian tried a fresh track.

'Do you miss London – or were you glad to get away from it? There's all sorts of stories going round. Well, you know how people gossip. "Don't ask me," I tell them, "I'm just her sister. I don't know." They reckon you must've been jilted . . . or lost your job?'

'I wasn't jilted,' Helen said, pouring more tea. 'There wasn't anybody to jilt me. And I still have my job, if I want it. I just fancied coming home for a bit. Mam and dad are getting on, you know. I want to spend some time with them . . . and with you and Billy and Karen. Karen's growing up and I hardly know her. Anyway, I'm enjoying it here. I get on well with David and Diana . . . you should've heard her today when those children arrived for a visit. "Get here, quick, Helen," she said, "I need you. This lot have me terrified."'

'*I need you, Helen,*' – so that was how it was! Not '*I need you, Lilian,*' after fifteen years. Oh no! '*I need you, Helen,*' after five flaming minutes. Lilian seethed inwardly for a moment, and then caught sight of a bowl on the mahogany desk, cracked from top to bottom and mended with rivets. 'Why, mind, our Helen . . . if you're down to putting cracked pots up, you should've said. I could have loaned you any amount of ornaments. You needn't be reduced to that.' She was getting a little bit of her own back, whatever Helen might be saying about Garret and Copeland or some such name – and just to score at all was balm.


It was still daylight when Howard picked Yvonne up at the crossroads, and the danger added spice to the meeting.

She climbed into the passenger seat and he leaned across her to secure the door. She had a shiny red camisole top on, one strap already falling down over her shoulder. He put out a hand and pulled the strap into place, letting his fingers linger on her cool young flesh.

'Where do you want to go?' There was the smell of grease about her hair and a faint, sweet odour from her body but it did not repel him. It was right that it should be so. They would couple and uncouple and then, when he got home, he would disrobe and wash it all away. He loved that cleansing ritual and the feeling of peace that followed it. He could pray then, on his knees beside the bath, the air moist and shimmering, no hunger in him any more.

The girl was pushing at him now, urging him to start the engine. 'Come on, Howard. I didn't come out to sit here all day. Let's go somewhere nice!' He half-smiled as he let out the clutch. 'Somewhere nice' meaning 'somewhere expensive'. Yvonne would scorn the frank offer of cash, but she meant to take it out in kind. She liked to squander his money, to order food and bizarre drinks and then leave them with a moue of distaste. She liked presents, her appreciation graded strictly according to their cost. Not for her the carefully chosen trifle in exciting wrappers – she liked his gifts to be the largest possible size, and was apt to get cross if they were wrapped in anything more demanding than a paper bag. 'She is a child,' he thought and was at once both ashamed and excited.

'There's a roadhouse just over the border into Yorkshire,' he said. 'Would you like to go there?'

Yvonne scowled. 'What's a roadhouse?'

Howard turned to look at her, at her rather protruberant eyes in their black kohl rings, her nose shiny and pored, her petulant little mouth. 'It's a rather posh pub,' he said, and was rewarded with a nod of the head.

He drove on through a string of villages to Scots Corner and then towards Richmond. The roadhouse loomed up, and he turned into the car-park. It would be light for an hour yet, an hour of plying her with drinks and trying to make conversation. She had two favourite topics, her fellow workers and his family, about whom she was endlessly curious. But he could talk to her about neither group without feeling intensely disloyal, and so their conversations were frequently awkward.

They were walking through the swing doors when he saw the Carleys, acquaintances and important clients. The impulse to turn and run was strong, but it was too late. He smiled at them and inclined his head, and hurried past, leaving Yvonne to teeter behind on her four-inch heels. 'You knew those people,' she said accusingly when they were seated at an alcove table.

'They're clients of mine,' he replied, shortly.

'So what? Why should you run away, even if they are clients? I'm not rubbish, you know, to be dumped if you see your fancy friends. If that's how you want it, let's pack it in now.'

Howard was torn between the need to placate her, because he couldn't do without her, and the knowledge, crawling now like some cold reptile up his spine, that her presence there with him was a badge of shame.


'There's only another half-hour before dusk,' Helen said, panting as she reached the top of the hill. Behind her Karen gave a groan and an extra push to the summit, and then flopped down on the grass. 'Sit down, Auntie . . . the grass is dry.'

Helen lowered herself to the ground and folded her hands round her knees. 'It looks lovely, doesn't it? Like a doll's town.'

Karen was nodding. 'I used to call it Lilliput when I was a kid, when dad used to bring me up here on Sundays.' She laughed aloud, throwing back her head at the memory. 'He used to say, "Let's stop up here, pet, till your mam cools off." She always got in a lather on Sundays, with the big dinner and everything. It was wise to keep out of the way.'

'She means well, your mam, though,' Helen said, realizing as she did so how easy it was to slip back into the idioms of home when you were there. London seemed a million miles away.

'You're sisters, but not much like one another,' Karen said. 'I've often wondered why you were so different, why you went away when mam stayed, and things like that.' Below them a dog was rolling in the grass in an ecstasy of freedom, and in the sky a kestrel hovered, beating its wings against the wind.

'There wasn't any special reason,' Helen said. 'We had different ideas about what we wanted out of life . . . and then your mam met your dad. I wasn't that lucky. But I think perhaps I was meant to go away. I've been very happy in London, achieved a lot of things I wanted. You'll go away, too, if you get your A-levels. Then you'll see what I mean.'

'I won't really leave Belgate, though. ' Karen's tone was emphatic. 'I want to come back and teach here . . . or in Darlasden. I don't think you ought to leave the place where you were born. You owe it something.' Her voice faltered a little as she realized what she was saying.

'Sometimes you can't help it,' Helen said. 'Things happen, and you have to go.'

'Was it a love affair?' Karen asked. 'Mam always reckons you got your heart broken at the Infirmary and you ran away to forget. She thinks it was one of the surgeons who was married, or something like that.'

'It wasn't anything so romantic,' Helen said.

'But was it a man . . . was it because of a man?'

Helen pulled her skirt over her knees to gain time. 'In a way it was. Because of a boy.'

'And is he still alive?'

This time Helen laughed. 'Yes, he's still alive. I'm not that old, Karen. Have mercy.'

'Well, why can't you and he get together? Does he still live here?'

In the distance Darlasden sprawled across the skyline. In one of its houses Michael was reading, or listening to music, or nursing his injured arm.

'He still lives here, Karen, but there's no chance of our getting together. I'm sorry, but this is real-life, and there are no happy endings.' Then, fearful that she had been too sombre, 'Well, that's not always true. You'll be happy . . .

like your mam. You'll marry some nice Durham guy, and boss him about, and have babies, and wind up a grandma.'

'And a headmistress,' Karen said. 'Don't forget the career . . . I'm more like you than you think, Auntie. Or so mam's always saying.'

'I've given you adjoining rooms,' Diana said cheerfully. 'Girls in this big room and Gary in this little one. And you can leave the doors open.'

It had been a hair-raising day, in spite of Helen's help in the afternoon and David's intervention after surgery. She lifted Gary's knapsack on to his bed, thinking longingly of the time when they would all be bedded down and she could just flop on the settee with a large drink, brandy for preference.

She let them all go off to the bathroom while she turned down the beds. She had put a rubber sheet on Gary's bed, as the social worker had suggested, and had covered it with a flannelette sheet for warmth. It was summer, but he was such a little boy. She turned down the twin beds in the girls' room, then went along the landing, but the bathroom door was locked.

'It's me,' she called, rattling the handle.

'What do you want?' Barbara's tone seemed hostile, and Diana felt suddenly guilty, like some old lecher trying to gain entry to a ladies' bath-house.

'Do you want any help? Be careful with the hot water . . .' The boy was little more than a toddler. She rattled the door handle again, and put her ear against the panel. She could hear only urgent female whispering and the sound of a running tap. 'Barbara! Let me in.'

'What for?' This time there was no mistaking the venom.

'Because I say so. Don't be silly. It's nearly nine o'clock, and you should all be in bed by now. Let me in, there's a good girl. I only want to help.'

There was no reply.

In the end Diana retreated downstairs to seek aid. 'They're locked in the bathroom,' she said dramatically

David half-smiled, but she could tell he was not amused. 'Locked in? As in "siege"?'

Diana realized she was wringing her hands, and tried to still them. 'No, don't be silly. But they won't let me in to help, and I'm worried about the little one. Barbara's a virago . . . God knows what she's doing to him in there. You'll have to go up.'

She expected him to reach for her hands and draw her close but he did not. 'Diana, those kids have been fending for themselves for several years. They probably quite like it by now, or they're so used to it that they can't imagine anything else. You can't come into their lives and be an instant mother, it won't work. Now pour yourself a large G. and T., and sit down. I'll go up in a minute and see what's what. In the meantime, stop flapping.'

Diana poured herself a drink but she felt no calmer. In fact his attitude had angered her, putting all the blame on to her as it did. She wanted to lash back at him and the words came easily. 'Well, I'm glad one of us is calm, David. But I have to point out that I was never full of optimism about this venture, and now that it's upon me I feel even less hopeful. Barbara's not a child, she's a geriatric harpy and Tracy is just her side-kick. I might as well be honest and say I don't like them.'

'But you do like Gary? Well, one out of three's not bad for a first day,' David said. His mouth smiled, but his eyes were angry. Diana sought a riposte but none would come. Instead she sipped her drink and thought how impossible doctors were as husbands and how nice it would be to be married to an ordinary, irrational, unqualified, but immensely sympathetic layman. When she'd emptied her glass she went out to the kitchen and attacked the potatoes and carrots until David appeared to summon her upstairs.

'Have a look at that,' he said. The children were all in one bed, the boy sprawled on his back in the middle, the girls clinging to an inch or two of mattress on either side. Barbara's arm was protectively around the others, and her mouth hung open in an O of exhaustion. 'Should we move them?' David said, but Diana shook her head.

'She's probably got the bed booby-trapped. Better leave well alone.'

Edward looked out on the London night while, behind him in the bedroom, Sylvia got on with the business of undressing. They had fallen easily into the old routine of sleeping at one home or another, and tonight they were in the Mews. He looked at the flat opposite, which had been empty now for four months. Today the joiner had vacated the workshop below it, and when the adjoining workshop closed next week the two buildings would be demolished to make way for flats. 'It's progress,' the estate agent had said, but to Edward it was one more break in the Mews' defences. If only Maria were still here – but she was lying in a hospital bed, oblivious of the life to which she clung. Twice he had been summoned by a sister to be there at her final hour, and twice she had proved them wrong.

He twitched the curtains into place and turned back into the room. Sylvia stood naked, arms above her head as she pinned up her hair for the shower. She saw his eyes on her and smiled. 'Do I pass?'

He nodded. 'Nine out of ten.'

She pouted. 'Only nine? Where did I lose a mark?' He pursed his lips and pondered. 'The neck? The shoulders?' He closed his eyes briefly as though seeking inspiration and then shrugged to indicate surrender. 'Maybe ten out of ten.'

Sylvia was beautiful and she knew it. But he wondered about what she would do when she no longer merited top marks, when the tilted breasts drooped and the taut belly sagged, when arms wrinkled and neck crêped. How would she cope? It wouldn't matter to him: there was beauty in a woman in all her seasons, as his mother and Maria had proved.

He pulled off socks and underpants and moved towards her, matching her thigh for thigh, belly for belly, feeling her breasts jutting against his flesh. He cupped her buttocks in his hands and squeezed. 'You're getting fat.'

Sylvia was confident enough to laugh, and he moved his

hands to the hollow of her spine. 'Let's shower,' she said, eager to get on with the process of loving.

They soaped and lathered and teased and kissed, putting off the climax of their loving for as long as it could be borne. He was sure of himself now, sure as he had never been in those early years, when it had been Sylvia who dictated, who led the way. He had been the novice, then, and glad to follow. But he had learned from the relationships that came afterwards, and now there was no need for her to guide, to provoke, to demand. He set his own pace and in the end it was he who gathered her, wet and slippery, into his arms and then to bed.

## 24

'Yes, you can laugh, Helen, but it's not so funny for me. I see that determined little face and my backbone turns to jelly. She honestly is a monster!'

Helen held out a filled coffee cup. 'A vixen in defence of her young?'

Diana took the cup. 'Thanks. Well, she perhaps may be, but I'm not trying to hurt her precious brood – anything but. She shouldn't be behaving like a little old woman, protective or not. She's an eight-year-old child. When I think of her coming again, I positively quiver!'

They were sitting in Helen's flat, looking down on the street below. 'I used to think I liked children,' Diana continued; 'well, I do like Gary and Tracy. But the Gorgon . . . I refuse to call Barbara a child . . . the Gorgon has convinced me I'm a potential child batterer.'

Helen smiled. 'Cheer up, she'll probably improve with time.'

Diana was looking around the room, changing the subject. 'You've accumulated some marvellous furniture. Did you have it in store, or something?'

Helen shook her head. 'No, I bought all this in sales around here. It's Victorian, not particularly valuable. That's a Dutch piece, that commode, late nineteenth-century . . . and these chairs are German.'

'How can you tell?' Diana asked wonderingly. 'They look really English to me, carved oak, wing backs . . .'

'It used to be my job, you know – I did fifteen years in the antique trade. You pick things up. I specialized in dolls eventually, and automata. I had . . . have . . . a marvellous boss, a friend really, who'd grown up in it and he taught me all I know. I hope you'll meet him eventually. He says he's going to visit me up here.'

'Is that who you see when you go to London?'

'Yes. I have other friends there, but he's the most important. I must go again soon.'

'You should meet my big brother when you next go down.' Diana's eyes were wide with significance. 'I'm prejudiced, but he really is nice. He's thirty-nine, divorced, six foot two. He's a civil engineer, and has been a bit of a lad in his day. I think he wants to settle down now, and you might be good for him. He worries about his kids.'

'Does he see much of them?'

'No, not as much as he'd like. Their mother married the man she ran off with and they now live in the States. Vic travels a lot, he's a kind of trouble-shooter, and she plays the usual game of withholding access unless he ups the ante. I feel sorry for him sometimes . . . when I'm not feeling sorry for myself at the thought of the Gorgon coming back. Why couldn't I get a nice, docile adoptee like Michael? David says you made a hit with him when he broke his arm?'

Helen felt the cup and saucer tremble and put them carefully down on the table. 'He seems a nice kid. What's his sister like?'

'Well, I like her, a lot. But she can be a handful. Nothing like our darling Barbara, but I've seen her throw a tantrum or two. Anne seems to bring the worst out in Susan.'

'But not in the boy?' Helen had tried to keep her voice nonchalant but it sounded strained.

'No, not the boy, not His Holiness. Anne can see the puffs of white smoke for Michael. I find it all a bit chilling, but David says it's none of our business.'

'Does he want to enter the priesthood? He's still very young, and boys of his age change their mind a dozen times.'

'It's hard to explain about Anne. I loathe her, frankly, but when it comes to saying why, I don't know. She gives to charity, she works for her church, I couldn't tell you one thing she's done wrong. She's never beaten the children, or put obvious pressure on them. But I know Michael would no more turn his back on her plans for him than on life itself.'

'What about his father?' Helen asked.

Diana shrugged. 'Oh, Howard is all right. He loves the children, but he'd never stand up to Anne. He's too goody-goody for words, not a bit like David . . .'

She giggled then, realizing what she'd said, and Helen laughed too, hoping her smiling face hid her unease.


Edward smiled at the retreating customer, and then turned back into the shop. The Edwardian seven-piece suite had only been in for forty-eight hours – that was the way to do business.

He sat down at his desk and began to open the morning's mail. The first one was from Malkin and Hope, the developers who had been after the shop and flat for years. They had now upped their offer to £250,000. His was almost the last remaining single-purpose unit. The developers owned the buildings on either side of him, so he was holding up progress. They said it nicely, but they said it just the same. It was time to take advice.

He reached for the phone and dialled. 'Philip . . . Edward Portillo here. Yes, long time no see. I was going to give you a ring anyway but something's come up . . .'

He was arranging to meet Philip when he saw the familiar envelope bearing Helen's handwriting. They talked often on the phone, but she seldom wrote. He fixed a meeting with Philip and cut short the conversation as politely as he could, before tearing open the envelope.

'Dear Edward . . .' She was well and thinking of him. 'I miss London and especially you, but I realize now that I have to stay here for the foreseeable future. Could you be an angel and arrange a tenant for my flat? Give it to whoever you think best. As for the business, I can't bear to think of you having any partner other than me, but I realize I can't be a dog in the manger. You've been very, very good to me, Edward, and I trust you completely. Make arrangements to dissolve the partnership on whatever basis you think fair. I can't keep taking a cut for something to which I contribute so little . . . I know you'll say "wait", but it isn't fair to you and I feel guilty. I'm writing this because you'd talk me out of it if I told you on the phone.'

Edward knew instantly that he couldn't sever the link. It was inconvenient managing without Helen, but he would have to do it somehow, or else employ temporary help. He sat for a moment trying to analyse his feelings: Helen had walked off a train and into the vacuum left by his mother's departure, and she was an indispensable part of his life now. Not just of his business – of his life. She was his friend.

He was planning to go north and argue with her when the phone rang. 'No, I'm sorry, Miss Clark is not here at the moment. I'm Edward Portillo, her partner. Can I help?' He listened as the dealer on the other end gave details of a doll collection coming up for sale in Manchester. 'I can get it for two-five, probably. It's worth four thou at least – but if she's not there . . .'

'We'll take it,' Edward said firmly. 'You say, it's Franz Schmidt and Pierrolli mostly, but at least one Bru . . . and the Kammer and Reinhardt is marked? Good. Two googlys . . . well, are they Heubachs or not?'

When he put down the phone he sat regarding it solemnly. The call had been an omen. He would keep Helen as a partner, and if dolls were the way to do it he would build the biggest bloody doll collection in Europe.


'And my client asks me to point out that further correspondence in this matter will be mutually wasteful. Yours sincerely etc, etc.' Howard sighed and closed the folder on his desk. On the other side Mrs Fraser's pen moved over her notebook. 'That's all, I think,' Howard said. 'No hurry for them today . . . why don't you go off at lunch-time? Your sons are home for the weekend, aren't they?'

Mrs Fraser closed her book and put her pen into the coiled wire along the top. 'Yes. It's lovely when they come home again.'

Howard nodded and smiled, pushing back his chair to stand up. 'I can imagine. All the more reason for you to go off, then. The girls can manage here.' Did her eyes flicker at that, or was it just his own guilty conscience?

'Thank you. That would be nice.' That was all she said – so why did he wonder all the time, trying to guess what was going on in her mind? She put her head round the door a little later to say goodbye, and he waved from the window, where he had been looking down on the Friday shoppers. 'Have a good weekend.'

Mrs Fraser had hardly shut the door when it opened again. Yvonne's face was thunderous. 'Why has she gone home?'

Howard tried to sound decisive. 'Because I said so. Her sons are coming up this weekend.' Yvonne was shifting her buttock on to the corner of his desk, the yellow skirt stretching across her black-nyloned thigh. 'And I suppose I've got to do her work, just because I'm young and I haven't got a son!' She looked down at her nails for a moment and then, cocking her head on one side, she looked up and held his eye. 'Well?'

'What do you mean? What do you expect me to say? I've given my secretary an afternoon off, Yvonne – don't turn it into World War Three. You can have a day off next week, if you want one. Fix it up with Mrs Fraser . . .'

Yvonne swung her legs to the floor. 'No, thank you. I'm not kow-towing to that bitch, not even for a week off. You can stuff your day off – just don't expect me to be at your beck and call when you feel like it. I'm being made use of, don't say I'm not. If I asked anyone, they would say it was true.' There was a terrible whining note in her voice, like a drill.

Howard felt anger rise up in him and his hands came together, fist against palm, with an audible thwack. 'Please yourself, Yvonne. I've done it now . . . she's gone. If you go on about it for the rest of the day we can't change anything.'

The force with which she slammed the door sent the papers rippling from his desk to the floor. He bent to pick them up, and then went down on his knees for them. It was getting out of hand. Slowly but surely his lust for Yvonne had ebbed, leaving only revulsion. How could he have been such a fool? And how was he ever going to bring it to an end?

'There now, get that inside you.'

Billy eyed the mince and dumplings Lilian had plonked in front of him and picked up his knife and fork. 'I love your dumplings, Lil . . . Lilian. They're ower stodgy in the canteen, real lead shot – but yours are like feathers. Crunchy feathers.' She ladled peas and carrots and chips on to his plate, and then sat down opposite him.

'So it's put you in a good mood then?'

Billy looked up, mouth full, eyes suddenly wary. 'What's up?'

She waved an imperious hand. 'Keep eating. Let your meat stop your mouth and I might tell you.' She kept him waiting as long as she could bear to stay silent and then she launched into her tale. 'Well, I've been thinking. I've been thinking about our Helen, if you must know. Waltzing back here and into a good job, buying this and that for herself, furnishing a flat front to back, just like that. What's she got that I haven't got? I'll tell you . . .'

'She's got O-levels,' Billy said, chewing. 'Qualifications. That's where we went wrong, Lily – not sticking in at school.'

'Speak for yourself, Billy Fenwick. I could've gone right to the top if I hadn't been needed to go out to work. It was my wage packet that let her stop on for her precious O-levels, don't forget that. Anyway, I wish you'd let me get on with my story. What has our Helen got that I haven't got? A wage, that's what she's got. So, I've done something about it. And before I speak, it's no good you harping on about it, Billy, because I've done it. I've got a job.'

For a moment Billy's knife and fork ceased motion and then he cut into a dumpling with exquisite precision. 'Where?'

Lilian shifted in the chair, crossing her arms under her breast. 'Greenwood's.'

'The fishy? You're going to work down the fishy?' His eyes were bright with amusement.

'Yes, the fishy, Billy. If I've got to stand over a stove all day I might as well be paid for it. I've been doing it for nowt for twenty years. And I'm going to be a fryer, not a counter hand. Now, if you'll eat that dumpling before it goes solid I'll fetch your rhubarb and custard.'

She turned at the stove. 'And before you get any ideas, Billy, my pay is my pay. Catch me paying all the bills out of me wages, like some round here.'

He was still bemused but there was a gleam in his eye she didn't like. 'What's that for Billy, that Cheshire Cat grin?'

'Nothing, Lil-ian. I was just thinking, if we have a bit more money coming in I could take the odd rest day now and then.'

'Rest day! Your life's one long rest day, my son.' She made a big yellow island in a sea of rhubarb and carried it to the table. 'Our Helen coming back has a chance to have changed my life, Billy. The worm has turned . . . from now on it's Number One all the way!'


Diana lifted the cucumber from her eyelids and peeped at the clock: five to four. Any time now the car would draw up at the door. She tried to quell her rising panic. Even if you combined their ages they were less than half her age. Their combined weights would be less than hers. She had twice the reach of Barbara, and had done a few karate classes at the village hall. So why was she scared?

'Because I'm afraid they don't like me,' she thought, the cucumber grown warm and useless on her lids. She stood up and walked into the bathroom, making a face at herself in the mirror above the basin. 'Eeny, meeny, miney mo, shall I stay or shall I go?' She rinsed hands and face and went down to welcome them. There were only a few more visiting weekends left, and then it was crunch time, the decision on whether or not to adopt. 'I can't do it,' she thought, 'but I haven't the guts to tell David!'

Resentment stirred as she thought of David's euphoria with his new brood, and then gave way to panic again as the car drew up at the door.

'He hasn't been well,' Tracy announced as they climbed out.

'He's all right,' Barbara said, pushing past Diana with Gary in tow. Lupi, the black labrador, was in the doorway, tail threshing, and the children fell on him with cries of glee.

'Hallo Diana,' she said aloud, addressing herself. 'Nice to see you Diana. We are pleased you're here, Diana. Just make the tea, wash up, cook, clean . . . thank you very much, Diana, three bags full, Diana.'

David's smile had not left his face since he got out of the car, carrying their bag over his shoulder, watching the children fuss over the dog. 'You know what it means when you talk to yourself,' he said, grinning fatuously at the group in the doorway.

'It means I'm mad,' Diana said. 'Well, I've known that for long enough. Seriously, doctor, if I'm psychotic, am I fit to be a mother?'

David leaned to kiss her brow. 'You will make the most wonderful mother in the history of the human race.'

'He won't take me seriously,' she thought as she followed him into the house. 'He wants this so much he won't let himself admit to any snags.'

Gary's eyes were wary as he stood in the hall, and Diana felt a shaft of fellow-feeling. 'He's scared too,' she thought and would have helped him off with his coat if Barbara had not been there before her.

'Who's hungry?' she asked, thinking of the carefully prepared meal all ready in the kitchen.

'Can we have sausages and beans?' Tracy asked.

'That's what we'd've got if we hadn't *had* to come here,' Barbara added, with emphasis on the word 'had'.

'I expect we can manage sausage and beans,' David said, looking appealingly at his wife.

Diana thought of the salad and egg mayonnaise, the wholemeal bread and butter, the ham cornettes she had spent hours rolling just to please them, and she decided to rebel. But Barbara's eyes were on her, expectant. 'She *wants* me to say no,' Diana thought. 'That's what she expects me to do. Well, I won't give her the satisfaction!'

'Sausage and beans it is,' she said, and swept into the kitchen.

Edward tossed the green salad while Sylvia chopped nuts and combined them in vinaigrette with grated carrot. 'Nice,' he said, sampling a spoonful. They carried the chicken and salad through to the dining-table and Edward poured the wine.

'Mmm, good,' Sylvia said. 'Was it expensive?'

'Not really . . . anyway, I'm feeling rich today. They've raised the offer for the premises.'

'How much?' Sylvia said, eyes widening. He told her what the letter had said and then refilled their glasses. 'I'm going to talk to a schoolfriend of mine, who's in property. I admit the sum is tempting . . . but when you think about the cost of starting again, it puts things into perspective.'

'But would you need to re-establish, Edward? You could invest all that money . . . and then you could dabble. What is it you call it, buy and sell on? You wouldn't need premises. And you could do something else entirely if you wanted to . . . anything that appealed. I could speak to my father . . .'

Edward smiled. 'No thank you, I don't want your father to be accused of nepotism . . . besides, I don't think I'm cut out for stockbroking.'

'I didn't mean you to actually work for him, but perhaps he could make suggestions. Don't you ever get sick of all the dust and the woodworm down there, and those two dreadful black boys at the foot of the stairs? Their eyes roll in the most disgusting fashion. I'd've thought you'd've been glad to get away from it. What would you get if you sold up the business?'

'As a going concern? And without the property? Fifty thou probably . . . but remember half of that is Helen's.'

Sylvia's voice sharpened. 'Half? But she hasn't been here five minutes, not in the real sense – it's an old-established family business. She can't be entitled to fifty per cent.'

'Well, I'm afraid she's an equal partner, so that's the way it would be. Anyway, this is an excellent wine and the food looks good and I can think of better things for us to do than to nit-pick over who owns what.' He had put on a Nat King Cole LP. '*Unforgettable, in every way* . . .'

'Do we have to have Cole?' Sylvia said. 'It always depresses me to think he died of cancer. You can hear it in his voice. Put *Evita* on: I love that show.'

Edward changed the record and tried to quell his sense of irritation by concentrating on the beautiful woman opposite, whom he would undoubtedly take to his bed before the night was over.


After the first hour the sweat had ceased to run down into Lilian's eyes, but her hair felt full of grease and her finger ends burned from pinching the chips to see if they were done. She was spooning batter out of the fryer into one of the heated compartments when she saw Billy there in the queue, as bold as brass.

She rattled the dredging spoon against the side of the vat, hoping to attract his eye, but his gaze was fixed on the piles of haddock and cod, jumbo sausages and corned-beef patties. The greedy bugger, he'd be expecting a buckshee supper! She moved round the side of the fryer and advanced to the counter. 'I'll deal with this one, Elsie.' She hooked a finger and drew him to the back of the queue.

'What are you doing here, Billy Fenwick?'

'I've come for me supper, Lily . . . seeing as you're not in to cook anything.'

'It's not two hours since you had a plate like Mount Vesuvius. Have you got a tape-worm?'

'I'm famished, Lily . . . that was me dinner, you know. It's supper-time now.'

'Supper-time? OK, Billy, I'll get you your supper.'

There had been a nasty little fillet among the fish, no bigger than a large sardine. She had battered and fried it, intending to put it in with a lot for someone she liked. Now she raked through the fish till she found it and placed it carefully on a greaseproof square. She took a scoop of chips and then knocked it against the side of the vat till half had fallen off. 'Salt and vinegar?' she enquired sweetly, and when he nodded she applied them generously.

'There,' she said, 'that'll be forty-five pence, please.'

She couldn't be sure which was best, the look on his face when he saw the size of the parcel, or his astonishment at having to fork out for it.

All in all, she was having a bloody good night.


It was the first time in her life that Helen had stolen anything, but she felt no shame. She held the photograph of Michael in her hand and looked at it, Michael squinting into sunlight, smiling. It was just one more snap to Diana; to her it was a lasting image of her son. Tonight he had come to evening surgery, complaining that his plaster cast was itchy inside. They had stood and joked, the counter between them, and she had watched his smile become more relaxed with each exchange, until David had appeared in the waiting-room to carry his nephew away.

She placed the snapshot in an envelope and put it into a drawer. It was still light outside, a lovely summer night. In London Edward was probably out with Sylvia . . . or in with her. She had never really liked Sylvia, all those years ago, but perhaps she had mellowed. As long as she made Edward happy, that was the only important thing. Helen closed her eyes and tried to summon up the shop, seeing the familiar objects, the things Edward would never part with . . . Mark and Antony holding their blistered torches, the gilt-gesso mirror on the far wall, the serpentine desk with its jumble of papers going back over the years. Every week Edward vowed to tidy them. Perhaps he never would, and one day someone would sort them and declare them a valuable archive.

She felt a sudden yearning for London, for Edward, for the life she had enjoyed. What good was she doing here? She was friends with Michael now, but not foolish enough to believe that he thought of her for a second once she had passed from his sight. He was being pushed towards the priesthood by a mother who was fanatical about her religion, but he wasn't really unhappy: no one could say that. Anne had brought him up . . . perhaps she knew him better than anyone else? But in her heart Helen felt that was just looking for an excuse for her own impotence, her inability to change the situation now, after all the years.

Perhaps Susan was the key? After all, it was Susan's anguish that had brought her back. Perhaps she should try to get close to Susan? Diana was suggestible . . . if she expressed a desire to meet Susan, it would be arranged. Helen was suddenly filled with resolution. She had come back to Durham because there was a possibility that Michael needed her, and she could not leave until she was sure that he did not.

She reached for a knitted jacket and let herself out into the warm dusk. She would walk for a while before bed, and tomorrow she would manoeuvre Diana into introducing her to Susan.


Howard made a show of eating, but the food was pallid and besides he had no appetite. He hated these evening meals unless the children were there. It felt like being in the dock, with Anne sitting at the opposite end of the table in judgement. He looked up and met her eyes, those dark, opaque, unfathomable eyes.

'You didn't go out tonight?'

Her question startled him. 'No, not tonight. I've had a lot of business meetings in the evenings lately, and it's good to have a night in.'

She was smiling and he felt sweat prickle along his upper lip. She knew. Any moment she would say, 'Come off it, Howard, I know about your "business meetings". I know

311

about the writhings, the couplings, the cheap lipstick smeared on the stubble on your face, the odour on you . . . the odour of sin.'

He found he had put his clenched fist to his mouth, and looked anxiously across the table, but Anne had returned to eating and his eyes encountered only the gleaming blackness of her downbent head, the parting white down the centre, leading to the coil knotted behind. He had dreamed once of uncoiling that hair, of letting it fall about her shoulders like a cloud, of lying in her arms, laughing with her, sharing, loving. If only it could have been like that.

He put his knife and fork neatly together and dabbed his lips. 'It was very nice, but I think I'm a little under the weather.' Anne frowned concern, and for a second their eyes met – but there was no real caring there. There was nothing at all.

What had come between them? Sex – her aversion and his incompetence? Or God? Anne had given herself to her religion in a way she never could give herself to him or to any man. But he had found other Catholics to be loving people in the main, warm and outgoing. Why was something that was so enriching in others so desiccating in her? Was it a true religion that could cut Anne off so from her husband and children? From everyone, really, for she had no close friends.

'There's summer pudding . . . do you want some?' She might have been a *maître d'hôtel* and he a regular customer.

'No, thank you. I think I'll take a walk round the garden and then turn in. Can I help clear the table?' It was a ritual question and received its ritual refusal. He went out into the garden, and as the stars appeared one by one in the marbled sky he gave himself up to grief.

## 25

'Lily . . . Lily, pet!' She could hear the voice pulling her out of the depths of sleep and she rolled on her face to shut it out. 'Come on, Lily, man . . . I should be in the cage by now. Take this tea.' She let go of the delicious half-remembered dream of Roger Moore and struggled on to one elbow.

'Put it on the cabinet, Billy. Use a bit of gumption. You wake a body out of a sound sleep and expect them to jump into action . . . anyway, what time is it?'

It was time Billy was off to the pit and he gave her a hasty kiss and hurtled down the stairs. Lilian sipped the hot sweet tea and snuggled down for a further five minutes. Since she started at the fishy she'd been feeling tired, although it didn't pay to admit it and have them all saying she should give up work. She had such plans for the house, new carpets and curtains first, and then the big stuff. A new bed for a start, so they didn't roll together in the middle. Thinking of rolling together reminded her of her pill and she groped with one hand in the drawer of the bedside cabinet, only then remembering that she had taken the last one yesterday and had meant to go for a repeat prescription.

It was a good job Billy was showing his age and not at it every night, like at the beginning. Still, she would go to the surgery on the way home from Darlasden. She switched on the radio for a time check: if she didn't wake Karen, the girl would sleep all day. But the announcer gave her five precious minutes more. Karen was a lazy young 'un, but she hadn't been a bit of trouble and please God she'd get safely married before long.

Lilian seldom allowed herself to remember the other child, the little girl Diana, but now she thought of what might have been: two of them in the next-door room, two to give her lip, two to hug her when she was down. She

had never cried much, for Billy's sake, but at times like this
. . . she turned into the pillow and cried until it was time
to get out of bed and wake her daughter.

'Karen! Have you left school? 'Cos if you haven't, you're
giving a good imitation . . .'


Edward started to unpack the dolls as soon as he came
down. They had arrived last night, well packed, just as he
and Sylvia had been on their way out to *Evita*. When they
got back they had both been tired, so the pleasure of seeing
the collection had had to wait. It was all that the dealer had
promised . . . and more. There were two Bru . . . he wasn't
as expert as Helen but even he could recognize a Bru.

He was repacking them temporarily when Sylvia came
downstairs, still in the robe that just skimmed her buttocks
and threatened to come asunder in the front. 'Watch it,' he
said. 'We'll have a crowd at the window if you're not
careful.'

She waggled her hips and handed him one of the two
mugs she carried. 'It could be good for business.'

'Thanks,' he said, sipping the coffee gratefully.

She was looking at the dolls, her brow wrinkling at the
sight of so many. 'God, Edward, they're awful. Look at the
mean little faces and the glittery eyes . . . that one's got a
finger missing.'

He picked up the doll and settled its faded petticoats.
'That, my dear girl, is a Bru and worth quite a lot, missing
finger or no missing finger.'

'It's not your kind of thing, though, Edward. Furniture,
yes . . . but this is little girls' stuff, surely?'

He knew she was getting at Helen and he felt his hackles
rise. 'It's a valuable part of the business, Sylvia. I don't
turn my nose up at honest profit. Besides, I think they're
rather splendid.'

He put the remaining dolls back in the crate and pushed
it against the wall. 'I thought you had an interview this
morning?' For some reason he couldn't fathom he wanted
Sylvia out of the shop. The sight of the long bare thighs
was annoying him . . . which, after last night, was strange.

'I have, but it's not till eleven. I've just put the heater on for a bath . . .'

He felt his tongue click against his teeth and had to school his face. 'I've told you, Sylvia, the water comes on automatically from six to nine. It's just gone off. There'll be gallons of boiling water . . .'

The telephone shrilling put an end to the conversation. 'Edward Portillo . . .'

It was the call he had been dreading. Maria Stepinska was deeply unconscious and suffering from a respiratory infection. 'Yes . . . I see. Should I come straight away?' He had seen her yesterday and known the end was near. 'I'll come in later today, then. Thank you.'

Sylvia had come up behind him and was sliding a hand between his arm and his side. He put down the phone. 'Not now, Sylvia,' he said.

She pulled a face. 'It'll be another false alarm,' she said. 'Why do you have to rush off like an errand boy?'

This time he let his irritation show. 'Because I damn well want to.'


Anne came down the stairs towards him, the pale blue silk suit setting off the sallowness of her face and neck, the glossy blackness of her hair. 'You look very nice,' Howard said. Her legs and arms were perfectly formed, the skin of her hands smooth, her nails pale unpolished ovals. She was putting on white gloves, her bag tucked under her arm.

'Do you think so? One is not quite sure what to wear for a Jubilee Lunch . . . I thought this might be appropriate.'

They drove to the Civic Centre through streets decked with bunting to celebrate the Queen's Jubilee. 'Everyone is making a fuss,' Anne said, idly surprised. 'It seems to have quite taken off.'

Howard nodded. 'I thought it would simply be the bonfires and one or two events in London, but the whole country seems keen to celebrate.'

It was the only exchange between them during the journey. They left the car in the Civic Centre car-park and

315

walked side by side through the imposing portals of the Mayor's Parlour, to be greeted by a Mayor and Mayoress burdened down by chains and sweating slightly in an under-ventilated room.

'Hallo, Howard . . . and Anne. Good to see you. You haven't been to Rotary lately, Howard – nothing wrong, I hope?'

He dared not look at Anne as he made his excuses and they moved on to the Deputy Mayor and other dignitaries. But he knew she would not refer to the Mayor's remark, or question where he had been if he was not at Rotary.

They took glasses from a waiter and moved together to a space in the crowded room. 'By the way,' Anne said. 'Have I told you I'm taking Michael to Yorkshire in the school holidays. We'll spend some time with mother and then go into retreat.'

'What about Susan?' Howard said, the stem of his glass brittle between his fingers.

'I rather thought you might see to Susan,' she answered, and turned her head to smile at a new arrival.


'This is nice, Lilian,' Helen said, when they were settled in a corner of Dembry's restaurant. 'Do you remember the day it opened and we had a snack . . .?' Too late she remembered Lilian, lumbering and six months pregnant with Diana. 'Sorry,' she said, 'does it hurt to be reminded?'

'No,' Lilian said. 'I was thinking about her only this morning. She'd be fifteen now . . . and a right handful.' She smiled a little tremulously and for a moment Helen was tempted to confess: *'I know how it feels, Lil,'* she could say. *'I know what it's like to lose a child.'* But the moment passed in a welter of choosing lunch, and afterwards she was glad.

'There's a lot of water gone under the bridge since Dembry's opened,' Lilian said as they ate their minestrone. 'Still, I don't have to buy everything on tick now . . . not now I'm working.'

'I've been meaning to ask how the job was going,' Helen said. 'Are you tempted to eat the chips?'

Lilian scraped the last spoon of soup and pushed her plate aside. 'I was the first day . . . not the chips but the batter. I was scrunching me way through that at the rate of knots . . . but after a while you get sick. I suppose it's the same with everything. Anyway, tell me about your job.'

They swapped news about the Whittingtons, Helen being careful to let Lilian have the edge, and then got on to their parents. 'You can see me dad's failing a bit. Me mam's not what she was but she's still wiry. I can see him going downhill bit by bit. He'd like to see you married, our Helen. He often says he'd like to see you settled like me.'

Helen smiled. 'I've told you before: find me another Billy. You don't realize what a jewel you've got there.'

Lilian tried to stay poker-faced. 'Who says I don't? Wait till we get into Menswear and see what I think of him then.'

'Where are we going first?' Helen asked as steak and kidney pudding and three veg. was replaced by apple crumble with fresh cream. But Lilian had not finished with sisterly advice. 'You want to think on about your age. You're what . . . thirty-three? Don't leave it too late to have bairns. They break your heart sometimes, but there's nothing like holding your own bairn in your arms, our Hel. You won't understand until you go through it – but don't leave it too late, that's all I say.'


'Thanks for being so understanding, Philip. And again, sorry about the short notice.' Edward had phoned Philip after the hospital's call and cancelled their planned lunch date to discuss the property developer's latest offer. 'I have to go to her, you see. I'm all she has in this part of the world.'

Philip had reassured him and told him to ring as soon as he had a free day. 'And don't worry, old chap. A property like yours can only appreciate.'

'Damn the property,' Edward thought, as he stepped into a cab. All he wanted was for the Mews to be as it had been twenty years ago, his mother installed on one side and Maria Stepinska on the other.

She lay in the high white bed, the sheet hardly rising and falling on her chest. 'Not long now, I think,' the sister said. 'I'll be sorry to lose her. She was quite a character.' He wanted to reach out and sob his gratitude, but all he said was, 'Yes – and you've been very kind to her. Thank you.'

He sat on throughout the afternoon, willing her eyes to open, for her to say just one word. He fancied she dreamed, for sometimes she whimpered slightly and once he could have sworn she smiled. She had seen two wars, she had loved a man and fled with him to freedom, she had survived and thrived on foreign soil . . . and all that life was reduced now to a small, fretful figure in an iron bed.

He tried to pray, but he was out of touch with God and nothing would come except, 'Please let it be all right.' They brought him tea in thick white cups, and he fancied he heard Maria's 'Tsk tsk' at the absence of porcelain. 'It might go on all night,' the sister said ruefully, a long while later. 'Are you sure you want to stay?'

She died at nine o'clock, as London began to quieten down and homing birds blew like leaves across the darkening sky. 'Sleep well, Maria,' Edward said, and went in search of a nurse. He had never seen anyone die before: now he knew that it was nothing more than the cessation of breath.

'You'll have to notify the Registrar . . . these are the opening hours. And could you possibly take her things? I know it seems awful, but we're so pushed for storage space . . . there's not much. You did say you were her executor, didn't you? There'll be arrangements to make.'

Edward walked for a while, down streets where lights turned rooms into goldfish bowls. In one a man and woman kissed, and then slid out of sight locked together. Maria would have liked that: 'Just a little bit wicked,' she would have said. He went on his way, smiling at how much of her he could remember.

\* \* \*

318

'Howard rang just before tea,' Diana said, when they had washed up and were settled in front of the television.

'What did he want?' David said.

'How do you know he wanted anything?' Diana asked.

'Because my brother isn't in the habit of making social calls, is he?'

Diana nodded. 'I suppose not. Well, it's all a bit odd. He says Anne is taking Michael to a monastery or something for a couple of weeks . . . well, a retreat . . . but she's not taking Susan, and he seems to be in a terrible flap about it. He wanted to know if we'd have her. I didn't say no, but I hummed and hahed. Well, you know what Susan can be like, and we'll have the kids here by then – I thought it might all be a bit much. I didn't say no, though, because I felt sorry for him . . . and sorry for Susan.'

'Don't pity her, it's young Michael you should be sorry for. My God, Anne's a bitch. She's never really cared about Susan, just her precious votive offering. That kid is a human sacrifice, or he will be – and we all sit around and let it happen.'

'You could try talking to Howard?' Diana said.

David grunted. 'Do you think I haven't tried? But he won't accept the responsibility of crossing Anne – I don't know why. I'd murder you for half . . .'

'Thank you,' Diana said.

'Well,' David said, 'you know what I mean. Howard's trying to offload Susan because he knows she's hell-bent on getting into trouble and he doesn't want the blame to land on him.'

'What are we going to do? I *could* make room for her, if I have to?'

David rubbed his forehead. 'We could ask Helen to take her . . . she's level-headed enough, and she was good with young Michael. Yes, why don't we ask her? And don't worry about our terrible trio . . . you'll cope!'

Diana smiled and nodded, but a bitter resentment was sour in her mouth, resentment at his taking her so much for granted. They had never fought, not in all their married years. Now it seemed to her that the children were spoiling everything.

\* \* \*

They had struggled back into their seats and Howard was in that uneasy post-coital state where he never knew what to talk about, when Yvonne spoke.

'Have you got a light?'

Howard pressed home the car lighter, and then held its glow against her cigarette. 'I've got something to tell you. I'm pregnant.'

She was opening Pandora's box, letting all the devils in the world loose.

'How do you know?' he asked, trying to keep the panic out of his voice, and in the darkness he saw her shrug.

'I just do. I've got all the signs.'

'But you can't be sure till you've seen a doctor?'

The cigarette glowed as she drew on it. 'I'm sure, all right. What do you want, a certificate?'

Howard tried to suppress his anger: he owed her that much. 'What are we going to do about it?'

Again she shrugged. 'It's up to me, I suppose.'

He was recovering his wits now. 'I thought you were on the Pill?'

'I was . . . but I forgot one day. One bloody day – and now this.'

If it came out, he would lose the children. They would never look at him again. For a moment Howard contemplated strangling Yvonne there in the car, in the dark, tipping her out amongst nettles and discarded Coke cans to lie in the lay-by till daylight. But that would be an even greater sin.

'I could get an abortion if I had the money.' A terrible cajoling note in her voice made his flesh creep, but there it was, the lifeline! Abortion . . . he thought of the strictures of the Church. He could burn in hell for that . . . or burn here on earth without it. Reluctantly he forced himself to reject the chance she'd given him.

'I hope it won't come to that, Yvonne. We can't be sure . . .'

She drew away to huddle against the door. 'Let's go home. If you're too mean to pay, I'll find someone else who will. Just start up and let's get out of here.'

'It's not that . . . I'll pay for anything that'll help you. But abortion is a sin . . .'

Her laugh cut the air with its harshness. 'And what's what we were doing five minutes back? I suppose that's holy? God, you've got some funny ideas.'

When she had come to work for him she had spoken carefully, with just enough of Durham in her voice to make it attractive. Now she sounded like a creature of the gutter. He drove on through the night, acknowledging that sins always had to be paid for. His day of reckoning was upon him.

'I'm so sorry about Maria, Edward. I know how you must be feeling.' At the other end of the line Helen sounded forlorn.

'I'll survive,' Edward said. 'Anyway, how are you?' He listened as she brought him up to date. 'So you're not much further forward? Well, here's something to cheer you up. You are now the proud owner of the Doubleday collection . . . yes, *that* Doubleday. He died six weeks ago, and his widow sold to a local man. He rang you, and I jumped at it on your behalf. They're quite something . . . when are you coming to look at them?'

He listened as she outlined again all the good reasons why he ought to dissolve their partnership. 'But I don't want to do it, Helen. I can't see a single thing to be gained for either of us. Let's look at the worst, the most extreme, possibility – that you stay there until Michael is a grown man. That's six, seven years. I can wait that long. But something may happen much sooner – he could decide to make his own decisions any day now. All mothers map out their children's lives – didn't yours? I was going to be a barrister, according to my mother. She never wanted me in the business . . . but in the end she accepted that I knew my own mind.'

Helen was struggling to explain that this was different, Anne was different, but she had nothing concrete to go on.

'Look, I'm not putting pressure on you to come back; you can stay as long as you like . . . as long as it needs.

Why don't we just leave it for now? I've got Maria's affairs to see to; you have your hands full up there. Nothing is spoiling for the time being.'

When she rang off he poured himself a stiff drink and carried it through to the kitchen. He hadn't eaten all day, but the fridge held nothing that appealed. He looked at his watch: eleven-thirty. As if on cue, the phone rang.

'Hallo Edward, you're back. I've been ringing all day. How is she?'

'She's dead, Sylvia. She died at about nine o'clock. I've just got back from the hospital.'

'I'll come over, shall I?'

Edward was filled with panic at the thought of what she would expect if she came. 'If you don't mind, I'd rather just turn in. It's been a hell of a day . . . no, honestly, it's kind of you, Sylvia, but I'd be lousy company.'

If Helen had offered to come he would have welcomed her. And yet he loved Sylvia, or thought he did. He certainly enjoyed making love with her. Not to her, but with her: there was a difference. He found a wholemeal roll in the breadbin and sawed through it with the bread-knife. Butter and the remains of Sunday's beef . . . it tasted foul and he left half of it on the plate.

On the television a man and woman in evening dress were singing their hearts out. Richard Tauber songs: his mother had loved Tauber. *'Is it well, who can tell . . . I'm a man and kiss them when I can.'* Edward watched the singers until they made their bow and were replaced by a picture of the Queen accompanied by the National Anthem.

It was a time of Jubilee, but not of jubilation . . . at least, not for him. He sat on until the picture receded to a white dot and then the screen shimmered in a storm of dots, fading to be replaced by an unbearable whine that finally drove him to bed.

# 26

It was strange to be quite alone together in the house, for the first time since Karen was born. She was staying with a friend in Darlasden. 'Do you think she'll be all right?' Lilian asked, turning in the bed and sliding her arm around Billy's waist.

"Course she will . . . she's a good lass,' he said, patting his wife's hand.

His touch was reassuring at first, and she sensed the very moment when it became something more. If she turned away now, it would be all right. He would subside and in a minute they could both get up and get on with the day. But the bed was warm and his back was solid and comforting against her cheek. She lay still while the patting turned to stroking and proceeded further up her arm. She lay still when he turned clumsily and slid one arm under her head.

'I love you, Lily.'

'So you say.'

'I do, Lil. I'm not good with words, you know that, but I think the world of you and the bairn.'

'You're full of soft soap, Billy Fenwick.'

'You love me though, don't you, pet?'

'If I do I must be mad.' Under her hand his back was muscled with work in the pit, work for her and the bairn. She felt ridiculous tears prick her eyes and bit the inside of her cheek. He would think something was up if he saw her going soft.

'Should we get up now, Lily?' He was pleading, and she felt her lips twitch.

'We should.'

'Yes, but shall we?'

'Please yourself.'

'I love you, Lily.'

'Well, get on with it then, you daft ha'porth.'

There might be greater lovers in the world, she thought, as he caressed her breasts with trembling fingers, but she would keep the one she had, thank you very much.

Helen had agreed to take Susan in as soon as Diana had suggested it. It had seemed like the answer to prayer. Now, waiting for Howard to deliver his daughter, she was less sure. Susan was, by all accounts, a handful and what did she, Helen, know about teenagers? Precisely nothing! There was another complicating factor, her own guilt at making use of Susan to get nearer to Michael. If only he could have been coming here instead. Still, at least they could talk about him, if she watched her tongue. Then she might find out what lay behind Anne's taking him to Yorkshire.

She flicked through the radio waves but since news of Elvis Presley's death there seemed to be nothing but 'Heartbreak Hotel' or 'Wooden Heart'. She stooped to select an LP, remembering when she had been a teenager and Elvis Presley the sulkily smiling boy of her dreams. Time was not kind.

She fussed about her appearance, anxious to make a good impression but unsure of who she wanted to impress. Did she wear jeans and T-shirt for Susan, or a governess-type skirt and blouse for Howard? She settled for a denim skirt and white cotton sweater, and sat down to await their arrival, her foot tapping to 'Hound Dog'.

She had seen Howard at a distance, an erect, rather handsome figure, always conservatively dressed and usually unsmiling. His appearance today, at close quarters, shocked her. There were circles beneath his eyes and flesh hung slack under his chin. He couldn't be more than forty-five, and he looked seventy.

'This is very good of you, Helen,' he said. 'I'm out such a lot you see . . . and my wife is visiting her parents in Yorkshire.' His eyes dropped as her own gaze flicked to Susan's slouching form. Her head was downcast as though in despair, and her hair needed combing. Why hadn't the mother taken both her children?

324

'I'm looking forward to your being here, Susan. I get lonely sometimes . . . you'll be good for me.' A spark glowed in the girl's sullen expression but was extinguished as quickly as it appeared.

Howard's mouth moved slightly and then he turned to his daughter. 'Be good, darling. And ring me.' He turned back to Helen. 'You know where to find me? My secretary . . . if it had been term-time we could have managed . . . but my hours are long. I think my sister-in-law spoke about expenses . . .'

They chatted for a few moments and then waved him off. 'Come on,' Helen said. 'Let's have coffee and get acquainted.'

She put an arm around the girl's thin shoulders to shepherd her indoors, but there was no response, only an infinitesimal shudder, whether of pleasure or revulsion Helen could not work out.


The instructions in Maria's will had been specific. She was to be buried in consecrated ground next to her Stephan, after a service in an Anglican church. It was all there, down to the hymns: 'The King of Love' and 'The Lord's my Shepherd'. It had not been easy to arrange but Edward had done it. Now he sat in the front pew, looking at the coffin with its single wreath. Beside him the solicitor mumbled his words, obviously unused to singing in church.

Sylvia had offered to come, but he could see she was only doing it to please and it was easy to turn down her suggestion. All the same, it would have been nice to have company. He felt uneasy about this so-English ceremony, even though it had been Maria's wish. She had been an exotic foreign flower; he was burying her like an English rose, in a church of another faith, in the country she had loved so much. He walked out behind her coffin, remembering the glittering eyes, the wide mouth, the teeth so often stained with lipstick . . . the generosity of her spirit. In the graveyard he stood with bowed head and then cast down a handful of English earth, thinking as he did so that it was an appropriate touch. Somewhere, beneath a layer of clay, Stephan was sleeping too: at least they would be together. He smiled as he turned away. Whatever Heaven they inhabited now, he hoped a little wickedness was allowed.

He walked the solicitor to his Rover. 'You'll come in tomorrow, then, and we can sort things out?'

Edward nodded. 'I thought her Scottish cousins might have made the effort to come – I sent telegrams and then letters, but I've had no response.'

'One of them is dead . . . the man. I heard from his daughter yesterday. And the woman is too old to travel. I expect she was here in spirit. Of course, latterly they weren't close. You were her prop and stay, she told me that several times.'

Edward stood for a moment, watching the departing car, then he turned towards his own.


Once or twice Helen glanced sideways and met Susan's eyes, bright with curiosity. 'She's enjoying this,' she thought and was glad.

'When does your thing come up?' the girl whispered, and Helen handed her the catalogue, pointing to '*Lot 141. Pair carved oak and upholstered wing armchairs.*'

'Why do you want them?'

Helen put her head closer. 'Wait till I've got them, and then I'll tell you everything, OK?'

Susan nodded and turned back to the rostrum. Lot 139 came up, and bidding was sluggish. Helen ran her tongue over her upper lip, speculating. It was a late George Second or early Third oak cabinet, with a fallfront, heavily damaged. If it went cheaply enough . . .

'Three hundred pounds,' she called out, and felt Susan tense beside her. A few moments and £50 later, the bureau was hers. The chairs started at £100 and went up in tens. They were knocked down to Helen for £210, which was about right. 'Let's get out of here,' she whispered to Susan and they made for the auctioneer's clerk. It only took a few moments to pay for the furniture and arrange for delivery, and then they found a coffee bar, and ordered open tuna sandwiches and Espresso. 'Now,' Helen said, 'this is how it is. When I was in London I worked for a man called Edward Portillo. I wasn't much older than you when I met him. He very kindly gave me a job in his antique shop.'

'Did you have qualifications?'

Helen laughed. 'Unless you count O-levels in total ignorance, no, I didn't. But I worked hard. I was interested. Edward taught me about the things I handled in the shop, so I know that those chairs were probably made in Germany about the middle of the last century, and we'll probably make a profit of 100 per cent on their resale. The bureau cabinet is riskier: it's probably George the Third, but it's been bashed about, and restoration is expensive. If we do it up, we'll get at least £1,000, but that won't leave us with much profit.'

'It sounds like a lot to me,' Susan said, eyes wide. And then, 'Who's "us"?'

'Edward and I . . . I'm still his partner. If I find good pieces up here I buy them and ship them south when I have a load.'

She knew it was coming, now, the question she always dreaded. 'Why did you leave London?'

Emptying her mouth gave Helen some valuable time. 'I got tired of London. Of the noise and the bustle and trying to get anywhere in the rush hour. Besides, I missed home.'

Susan's snort was fervent. 'You must be mad!'

Helen smiled. 'Why do you say that? Wouldn't you miss your home?'

Susan shook her head, the freckles suddenly standing out on her pale, intense face. 'I can't wait to get away. I'd go now if it wasn't against the law. I can't go till I'm seventeen, and then I have to go somewhere respectable: I know because I made enquiries.'

Her eyes on Helen's were hard and defiant. 'She means it,' Helen thought but she said nothing.

'I know I should be grateful,' Susan said. 'I'm adopted, and so is Michael. But I'm not grateful. Well, to daddy a bit. But I really just want to be on my own and live my own life.'

'I can't handle this,' Helen thought. 'I can't pump this

327

kid for information, there's too much pain there. I simply daren't take off the lid.' Aloud she said, 'Shall we go for a walk this afternoon? I like going up on to the hill . . . you can see for miles.'

Ahead of them in the park the two girls, Barbara and Tracy, walked side by side, Gary gambolling in front of them. All three were with them to stay now, legally theirs once the procedures were complete. 'How does it feel?' David asked.

'Nice . . . scary,' Diana said ruefully.

He took her hand and pulled her closer. 'Why scary? We can afford them, and they're basically nice kids. You can have as much extra help in the house as you want. What are you afraid of, Diana?'

'It's not the extra work, David, don't be stupid. It's . . . well, it's emotional things. I mean, at the moment we're all polite, we circle round one another, trying not to offend. I know I do it and so do you, whether or not you realize it. The kids don't put a foot wrong . . . even Gary, and he's just a baby, knows he's on a kind of probation. It's awful that it should be like that, but it is! What worries me is, what happens when we drop our defences, our pretences if you like? What happens when we have a row, or I tell Barbara not to do something? Will she turn round and say, "And who the hell are you to dictate to me?"'

David was taking her questions seriously for once, and she felt herself relax. A glib answer would have been the bitter end. 'I don't know, so I can't give any firm assurances. But I know one thing . . . we wanted kids, and those kids want parents. They may not even know it yet, but there's also a longing inside them for someone who will say "no" occasionally, and even whack their backsides if they get out of line – as long as it's done out of love. So it seems to me that if A wants B and B wants A, it damn well ought to work in the end.'

Diana nodded, still unconvinced. 'I suppose you're right . . . but that doesn't stop me from worrying.'

He squeezed her hand. 'I know. For the moment let's just take it one day at a time, shall we?'

They walked on, each with their private thoughts, their eyes on the children ahead, on the park's broad pathway.

'Susan went to stay with Helen today, didn't she?' David asked at last.

'Yes. I still don't understand why Howard didn't let her stay at home with him. She's fifteen . . . she should be looking after him, for goodness sake.'

'He has no confidence in himself,' David said. 'He's so guilt-ridden now that he can hardly function outside his office. He's all right there, with his dusty conveyancing and his probates. But outside, in the real world, he's . . . oh, well, what's the point?'

'What was he like when he was a child?' Diana asked.

'OK. There were three years between us, and he was a bit of a swot, a bit introverted . . . but we got on. He did the things we all did, although he was always a bit self-conscious with girls. You could've knocked me down with a feather when he produced Anne. Still, that's water under the bridge . . . Helen's been a brick about Susan, that's the one bright spot.'

'Yes, Helen is all right. As a matter of fact, I mean to get her for Vic.'

David chortled. 'The wayward brother! You're a schemer, Mrs Whittington. Still, it's not a bad idea.'

They walked on for a while but she could see something was troubling him. Gary was beginning to tire: any minute now the children would need attention, and the moment would be gone. 'What's on your mind, darling? I can see something is. Why don't you tell me?'

'It's nothing. It's stupid, really . . . and disgusting. I'm ashamed of myself for thinking it.' David looked at her a moment, and then plunged. 'The thing is that I think Howard doesn't want to be left alone in the house with a nubile adolescent. Not for any good reason, not because he lusts after his adoptive daughter . . . but because his wife has created such a sin-ridden atmosphere in that house that he daren't risk it.'

Diana was lost for words. The idea both shocked and satisfied her. Dreadful as it was, it would explain everything. 'You might be right. If you are, it's unspeakable, isn't it?'

They stood still, staring at each other and then away in embarrassment. It was a relief when Gary came running back to them to show David a ladybird, red and black and normal, in the centre of his palm.


Howard pulled into a lay-by and switched off the ignition. Yvonne sat sulkily in the passenger seat, huddled against the window as though to separate herself from him. A state of war existed between them now. He had refused to give her £200 for an abortion, but he was still uncertain about his motives for refusing. Abortion was a sin . . . but it was something more than that. In some recess of his mind the idea of a baby, an embryo, growing, developing, was not unwelcome.

'Well?' Yvonne said, looking at him through narrowed lids, 'do I get it or don't I?' Howard put his hands together and raised them to his lips. 'I'm going to help you, Yvonne; I want to help you . . . but giving you money isn't the answer. Not in that way. That would be too easy.'

'Easy! Easy for who? Not so easy for me, chum, getting cut about.'

He shook his head. 'I'm sorry, that was stupid of me. What I mean is that abortion is not the only option. There are other ways in which I can help you. I can make sure you never want for anything, you or the baby.'

'I'm not having it. Don't start on about that, because it's not on. Anyway, you must be mad! What's your wife going to say, or your precious Mrs Fraser? Not to mention the clients!'

It was not his clients he worried about, it was his children. But this too was his child, growing in the womb. 'Just think about it, Yvonne. I'm not asking you to decide now . . .'

'That's good, because there's nothing to decide. I'm getting rid of it, Howard: R – I – D. All I want from you is the cash. Just give me it, and let it go at that.'

He turned in his seat and reached for her. 'Yvonne, please, let me help you. I'll make arrangements for the baby, I'll see that it has everything, every advantage . . .'

She was struggling free now, pushing at his arms. He noticed that the maroon polish on her nails was chipped where she had nibbled the edges, and a wave of disgust overcame him. He must have been out of his mind to lust after her as he had.

'OK, that's it! Show over. Take me back into town, anywhere near Dembry's – now!' Yvonne was reaching for the ignition but he took out the keys.

'Not yet, Yvonne. We have to decide about the baby.'

'There is no baby.' She said it flatly, and he knew instantly that it was true. She had done away with it already.

'Why did you do it, Yvonne? I told you . . . *why* did you do it?'

'I didn't do anything. There wasn't any need, there never was a baby. I got it wrong, that's all. Now for God's sake take me back to the town and shut up.'

There would be no scene with Anne, no disgust on his children's faces, no gossip at Rotary, no discredit in the office. His appalling dilemma had vanished. So why did he feel so sad?


Sylvia wore a green silk blouse with the *plique-à-jour* enamel brooch he had given her yesterday at her neck. The lights in the restaurant reflected in her red hair and threw her face into shadow. She looked good.

'Now, what are we going to eat?' he said. 'And, more important, what shall we drink?'

They chose duck and drank a good burgundy with it, finishing with syllabub.

'Lovely meal,' she said, covering his hand with hers, as coffee was delivered to the table. 'Now, are you in a good mood?'

Edward smiled. 'I don't like the sound of that. What comes next?'

'I have a proposition to put to you.'

Oh God, he thought, she was going to suggest moving into the flat and he wasn't sure he was ready for it. She almost lived there now, but there was a gulf between 'almost' and 'actually' which he was not yet ready to bridge.

'I want you to take me into the business, Edward. I can buy my way in: I'll have money once the divorce is through, and besides, there's always the parent. I don't want to go back to journalism and I've got such plans. If you sell out to those developers and I put my money in with yours, we could set up somewhere else and expand. Operate on two levels . . . you do the genuine stuff which doesn't move quickly, and I start up a line of good reproduction. Only the best, the kind of thing you or I would like to have in our homes . . . real wood, real craftsmanship. You could design it.'

'Just a moment, Sylvia . . . you're going too fast. I don't particularly want to expand, and if I did it wouldn't be into reproduction stuff. I'd sooner operate a whelk stall.'

She had withdrawn her hand and the atmosphere around the table had cooled. 'Well then, how about a partnership in the business as it is? After all, we're pretty much of a partnership already, aren't we?'

'But you don't know anything about the trade, Sylvia. I've never seen you show any real interest in it. Are you sure this isn't just a whim?'

He had said the wrong thing, and if he had not known it as he said it, he would have seen it in the set of her lips.

'I know as much as, or more than, your precious Helen knew when you took her off the street.'

He seized on the excuse. 'That's another thing, Sylvia: Helen is already a partner, so it wouldn't be my decision alone . . .'

'Don't hide behind Helen, Edward. I deserve better from you than that.'

'You're right, of course. Very well, then, I don't want a second partner, I have no present intention of expanding or altering the nature of my business – I'd like to change the subject before we spoil what, up to now, has been a pleasant evening.'

* * *

They bathed and got into their dressing-gowns early so that they could watch the black-and-white movie on ITV. 'I love Bette Davis films,' Susan said. She looked much more relaxed, her hair still damp from the steam of the bath and curling around her face.

'You suit your hair loose,' Helen said. 'Biscuits?'

Susan took a Bourbon and dunked it in her coffee. 'Ooh, sorry. Disgusting habit.'

Helen kept a straight face. 'Only if it drops off in the cup and disintegrates. That's disgusting. If you get it into your mouth intact it's just about permissible.'

They giggled and went on dunking as *The Little Foxes* unfolded, taking turns in the commercial breaks to dash out for coffee or apples or crisps.

'I'm not sure,' Helen said, 'that this is what I'm supposed to be feeding you. I believe balanced diets were mentioned.'

'We can eat sensibly tomorrow,' Susan said.

'When she smiles she is positively pretty,' Helen thought, and resolved to make her smile more often. After the film was over they sat on, talking companionably. Sometimes Susan had to grope for words but Helen resisted the impulse to prompt her, even when chances of introducing Michael into the conversation came and were lost.

At last it happened quite naturally. 'I think I'm going to be a nurse,' Susan said. 'I quite like the idea, and if my parents say I can't I won't let it stop me. You earn while you learn with nursing. If they had to keep me, they could stop me – but not with nursing. So I'm lucky, not like poor old Mike.'

'What's he going to be?' Helen already knew, but still feared, the answer.

'He's going to be a priest. He goes away in September. He says it's what he wants, but I know it's not – all he's really ever wanted was to be a sailor. And once he wanted to be a bus-driver, but that was only for a week. Anyway, I've told him he's mad but he just smiles. He never fights, even when you do something terrible to him. He'll be a rotten priest, because what priests do is tell people off all the time and threaten hell-fire, and Michael just won't be able to do that.'

'He does seem nice,' Helen said as casually as she could.

'He *is* nice, really. If only he'd stand up for himself a bit more . . . and for me. He does sometimes, if he thinks Mum's been really beastly, like when she wouldn't let me have stockings for school when Reverend Mother said they were OK and all the other girls got them. But most of the time . . .'

'My God!' Helen said suddenly, sitting upright. On the screen a suntanned young god was teasing a girl with a chocolate bar. Susan was looking alarmed. 'Sorry,' Helen said, 'It's just that I know that guy in the commercial. His name's Patrick Sheen.' She forbore to mention that he had been her lover. 'He was an out-of-work actor when I knew him. I'm glad to see him earning some money.'

'He's gorgeous,' Susan said. 'Look at those muscles.' Her eyes slid sideways to see what effect her words were having on her listener.

Helen grinned. 'He should be, he spends all his time doing press-ups . . .' She finished, 'and making love,' under her breath. She was trying to bring in a more relaxed regime for Susan, but there were limits.


## 27


'The week-end's gone and I feel as though I've just got here,' Helen said.

Across the table Edward was buttering toast. 'Time seems to go faster as you get older.'

Helen nodded. 'I thought that last night . . . when I was in your mother's bedroom. It seems like yesterday that I was first in there, and it's nearly fifteen years.'

'You were a funny kid, then, . . . like something out of Dickens.'

Helen laughed. 'I thought you were an old man. Honestly, I thought you must be in your mid-thirties . . . and you were twenty-seven.'

'If you'd known what a young, virile, handsome guy I was, would you have been so trusting?'

'Yes, of course I would. I'd've trusted you with my life.' She said it so easily that it irked him.

'I'm not as harmless as all that, surely?'

But she was still smiling indulgently. 'You are to me.'

They got down to business then. The new load of furniture from the north had arrived safely, and Edward was pleased with the standard. Helen had crowed with delight over the doll collection, and now she gave him detailed instructions about selling it on.

'I wish you needn't go back today. Couldn't you make it tomorrow?'

'No. David was good to give me Monday off, and I couldn't ask for more. But I'll come back soon, if you can put up with me. And I'll be back for good eventually, Edward. When Michael leaves . . . *if* Michael leaves . . . there'll be nothing to keep me in Darlasden.'

'Has it been worth it?'

'Going back? Oh, yes, it's been worth it. I'm proud of Michael, Edward, and I love him. In a funny way I love Susan, too. That's a bonus. She's a funny kid; she almost strangled me when it was time to leave – so much pent-up affection that she can't give Anne. I realize now that it is possible to care for someone else's child, and I think that Howard loves the children. It's strange, really: sometimes, over the years since I first saw him I've thought . . . what if I was wrong and Michael is not my son? It could be – it's unlikely, but I could have got it wrong. Anyway, the point is, it doesn't matter. I still want him to be happy.'

She sounded as though she intended to make sure he was happy and any hopes Edward had cherished of her early return were dashed by the steely note in her voice.

'What time are you going back?'

'I'm meeting Diana's brother for lunch, since she wants me to collect a package of some sort from him. I'm hoping to go straight from there to the train.'

Edward tried not to show his disappointment. 'So I won't see you once you leave here? I was hoping to give you lunch myself.'

'Come and join us, Edward. I'm sure Victor won't mind. He sounds just like Diana, and you know how friendly she is.'

He shook his head. 'No, thanks, I've got lots on here . . . which reminds me, I'd better open the shop.'

There was mail on the floor and he gathered it up before loosing the bolts, sitting then at his desk to open the letters. Helen moved about, touching remembered objects, examining new stock, smiling at the faithful Mark and Antony still guarding the stairs. He put two bills aside and opened a white foolscap envelope. It contained a single sheet of paper, whose heading was the solicitor's who had handled Maria Stepinska's estate. Papers were now ready for his signature as joint executor. But it was the final paragraph that caught his breath: 'The estate was larger than we had anticipated and, as principal beneficiary, you would appear to have a substantial bequest due to you. We will be happy to discuss investment possibilities, if you so choose. Please ring my secretary . . .'

'Trouble?' Helen was looking concerned.

'No, no trouble, just a surprise. Maria Stepinska has left me something in her will.'

'That shouldn't be a surprise, surely? You were the apple of her eye.'

He folded the letter and put it back in the envelope. 'No. I knew she'd left me something . . . but they say it's a considerable amount. Anyway, let's not think about that now. I have a little present for you.'

The automaton was faded but perfect inside its glass dome. 'It's a Leopold Lambert,' Helen said, her mouth open in amazement, as he wound it. The girl in the velvet dress bowed and turned, lifting a hand to her mouth to blow a kiss while the music tinkled out: *'My love is like a red, red rose . . .'*

Her arms were round his neck, her lips were against his cheek. . .it was the kiss of a grateful child, no more, but he was surprised at how pleasant a sensation it aroused in him.

\* \* \*

Howard had always hated Mondays, but now he dreaded every day he had to come to the office. There was contempt in Yvonne's eyes, distaste in the set of her mouth. He stayed in his room as much as he could, trusting Mrs Fraser to keep him in touch with what he should know, but there was still the gauntlet to be run, four times daily – from the street to the sanctuary of his room, and back again. Would they all look up laughing, or draw away the hem of their garments? Would she stand up and block his entrance, forcing him to turn and crawl away? By the time he got into his room his hands were always shaking, sweat running in a rivulet between his buttocks, his heart pounding uncomfortably, reminding him of the ephemeral nature of man.

Today, though, Yvonne was not there, only the juniors, heads bent over their work. Mrs Fraser stood by the photocopier, waiting to collect something that looked important. He mumbled good morning, not resting until the door was shut behind him. Where was she? What would he do if she stayed away and defied him not to pay her?

The phone rang and he picked it up. 'Neville! Yes, of course. I'll bring details to the committee tomorrow. We can hire a disco, or there's a band who'll donate their services since it's for charity. I'm not sure about the standard of their playing, that's the difficulty.'

It helped to have something to talk about, suggestions to make, arrangements to confirm. He would miss Rotary if . . . *Where was she*? He longed to go to the door and look out into the office, to ask questions as to her whereabouts if she was still missing. But terror kept him in his seat.

At ten o'clock Mrs Fraser brought in his coffee – perfect coffee in a Wedgwood cup, two Marie biscuits in the saucer.

'Mrs Willis is due at ten-thirty – is this the seventh edition of her will, or the eighth? And you're meeting Mr Bascombe at the Swan at twelve-thirty. The details are all in this folder.'

She was at the door, her hand on the knob, when she turned. 'Oh, and by the way, we won't be seeing Yvonne again, I'm afraid. We had a difference of opinion late on Friday and agreed she wasn't quite right for the firm. I gave her wages in lieu of notice: I thought it was within my jurisdiction. I hope I was right?'

Howard nodded, swallowing hard before he could say: 'Of course . . . and see to a replacement, will you? No need to consult me.' He smiled reassuringly until Mrs Fraser had closed the door behind her, then he put his head on his arms and wept with relief.


Lilian knew she couldn't be pregnant: there was her age, for one thing, and they hadn't taken that many risks. Armoured by age she sat confidently in the waiting-room until the number one light flashed and it was her turn to see David.

'Hello Lilian. Sit down and tell me what's wrong.'

She loosened her coat. 'Is Diana all right? I've been meaning to call . . . she'll have the kiddies now? That'll keep her occupied.'

'Yes. They're settling in well and Diana is coping with them marvellously. But she'd appreciate sight of you when you have a moment. Now, what's the trouble?'

Lilian confessed to a missed period, a sickly stomach and a terrible tiredness. 'I could go off to sleep where I stand, just like that. I think I've got the sleepy sickness, or something like that.'

He was studying her case-notes. 'You're still taking your contraceptive pills?'

She didn't answer and he looked up sharply. 'Well?'

She would kill Billy for this. Kill him! She twisted her headscarf in her hands, making believe it was his neck, until David put down the notes and got to his feet. 'I think we'll have you up on the couch, Lilian.'

He was whistling softly as he examined her and she knew he was passing sentence. Then he helped her down and went back behind the desk. 'We'll send off a specimen but I'm fairly sure . . . about six weeks, so it's very early days.'

Six weeks! So she had fallen as soon as she had missed a

pill. Lilian felt at once outraged and rather pleased at her own super-fertility. All the same she *would* kill Billy . . .

'How would you feel if it was confirmed, Lilian? Karen is how old?'

'Eighteen, nearly. It's fifteen years since I had Diana.'

'Did you ever think about having another baby? I know you took precautions . . . that's why I'm surprised you've been careless now . . . but did you ever seriously consider it?'

'Not really. I never was one for a lot of bairns. When Diana went I thought about it, but there'd never have been another one like her.'

David was nodding sympathetically. 'She was a special little girl. Well, Lilian, if this is a baby you have decisions to make. I think we could make out a case for termination: you're not young, and it's a long time since your last pregnancy. Fortunately, the obstetricians in this area have a liberal attitude to termination. However, it's not something to be done without thought. How would Billy feel about being a father again?'

Billy would take it in his stride, Lilian thought, as he took everything in life. And if she decided not to go ahead, he would accept that too. However it turned out, it would be up to her.

'He'd be all right about it – you know Billy. It's our Karen I'm not sure about.' Suddenly she stiffened, looking at the case-notes. 'I wouldn't like our Helen to know. Not just yet.'

David nodded.

'She's in London today, so you're quite safe. I'll keep your notes in my drawer. Bring the specimen in this afternoon, wrapped up, and make sure it gets to me. I'll see it's kept quiet until you've made your decision.'

She thanked him and came out into the sunlight. She knew she was pregnant – somehow she'd known it all along. So she still had it in her after all. And so had Billy. Well, bugger a hell!


Vic was very like his sister, with the same blue eyes and same thick sandy hair, but bigger and taller. 'It's nice to meet you at last. Di has given you an awe-inspiring build-up.'

Helen laughed. 'Snap.'

He leaned across the table. 'Do you think she's doing a little matchmaking?'

Helen nodded solemnly. 'I'm sure she is, but we won't let that influence us, will we?'

He was easy to talk to and he seemed to have been everywhere. They talked about the first space shuttle that was dominating the newsboards. 'I worked on a NASA project once. They're a dedicated bunch.'

'What do you do?' Helen asked.

'I'm a building engineer – or I was. Now I'm a trouble-shooter . . . and don't ask me what that is because it's not easy to define. I iron out hold-ups, that sort of thing. But tell me about you. I know you're David's secretary or receptionist or whatever, but my sister thinks you're some-thing of a mystery-woman. She says you were some high-powered business lady here in London, but gave it up for an affair of the heart. True?'

His eyes were challenging but kindly. 'I like him,' Helen thought, a little frisson of excitement catching in her chest. Aloud, she said, 'Something like that. But I wasn't a high-powered executive, I was . . . I am . . . a partner in an antiques business. I . . . well, there was a relationship with a certain young gentleman . . . I thought I'd go north for a while. That's all.'

'Well, if he let you go he was a very foolish young gentleman. Now, what are we going to eat?'

It was a long time since she had sat like this with a man, a powerful man, a man who made her feel . . . she sought for a word. Amorous? Randy? No, Patrick had made her feel randy. This was something more.

Vic took her arm when they emerged on to the pavement, holding both her bags easily in the other hand while she carried Edward's gift and the package to deliver to Diana.

'Don't go back now – this is crazy. We've only just met, and you're off. Catch a later train. Better still, go tomorrow.'

It was tempting but Helen resisted. 'It's got to be the

three o'clock. But I'll be coming back – and you should visit your sister. She's always hoping you'll come to Darlasden.'

'I will now!'

He charmed the man at the barrier into letting him accompany her to the train, and saw her safely into a seat. After stowing her things, Helen walked back to the door and stood there while Vic descended to the platform.

'Goodbye, Vic.' She held out her hand and he took it, stepping up again until their faces were level in the doorway.

'Au revoir, Helen. You're the nicest thing that's happened to me for quite a while. You'll see me again.'

His lips were warm and dry, and just questing enough for a brief acquaintance. Long after she was in her seat and the train was speeding out of London she remembered the sensation of his mouth on hers, his cheek warm and slightly abrasive against her own.


Diana selected an armful of bright clothes from the rails and carried them into the fitting-rooms. 'I'm guessing your sizes,' she said. 'Next time it'll be easier.' Barbara and Tracy didn't look like two little girls who were on a shopping bonanza: they looked scared stiff.

'Come on then, let's start trying on.' Diana sat on a chair while they took their clothes off, folding them carefully and putting them in a neat pile. For reasons she couldn't understand the precision of their actions brought a lump to her throat. They were like little old women. At their age she had been helpless, needing assistance with buttons and straps, dropping her clothes everywhere. God, they were so careful! She ached to help them, but she didn't have the courage so she sat as they struggled into the new clothes and turned obediently for inspection.

'Well?' she said. They looked at her blankly. 'Well?' she said again, 'what do you think of them?'

Tracy looked down at her brightly patterned dress with its scarlet trimmings. 'It's nice,' she said, without enthusiasm.

'Do you want it?' Diana asked. The child's eyes slid to

her sister's face and stayed there. Barbara looked at Diana and her expression said, 'Where's the catch?'

For some reason she couldn't understand Diana felt a sudden overwhelming irritation. 'I asked you, Tracy, not Barbara!'

Tracy's eyes began to brim. She looked first at Diana and then at her clothes, folded neatly on the chair.

'I'm waiting, Tracy. *Do you like it*?' – the words trembled on Diana's lips, but she bit them back as Tracy moved to the chair and gathered up her old clothes, clutching them to her chest.

For a moment Diana was baffled, and then it all came clear. 'They're her security,' she thought. 'Those clothes are familiar, and they're hers, and she's frightened I'll take them away.' Half of her was consumed with pity for the child, the other half was furious with David. Where was he when she was under stress like this?

She turned to Barbara. 'Do you think the dress suits her?' she said, acknowledging the older child's superior knowledge.

Barbara looked back haughtily but her shoulders rose almost imperceptibly. 'It's OK.'

'Right,' Diana said. 'Take it off and put your own clothes back on, Tracy.' She turned to Barbara as Tracy began to scramble out of the new dress. 'Now what about yours?'

The pink dress did nothing for Barbara. Above the frilled collar her face was pinched, her hair still drawn back into unbecoming bunches. 'I don't like that one,' Diana said. 'Try this.' The grey and lemon Liberty print brought out the green of Barbara's eyes and lent colour to the thin cheeks. 'It looks marvellous,' Diana enthused. Barbara's lips twitched approval, and then she sucked in her cheeks and dropped her eyes.

'I'm overwhelming them,' Diana thought and cursed her own insensitivity. 'Do *you* like it?' she asked again, gently this time.

Barbara turned to the mirror and slowly nodded at her reflection.

'Right,' Diana said. 'Get dressed again, and I'll pay for these.' She carried the dresses, one for each child, to the cash desk and got out her chequebook. 'I think they're too tired to try everything on today,' she said. 'I'm sorry, I've left the rest in the cubicle. We'll come back another day. In the mean time I'll take these two . . .'

While she was waiting she saw both children check the cubicle carefully in case anything had been left behind.

They were nearly at the park where David and Gary were waiting when Barbara spoke. 'Will our Gary get something too?'

Diana smiled. 'His turn next, Barbara, you can be sure of that.'

Ahead of them, David was pulling at the string of a kite, a cheap thing that had come with petrol. Gary was craning his neck to watch as it bobbed above the ground, and then David was running and the kite was taking the air. Diana glanced sideways and was taken aback by the grin of pleasure on Barbara's face.


'Well you've done it now, Billy Fenwick.' He had come in from back-shift, and Lilian slapped his meal in front of him.

'What've I done now, then? I'm never out of the dog-house with you, Lily pet.'

'Don't Lily-pet me, Billy. You've got me pregnant, that's what you've done. You've done it to be spiteful . . . you've never liked me working, but I didn't think even you'd stoop to this.' She knew the weak line in her case: it took two to tango. But if he said that she'd slaughter him. 'Well . . . what've you got to say, Billy. No good sitting with your mouth open. That'll solve nothing.'

'I'm pleased, Lily. If you want to know the truth I'm flabbergasted . . . but I'm pleased, too. I'm over the moon.'

'I might've known. I might have known you'd think you'd been clever. Not a word about me! I can hear them talking now, in the corner shop, down the club. We'll be a laughing-stock. And all because you couldn't control yourself . . .'

'Now, hold on, Lily . . .'

Here it was, the get-out. 'Lilian! My name is Lilian. Lily-*ann*. God give me strength, we've been married for seventeen years and you can't get me name right. And I'll tell you why, because you keep your brains in your trousers. That's the only end of you that works. Well, I'll tell you this . . . I've taken a sample down the surgery, and if it comes back positive you'll live to rue the day, I promise you that. And don't tell me to hold on! You're the one who should've held on! If this turns out to be definite, I'll show you what holding on means!'

'You mean it's not definite?' Billy sounded disappointed, and she felt a glow of pleasure. He wanted it, then! All the same . . . 'You better eat that meat and veg, Billy Fenwick. It has a chance to be your last!'


Helen had meant to work on the train, on the sheaf of business letters and catalogues Edward had given her, but she found herself in a strange, reflective mood. Going back to London had reminded her of what it was like to be free, an independent woman living and working in a metropolis. And then there had been Vic. She had known in the restaurant that something special was happening, some indefinable chemical reaction that made even the picking up of a fork a significant thing. And then his lips on hers on the train steps, like teenagers! She kept wanting to close her eyes and relive the moment. Again and again. She hadn't felt like this since Alistair.

Outside the train window the late summer countryside suited her mood; mellow and fruitful. 'I think I've fallen in love,' she thought, tried to dismiss the idea as ridiculous, and then gave way to it completely until the train came to a halt in Darlasden.

She got a cab outside the station, feeling an odd sense of regret at all she had left behind. It had been such fun to look at those dolls. On the seat beside her the parcel containing the automaton, Edward's present, was a link with that London life. She took out the cab-fare and her door key, picked up parcels and bags, and struggled out of the cab.

'Hello.' Susan came up beside Helen, her face flushed with pleasure.

'Hello,' Helen said in surprise, turning to thrust coins through the cab window. 'How did you know I'd be coming back now?'

'Aunt Diana told me . . . anyway, we thought we'd just wait around until you turned up.' Helen was about to question the 'we' when she saw the figure in the background. 'Hello, Michael,' she said as calmly as she could, and unlocked the door into the house.

In the kitchen she got out cups and saucers, put on the kettle. 'Only biscuits, I'm afraid. And I'm quite hungry.'

'I could go to the corner shop for you,' Michael offered.

Seeing he was eager to please, Helen reached for her purse. 'OK. I'm famished, I don't know about you two. Let's have a feast.'

They ate frozen chips and fish portions with tomato sauce. 'Better than school,' Michael said. He still had the hearty appetite of a child, and whenever she caught his eyes they were smiling although his mouth was in repose. She saw, too, the bond between brother and sister: so much for ties of blood, these two had no consanguinity, but would probably die for one another if the need arose. 'She has driven them together,' Helen thought and for the first time since Easter felt grateful to Anne Whittington.

'Now the *pièce de résistance*,' Helen said, taking the frozen cream sponge from its box. It was still hard in the middle and resisted the knife.

'I like it like this,' Susan said. 'It's like ice-cream, only extra creamy.'

'Next time you come I'll make you a proper meal. What do you like: Indian? Italian?'

Susan's eyes rolled. Michael shrugged. 'I don't know.'

'You've never had Italian food? We'll have to remedy that. I could take you out to a meal some time . . . but how would that go down at home?'

Again the exchanged glances. 'We wouldn't tell her,' Susan said defiantly. 'Or Dad. He wouldn't mind, but it's just best to leave him in the dark.'

Michael was looking uncomfortable. 'We don't lie, we just . . . sometimes don't say things.'

The look Susan gave him now was almost contemptuous. 'I'm not ashamed – and I do tell lies. She spoils things if you don't keep them quiet.'

'It's really for our own good.' Michael's eyes were desperate on Helen's.

*'He wants me to get him off the hook,'* she thought. Aloud she said, 'Well, enough of this. We'll fix up an expedition . . . what and who you tell is your own business. Now, come and see what I've got.'

As the automaton waved and blew kisses she blessed Edward, who always came up trumps at sticky moments. She half hummed, half sang to the music: *'till all the seas gang dry, my love, and rocks melt wi' the sun . . . oh, I will still love thee, still my dear, while sands o' time shall run.'*

'I think I'm in love,' she thought, 'and Edward is my friend . . . and my son is here, under my roof.' If she had a cup, it was truly running over.


Edward had bathed and changed and was fastening his shoelaces when it came to him, a revelation at once incredible and utterly believable. 'I love Helen,' he said aloud. 'My God, I love Helen.' He had been thinking of her pleasure at the automaton, of the way she had laughed as it dipped and swayed, and suddenly he had realized that more than anything he wanted to be within the sound of her laughter for the rest of his life. More than that, he wanted her . . . as he had never wanted any woman, not even Sylvia. He laughed aloud, thinking of the difference between what he had felt for Sylvia and what he was feeling now, this fire in his blood.

He stood up and walked to the window, suddenly short of breath. He must persuade Helen to come back to London. If not, he would have to go up there and take her by storm. 'I will woo her,' he thought, feeling ridiculously like a boy again. 'I will woo her until she sees me as a man, not as dear old Edward who rescues damsels from railway stations, but as a living, breathing lover.' He found he was grinning like an idiot and to pull himself together he addressed himself to the problem of what to do about Sylvia, who would shortly let herself in with her key.

In the end he opened a good bottle of wine, put Mahler on the record-player, and came straight to the point.

'Sylvia, I've been thinking over what you said. And of course Helen has been here over the weekend, so I've had time to talk and assess how the business is going, how it will go in the future. You know I'm fond of you . . .' The lie surprised him: he was not fond of her at all. Somewhere along the line he had begun to dislike her very much indeed. 'But I don't think we could work together. And, if you'll forgive me for giving advice, I think you should go back to what you're good at. To what you really enjoy – journalism.'

He saw her lips quiver and then stiffen, but she didn't speak.

'I realize that you may resent this decision, and I'm sorry. If you feel that, in the circumstances, you don't want to go on . . .'

She sat up straight at that, and cut across his words. 'You're dumping me, Edward!' Her eyes were two circles of green glitter, her face white in its auburn frame. 'My God, you're giving me the bum's rush!'

She stood up, swinging the end of her green and blue Liberty shawl over her shoulder. 'Thanks for the wine . . . it's good. Enjoy your business, Edward. I won't occupy any more of your time! And . . .' She paused in the doorway. 'Sod you, Edward!'

He heard her heels clatter on the stairs and then the shop door jangling closed.

His breath came out in a sigh of relief and he leaned to refill his glass. He had been fond of Sylvia . . . once . . . but they would never have made a lasting relationship. He wondered uneasily if she would return her key to his flat, and then dismissed the thought as unworthy. Besides, enough of Sylvia. He dialled Helen's number, fingers crossed that she would be there.

'Helen? So you're back safely, good. Oh, the usual Saturday. They were? That must have been nice. . . .' He

347

listened as she enthused about her departed visitors. In a moment he would speak out, and damn the consequences. And then he heard the note in her voice as she spoke of Vic, and started to listen properly to what she was saying.

'It sounds crazy after one meeting, not much more than one hour . . . but I just know this is different. And I think he knows it too.'

It was funny. It was hilarious really. When Edward put down the phone, he found he was laughing quietly and shaking his head. He had let it slip through his fingers. He had failed at the last hurdle. He had been pipped at the post. He wrapped himself in comforting clichés, but the uncomfortable truth still penetrated. He loved Helen, but Helen did not love him . . . not in the same way. And now that she had met this apparent superman, Vic, she probably never would. If only he had realized how he felt just one day sooner.

As he finished the wine, he tried to pinpoint the fatal moment. Was it when he had allowed her to drop everything and run back to Durham in pursuit of a dream? Or before that, when he had encouraged the damned Easter pilgrimages? Without them there would have been no Diana, and without Diana no Vic. But the real truth was that he had been blind all along and now he was paying the price.

At least his rival was here in London: 250 miles separated him and Helen, so Vic was as bereft as he was – tonight at least. And while Michael was in Durham, Helen would be loath to leave it, even for the man of her dreams. Who would win the tug of love, Michael or Vic? Whoever won he knew with certainty that he, Edward, would be the loser.

# BOOK FOUR
### *1981*

# 28

'Just keep still another minute, Lilian.' Helen gripped her sister's hair with one hand and inserted a heated roller with the other. 'One more minute . . . don't pull.' Lilian was fretting over things undone and things already done that would have to be undone.

'If I don't get up there, Helen, God knows what he'll be up to. "Bath the bairn," I said. It sounds as though he's drowning him.' The sound of Lilian's three-year-old son causing mayhem in the bath was percolating down the stairs. She closed her eyes in anguish and opened her mouth. 'Billy! Billy . . . what are you playing at up there? Fetch him down.'

There was a clatter, and Billy appeared, the towel-clad boy in his arms. 'We were only having a bit fun, Lily. Weren't we, son?'

The boy balled tiny fists and pummelled his father about the head. 'Boom! Boom! Boom!'

'There,' Helen said, pinning the last roller.

'Thank God!' Lilian said. 'Now let me get this wedding sorted. Put that bairn down Billy, and get cracking. In case you've missed it, your daughter's getting married today. Have I got to do everything? Helen, take that bairn . . . his clothes are on the chair. Keep a hold on him once he's ready . . . No, wait. Give him to me and you go up to our Karen.'

Upstairs, Karen's room was a haven of quiet. The bride lay in bed, hair tousled, face serene. 'Your mam's getting a bit agitated,' Helen said, laughing.

Karen rolled on to her face. 'I can hear her.'

On the wardrobe door the wedding dress hung in snow-white splendour. 'Can I do anything?' Helen asked.

Karen turned and pulled herself up on the pillows. 'Yes, Auntie Hel, you can take me mam and our Andrew out for a couple of hours and let me get meself ready.'

'Yes,' Helen said drily, 'but apart from the impossible?'

'I know,' Karen sighed. 'She's really enjoying it, isn't she? I shouldn't begrudge her.' She swung thin legs out of bed and stood up. 'It's nine o'clock. Heather and Brenda are coming at ten; they'll get ready here. Auntie Diana is bringing the girls round, all ready, at half-past. I hope me mam doesn't get our Andrew dressed too soon . . . he'll murder that page-boy suit, and it's got to go back tonight.'

As her niece moved round the room, assembling the things she needed, Helen marvelled at how calm she was. 'If this were me,' she thought, 'on my wedding day . . . how would I feel?' Thinking of weddings reminded her of Vic, who would be awake in Diana's house now, preparing to be a wedding guest. In two hours they would stand side by side in the church, listening as Karen and her Brian exchanged their vows. Tonight, Vic would probably propose . . . for the third time. She picked up the veil from its tissue wrap and held it away from her to admire.

'Try it on, Auntie Hel,' urged Karen, coaxingly. 'Go on, I bet it'll suit you.'

In the mirror Helen's face looked back at her, old and lined. 'Careworn,' she thought, suddenly depressed. 'I'm thirty-seven years old, and I look it.'

Karen was settling the silver tiara on her aunt's head, the while tulle flying. 'There now, you look lovely. If Vic could see you like this . . .'

Tonight she might tell Vic about Michael. But could she trust him to keep such a secret from Diana, and the family? Now, she could, and for as long as he loved her – but what about when love faded? She took off the veil and looked about for something practical to do.

Edward came down the stairs, looking into the shop filled now with sunlight that showed up the dust. They were getting a good day for the wedding, if it was like this further north. He thought of his invitation upstairs on the mantelpiece . . . perhaps he should have gone, after all? He had intended to go until he heard that Vic was going to be there. He slid back the bolts and stooped to pick up the mail and the papers.

The front pages were still full of the Gang of Four and the new Social Democrat Party. And Auchinleck was dead. Field Marshal Auchinleck . . . he could dimly remember that name from the war. So even war heroes went to dust in the end. He put the papers aside at the sight of a letter from Helen and sat at his desk to read it. She did not ring him so often now, and letters were doubly precious.

It was full of talk of the wedding, and Edward's lips twitched at details of Lilian's latest exploits. And then came the news he had waited for for so long: *'Michael seems to have settled at the seminary and Susan has been accepted at Guy's Hospital to train as a nurse, so I should be free to come back to London in a few weeks' time. You have been an angel, keeping my place for me all this time. I'll try and make it up to you when I come back.'*

He put the letter down, his eyes misting suddenly so that the graceful artefacts in front of him lost their clear outlines and wobbled in his view. The cheval mirror reflected a dusty antiquarian. He would have to do something about his clothes, smarten up a bit. He could afford it – Maria's money was compounding itself in the bank! If he didn't come to a decision about selling the shop soon, he would have to invest it properly, maybe expand.

He got to his feet and walked towards the mirror, trying to quell the excitement mounting in his chest. Helen was coming back. He put out a hand and fingered the mirror's frame: satinwood and tulipwood, crossbanded, crafted for someone around the time that Victoria ascended her throne. And still here. Enduring. Behind him in the glass, he could see Mark and Antony, eternal torch-bearers. If Helen agreed to any move, they would have to come too.

He felt the same old mixture of joy and anguish that came now with thoughts of Helen, so that he could not resist thinking of her and could not bear to think of her at one and the same time. He had come to terms with the fact that she would marry Victor: they were right for one another. But he could still love her – no one could take that from him. Just as she had loved Michael across the years without ever betraying how she truly felt, so he would love her. She would marry and have children and he would be a part of their lives, a godfather bearing gifts for children that might have been his own. The thought saddened and pleased him at the same time, and he smiled.

He might have gone on standing there if the bell had not jangled to herald the first tourists of the day, anxious to secure a piece of history.


Upstairs David was banging on the bathroom door, begging whichever girl was in there to come out. Vic was in the shower. Gary was still in the garden with the dog. Diana sat at the kitchen table, listening to the dishwasher agitating away and enjoying one last cup of coffee before the mêlée.

Barbara and Tracy were to be got into their bridesmaid's gear, and if the excitement of the rehearsal was anything to go by that would be no easy task. Gary still had to bath and then dress; David would need inspecting to make sure he had on the right shoes and tie. Only Vic could be trusted to be at the front door, immaculate, at ten-twenty. With luck she herself might get her dress on, but that was about all.

'Any coffee?' Vic was still towelling his hair, his legs bare beneath the short blue robe.

'Help yourself. Has David got into the bathroom yet?'

'I think so. Barbara floated past me on the landing looking like the Virgin Queen, and Tracy's tonging her hair on the stairs – so he must be in. How much longer have we got?'

'Half an hour or so. Are you picking up Helen?'

'No, she's going with the bridesmaids. I'll bring her back.'

'I wish it were you getting married today.'

'You and me both, sister. It's not that simple, though. I've asked the lady, but she won't say yes.'

'You can't hurry Helen, she's – well, she's a strong character.'

He had slung the towel around his neck. Now he sat facing her, nursing a cup between his hands. 'How much do you know about her, Di? I don't mean background or gossip, I mean about what makes her tick.'

'Why do you ask? You surely know her more intimately than I . . . and that's not a dig! What can I tell you? She doesn't go in for girl-talk, if that's what you mean.'

'I don't know what I mean. It's just that there's something, a quality of . . . well, not remoteness. Containment, I think that's what I mean. She's warm, she's loving, she's honest and friendly. But there's that little cabinet inside her to which she does not provide a key.'

'Yes,' said Diana thoughtfully. 'When she came here, we wondered about her. She's capable of much more than being a doctor's receptionist, and she has that business in London. David said it was a broken love affair, but if it had been that surely she'd have licked her wounds and then gone back to her old life. Instead, she's stayed. I know she's fond of you . . . I can't think why, darling brother, but I know she is. So why doesn't she say yes to you? It can't be the fact that you've already got kids, because she loves children. Ours adore her, and she's made such a difference to Susan! If Anne wasn't so utterly uncaring, she might ask herself why her daughter spends all her time with another woman. But of course she doesn't.'

'Hasn't Anne changed towards her since Michael went away? I thought she might switch her affections once she no longer had him at home?'

'Don't ask me, I see as little of her as possible. Now, can you get out of here and get ready? I'll need some help nearer the time. When you go up, tell David I'm sending his son up for descaling . . . he's in that bed where we buried the tortoise again. That'll be three times he's had it up.'

'Necrophilia?' Vic asked as he made for the door.

'Curiosity,' his sister said and went to summon her son.

Down below in the market square the Saturday crowds were hurrying backwards and forwards. The north was supposed to be depressed but there was still clearly money around. Howard turned back to his desk and got out the bottle of Glenlivet from his bottom drawer. He liked these Saturday mornings alone in the silent offices. It was a chance to catch up on work, but most of all it represented peace.

The whisky was warm on his tongue, fire in his throat. He opened his paper and looked at the headlines. David Owen and Shirley Williams . . . the new party would be a flash in the pan no doubt. He turned to foreign news . . . the wife of the dead dictator, Peron, jailed for corruption, and a middle-aged teacher jailed in America for killing the inventor of the Scarsdale diet, whatever that might be. He refilled his glass and looked around the room. It needed redecorating, but he couldn't stand the thought of all the disruption.

Down below there was a thud which sounded suspiciously like the outer door. But who would be here on a Saturday? He sat, tense, head turned for the sound of footsteps. It was a woman. Her heels were clicking their way up towards him. Not Anne, she would be safely in church at this time, as she was every day. And Susan would have called out to him as soon as she entered the building.

A moment later Mrs Fraser appeared in the doorway.

'How did you know I was here?' Howard said stupidly, not sure whether or not he welcomed interruption.

'I saw you at the window just now. I was coming out of Dembry's when I saw someone, and I knew it would be you.' She was shrugging off her cream swagger coat and folding it over a chair, and it perturbed him.

'There's no need for you to work today, Elizabeth; I'm just pottering . . . it can all wait till Monday.'

She had vanished into the outer office and he heard the

lid of the electric kettle. A few moments later she had placed a tray on his desk, two cups of coffee and caramel shortbread. His favourite!

'How are your boys?' and for a few moments they swapped family news. Mrs Fraser had worn well. Her figure was still trim, the lines on her face were lines of good humour, and her mouth was kind.

'Have you planned a holiday yet?' she asked him. 'I'm thinking of going to the Lakes again. Well, I like walking . . . and there aren't many places you can go on your own. The other possibility is a painting holiday.'

'Do you paint?' Howard asked, astonished. They had been together almost every day for twenty years and still he didn't know her.

'A bit . . . I'm not good. Well, I'm not bad, actually! I'll show you some time.'

He had a sudden desire to get closer to her. Not physically: he never wanted to get close to a woman like that again. But it suddenly seemed desperately important that she should like him. 'Tell me about it,' he said.


It was too late now to worry, Lilian thought, settling into the pew. Might as well relax and enjoy it, for God only knew how it was going to be paid for. Still, she had promised Karen a proper wedding and that's just what it was going to be. There were flowers on all the windowsills, to match the altar flowers. The bride's dress had cost £180 – nearly the price of a bungalow – but that was the going rate, nowadays. The reception at the George was £5.50 a head, but they had promised her a good feed and they had a good reputation.

By the time Lilian had reviewed all the arrangements in her head, the organ was pealing out triumphantly. She turned to see Karen, radiant on Billy's arm, the bevy of apricot satin bridesmaids behind her – but all she could think of was that the little dead Diana should have been there. Eighteen, she would have been. Eighteen, and the essence of impidence.

Tears started to gather and then to trickle down her

cheeks – until she saw Andrew, the lacy shirt making him look like an angel, one strap of the blue velvet trousers falling from his shoulder, meandering down the aisle, smiling right and left. 'He's enjoying it,' she heard someone behind her whisper. She put her dead child back into the recesses of her mind, and concentrated on admiring the live ones.

After that, it was all over in a flash, and she was chatting in the vestry, posing for the photographs, making sure everyone had a lift to the George. Helen's fancy man was a good help, rounding people up and checking for stragglers. 'You want to snap that one up,' she hissed as Helen passed her in the doorway of the George, but as usual her words fell on deaf ears. And Helen was starting to go at the neck. She'd be left on the shelf if she didn't watch it.

The chicken and salad was all right and the Black Forest gâteau suitably creamy. She heard one or two people remark favourably on the Asti Spumante, and was beginning to feel quite pleased until it was time for the speeches. She had coached Billy and even written it all down for him, but when he stood up he had nothing in his hands. Lilian tried tugging at the sleeve of his jacket, but he took no notice and then he was launched and it was too late.

'Ladies and gentlemen, I think Brian's a lucky man to get our Karen.' This was not what she had told him to say! 'Not just because she's a bonny lass and a good girl to her family. Not because she's a hard worker, although he'd go a long way and not do better. No, the reason why he's lucky is because she's her mother's daughter. And I can tell you, ladies and gentlemen, that they come no better than my Lily . . .'

She compressed her lips and schooled herself not to cry. She would kill him when she got him home, if she didn't die of pleasure first – or remorse, for all the times she'd given him the rough edge of her tongue. She looked up and saw him looking at her fondly, as though she was a favourite bairn.

'Sit down, Billy Fenwick! You've got me going from a salve to an oil.' But he was in no mood to obey her today and she contented herself with spreading her hands in a gesture of resignation.

'Proud of them?' David whispered, as Barbara and Tracy went back and forth among the guests with silver baskets of cake. They looked like flowers in their apricot dresses, their faces solemn as vestal virgins. When Lilian had asked them to be Karen's bridesmaids Diana had thought it would be a fag, but it had really been a pleasure. She looked across at Lilian, her face relaxed today under the broad-brimmed turquoise hat. Was it really almost twenty years since they had met in the hospital? Twenty years, and five dead babies. She had the girls now and Gary, half-asleep on David's knee. But they were not her children. She cared for them, but they were not flesh of her flesh. David's cheek was resting on Gary's hair – for him it had always been different, an instant bonding. If she was honest, that had sometimes come between them in the last few years.

Across the table Helen and Vic were sitting close, probably holding hands under the table. There would surely be a wedding there before long. Helen had met his children and liked them – but would she ever love them? Perhaps other women loved all children automatically. Was she the odd woman out? The old angst stirred in her and she tried to ignore it by watching her daughters carry out their ceremonial duties.

As though she sensed Diana's perplexity Tracy moved to her side. 'I've done ever such a good job, haven't I? Everyone says so.' She sighed slightly as though at the weight of the silver basket and Diana felt her lips twitch.

'They couldn't have done without you, darling.'

Tracy nodded solemnly and sighed again. 'I know.'

David put his lips to Diana's ear. 'It's a hard job being perfect, isn't it?' She looked at him and smiled, but his smile was for his second daughter, basking in her bridesmaid glory.

Diana looked quickly away, and met Barbara's eyes, cool

and contemptuous as ever. 'Three years,' Diana thought, 'and still she keeps her distance.'


Edward had heard clattering and banging in the next but one building all day, in spite of its being a Saturday. Now, as he bolted the door for the night, he saw the workmen leaving the site. There would be five luxury flats when they were finished, where once there had been two dwellings: that was progress, or so they said. He stood for a moment, his hand still on the door catch, as the last workman ambled past, lighting up a cigarette. They would probably be back tomorrow, hammering away at eight o'clock.

As he went upstairs he wondered again how much longer it would make sense for him to stay. Still, he had made a short-term plan. Helen's flat was leased to a tenant, and would continue to be for six months more. When she came back to London she would have to stay with him, so he had booked an interior decorator to redo his mother's room. It was time for a change, and when it was redecorated he would fill it with pieces that would please her, specially to welcome her home.

He pushed open the door as he passed and looked in. He had not realized how shabby the room had become, and it was a shock. His mother's things were still in place on the dressing-table, some of her clothes still in the wardrobe. Helen had slept there occasionally but only as a temporary measure: now, for a while, it was going to be her home. He wanted to get a pad and make a list of treasures for the new room, but he had a job to do first.

He sat down at his desk and wrote out a cheque to the SDP: he had lost faith in the Labour Party, and Mrs Thatcher was beginning to scare him. Perhaps the new lot would do better. He sealed the cheque in an envelope and put it ready for posting.

The decorator's fabric samples were on the top of the desk and he touched them, enjoying the textures and the fabric he had chosen, a delicate shade of aquamarine with a vivid geranium motif. He was suddenly struck by a thought. Downstairs, at the back of the shop, there was a stool which Helen had once admired. Walnut, George Second, red velvet sides, its original top replaced by some Victorian lady's beadwork in shades of grey and aquamarine. Perfect for a dressing-stool. He went downstairs and located it, putting it ready to go for repair.

Then his eye was caught by a pole screen, also in shades of turquoise. He felt the familiar excitement of the collector – but this time he was collecting for something so important . . . he tried not to let his imagination run away with him. After all, she might elect to move in with Vic . . . But he went on choosing and discarding, while the roar of the London traffic in the High Street dwindled until it could not be heard.

'It's been a lovely wedding,' Vic said, holding Lilian's hand and gazing into her eyes. She looked at him intently, trying to decide if he was getting at her or not, and then inclined her head. 'I'm glad you enjoyed it.'

He let go her hand and took Helen's elbow. 'Now I'm going to carry off your sister, if you can spare her?'

Lilian gave him an old-fashioned look and Helen smiled inwardly. 'Come on, idiot. Take no notice of him, Lilian. Seriously though, is there anything I can do?'

'No thanks, Hel. You've been a big help, but all I want to do now is get home and put me feet up. Billy'll have to get the bairn to bed, and then he's off down the club with the other side. They're going to have a knees-up. It wouldn't do for me – I'm glad I've got the bairn as an excuse.'

'Well, it was a lovely wedding. You should be proud,' Helen said. For a moment they looked at one another and then Lilian held out her arms.

'Come here and give us a love. I'm glad you were still here. It wouldn't've been the same without you.'

'I'd've come back,' Helen said. 'For Karen's wedding, I'd've come back from Baluchistan.' She smiled, feeling tears prick her eyes. It was the closest she had been to her sister.

'I would like to sleep with you tonight,' Vic said as they walked to the car.

'Will you lower your voice!' Helen said, looking around. 'This is Belgate, not Chicago. Well, you can't have your wish . . . for the very good reason that your sister would wonder where you were.'

'I don't have to do what my kid sister tells me, my darling. I'm quite a big boy now, in case you haven't noticed. With all a big boy's needs.'

'Oh, I've noticed, all right. You can come round to my flat a bit later on, and say we're going out for a drink. But on the stroke of midnight, home you go!'

He pulled a doubtful face and looked at his watch. 'Midnight . . . well, I suppose it might do.'

He dropped her on the corner and she walked up to her door, fishing in her bag for the key. She had the door half-open when she sensed someone behind her. 'Michael!' she said, turning and clutching her bag to her chest. 'What are you doing back here? I thought you were at the seminary?'

He was looking right and left. 'Can I come in? I haven't been home yet, so I don't want anyone to see me.'

Helen could see from his face that something was wrong, and agitation gripped her as she ushered him in and shut the door. 'Come in. I'll make some coffee, and then we can talk.'


Sitting in the outer office of Cotton, Whittington & Grey, pretending to read a back copy of *Punch*, Helen analysed her feelings. She was calm, but it was an unreal serenity that gripped her. Would she break down when it was time for the inner sanctum? Would she stammer and stutter, or give away more than she should? She turned her head to the sheaves of leaflets . . . *How to Invest, Use your Solicitor, The Northern Building Society, Planet Insurance* and, incongruously, *Catholic Marriage Guidance*. Of course, that would be Howard Whittington's idea.

The grey-haired woman who had taken her name came out of the inner office, leaving the door ajar. 'Miss Clark, Mr Whittington will see you now.'

Suddenly Helen's calm deserted her. She stood up, reeling a little so that she had to put out a hand to steady herself. 'I'm sorry . . . I lost my balance.' Was it her imagination or did the woman lean towards her as though to smell her breath? The next moment she was in Howard's office and he was rising to greet her.

'Helen. Do sit down. Now, how can I help you?' Howard seated himself behind his desk again and smiled at her expectantly.

'It's difficult to know where to begin. I . . . I hope you'll understand . . . it's really none of my business . . .' His face was changing now as he realized that she was not here on orthodox business. Should she tell him the whole truth? Would that help her cause, or hinder it?

'It's not Susan, is it?' He was looking at her anxiously and suddenly she found the words.

'Michael came to see me last night, before going home to you. I know it seems strange, but he came to talk to me about something rather than to you or his mother – or his uncle and aunt. I think I know why he did. He knows me, he likes me a little even, but there are no emotional ties. He can be honest with me without feeling he's hurting me or letting me down, because I'm not involved.'

'Is he in some kind of trouble?' Howard's tone was sombre, his hand moving along the edges of the papers on his desk like a blind man feeling his way. Helen had half-expected him to be hostile or at least annoyed by her interference, but he was not. She gathered a little confidence, and went on.

'Yes, he is – but not the kind of trouble you mean, I think. He feels he's not cut out for the priesthood, that his heart's not in it. But he also feels that if he comes to you or his mother and says so, you'll be terribly disappointed. His words to me were, "It'll break their hearts." He didn't come to ask me for help in getting out of it; he's determined to go on and be ordained. Mine was just a shoulder to cry on; it was a chance to talk out all his feelings before he puts on a brave face and carries on. But I felt I ought to tell you . . . you in preference to his mother, because I know you better – no other reason.'

Did Howard detect that lie? In a funny way, though, he was looking relieved, as though her news might have been worse, the problem more intractable. But was he going to help?

'Michael never said anything about this last night. He seemed to us . . . quite as usual. However, I'm not doubting your word. Michael – ' He was standing up and moving to the window so that she could not see his face. 'Michael has not been encouraged to exhibit his feelings. My wife is a very devout Catholic and she feels problems are best shared with one's confessor . . . or with God. Has Michael spoken about this to his priest?'

He did not seem to find it at all odd that a comparative outsider might know more about his son than he did, and Helen found that strange. 'Yes,' she said. 'I gather that he's discussed it with his tutors and with his priest, and they have told him it must be his own decision. They also suggested he should talk to you and to his mother. That was the purpose of his visit home.'

'I wondered why he had come,' Howard said, turning to face her. 'But, in fact, he doesn't intend to speak to us?'

Helen nodded. 'He thinks it would upset you both far too much. So he's going back tomorrow . . . unless you do something to stop him.'


'Will I play in the sand-pit?' Andrew's eyes were on her, bright with excitement.

'If you're a good boy.' His hand in hers was so little, so trusting. Lilian had dreaded this moment, but it had to be done. Nursery gave you an advantage when you went on to school: Diana had said so, and it must be true. Her Gary had gone, and look at him.

'Will I come home for me dinner?'

Lilian nodded. 'I told you you would. You never listen.' If he got in the top stream at school in his first year, he would be away. The top stream always got on. They could call it comprehensive or anything else they liked, but it was still sheep and goats. If your elbow was out of your jersey and your mam set her lip up to the teacher, you'd had it –

but she meant to box clever this time. She'd been slipshod with Karen, and look what had happened there. A-levels never taken and four months pregnant. Still, it was different for girls, they got married.

She turned the corner and there it was before them, windows marked by coloured stickers of flowers and animals. When they had made their visit last week the place had hummed with activity and children's laughter. Now, somehow it looked less inviting. If she missed him too much she could come and see him at playtime. Not right up to the railings, they'd been warned about that. But there was a shop on the corner opposite, where she could stand in the doorway and peep out.

A girl had come up behind her with a baby in a pushchair and a toddler by the hand. 'Is he starting nursery too?' she said, nodding at Andrew.

Lilian inclined her head. 'Yes, he's all fixed up. Is yours going?'

The little girl had disentangled herself from her mother and was trying to capture Andrew's hand, but he was having none of it. 'Get off,' he said and looked appealingly at Lilian.

'Girls are pushy, aren't they?' the young mother said. 'Leave off, Kim, you'll have him over in a minute.' She turned back to Lilian. 'I'll be glad to be rid of her three mornings a week, I can tell you. She's a right handful.' She looked at Andrew. 'Does his mother work?'

Lilian struggled to comprehend and then light dawned: 'She thinks I'm his grandmother! The cheeky monkey!' She seized Andrew's hand and held it firmly. 'I don't know what you mean – I'm his mother.' The girl was looking as though she hoped the ground would open and swallow her up, but that was small satisfaction to Lilian. When Andrew went inside she would be left to walk away with a group of girls hardly out of nappies themselves.

It was a daunting thought but she knew how to counteract a single worry: bury it in something else, that was the answer. She thought about the bills for Karen's wedding, mounting on the sideboard. God knows how they would be paid. Still, she would manage; she always managed.

And she would make sure she lived long enough to see Andrew up and thriving, which was more than could be said for the pasty-faced lass with the pushchair.

Lilian mounted the steps to the Nursery door, and prepared to surrender her son to higher things.


'They're at a loss now the other kids have gone back to school,' Diana said. In the garden Tracy swung languidly on the swing, Barbara was full length on the grass reading, and Gary was rolling in the flowerbeds as usual. 'He's going to be an exavator,' David said gloomily. 'He has to be digging holes in something. It's in his blood.'

Diana joined him at the window, slipping her arm around his waist. 'He's going to be a barrister. I can just see him in wig and gown.'

David shook his head. 'Barbara will be the barrister, Tracy will go in for the theatre, and Gary will take up roads for the Gas Board.'

'Lilian wants Andrew to be a doctor, did she tell you? She's got it all mapped out. He starts Nursery today, by the way. She'll be lost.'

'She'll survive, she's a survivor, the old News of the World. And that's a bright boy she's got there – he could well make the profession if he gets the right schooling.'

They both fell silent, uneasy about the whole question of education. At last Diana couldn't resist putting her thoughts into words. 'It makes you feel guilty, doesn't it? I mean, our lot are all getting a good education because we can afford it . . . just. But if we keep pulling our kids out of the state system, how will it ever improve?'

'There's a certain arrogance in that argument, my darling. It implies that our kids are somehow necessary to the process of good schooling. In fact, they're not – or they shouldn't be. The quality of what's on offer should be the same, public sector or fee-paying. All the same, it does make for divisions. Our kids are out there, bored, while the kids they play with, their friends, have gone back to school. So already they know there's a difference. Just as Michael and Susan have never made friends with their neighbours' children, because they, in the main, are Protestant and go to a different school.'

'You could make out a case for saying all kids should go to a single state school . . .'

'Except that that would be an unwarrantable intrusion into the rights of the individual. Do you know what I think?'

'What?'

'I think we should get off this subject now before we get even more depressed. At least they're all healthy, and if we educate them all to be leaders of society they can do a better job of it than their parents ever did. Now kiss me, and then go and put the kettle on. I am going out to teach my son overarm bowling . . . if I can get him away from his tunnelling.'

Diana wanted to talk to him now, to tell him again of her long-held doubts, but she knew from experience that it would be useless. He couldn't understand her lack of maternal feeling for the children because his own feelings for them were so overwhelming. It was the subject on which they could find no meeting-point, and she found it increasingly hard to forgive him his lack of understanding.


Howard sat at the back of the church, keeping his eyes closed as though in prayer. It was not his own church, it was not even a Catholic church, but he could sit here without anyone noticing and engaging him in conversation. 'Help me, God. Let me do what is right. I need to be strong and I am weak.' In his mind's eye a vision of the Virgin arose, pale-blue and perfect. He opened his eyes to the comparative bleakness of the Anglican decor, but the image remained. 'Holy Mary, Mother of God, have mercy on us . . .' It was the mercilessness of women that was to blame for his misery, for his son's misery. He got to his feet, checked himself when his knee would have bent to the altar, and went out to his car.

On the drive home he willed himself not to think. If he tried to find a formula of words, he would surely fail. He thought about Darlasden, about Dembry's store, chanting the departments aloud so that they excluded any other thought from his mind. 'Haberdashery, Hosiery, Stationery, Clocks and Watches, Books, Gloves, Belts and Handbags . . .' He parked the car in the drive and went into the house.

Michael was in his room, lying on his bed, a copy of Cervantes face down beside him, and Howard spoke out before he lost his nerve. 'Michael, I want a straight answer. Do you want to leave the seminary? I'm not asking whether or not you *should* leave it but whether or not you want to? What would you do with your life if neither your mother nor I existed, if you were alone in the world without a single obligation to anything or anybody? I know you have never lied to me – not directly. Now I order you to tell me the truth.'

Edward swung back the door of the encoignure to reveal a glowing interior, unfaded by sun. 'It's expensive I'm afraid. It has all the features . . . serpentine front, the top is white Carrara marble, brass inlay on tortoiseshell, internal drawers and shaped shelves. It's *circa* 1860. A very nice piece.'

The customer obviously knew his furniture, and had nodded agreement as Edward spoke. Now he ran gentle fingers over the piece and closed the door. 'How much?'

Edward pondered for a second. 'Six-fifty. I have one other, similar, not quite so pleasing, but cheaper. And of course there's the tulipwood over there at £1,500.'

The customer laughed. 'Quite. Let's stick to this one. I take your point about the interior, and of course they're coming very much into vogue . . .'

'They've never been out of vogue for me,' Edward said. He liked the look of the man. He particularly liked the way he was caressing the cabinet work. If it went to him, it would be cherished. He made rapid calculations. He had bought in at £300 and spent a further £100 on its distressed state. 'I could come down to £575,' he said.

When the man had gone away, satisfied, Edward sat down at his desk and spread out the invoices he was checking for the accountant. Helen had always been so good with the paperwork. He had just uncapped his pen when the doorbell jangled as the shop door opened. The woman entering had a child in her arms, rosy-cheeked, with hair like a Botticelli cherub, and was beaming at him. He rose to his feet. 'Celia! How nice to see you. Come in.'

He locked the shop door and shepherded them up to the flat. When he had made tea, and taken orange juice from the fridge for the child, he sat down beside them. 'He's beautiful, Celia.' He held out the twin-handled Vienna beaker and the child took it from him, large blue eyes searching his face until the lashes drooped over the cup. If he had married Celia this might have been his child, this beautiful infant with hands like agitated butterflies, curling and uncurling around the handles.

'It's not a good cup, is it?' Celia asked nervously. The Vienna beaker, with its precisely painted flowers, was probably worth £300, but it had been made for a child's hands more than two centuries ago. 'No, it's not a good one,' he said soothingly. 'Old, but not too valuable. You look well, Celia. Marriage suits you.'

She was blushing. He had forgotten how natural she had been, how loving. 'I'm a lot fatter, if that's what you mean.'

He shook his head. Why had he not married her when he had the chance? What a fool he had been. 'Let me give you some tea,' he said, 'and then we can catch up on the last few years.'


'Come on . . . last one to the top washes up supper.' Susan was bursting with energy and good humour, but Michael was quieter than usual. Helen looked at him as they toiled slowly up the slope, the April evening turning to dusk around them. In the west the sky glowed molten red, lending an eerie glow to the landscape and making him look at once older and more vulnerable than his years.

Susan had already cast herself down on the hilltop and was out of earshot. Michael spoke hesitantly. 'Dad says you went to see him today.'

'Yes, I did. Do you mind?' Helen braced herself for disapproval if it came, but there was no anger in his voice.

'No. I suppose it makes sense. I should have talked to Dad myself, though. Now I feel he'll feel . . .'

She broke in. 'Michael, perhaps you feel too much. It's right to care about your father, but not at the expense of your own happiness. He doesn't want that kind of sacrifice from you, he told me that this morning. He only wants what is right for you.'

She had lost him. She had probably won him his freedom, but his face was closing against her now as he battled with divided loyalties. She remembered Howard's remorse this morning: *'It's my fault. My fault. I haven't been what I should have been, to the boy or to the girl. I'm to blame.'* But she herself had been to blame, too . . . and Anne, who had acted according to her lights . . . and Alistair . . . She saw Susan's eyes on her as they neared the summit, and summoned up a smile. 'You're a right little opportunist, madam. You wait till you're ten yards in front and then decree a race. What a swizz!'

'She's like that,' Michael said, smiling indulgently at his sister. They wrestled playfully as Susan teased him with a piece of couch grass. Perhaps it was going to be all right. Helen sat down on the turf and looked down at Belgate on one side and Darlasden on the other.

'Watch the lights springing up,' Susan said. 'It's like fairyland.'

'All those people,' Michael brooded. 'Living and dying down there . . . but it still goes on, doesn't it?' He seemed to have got over his unease. Perhaps it would be alright after all. He tried to tie a knot in a blade of grass and failing, cast it to the wind. 'Do you have, well, a kind of loyalty to Durham, Helen? I mean, not just a family thing but a sort of affinity to the place itself?'

'I used not to,' Helen said. 'I couldn't get away from it quick enough once.'

'Why did you come back?' Susan said, suddenly interested. 'Everyone has a theory, what's the truth?' Michael was looking askance but his sister was unperturbed. 'Don't look like that, Michael. I want to know.'

'I came back because of a man,' Helen said.

'A nice man?' Susan was sitting forward for a reply.

'A very nice man,' Helen said firmly.

'Nice men are boring,' Susan said, making Michael shake his head in mock-disapproval. 'Wrap up, Michael. Just because you're going to be a cardinal, you don't have to be pious.' So Susan didn't know yet, Helen thought. That meant it still hadn't been discussed in the home.

'You said a nice man,' Susan persisted. 'Better than Uncle Vic?'

Helen stood up. 'In a different age-group, Miss Impudence.' Below them Darlasden was a web of streets and highways, strung now with lamps, gleaming faintly in the dusk.

'It'll be odd to leave here,' Susan said suddenly, sounding reflective.

'You could train in Darlasden,' Michael said. 'At the Infirmary.'

'No thank you, brother dear, I am going to spread my wings . . . and so will you, if you have any sense. Won't he, Helen?'

'He must make up his own mind,' Helen said. 'Now, stop bullying him or you can cook supper *and* wash up.'

She walked down the hill, treading warily in the gathering dark, the outline of her son's head before her so familiar now that even when she closed her eyes she could see its well-loved contours.


Howard knocked on the door and entered without waiting for permission. 'Anne, I want to speak to you.'

She continued to tie the belt of her négligé as though nothing had happened, and yet he had not entered her bedroom unbidden since that night on the stairs when she had banished him to the spare room.

'It's very late, Howard. Won't it wait until morning?'

He moved forward, between her and the prie-dieu. He had seen her eyes slide to the beads lying on the coverlet. When she sank to her knees she could always freeze him out, but tonight he would not allow it.

'No, Anne, it won't wait. I am well aware of my own limitations, and if I sleep on it I will lose my nerve. My son's happiness is too important to be sacrificed to my inadequacy.' He had scored a hit, he knew it from the way her eyelids dropped, just for a second.

'What is it then, Howard? Please be quick. I spoke to Michael before I came up, and he seemed perfectly all right to me then.'

'Did he? Did he really, Anne? How do you measure your son's happiness? Do you care enough to try?' Even to his own ears his voice sounded harsh, like that of a hostile stranger.

'I won't listen if you are going to be abusive, Howard. We'll talk in the morning . . . if there is anything to talk about.'

It was the terrible certainty of victory in her tone that riled him. She was dismissing him! He moved forward and reached for her shoulders. 'Now listen to me, bitch. Bitch, bitch, bitch! I have let you ruin my life with your hatred of every single thing that is human and natural, but I will not let you shut out my son from the simple happiness that a man can get from a loving woman. Did you always mean to deny me, Anne . . . or did I repel you when it actually came down to it? That's what I've asked myself a thousand times. "Her or me?" I wondered. "Her fault or mine?"'

Anne was not flinching. He could feel skin and flesh moving over bone as he gripped her, but she gave him eye for eye, unmoved. Tomorrow she would bear the marks, and for her they would be stigmata.

He released his grip and moved back from her. He had wanted to wound her, but she could not be wounded by anything he could say. He could still spoil her plans, though – her precious plans to give God her son.

'Listen carefully, Anne, and believe me. Michael is not going back to the seminary. He wants to be a sailor, and tomorrow morning I am taking him to the Naval Careers Service. Don't work on him in your usual way, because if you do I will kill you. You don't fear death, I know that, and martyrdom would suit you. But if you die he will go to the Navy anyway. So either way, I win.'

As he moved to the door he half expected her to sink to her knees, to hear the clicking beads, to see the restless lips. But as he turned in the doorway he saw that she was standing where he had left her, hands by her sides. He moved along the landing, trying desperately to enjoy his triumph, and finding only a terrible feeling of futility.

# 30

Helen already had her ticket. She was first through the barrier, moving to the end of the platform, standing behind a pillar. She wanted to look and see if Michael was there, but she dared not risk it. When the encounter came it must seem completely unplanned.

On the opposite side of the railway lines the trees were already changing colour. It was less than four months to Christmas, and still she clung to Darlasden as though afraid of breaking away while Michael was here. The loudspeaker gave out a garbled message, and then the train appeared in the distance. She picked up her bag and got ready to board.

Until the train was well out of Darlasden, Helen sat in the first available seat, but then she got to her feet and began to make her way down the swaying aisle. She found Michael in Coach G, his rucksack on a seat beside him, his case with its 'HMS Raleigh, Torpoint' label on the rack above. 'Michael! I didn't realize you were getting this train. What a nice surprise. Do you mind if I sit beside you?'

Her heart warmed at his beaming welcome. 'You never said you were going to London? I didn't see you on the platform. Dad came to see me off.' His face clouded briefly and she knew he was thinking of Anne.

'I didn't realize I was going,' she said easily. 'When we said goodbye yesterday afternoon, I had no idea. Then my partner rang last night, something rather urgent. I had today off, so . . . here I am.'

'Will you see Uncle Vic in London . . . or is he still in South Africa?'

They talked a while of Vic and David and Diana, and then Michael stood up. 'Can I get you coffee or something?'

He grinned and she suddenly realized how much he had changed in the months since she had spoken to Howard. 'I'm rather flush. Dad was generous with the going-away money . . . and I'm famished.'

'Didn't your mother cook breakfast?' Helen regretted saying it but she couldn't help it.

'She didn't come down,' Michael answered. 'I said good-bye to her in the bedroom. I don't think she's awfully well at the moment . . .' The old loyalty surfaced. 'She's been very good about things. It's not what she wants, but she gave me her blessing.'

There was a queue at the buffet and Helen watched as he joined it. He was tall now, broadening, his wrists starting to shoot from the cuffs of his jacket. A terrible pain grew inside her: this had been a mistake, this grand idea of hers. She had wanted to see him on his journey to a new life, to be with him for just a few hours at a vital moment. He was on his way to Torpoint, to HMS *Raleigh*, to do his basic Naval training. He had told her a dozen times in the last few weeks, so that she knew the details by heart.

She looked out at the countryside flashing by, but all she could see was the scene in the bedroom this morning – the boy craving his mother's blessing on his enterprise. And receiving it . . . or so he said. Did that fit in with everything she knew of Anne? In any event, it was not enough. He should have had arms around him, loving arms, someone to say: 'I'm proud of you, Michael. Go out and conquer the world.'

'I *have* to tell him,' she thought suddenly. 'I have to tell him now that he is loved and wanted, that since I got to know him I have never stopped loving him for a second.' But then he would have to know it all, not least that she had lied to him, that their whole relationship was a sham.

He was coming back to the seat, a cup in each hand, grinning as the train rocked and coffee slopped over the sides. She saw a girl look up at him and smile, saw the Adam's apple in his throat bob at the overture. 'Oh, my son,' she thought, 'I so much want you to be happy.'

'There you are . . . and it's on me, so stop reaching for your bag.' He leaned forward. 'You've been a good friend

to me, Helen. The best. To Susan, as well. I'll miss you.'
He reached into his jacket pocket and pulled out a sandwich pack. 'Bacon and lettuce, one each. Don't say I don't
do ladies proud.'

She smiled and took a sandwich, chewing it carefully to
obviate the need to speak. Outside, the autumn countryside was golden-brown, blurring as she fought back tears.
She was here with him, that was the important thing. For
three hours she would have him to herself. 'I think this is
the nicest breakfast I have ever had,' she said and smiled
at her son.


Howard stood by the window, looking down on the market
square. Everyone was rushing, in a hurry to beat the nine
o'clock deadline and be in time for work. He had spent the
last hour in church, at peace and giving thanks. Michael
was off and running. Susan would go to Guy's in two
weeks' time. Then he and Anne would be left alone in the
empty house, as they had been all those years before.

In the end, it had all been easier than he had feared. She
had tried to retrieve Michael, but he had countered it. He
had watched as the boy, torn in two at first, finally decided
to give up the priesthood and join the Royal Navy.

Now, though, he had to think about the future. He was
fifty years old – not a great age, nowadays. He would
probably live for another thirty years. Could he spend them
with Anne? Could he live without her? Were they inextric-
ably bound together, the one intended as a scourge for the
other?

Mrs Fraser came in with tea. 'I thought you'd like a cup.
Did Michael get away?' They talked the easy talk of parents
whose offspring are doing well. He liked the feeling. He
liked this simple tea ceremony, the shared coffee, the
occasional meal they had together when work demanded
it. Perhaps if he watched the children grow and flourish,
making their own lives, if he had this oasis here, he could
live out his life with Anne? Perhaps he could even find pity
for her eventually?

'Well,' Mrs Fraser said, collecting his cup, 'I suppose we must make a start.'

He nodded. 'Yes, it's a full day. I'm in court at eleven. Can you ring Dowson at Lawson and Sparkes and ask about exchanging the Wear Street contracts? And could you put in my apologies to Rotary? I'll be in Newcastle tomorrow.' She was nodding as she moved to the door.

'And would you send my wife some flowers – you'll know the right sort. It's not every day you lose a son, is it? It ought to be marked.'


Lilian watched as Andrew went through the Nursery door without a backward glance. 'Be proud he's not a mammy's boy,' she told herself but it didn't help. Still, Billy was on back-shift and would need his breakfast. She hurried back to the house to fry his bacon and black pudding and turn out a perfect fried egg on toast.

'I've been thinking,' she said, sitting opposite him to pour two mugs of tea. 'I've been thinking about money.'

He emptied his mouth to click disapproval. 'Never do that, Lily, pet. It leads to an early grave.'

'Worry's what leads to the grave, Billy, not thinking things through. We've got a lot of bills off our Karen's wedding, and a loan to the Provvy. I know you're doing your best with SatSuns – I could call you a lot of things but you're not lazy. Anyroad, I reckon it's up to me. I'm going to get a job again, only this time I won't ruin everything by falling wrong.'

He grinned at her wickedly above a forkful of black pudding. 'You can never tell, pet . . . a luscious, loving woman like you, it's enough to drive a man mad with passion.'

She aimed a blow at his arm, not at all displeased with his words. She had been feeling a bit down since yesterday with that lass mistaking her for a granny! She had a few good years left in her yet, and they'd better all realize it.

'What kind of job are you thinking of, pet?' Billy asked. 'You're not getting any younger, you know. I don't want

376

you knocking yourself up. It's up to me to do the providing.'

She gave him short shrift after that, bundling him out to the pit, bait can and all. She would give him 'not getting younger'! But the face in the mirror in the bedroom stood witness to what he had said. 'I look a hundred,' she said out loud. She had been a good-looking girl only yesterday, or so it seemed, but now the colour was going from face, eyes, hair, as though life were draining out of her, bit by bit. She opened the drawer of the dressing-table and pulled out the jar of body cream Helen had given her for her birthday. It smelled like a Chinese brothel, but when she stuck in a finger it was cool and creamy, vanishing instantly when she stroked it behind her ears.

It was years since she had bought herself any perfume. It had been Coty L'Aimant then, guaranteed to drive Billy wild. But the bairns had come along, and the bills, and she had been content with soap and water and plenty of it. Her skin was parched, that was it – cracking now like the ground in Africa, on the telly. She couldn't go and spend money on it though, even supposing her skin flaked off and left her like a battered pluck.

She stood up suddenly and went into the next bedroom, so recently vacated by Karen. Treasure trove! Half-empty pots of goo for everywhere short of your armpit, and even a spray for that. Lilian picked up a lipstick and outlined her mouth with a shaky hand. She was out of practice but it would all come back. She sped in search of a bath and a new start.

'What do you think?' Susan's face was anxious above the clinging green dress.

'Stunning,' Diana said firmly.

'You don't think it's a bit, well . . .?'

Diana nodded gravely. 'Yes, it's very "well . . ." But why not? You have the figure, the legs, and age is on your side. God, if I could get one leg in it, I'd be happy.'

'You're not fat, Auntie . . . you're cuddly. But are you sure it's me?'

Diana nodded and smiled, groaning inwardly at the thought of the next two hours. Howard had told her to spare no expense, so they might still be here at midnight! Still, it was fun. What a fool Anne was to miss all this. 'What does your mother think about your going to London?' she said aloud.

Susan shrugged. 'I don't suppose she's noticed, you know what she's like. I should be grateful to her, and I am – but she never really wanted me. I've often wondered why they took me . . . well, Dad loves me, I suppose, but even he's lukewarm. They won't care when I'm gone. Dad'll make sure I don't want for anything, and he'll quite miss me . . . but it won't be like you and your lot. No one will die of grief for me.'

Diana sought desperately for a lie, a good lie, one she could make stick. 'It's not like that, Susan . . .' But the girl in front of her, honest eyes on hers, deserved better. 'They're a bit different, your parents, I'll grant you that. They're not the type to coo and fuss . . . David says I smother the kids and he's probably right. But it's not strictly true to say they don't care . . .'

Susan's eyes were scornful, but that was the least of Diana's problems. Inside her head the girl's words were repeating and it wasn't comfortable: *'Not like you'*, *'not like you.'* But was she any different from Anne: she didn't feel Barbara, or Tracy, or even Gary, was her child. They all were her responsibility and she would never harm them, not even by one inconsiderate word. But she didn't, *couldn't*, love them as she had loved the five dead babies she had carried under her heart. And if Barbara was typical of the three, they didn't really want her love.

Aloud she said, 'We'd better get a move on. Your father said pull out all the stops, so you've got some serious spending to do before we can have tea.'

'It's a bit ridiculous,' Susan said, wriggling into a yellow jersey shift dress and tying the belt. 'I'll be in uniform all day at Guy's and too fagged out at night to dress up. All the same, I suppose I might meet some handsome stockbroker and start to live a life of total debauchery . . .'

'Knowing you,' Diana said, 'it'll probably be an anarchist

with a ring in his nose who'll teach you to make bombs and subvert the nation. I can just see your father's face when it comes out in the *Sun*.'

Susan was smiling. 'I'd like that . . . but it won't happen. Anyway, I'll have my lovely Helen to keep an eye on me. She's going back to London soon, isn't she?'

Diana stood up to twitch the yellow shift into place around her niece's knees. 'She's going down there to be with Uncle Vic . . . don't you dare be a gooseberry. I have great hopes of that affair, and if you behave you might be bridesmaid. Helen is just daft enough to let you. I don't think that dress suits you – let's try something else.'

Edward was on the phone when he saw Helen through the glass door panels. 'I'll ring you later, Philip. I see a customer.' As he got to his feet and moved to the door, he could see she had been crying, but he was not prepared for what happened when she was safely inside the door. 'Helen, what's wrong . . . has something happened?'

She was in his arms, sobbing now against his shirt, while he held her, soothed the curly black hair, touched the wet cheeks. He wanted to kiss the damp eyelids, to hold her so close that he would blot out everything that could cause her pain. Instead, he held her at arm's length and spoke sharply. 'Stop it, Helen. Tell me what's wrong?' She looked up, shaking her head wordlessly. 'Come on, now, why are you crying?'

'I came to London with Michael, Edward. I must have been mad. Sitting there, watching him – and then, when we got to King's Cross, "Goodbye, Helen," he said. "Goodbye, Helen," and then he walked away. I love him, Edward. I've tried not to, I've really tried . . . but I do love him, and I want to hear him say I matter to him.'

Edward drew her close again, holding her gently, content that she had come to him. 'There, there,' he said. 'There, there.'

He went on holding her till she drew back and smiled at him. 'Idiotic, isn't it? After all these years . . . I must be losing my grip.'

They went upstairs, the shop door locked behind them. She turned when they were inside the living-room and moved back into the shelter of his arms. 'Oh Edward,' she said, 'what on earth would I do without you?' She looked up suddenly. 'If you ever marry, will we still be friends?'

He let her go and went into the kitchen. 'I expect so,' he said, trying hard to quell the earthquake inside him. He left the kettle beginning to moan and began to set a tray. 'Anyway, I have no firm intentions at the moment with regard to marriage, so let's not speculate. Michael's gone then . . . does that mean you're here for good?'

Helen had come down on a flying visit, simply to share the journey with her son. 'So you see I must go back tonight, on the sleeper, and tell David I'm leaving next month. I'll give notice at the flat, and clear things up there. Michael said we might meet in London . . . he'll want to come here and see Susan.'

'There you are, then,' Edward said. 'So you're not going to be separated from him at all.' Desperate as he was to cheer her up, in his heart he was dubious. The situation was getting out of hand. Sooner or later she was going to tell the boy the truth, and what would happen then?

He drank his tea but all he could think of was the feeling of her in his arms, at once more slender and more vibrant than he had ever imagined. He wanted her so much, but he would probably never hold her like that again unless in further grief – and he loved her too much to countenance such a price.


It felt good to be back behind the fryer, deciding who would get chips and when, picking out big fillets for those she liked and warped bits for those she didn't. Lilian had called in at lunch-time on the off-chance, and been greeted with open arms. 'When do you want me to start,' she'd asked and had been told, 'Yesterday.'

She noticed one or two, now, giving her the eye but pretended not to see them. She felt good, smelling of Max Factor from head to foot, her hair tied up in a chiffon scarf except for a curly fringe, eyes, cheeks and lips all made up to tone. She would have to speak to Karen about extravagance – if that was what she had left behind . . .

She pushed back a gleaming chrome lid and inspected the seething fat. In with the slatted ladle, lift, shake, nip a chip, drop them back, close the lid and look at the queue with the sombre face of a High Court judge. She had them by the short and curlies, and there would be a pay packet at the week's end. Money for jam. She had left Billy a note, explaining her whereabouts and asking him to collect Andrew from two doors down. Her neighbour had gawped when she answered the door. 'Eeh, mind, Lilian . . . you don't half look different!'

Billy would come in, no doubt about it – looking for a cod lot and batter, and all for nothing. He would notice the headscarf first, and then the mascara and lipstick. That would learn him to talk about 'getting on': she wasn't even in the change yet, but regular as clockwork. They had tied her tubes when Andrew was born, so she had no need of the pill. But the operation could be reversed in an emergency – they had told her that before they did it, and she had had to hold in her laughter at the very idea of ever wanting to be put through that lot again.

Now, though, she was not so sure. What would happen when she no longer had a period, when Billy no longer wanted her? Some women started the change in their thirties. She was forty-three. But she had started early, at twelve, and they said if you started early you finished late. Lilian felt quite cheered at remembering this, and decided to release some cod for the peasants queuing patiently beyond the counter.

It was then that she saw him, leaning on the counter talking to a young wife in an anorak with sleepers in her ears and a mole on her cheek. 'Billy!' She moved round the fryer and picked up a piece of greaseproof. 'What do you want, pet? I'll get it for you, save you standing.' She looked at him sweetly, letting her lashes flutter a little, her lips getting ready to make light of his compliment.

'Cod, please, Lily . . . salt and vin . . . plenty batter. And don't go easy on the chips, I don't have a weight problem.'

'What do you mean by that, Billy Fenwick?'

The dark-haired wife was watching him and he knew it, the sod.

'Why, I don't mean anything, pet. Howay, givvus the cod . . . Eric Bristow's on the telly. Let the dog see the rabbit.'

He had never even noticed the lips and the lashes, much less smelled her Geminesse. 'Men?' she said as she moved to the fryer. 'Give me alligators!'

They had walked round the hall admiring the work exhibited there, trying not to beam stupidly if they found a piece marked 'Whittington, Second Form'. David had talked to the Head and Diana to the Senior Mistress. Now they moved towards the queue for Barbara's form mistress.

'What d'you think she'll say?' Diana whispered as they shuffled along the seats towards the desk.

David moved his head closer to hers. 'The truth, of course. That she is brilliant, unique, wonderful and a credit to her parents.'

In the event, it was almost precisely what the Form Mistress did say. '. . . so she's got a very bright future, all being well. Next year we'll have subject options . . . but I think Barbara will be all right, whatever she chooses.'

They moved outside in a glow. 'See?' David said. 'Told you.' He opened the car door. 'Fancy a quick drink on the way back? They'll be all right with Susan for another half-hour.'

'I'd like a drink, darling, but we'd better get back. Gary was a bit droopy today, and I promised we wouldn't be long.'

He folded her into the car and came round to his own seat. 'You're at it again – over-protecting. And you were the one who had doubts before we took them . . .'

There it was again, that unintended prick to her conscience. Perhaps she over-mothered them to compensate for maternal feelings she didn't have? She glanced sideways at David, seeing the contented set of his features, and had a sudden, irrational desire to wipe the smile off his face. 'It hasn't all been beer and skittles,' she said and felt a savage satisfaction as the shot went home.

Howard had dreaded dinner ever since he learned that Susan would not be there, and that was odd because evenings lately, with Susan full of rebellion and Anne so curiously detached, had been nightmarish. He went into the kitchen at five minutes to eight and offered to help, the ritual offer ritually refused.

In the dining-room he poured himself some wine and wandered across to the mantelpiece. Susan and Michael on the day of their first communion; Anne as a girl, grave even then; he and David in a rowing boat, squinting at the sun. He had found that on his mother's bedside table after her death and brought it home with him. The two of them had been so close then, a regular David and Jonathan. Now they hardly spoke except on state occasions. They were brothers, and yet were less close than Michael and Susan who had no blood ties at all. They should have been a comfort to one another, both afflicted by childlessness. But their cases had been so different. At least David had proved his manhood by fathering five children. He himself had not even achieved that, and the one time he had believed it to be true it had been a tawdry lie.

'Shall we sit down?' Anne was putting the tureen on the table and he moved to adjust her chair. She had grown even thinner of late; there were cords in her face, veins upraised on hands and forearms. He felt a sudden inexplicable tenderness towards her.

'How was your day?' She was handing him a plate and removing the lid from the vegetables.

'Ooh . . . much the same as usual,' Howard answered. 'I seem to be in a bit of a backwater now. I get the rather dull, prestigious clients, and the younger partners get the exciting stuff. I've been thinking, Anne – I could easily get away after Susan goes. What about the Scottish lochs, or a fortnight in Cornwall? I could do with a break.'

If only she would display some emotion – even hate for the battle he had fought and won over Michael – that would be better than this utter absence of feeling. 'If you'd like to go, we could make some enquiries?' he said again, coaxingly.

Anne smiled, but she didn't speak. She wouldn't even say no to him. They went on eating in silence, each conscious of the empty chairs at the table, each locked in a strange, separate Hades which they carried into the sitting-room along with the coffee and then upstairs to their silent rooms.


Helen felt better now, in the restaurant, her face cooled from the weeping of the morning. 'This is nice, Edward.'

He turned from ordering wine and smiled. 'That's better. Now, let's make some plans. Business first, then we'll get round to the other stuff.'

'The unimportant stuff?' she said, laughing.

'That's right,' he agreed. 'The unimportant stuff like love and holidays and where to live. You should have a holiday, you know. Why don't we fly to Malta or the Canaries . . . or the Gambia. I could do with some groundnuts – wasn't that the Gambia?'

'I don't want a holiday, I want to get back to work. Do you think I'll be able to pick up where I left off? I feel out of touch – you know how prices change and fancies fluctuate. It took me fifteen years to master the business . . . now I'm four years behind.'

'Not really,' he said, reaching to pat her hand. 'You get things wound up in Durham and we'll soon have you back in the swim. You've never lost touch with the dolls, you've always advised me there. And you'll soon pick up the rest, with a few days in the shop and one or two good sales. You have a feel for it, Helen.' He didn't want to mention Vic but he couldn't resist it. 'When does Vic get back?'

He saw her face break into a smile, the foolish indulgent smile of the lover. 'This week-end. He's here until Christmas at least: isn't that nice? And I might see Michael before then. He says he does six weeks basic training and then four weeks at HMS *Sultan* at Gosport . . . that's his actual mechanical training. He gets a weekend at that stage, and then it's back for more training – but he'll have those precious few days. And after that, of course, there's Christmas.'

'Won't he want to go back to Durham for that?'

She shook her head perplexedly. 'I don't know. I think he'll feel he should . . . but he'll also want to be here with Susan. It will be quite a tug for him.'

'Do you still want to tell him?'

Helen lifted a finger to her mouth. 'I don't know. At times the need for the truth almost overwhelms me – and then I think of the sheer impossibility of telling him. How can he ever understand, Edward? How do I explain why I've lived a lie for four years?'

'And there's another thing . . . when and how do I tell Vic? And if I tell Vic, will he tell Diana? I don't think I could bear Diana to know about all the lies over all the years. Do you think I should tell him? How much of your past do you owe to a lover?'

Edward felt shocked by the use of the word 'lover', as shocked as if she had blasphemed. He couldn't bear the thought of her in bed with Vic, and he certainly didn't want Vic to know about her son. It was the one part of her that belonged to him alone, and he meant to keep it like that.

'I don't think the past is relevant, Helen; it's what you are now and what you will be to one another in the future that counts. Besides, didn't it all happen a lifetime ago to a different girl? You've changed out of all recognition. If it were happening now, you'd probably make a different choice.'

'You mean I'd keep a baby, now? Yes, I suppose I would. But it isn't me who's changed, Edward, except superficially: it's the times that have changed. Back then, I wouldn't have dared confess I was carrying a baby unless I was getting married. Now they don't confess, they boast. It gets them the key to a council flat.'

'But it isn't necessarily better for the baby for a young girl to keep it.' He saw her face darken, and rushed to explain. 'You were unlucky, you gave up your baby with the best of motives . . . to the wrong couple. But look at Diana and David: it's worked there, hasn't it?'

Helen was silent for a moment, considering. 'It's worked. I mean, they're an ideal family. But Diana once told me she couldn't feel for the children as though they were hers . . . and she's never retracted that.' She frowned, a little, then changed the subject. 'Still, give me some more wine, and start to gen me up on prices. In two weeks' time I'll be back in business!'

# 31

It was still sad to enter the Mews and see how much it had changed. Helen walked down towards the shop, remembering the glass shopfronts, the workshops, Mrs Stepinska's window-boxes, the laughter and the comradeship of 1962. Now there were expensive brick fronts, imposing doors with bull's-eye glass, garage doors that looked like drawbridges, drawn up against all comers. It was closed, anonymous . . . only Edward's shop still standing and the old joiner's place down beyond Gossett's Yard, although that already belonged to the developers. How much longer could Edward hold out?

She pushed open the door and went inside, relishing the smell of old wood and beeswax. 'Hi! Sorry I didn't call last night, but by the time I decided to stay at Vic's it was too late to ring.' Did Edward look disapproving or did she just imagine it?

'Coffee?' He had a pot and two cups on his desk, so he had been expecting her. She poured a cup and drank as he scanned the morning post. Soon she would have her own flat back and not be answerable to anyone. In the meantime she couldn't help feeling like a naughty little girl, caught out in hanky-panky.

'Anything in the mail?'

He shook his head. 'Not much. There's a sale coming up in Lincoln that sounds promising, and one in Hexham. I could do Lincoln and you could cover Hexham . . . give you a chance to go home?'

They leafed through catalogues, comparing notes from time to time, the atmosphere easing between them. 'Did you enjoy the Puccini?' Edward said at last. He was asking about her night at the opera with Vic and she recognized it as an olive branch.

'Very much. I cried when Butterfly died, just as you predicted. Vic says he won't take me again if I can't restrain myself.' She was about to offer to make more coffee when the doorbell pinged and the bright white macs of the American tourist entered the shop. 'I'll make coffee, you take the punters,' she hissed, beaming welcome to the newcomers.

'Would you happen to have a Pembroke table?' the man said. 'My wife has set her heart on a Pembroke table . . . no other.'

Helen, ascending the stairs, smiled at the enthusiasm in Edward's voice as he responded. 'I do have a very fine Pembroke . . . oval top, turned legs I'm afraid, but some very nice marquetry. It's over here, if you can just come round by the commode.' He loved his furniture; every sale was a little death for him because it meant a parting with some precious object.

In the kitchen, while she waited for the kettle, she thought of last night, lying in Vic's arms, talking about the future. She had wanted so much to tell him about Michael, but the secret had grown so immense now that it defied the telling. *'By the way, Vic, you know your sister's sister-in-law's adopted son . . . well, I'm his natural mother. Yes, me, your swinging liberated career woman, the woman you trust so much – I've lied to you systematically for four years, or if I haven't lied I've certainly deceived you . . .'*

She abandoned the imaginary scenario and made the coffee, lingering on the stairs as a deal was struck downstairs. £900: it was going to be a good day!

Howard signed the last letter and shuffled them neatly back into the folder. 'There, that's splendid. Now, shall we have coffee?' He pulled the chairs into place and picked up the pot.

'Seven weeks to Christmas,' Elizabeth Fraser said, accepting a cup. 'I'm so looking forward to seeing the boys.'

Howard knew she would ask about his own arrangements soon, and he didn't want to discuss them. 'What do you think about the Havers bomb? He had a lucky escape.' A bomb had exploded the day before at the home of the Attorney General. It was as good a topic as any.

Elizabeth shook her head. 'I've never understood the Irish. There's so much unrest in the world, I wonder sometimes if we should be exploring space when we can't work this world out. Still, it doesn't pay to think about such things. Tell me about your plans for Christmas.'

So he hadn't escaped after all! 'Oh, I suppose we'll have rather a lonely time this year, with Michael in the Navy and Susan in London. We'll see my brother and his family, I suppose . . . but Anne hasn't been awfully well lately, so I don't think we'll do too much.'

'Does she miss the children? She was always so fond of Michael, wasn't she?' Was there a barb in the words, a suggestion that Susan had come off less well? Surely not. Elizabeth was not a spiteful woman, it was one of the things he liked about her.

'I'm sure she does miss them. And she was disappointed when Michael chose not to go into the priesthood. But she's accepted it, of course.'

'You've been lucky with the children, they've turned out well. Not that I'm suggesting adoption is any more risky than having a child of one's own . . . in some ways it's less risky. But any child is a gamble. We've been lucky, you and I.'

Howard thought of those words an hour later, safe in a back pew of the town-centre church, which was his sanctuary now at lunch-time. Had he been lucky? Had he had a day's luck, a day's happiness, in his entire adult life? The heady days when he had been accepted into his profession and courted Anne . . . he had been so excited then, but so blind. Afterwards, life had been a torment.

Whose fault had it been? She had never refused him, never commented on his failure, had never taxed him with his inability to give her children. He had proved himself a man with Yvonne, though. He had taken her, again and again. Howard thought of it, reliving each moment, until he looked up at sunlight coming through blue glass and red. Oh, God to think those thoughts in such a place! He slipped forward on to his knees and bowed his head.

'You could put a larger part of your income into a pension plan, but let's wait until you see the accountant. In the meantime if you'll sign, I'll call my clerk.'

The will was short and simple. Edward had left his Aunt Dorothy the sum of £15,000, and if she should predecease him the money was to go to her daughter. The rest of his estate was to go to Helen Margaret Clark, of 14, Ranelagh Road, Shepherd's Bush, London. He was slightly astounded by his own affluence. He had always been comfortably off, but now he was rich. He signed against the pencilled cross and then watched as the solicitor and his clerk appended their signatures.

'Now, that's out of the way,' the solicitor said, leaning back in his chair, 'tell me about the developers.'

'Their latest offer if £300,000. I also got a whiff of "last chance" in the wording of their letter . . . and a rather smooth gentleman on the phone gave me to understand I had a limited time to accept – or decline.'

'They can't afford to withdraw just yet.' The solicitor was smiling complacently. 'They already have the property either side of you. Separate development will bring them much less than they'd get if they developed the block, and well they know it.'

'What should I do?' Edward asked.

The solicitor shrugged. 'Whatever you think will be best for you. Don't allow yourself to be hustled out of home and business simply to satisfy their impatience. On the other hand, I don't need to tell you that £300,000 could be the key to a number of things. Properly invested, it could bring you a comfortable income. Take time to think. How is business, by the way? We've been too busy with these other things to talk about that.'

Edward smiled. 'Business is booming. Helen is back, of course, which frees me to look a little further. Antique silver has been a very volatile market for the past year or so, but it's beginning to recover, although prices are still ridiculously low. I'm buying in, and I hope to do quite well eventually. I've actually got something I think you'd like. I let you have that German hare I got in Dublin, didn't I? I've got another, a splendid chap, twenty-two ounces.'

'I'll come in later this week. Meanwhile, sit tight. You have time to make up your mind. Now, shall we have a glass of sherry? It's not every day you make your will.'


'What do you think?' Diana had decided to stay down in the hall while David examined Gary, not wanting to alarm an already fretful little boy. Now she peered up at her husband, knowing from his failure to meet her eyes that the news was not good.

'I don't know, darling. I'm not putting you off, I just don't know. He's not well, any fool could diagnose that. I've gone over him from top to toe, and there's nothing specific, but all the same . . .'

'Let's take him to Sandy Barbour. Ring him now, and he might see us straightaway. Please, darling, better be safe than sorry.'

She wanted him to say 'No', to refuse to bother the paediatrician, to tell her her fears were groundless. Instead he said, 'OK. You go up and settle him, I'll give Sandy a ring.'

She stood on the landing as he dialled. 'Sandy . . . David Whittington here. Yes, problems. Close to home actually. Our youngest . . . his glands are a bit up . . .' She was craning her neck to hear when she became aware of Barbara standing in the door of her bedroom. 'She knows,' Diana thought. 'She knows something is wrong.'

She moved across the landing and gently pushed Barbara back into the room. 'Daddy is ringing up another doctor because Gary isn't well. But it can't be anything serious, because if it was Daddy would have spotted it.' They had found it so easy to call David 'Daddy'. They avoided calling her by name at all, if they could help it.

'Why is he phoning someone else then?' Barbara's eyes were on her, offering no quarter.

'Because he wants to be sure, that's all.'

There was fear on the child's face and Diana wanted to reach out and hold her, soothe her fears. Would it be welcome, though? That was the problem. 'Don't worry, darling, you know what a good doctor Daddy is. Even if Gary is . . . well, if he's . . . if something's not quite right, Daddy will know what to do. Now, why don't you go in and read Gary a story and I'll go down and get him some orange juice.'

'He was all right yesterday,' Barbara said.

'Yes,' Diana agreed, 'that's what's so funny. He's bright as a button one day, and down the next. Which probably means there's nothing at all wrong.'

In the next room Tracy was singing to her doll: 'Ring-a-ring-a-roses, pocket full of posies, tishoo, tashoo, all fall down.'

David was replacing the receiver as Diana came down the stairs. 'He'll see us now,' he said. 'So we won't have much longer to worry.'


'It's fantastic.' Susan was open-mouthed in front of the automaton as it dipped and whirled. It was a young girl dressed in yellow silk, holding up its lace petticoats to curtsey, bow and twirl to the tinkling music of its base. 'It is nice,' Edward agreed. 'It's a Tête Jumeau . . . French. Probably made about 1895. Helen will tell you better when she comes in. She's the expert.'

'I know absolutely nothing about things like this,' Susan said regretfully. 'I remember you gave Auntie Helen one a few years ago. She brought it back to Darlaston on the train, and we all sat round the kitchen table watching it. You and Auntie Hel are clever, understanding antiques and dates and things.'

'Not as clever as you, dealing with life and death. How's it all going at Guy's?'

'Well, I know the difference between metacarpals and metatarsals now – at least I think I do. They're like stalactites and stalagmites, one's up and one's down . . . you know . . .'

They turned as the shop door rang. 'Hallo,' Helen said, advancing on them. 'What are you doing with my courtesan?'

'Your what?' Susan said.

'Courtesan,' Helen said firmly. 'Look at the gleam in her eye and you'll see she is definitely a lady of easy virtue. And look at the amount of leg she's showing . . . shocking! But how are you? Let's go upstairs and be comfortable.'

'I've heard from Michael,' Susan said as they sat around the kitchen table.

'How is he?' Edward said, knowing Helen was longing to ask but daren't.

'He's fine. His basic training's over, so that's bucked him up. He says you were good company on the train down, Auntie Hel. He felt a bit queer, wondering was he doing the right thing and all that, and you cheered him up. He said to give you his love.'

Edward could see the colour fading from Helen's face. 'What branch of the service is he in?' he asked quickly. 'I know it's the Navy, but what's he going to be?'

Susan pulled a face. 'Marine engineering mechanic, whatever that may be. He says it'll take a while, but that's what he wants to do. He's very odd, that brother of mine. Dad wanted him to be an officer, to go in with a commission – you know how many A-levels he's got. He doesn't count them, he weighs them! But he said no, it had to be in the ranks.'

'He can move up later,' Edward said. 'Lots of blokes do that . . . go in and work their way up.'

Helen had regained her composure. 'As long as he's happy, I don't think the rank matters. When does he get his leave?'

Down below the shop bell rang. 'I'll go,' Edward said. As he crossed the landing he heard Susan sigh: 'He is gorgeous, Auntie Hel. Has he got a woman in his life? He's just like Nigel Havers.' He hovered on the top step, hoping to hear Helen's response but all she said was, 'Do you want some coffee?' So she didn't consider him dishy enough to comment. He went on his way downstairs, whistling softly between his teeth.

'But I still can't believe it.' Diana tried desperately hard not to cry but tears were forming inside her lids and threatening to spill over. 'Last week he was rushing around in the sunshine, he had almost too much energy. Now you say it could be . . . myeloid leukaemia. Leukaemia! That means he's going to die!'

'No,' David and the paediatrician spoke sharply and together.

'No, it doesn't,' David said more gently. 'Now, let's listen to the expert, Diana, and not lose our heads.'

'Sorry.' She was nodding fiercely and fumbling for a hanky. The paediatrician twitched two tissues from a box on his desk and handed them to her. 'Thank you.'

'Your son may have myeloid leukaemia. *May* have! The tests may prove my initial diagnosis right; they may not.'

Diana shook her head as though to clear her thoughts before she spoke. 'And if it's not?'

The paediatrician pursed his lips. 'It could be glandular fever . . . or a simple virus. And even if it's leukaemia, it's not necessarily a death sentence.'

'It would be a time-bomb,' Diana said dully.

'If you like, yes. But we have ways of defusing time-bombs nowadays, Mrs Whittington. In Gary's case I think the answer would be a bone-marrow transplant: close relatives have a one in four chance of being donors. I understand that Gary is your adopted child – '

'Does that rule us out?' Diana said, not caring that she was interrupting.

'No. It means your chances of being a donor are fewer, but they still exist. If all else fails there is a donor register, but the complexity of the tissue-matching tests means it takes at least four weeks for each attempt to find a donor . . . so it can take time.'

She knew her voice was rising but she didn't care. 'And meanwhile, this thing could be waiting to tear him apart . . . is that what you mean?'

'Diana!' This time there was anger in David's voice.

'I'm sorry.' Suddenly she felt calm. 'I'm sorry, I'm being stupid. We're not going to beat this thing with hysteria.'

'There may be nothing to beat. And don't be too hard on yourself.' The paediatrician's smile was resigned. 'Anger is a fairly typical maternal reaction. Get angry and you don't have to face the fear, the grief. So get angry if it helps . . . in the mean time, let's get cracking. In case the tests are positive, let's make plans. I don't suppose you know the whereabouts of any of Gary's family?'

'We've got two of them,' David said, suddenly grinning like a boy. 'His sisters . . . they're our children too.'

'So if it's one in four for a relative, that means we'd have a one in two chance?' Diana said.

The paediatrician laughed out loud. 'I'm not sure about the arithmetic, Mrs Whittington, but that's something like what it means.'


Lilian counted the loops again, positive something was wrong. She couldn't see the damn thing, that was the trouble. The mascara had clogged on her lashes and now, as she rubbed her eye, it transferred itself to her finger and had to be licked away.

'Feel like a cup of tea, pet?' Billy said plaintively. He was sitting on the other side of the hearth, reading his evening paper.

'I suppose you mean, will I get up and make one for you?' she said, stabbing needles into wool.

'I'll make it,' he said, not moving from his chair.

She filled the kettle and clattered cups on to the table, so that Billy scented trouble and tried to divert her with, 'What're you knitting, pet?' She poured tea into mugs. 'I'm not knitting anything now, Billy – I'm running after you, as usual. It's a matinée coat for our Karen's bairn, if you must know. But what a pattern! It's got me stumped.' She ran a finger round the top of her new skirt, trying to ease the waistband that was biting into her flesh. She had spent half an hour getting dolled up, but for all the effect it had had she could have saved herself the trouble.

'I see that space craft's in trouble,' he said, putting aside the paper. 'And they've bumped off another one in Ireland, by posing as workmen. A politician and another man. It's a bloody war over there now, like it or lump it.'

'Can you not say anything cheerful, Billy? I wait all day for you coming in with a nice bit of news or a joke or something, and what do I get . . . "Isn't it a bloody awful world, Lilian? Get your hanky out, Lilian. I see there's another one gone, Lilian." I'm glad you came in!'

'Well, what d'you want to talk about, pet?'

'Oh, don't bother about me, Billy. I could be just wallpaper around here for all the notice you take.'

'No, you're not, pet. I take a lot of notice of you, you know that.'

'Well, then, tell me if you've noticed anything different about me lately. Come on, just say.'

'Well, yes, I have noticed. Your hair's different. More curly. And you wear your good clays a lot . . .'

'Clothes, Billy, clothes! You're not down the pit now. What else then?'

'Well, you do yourself up . . . and you always have your earrings in. That's about it.'

'So what do you think, then, Billy? If you've noticed . . . which I'm surprised about . . . what do you think?'

The long silence told all but she held her peace. 'Well, it's very nice, Lily. I mean, you look smashing. But, if you want the truth . . . I liked you better the way you were!'

She was not going to dignify him with a row. Instead she pulled her needles from the wool and began to knit again, chanting under her breath, 'in, over, through and off,' just as she had done when she learned. It was that or kill him, and she was not going to hang for the likes of him.

\* \* \*

'Comfy?'

Helen stretched and wriggled her head into the niche of Vic's shoulder. 'Yes. Blissfully.'

He squeezed her gently and put his lips against her hair. 'Good.'

They were lying in front of the fire, his back against a chair, she held in the crook of his arm. On the stereo the Man from La Mancha was exhorting them to ride out to glory, but neither of them wanted to move. Outside, rain spattered the windows and street lamps had already sprung to life.

'I love you Helen, did you know that?'

She felt the usual pricking of alarm and hoped he would not sense her rapid heartbeat. 'I seem to remember you told me once or twice before.'

Last night he had paused in their lovemaking to say, as though surprised, 'My God . . . I love you, Helen.' Now, they both remembered.

'How do you feel about it?'

'What?' She was playing for time.

'About the fact that I love you?'

'I like it. But, Vic . . . loving is one thing, doing something about it is another.' She paused for a momemt. 'Are you talking about marriage?'

'Yes,' he said simply.

Helen played for time. 'I'm not sure I'm ready for that.'

'Do you mean you want to be free to sleep with other men . . . because I have killed for less?'

'Idiot! You know that's not what I mean.' He moved his hand to cup her breast, comfortably, more as a sign of friendship than passion. 'Explain . . . because up to now you have made no sense at all.'

She closed her eyes, wishing she could close her ears to the music. How strange life was, in the way that it pointed up the moment. Aldonza was singing her heart out, explaining to her Lord of La Mancha that she was far from pure, and was nothing and no one, only Aldonza the whore.

'What about the past?' Helen said desperately. 'I mean,

we're not just here and now, we're background and history, and a whole host of things.'

'Good point,' Vic said teasingly. 'Well, I once stole a bicycle repair kit from Woolies. Worse still, I enjoyed possessing stolen property, and seriously considered a life of crime, but I went in for engineering instead. I married Jennifer . . . which could be construed as an act of criminal lunacy . . . I fathered two kids and I'm not exactly this year's model. However, I've survived to forty-three, so who knows, I might last to the half-century. Now, what about you: you've been married three times, widowed twice in mysterious circumstances, you had two children by the milkman . . .'

He was making a joke of it and she couldn't interrupt him with the truth. 'OK,' she said, moving away and getting to her feet. 'Let's eat, I'm starving. You can't live on love, you know.'

His hand was round her ankle and he would not let her go. 'Let's try,' he said. 'It sounds much more appetizing than anything that ever came out of a kitchen.'


David was trying to soothe her. 'Even if it's confirmed, darling, we'll have every chance.'

'Chance? I don't want "chance" for him, David . . . he's not some gamble, he's our child. I can't believe this; I can't believe lightning can strike twice in the same place. What is it about this family? Howard and you, you've done no harm to anybody, but neither of you could have children. Now Howard has Anne growing stranger by the minute, and we have this. Are we jinxed?'

She expected him to soothe her again, was even half-prepared to push him away. Instead he stood up and held out his hand. 'Come on, Diana. The girls are in the kitchen, and now is as good a time as any to tell them what's going on. It can't be as bad as whatever it is they're imagining.'

Outside in the garden she could see Gary's wheelbarrow, his miniature hoe and fork sticking up, mute emblems of their owner. He had loved to follow them round when they were gardening, hoeing away, standing back to dust his hands when he finished, the action a carbon copy of David's.

'If it is leukaemia,' David said carefully, 'and if Tracy happens to be the only tissue match . . .'

Diana looked at him steadily. 'Yes?' she said.

'Would we have a right to ask her?' David said.

'I've been thinking about that too, David – the ethics of it, the sheer difficulty of explaining to an eight-year-old why something uncomfortable might happen to her for no apparent reason. If we coerced her, she'd do it . . . Barbara would help us there. But would we have the right? I think we'd have no choice, David, and I'll tell you why. Today Tracy is eight, but one day she'll be eighteen, and if we hadn't gone ahead I don't think she'd understand why we let her brother die when resolution on our part might have saved him.'

'Well,' David said uncertainly, as they went into the kitchen, 'perhaps it won't come to that.'

They sat round the kitchen table, Barbara white-faced and intense as usual, Tracy bewildered and inclined to tears. 'When's Gary coming home?'

David reached out and pulled her to him. 'We don't know. Quite soon, I hope. That's what we want to talk to you about. Gary *may* have an illness, quite a serious one . . . but there are lots of things they can do about it if it's true.'

On Barbara's nose the freckles seemed to darken even as Diana watched. 'Will he die?'

'No,' David said evenly, 'I don't think so. There's a thing they can do called a bone-marrow transplant. They take a bit from someone who is well and put it into someone who is sick, and the good bits will conquer the bad. Does that make sense?'

Tracy nodded but it was obvious she was simply anxious to be agreeable. 'She's too little,' Diana thought, 'she can't take it in.'

'How do they do it?' Barbara said. David put an arm around her but she resisted him.

'Well,' he answered, withdrawing his arm, 'remember it probably won't be necessary but if it is, what happens is this. They find out first who has the right kind of bone marrow. Not everyone can give it to everyone else. When they find one that's compatible – that means one that matches the sick person's own bone marrow – they take some out of them . . . in hospital . . . and give it to the person who needs it, to make them better.'

'We'll be tested,' Diana said, 'if they do find it's necessary. Daddy and I . . .' She was going to say 'and you too', but Barbara was flying at her, lifting a fist to strike her arm.

'Not you, not you! He's my brother and I'll do it. Not you!' She stopped suddenly, her hand still upraised, looking at their shocked faces.

'How dare you?' Diana heard herself say, and then Barbara had flung out of the kitchen.

There was silence. 'I'll go to her,' David said, and left the room. Diana busied herself at the sink, her back to Tracy, trying to calm down, get herself in hand. How Barbara must hate her if the thought of her mingling her tissue with Gary's was so repellent.

'Do you want a biscuit?' she asked Tracy, trying to speak lightly, but the little girl had finally given way to tears. 'Tell you what,' said Diana, putting an arm round her, 'why don't you go and see if Pamela wants to play?'

Tracy sniffed, and then gave one of her heavy sighs. 'I expect I will,' she said, and made for the door. Diana watched her go, and then sat down despairingly at the table again, her head in her hands. In the now-empty kitchen the clock ticked alarmingly, as though to signal that time was running out.

She lifted her face as David came back into the room. His eyes were wet, but there was a faint smile on his lips as he sat down opposite her and reached for her hand. She waited for him to speak, to make excuses for his precious Barbara's behaviour, but nothing came.

'Is she all right?' Diana said at last, her voice deliberately cold.

The pressure of his hand on hers increased. 'Do you know why she said that?'

Diana shook her head.

'Because she thinks transplants are dangerous. She doesn't want you to take the risk, because the others need you so much. If anyone is going to have to chance it, she wants it to be her.'

Diana wanted to disbelieve him, but she could not. It was true: She knew that beyond any doubt. 'Oh, David,' she said, and then again, 'oh, David!' Then she got up from her chair and went to mount the stairs.

In Barbara's bedroom the light was fading but the thin figure was sitting defiantly in the window seat. 'Come here,' Diana said, holding out her arms, certain now that she would be obeyed. Barbara came to her and she locked her tight. Inside her arms the thin body was at once fragile and intensely alive. Against Diana's cheek the child's own cheek was wet.

'You silly!' Diana said, holding her at arm's length so that she could stroke away the damp wisps of hair. 'You silly, silly girl. I love you so much, Barbara.' There was a sudden leaping inside her, a sudden jubilation as the truth went home. 'I love you all, and I'm going to keep you all safe, just you wait and see.'

## 32

Helen's hands were shaking as she set the tray and beat up the eggs. It was crazy, really, to be excited like this. Like a child. She moved to the door of the guest room and laid her ear against the panel. Not a sound. Michael must still be asleep.

She pushed open the door carefully and moved inside the darkened room towards the bed. He lay on his side, one arm thrown out, the other curled up towards his chin. In the dim light she could see the shadow of stubble on his chin. Her son was a man. The arms were muscled and strong, the jaw determined. She had watched him grow, but manhood had come upon him suddenly, catching her unawares. She wanted to reach out and touch him, stroke his skin, kiss the place where hair was rumpled on his brow. Fear of his waking held her back – but couldn't she explain, sit down on the side of the bed, and tell him that it was not seduction but something else, love of mother for child?

Last night he had talked of his mother, calling her 'my natural mother'. 'I often think of her, you know. I sit opposite someone on a bus and I think "That could be her." Then I think, "No. She looks too kind, she wouldn't have given me away," and I know it isn't her.'

She had wanted to tell him then, but he was still speaking. 'Still, I haven't really missed her. I've had Dad and mother . . . and you, Helen. You've really been a good friend to Sue and me. We're grateful.' She had stood up then and gone to make coffee in case he saw her cry. Now she looked down at him, put out a tentative hand, withdrew it, and turned on her heel.

Back at the kitchen table she picked up the paper and smoothed it out. A résumé of 1981; the usual New Year's Eve predictions; trouble still in Poland; and reports from America about a new type of disease that was attacking homosexuals and defying attempts to cure it. Cheerful stuff. She went back to the cooker and gave the eggs another stir. She had asked him last night what he would like for breakfast and he had said, 'Scrambled eggs and toast. Not together, it makes them soggy. But separate, with lashings of butter.'

She put her hands to her mouth, quivering with excitement, and then put them down by her sides. She had to stop this or it would all get out of hand. He was here for two days, that was all. In less than twenty-four hours he would be on his way to join his first ship and he might never sleep under her roof again.

She heard the radio start up in the guest bedroom and switched on the hotplate.

She took juice from the fridge, but when she carried the glass into the bedroom the bed was empty. Michael must be in the bathroom. She put down the glass and was about to leave when she saw the dint in the bed where his body had lain. She bent and put her hands into the still-warm place, and left them there until it was time to hurry back to the kitchen.


They were in the locker-room at Queen's and the pleasure of beating Philip 3–2 at squash was balm to Edward's aching legs. 'Good game,' Philip said, pressing a towel to his beetroot face. 'Still, I wonder if we're getting past it. I get this moment of panic now when I'm in the court and the damn ball starts ricocheting all over the place. Did I ever tell you about my boss . . .'

'. . . who got the ball clean into his eye-socket? Yes, you did,' Edward completed. In his hand the small ball was hot, proof of their hour-long exertion. He dropped it into its holder and zipped the headcover of his Dunlop Maxply. He still liked the classic wooden racquet: Philip could keep his carbon-fibre, or whatever marvel of technology had lost him the match.

Philip was still complaining. 'It was different when I could play regularly. I hardly felt it then.'

'Don't be a wimp, Philip. You're becoming too fond of the flesh-pots. Exercise is always good for you . . . get your shower and I'll have the lager set up before you're dressed and out.'

They sat over their drinks, feeling virtuous, limbs tingling pleasantly, and talked politics.

'You've got to hand it to David Owen,' Philip said, contemplating his misty glass. 'I can't stand the man . . . and he was a party to sending Peter Jay to Washington as ambassador, which must be the greatest piece of nepotism since the Pharaohs . . . but all Owen had to do was keep his mouth shut and he'd be in Downing Street by now. There's no one in the Labour Party who could have stopped him. He's thrown all that away for a principle . . . It's brave but foolish. The SDP'll never amount to a row of beans.'

'I've sent them my few bob,' Edward said. 'They're better than the other lot . . . both other lots. All three other lots, come to that.'

'Yes, splendid,' Philip said, 'but doomed. Now . . . about this deal of yours. I think you must make up your mind soon. You're the only original owner left in the Mews. The developers could redesign, using the two sites they do have, if you don't buy this time. It wouldn't be so lucrative for them, but then they're losing substantial sums of money all the time you keep them waiting.'

'What would you do?' Edward asked.

'I'd sell, like a shot. And live like a lotus-eater on the investment income. However, as I know your penchant for your trade, I'd advise you to look for new premises in an area that's coming into its own. What about your partner?'

'The property is mine: it's the business which is jointly owned. If we re-locate, we'll go on in partnership; if I decide to withdraw, she can keep the name and the stock, and start up herself elsewhere. I'd help her find premises, and would retain a financial interest. We'd come to an amicable agreement, I know. The only problem is – do I stay in Inkerman Mews, or do I go?'

It wasn't quite the only problem – post-squash fatigue was setting in rapidly, and Edward was glad it was Philip's turn to order the other half of lager.


Lilian waited impatiently for the ward doors to open. She could see them in there, laughing and chatting, refusing to open up. Nurses weren't what they used to be, not by a long chalk. She was quivering with excitement at the thought of seeing her grandchild again. Karen's man came in every night, but the afternoons, while he was at work, were hers – and today she had a special mission: Helen's letter with the cheque for £50 was in her handbag. Fifty pounds! Wait till Karen saw it.

A nurse was pulling back the doors and bolting them ajar. 'Ooh, are we actually going to be let in?' Lilian said as sarcastically as she could, but the nurse just ignored her, cheeky bitch!

Karen was sitting up in bed, looking expectantly at the door. 'Hallo, mam. Did you bring me *Woman's Own*?'

Lilian decanted magazines and fruit and bottled drinks on to the bed. 'Yes, I did. Brian brought it round this morning. He says he'll see you tonight, and he's got everything ready for you coming home. Now, where's this precious bairn? And wait till you see what your Auntie Helen's sent!' Karen oohed at the cheque, but all Lilian could see was her grandson.

The baby was red-faced and solemn, his hair a dark crest, his fingernails of an incredible smallness. 'Look at those fists,' Karen said indulgently. 'He's going to be a boxer.'

Lilian picked him from the crib and cradled him in her arms. 'No, he's not, he's going to be a lawyer in a wig and gown and everything. Getting people off and saying, "I rest my case."'

Karen leaned over to cluck at the baby. 'Where's Perry Mason, then? Where's the little judge?'

'Your dad's coming in tomorrow afternoon, with Brian's mam. It's to be hoped she's going to watch her language in front of this bairn, mind.' She looked down at the child again. 'Nothing but the best for you, my son, you're that precious!' She shook her head solemnly. 'It's awful, isn't it, the hold they have on you right from the word go? You couldn't bear to lose them.'

Karen was reaching out for the baby and hugging him to her. 'It doesn't bear thinking about, does it?'

'No,' Lilian said. 'You never give it a thought until it happens.' She was remembering a determined little figure running ahead of her, turning to exhort: 'Come on, mammy. Come on!'

'You're thinking about our Diana, aren't you?' Karen said, and then, holding out her firstborn, 'Take your grandbairn, he'll make you feel all right.'

Lilian looked down at the baby. 'You're right there, our Karen. You never said a truer word.'


Howard moved slowly along the supermarket aisle, pushing his trolley. 'Don't forget soap powder,' Elizabeth Fraser said, 'and washing-up liquid. It's so terrible to be without. I can't think how we coped before we had detergents.'

Howard dutifully took down everything Elizabeth suggested, and added a few items of his own. He had been doing the shopping for a month, since Anne's indisposition, and had discovered all sorts of delicacies that she never bought: delicious Dutch biscuits and tinned herring roes, pink taramosalata and Scotch mutton pies, thick with grease and melting in the mouth. He had to hide them from Elizabeth, who would condemn them as rubbish, but it was a delight to unpack the carrier bags when he got home and secrete his treasures where Anne would not find them.

On the way to Elizabeth's neat house he thought guiltily of Anne, alone in her shadowy room with only the plaster faces of saints for company. But even if he were to go home, he would make no difference to her.

He carried Elizabeth's groceries into the hallway and put them on a low table. 'Now sit down and get comfortable,' Elizabeth said, reaching for his coat. 'We must have one small drink . . . I'll be alone tonight, so I shall have my New Year's Eve dram now, with you. It's going to be a good year, I can feel it in my bones.'

Howard sank into the chintz armchair that had become his usual seat and listened to the clink of glasses and bottles at the drinks trolley. At the edges of his mind all sorts of fears and anxieties skittered, demanding attention. He put them resolutely away. For the next half-hour he was going to relax, and nothing and no one was going to spoil it.


Diana walked into the ward and waved. Gary was sitting in a small basket chair, dressed now in his own clothes, once more a happy little boy.

'Well, then,' she said, taking his hand, 'how have you been today?'

'Where's Dad?' he said, looking back towards the ward door.

'He's coming, darling, as soon as he's done his visits.'

'What've you brought?' he said, rummaging now in her bag.

'Ha ha,' she said mysteriously. 'Wouldn't you like to know?'

'Come on,' he said, climbing up to twine his arms round her neck, 'Come on, Mammy! You said . . .'

'Said what?' she said, grinning at him, both of them enjoying the joke.

'You said presents,' Gary insisted. 'Dad said . . . you know. . . . *vroom, vroom!*'

'*Vroom, vroom*? I don't know what *vroom vroom* is. We'll have to wait till Daddy comes.'

'Please. Please . . . oh, please.' He put his head on one side, imploring.

'Well,' Diana said, 'There is a little parcel in my pocket here.' She took out the parcel and shook it against her ear. 'It doesn't go *vroom vroom*.'

He seized it and was tearing off the paper to reveal the small cardboard box with the miniature vehicle inside it.

'It's a dumper . . . just what I wanted!' He rolled it along the arm of her chair. '*Vroom, vroom*. This is the best one I've got.'

'You always say that about new ones! It is nice though. Don't forget to bring it home with you when you come.'

'When will I come home?'

'Soon,' Diana said, 'very soon. Daddy is going to ask today.'

'Dad!' Gary was hurtling down from her knee, running towards the door to cling around his father's leg until he had to be dragged like a weight.

'They look right together,' Diana thought. Aloud she said, 'He's found this dumper truck in my pocket. Do you think it's meant for him?'

'I expect so,' David said, squatting down to examine the new vehicle, and vroom, vroom-ing with Gary. Then he looked up at her. 'Hallo, Mum,' he said.


Howard put two glasses on a tray and half-filled them with Cointreau: Anne used to like Cointreau. He had seen it in the supermarket and remembered. Now he carried it upstairs and into her bedroom, more conscious of the silence since the children had gone back after Christmas.

She was on her knees, the beads moving between her

fingers, and he waited for her to rise. 'I brought you a drink,' he said, trying to smile.

Anne moved towards him and took the glass, breathing in its aroma. He suddenly realized that she looked somehow happier than he had seen her look for a long time. 'Cointreau?' she said. 'How nice.'

Howard held out his glass. 'To the New Year, Anne.' His courage faltered but he ploughed on. 'I want it to be a good year, for both of us. I know you miss the children. So do I. Can't we be a comfort to one another?'

She was smiling now and he felt a sudden surge of relief. For a second the girl she had been looked out from the haggard face, and he wondered what would happen if he leaned to kiss her cheek. It had always smelled delicious in the old days.

'I have something to tell you, Howard,' Anne said quietly. 'I have a lump here.' Her hand with its pale oval nails moved lovingly over her left breast. 'I found it some time ago. I haven't done anything about it because there is nothing that can be done. And I'm quite at peace. It's God's will.' She raised her glass in a small salute and then put it to her lips.

Howard was staggered. How long had she known this? Why had she kept it to herself?

'We'll find a specialist,' he said, at last, still trying to comprehend her words, to understand her acceptance of something so unacceptable. 'David will know the best man . . .'

And then, as Anne shook her head, he realized that this was exactly what she wanted . . . she would achieve that prized conclusion to a religious life – a martyr's death.


Lilian wiped the edges of the fryer and rinsed the cloth. 'That's it then, lasses.' They hung up their overalls and turned the *Open* notice to *Closed*.

Outside the night sky twinkled as Lilian locked up the shop and made her goodbyes. 'Don't get drunk, Vi. See you in 1982, Elsie. Remember, pop in for your glass if you're passing.'

The pavement sparkled with frost as she walked home, but she felt warm inside her thick coat and only pleasantly tired. Andrew was stopping the night with his friend, and Billy would be at the club until midnight. He'd better be back in time to first-foot, or she would have his eyeballs for earrings. But she didn't begrudge him his night whooping it up; he worked for his money, unlike some.

As she rounded the corner she saw the firelight flickering behind her front-room curtains. When she got in she would kick of her shoes and her roll-on and flop for a while. A nice cup of tea, and then she would get ready to welcome the New Year. A good wash and dab of Youth Dew would do it, and her nice new blouse, polyester crêpe de Chine and as good as silk any day of the week. Her legs were aching slightly with a night's standing, and that was after an early finish. She put her key in the lock and felt the magic of her own home enfold her.

As she was fumbling for the light switch, the lights sprang up. 'Welcome home, Lily!' Billy said, beaming at her from the hearth rug. He had a bottle in his hand. 'Asti Spumante,' he said proudly, and popped the cork.

'Why aren't you down the club?' Lilian said suspiciously as she accepted a glass. 'And don't say you preferred to stay in, or I'll be straight on the phone for the doctor.'

'I decided', he said, speaking posh, 'to treat my little wife.' This morning she had tipped the scale at fourteen stone, but you could see from his face that the silly bugger meant what he said. He was turning to the range and opening the door on a collection of cartons, keeping warm on a baking tray. 'Egg Foo Young, fried rice, prawn crackers, crispy pancakes, two portions of curry and mushy peas. And . . .' he moved to the table and twitched aside a clean tea-towel . . . 'Fruit cocktail and double cream.'

'You've got a tile off,' Lilian said, feeling for a chair back.

'No, I haven't,' he said. 'I got the jackpot at the club last night . . . £40! And I got a win on the pools: £584 between four of us. So I kept it quiet, and I planned this.'

'Where's the rest of the money?' Lilian said, and then could have bitten off her tongue.

'It's here, Lily . . . I had a feeling you'd ask that, so there it is: £134. I bought the lads a pint.'

She looked around, uncertain whether to kiss him or crown him. She was lost for words. 'By God,' he said suddenly, 'I think I've got you bested, Lily Fenwick. Well, bugger me!'

She would have given him the length of her tongue, but foolish tears had robbed her of words. A grandchild and a man in a million – it was too much for one woman and that was a fact.

'Well, get it out then, Billy,' she said at last. 'If you've paid for it, I suppose we'll have to eat it.'


They were all gathered in Helen's flat to see in the New Year, Vic and Edward, Susan and a gangling young medical student, Michael and a very pretty probationer called Charlotte who had come with Susan but was now glued to Michael's side. Edward watched as Vic moved about, playing the host. He and Helen looked right for one another; it pained him to admit it, but it was true. He watched now as they leaned against one another, listening to one of Susan's outrageous hospital stories.

He dared not even fantasize about her now, when holding some other woman in his arms. He had to cling to the fact that she and Vic would be married before the year was out, would have at least three children, and would live happily ever after.

'Refill?' Vic was hovering with a bottle, and Edward inclined his head. 'Thanks.' It was strange to be here, like this, but no stranger than the rest of it. A chance meeting on a train had changed the whole course of his life. He would never marry now; he knew that and accepted it.

The phone rang and Helen moved to answer it. 'Hallo, David! How nice . . . yes, Vic's here.' The buzz of conversation in the room gradually dwindled as they all watched Vic's face grow grave, and then lighten again. He put down the phone and turned into the room.

'Good news! Gary's been rather ill and they thought it

might be serious, but apparently it's only glandular fever. He's still poorly, but the outlook is bright.'

'Let's go up and see them, Vic,' Helen said, 'as soon as we can get away . . .'

They talked politely then, and ate the food from the buffet, but somehow the night had lost its sparkle. Perhaps the news of a childish illness had reminded them that nothing in life was certain. Though Susan turned on the stereo and they began to dance, changing partners and laughing and talking, each of them was suddenly aware of mortality.

'Good party,' Edward said when Helen was in his arms. A Nina Simone record was playing now: 'Cherish is a word . . .' He had forgotten what a nice word 'cherish' was, implying so many loving feelings. He bent his head and began to sing the words softly against Helen's hair.

'I didn't know you could sing,' she whispered, smiling at him.

'I'm a man of many parts,' he said, and brushed his lips lightly against her temple.

'It's time I was going out,' Vic said, reaching for the bread and salt and silver that Helen had put ready. 'Do I have to do all this mumbo-jumbo?' he asked plaintively, but Helen was adamant.

'Yes, it's a northern tradition.'

'But I'm a southerner!'

'Oh, get out and do it, Uncle Vic,' Susan said. 'Can't you see you're outnumbered?' They had a head count of north versus south, and then Big Ben was chiming from the TV set and Vic was coming through the door to take Helen in his arms, and there was kissing all round.

'To 1982,' Edward said.

Helen raised her glass when they all had drunk to the year: 'To Edward . . . prosperity. To Susan and Charlotte . . . success in their training. To Vic . . . a better way of life.' Her eyes were dancing and then she turned to Michael.

'She's brave,' Edward thought and raised his own glass as she spoke.

'To Michael . . . success on his new ship, HMS *Sheffield*.'

'To Michael,' Edward said and let his eyes lock with Helen's. At least he shared her secret. That was something he had that not even Vic could take away.

## 33

'This is getting ridiculous,' Edward said out loud, throwing down the letter and then having to extricate it from the butter dish. Their latest offer was £350,000 plus help with his relocation.

He stood up and moved to the window, looking out on the Mews, basking now in April sunshine. Why did he cling on, when it had all changed so much? It was almost entirely residential now, which meant there were fewer passers-by to call in at his shop. Customers came anyway . . . he was well enough known in the trade . . . and even if they didn't, he would survive. Money seemed to breed at an alarming rate, rather like greenfly . . . or was it grasshoppers?

Damn them all, he wasn't in the mood for decisions. He was in the mood for a holiday, that was it! He would go away – the Algarve? – and forget it all for a while: then he would come back and make decisions.

He was pouring more coffee when he heard the radio announcer's voice and stopped, percolator in hand, to listen. 'Informed sources believe that an Argentine attack against the Falkland Islands is imminent. The President of the Security Council has requested that both Britain and Argentine refrain from the use or threat of force, and continue to search for a diplomatic solution. There has been no Argentine response to this request. Sources here in London say that all appropriate military and diplomatic measures to sustain British rights under international law will be taken in accordance with the provision of the United Nations Charter. In our radio car we have the Shadow Minister . . .'

Edward crossed to the window again. Down below

people were moving about, laughing, talking . . . casting off their winter coats and folding them over their arms. My God, Britain was on the brink of war! What would happen, now? He suddenly needed to talk to someone but Helen had gone north with Vic. He sat down, remembering that other war, his mother holding his hand, putting him on the train, the pain of separation.

This would be a different war if it came. The Falklands were a million miles away, a rocky outcrop in an unfriendly sea. He reached for the radio and switched it off. Perhaps it would all fizzle out by tomorrow – like the Cuban crisis. Anything else was unthinkable.


Howard poured milk into the jug and put the bottle back in the fridge. He checked the tray: teapot, two cups, milk, sugar, biscuits, tablets. He picked it up and went to mount the stairs. In the hall Mrs Bickerstaffe was dusting, and he smiled at her as he passed. 'I could have done that, Mr Whittington,' she said but he shook his head.

'It's all right, you have your hands full. Besides, I like to see how she's getting on.'

Anne was lying with her eyes towards the corner of the room. 'I've brought you some tea,' Howard said, putting down the tray and moving to ease her up on her pillows. He saw her wince as he put his hand beneath her shoulder. 'There,' he said. 'Are you comfortable?'

She smiled at him, the curious wolfish smile that made her teeth bulk large in her wasted face. 'I'm fine. Why aren't you at the office?'

He poured her tea and held the saucer while she raised the cup. Her hand shook and her fingernails, grown long from neglect, clinked against the porcelain. 'I'm taking a few days off,' Howard said.

Anne put the cup on the saucer and sank back on her pillows. He put down her cup and saucer and moved to get his own, carrying it to the basket chair by the window. He often sat here now, and he sensed that if she did not actually welcome his presence, she didn't mind it.

'Mrs B. is downstairs, so everything's under control. I

think Susan is coming up this weekend. She intends to come, if she can get away.'

It didn't matter to Anne. Her mouth had curved slightly, but only in polite recognition of his remarks. He had decided not to tell her about the crisis in the Falklands in case it made her fearful for Michael, but now, seeing her lethargy, he doubted that she would care.

Had she ever cared for any of them, except in so far as they had served her purpose? And yet she had not been a wicked woman; it was he who had been the sinner, in deed and in thought. Lately, though, he had found it easier to banish evil from his thoughts. He had something to do now, a duty.

Perhaps that was why Anne's cancer had happened – to bring him to book? He had been growing fond of Elizabeth, but he had put that behind him now. 'I want to be good,' he thought. 'I so much want to be good.'

Anne was moving in the bed, struggling to reach the tissues on the bedside table. Where the ruffled nightgown fell away, her neck and shoulders were thin to the point of emaciation. She was dying before his eyes, and it was what she wanted. He had called in doctors but it had made no difference: Anne had refused all treatment, and no one had been able to change her mind.

Howard stood up suddenly, so that tea slopped in his saucer. 'Let me get those for you.' He put a tissue into her bony fingers and turned to the window as she raised it to her lips. 'We must take up chess again when you're well, Anne. Remember how much we used to enjoy it?'


Ever since she had heard the news on the car radio, Helen's mind had been scrabbling for comfort. 'What do they mean by an Argentine attack – there's nothing there, is there?'

Vic's gaze was on the road, so he could not see her anguished eyes. 'Only sheep,' he said cheerfully.

'But will we retaliate?' Helen insisted, thinking of Michael on his ship. She had had one postcard from him since he had flown out to join HMS *Sheffield* in January. He had said the ship had been at sea since November and would be back in port at the beginning of April. What would happen now? The *Sheffield* was a warship . . . a guided-missile destroyer. Did that make it safer? Or more dangerous?

She wanted to confess her anxieties to Vic, but it wouldn't do. Now, when she was in such a state, was not the time to tell him the truth. As soon as she could she would ring Edward. Till then, she would have to suppress her agitation and wait.

The car flashed over the border between Yorkshire and Durham. 'Not long now,' Vic said, glancing sideways to smile.

'Do you want me to drive?' she offered but he just grinned.

'I quite like living,' he said, 'so no thanks.'

'Chauvinist,' she countered but her reply was mechanical.

'I'm not actually looking foward to this visit,' Vic said as Darlasden came into view. 'On the other hand, Diana needs cheering up. First there was that worry about the kid . . . and now the weird sister-in-law is, by all accounts, simply fading away.'

'It can't be much fun for her husband,' Helen said, 'or for their children. Susan is coming up tonight, if she can get away. I offered her a lift, but she said someone else was travelling north so we needn't hang on. I talked to Diana on the phone last night, did I tell you? She said she was looking forward to seeing us, but apart from that it was all about the children. You know how she idolizes them.'

'Do you think you could love someone else's child?' Vic said, slowing as they entered the built-up area. 'I don't know how I'd feel if you had one . . . I'd be good to it, I'd even like it because it was part of you, but could it ever be the same to me as my own? I don't really think it could. That's why I wonder how you feel about my kids?'

Helen put out a hand and patted his arm. 'I like them,' she said, and let the matter rest there.

\* \* \*

Lilian was feeling contented today. If war came, it came. Billy was too old, Andrew too young, and Karen's man would be needed down the pit. You couldn't run a war without coal. She had wanted something better for Karen than a miner, but it had all worked out for the best. Still, there was lots of lads around the doors that might get drawn in if it went on for long. And lots of lads that had joined the Army already because there were no other jobs for them.

She stood at the sink, peeling taties, thinking of her luck: two healthy bairns and a grandbairn that would win prizes; Billy toeing the line; and a chance to buy their house off the council. It would be funny to own property. She wasn't sure she approved of it really, but you couldn't pass up the chance of having something to leave your children. For a moment she thought briefly of dying, and then she remembered what she and Billy had got up to last night and the memory rejuvenated her.

She rinsed her hands and dried them on the tea-towel before she reached to switch on the radio. You couldn't be too careful with electricity. They were still on about the Falklands: she'd never heard of the bloody place till yesterday, and now you couldn't get away from it. It sounded as though it was all Maggie Thatcher's fault, but she wouldn't be the one to go to fight, she would just sit back in Downing Street, waited on hand and foot, while other people's bairns got shot. They wouldn't send *her* lad, that was for sure. He'd never be able to find the bloody place! On the radio someone was discussing Prince Andrew: would he go to war if war broke out, or would he be kept at home? Lilian didn't fancy anyone's chances of keeping that young man anywhere he didn't want to be. Still, it was up to the Queen.

She sat down at the table pondering the state of the country. Three million out of work, even that Freddie Laker – although that had been a fiddle by the Yanks, according to Billy. And now a war, most likely. She wondered whether or not she would go in for the black market if it came to the crunch. According to her mother, you dealt in the black market or starved in a war. Well, if it was the only way to feed her family, she would be in it up to her neck.

Looking out at the back garden, Lilian pondered the possibility of hens. If she did get a few, she could keep them on taties and a bit of chicken meal. Fresh eggs were good for you, everyone knew that. She would give half a dozen a week to Diana's bairn, God love him. That would set him up.

At last she got to her feet, remembering that Helen was coming up with her fancy man today and might well pop in. It wouldn't do to let her down. She was gettng a bit long in the tooth and needed all the help she could get to land a feller. Jealousy reared its head as she thought of Helen actually marrying into a doctor's family but it didn't last. She switched to Radio One and heard the twinkling sounds of 'Chariots of Fire'. Billy was taking her to see that at the weekend, if they hadn't all been blown up by the Argies. She laughed out loud at the very idea and got on with preparing the meal.


'I don't feel well,' Tracy said. Since Gary had been ill and the centre of attention, she had adopted an air of languor. 'If I have to go into hospital, will it hurt?'

David kept his face straight. 'It depends what's wrong with you. You might need an operation.'

Tracy tried to look apprehensive and brave at the same time. 'Will an operation hurt?'

'Perhaps a little bit,' David said, 'but not much. Do you remember when you had your sore knee? Well, about as much as that, and you were quite brave then.'

Tracy nodded gravely. 'I expect I'll be all right.'

Diana cuddled her closer. 'Try and get better without going to hospital. Now that Gary is well again, we're all going off on holiday, to the sunshine. Daddy is buying an apartment in Spain, where it's sunny all the time, and we're going for a whole month.'

Barbara had been sitting quietly by. Now she looked up. 'What about school?'

Diana smiled at her. 'You're going to play hookey . . . or what do you call it now – dolling off?'

Barbara looked scandalized. 'We'll get wrong.'

'No, you won't,' David said firmly. 'I'll see the Headmistress and explain, and it will all be all right. Now . . .' He never finished his sentence because at that moment Helen and Vic arrived, and there was an orgy of greetings and gifts and exclamations over who had grown taller or thinner or more alike.

Diana went into the kitchen to make coffee, pleased at the affection she had sensed between Helen and Vic. If they got around to a wedding, she would really splurge on her outfit!

Helen sank to her knees in the Durham cathedral pew, her eyes fixed on the glorious rose window. 'Oh God, please take care of them all. Don't let there be war. Keep Michael safe at home in quiet waters.' Beside her Vic was already fidgeting, his prayers said. He had never been in the cathedral before and was anxious to see all its spendours. She slipped back into her seat and reached for her bag. 'Come on,' she whispered. 'Now you get the guided tour.'

They moved down the aisles, past the Miners' Memorial . . . *'Remember before God the Durham miners who have given their lives in the pits of this county and those who work in darkness and danger in those pits today.'*

'Impressive,' Vic said, looking at the seventeenth-century woodcarving, the fat cupids and fruited vines. They moved on, beneath the window of Oswald, bold King of Northumbria, bestriding the aisle. Beyond lay the Bede chapel, grey and quiet, with its prayer to Christ, the Morning Star.

Helen stood for a moment, still thinking of Michael. He had only begun to live, to enjoy life. He and Charlotte were lovers, she knew it from their glances, their touching hands. On his last day of leave they had talked about his time at the seminary. 'The monks said it was dangerous to touch too much. I never understood what they meant, until now.' She had known then that he had made love to a woman and a feeling of anger had filled her, an anger more than tinged with jealousy that some other woman had possessed her son. In the end, though, she had been happy for him, for his obvious delight in living and loving. Now, all that might be swept away because of some stupid territorial argument.

'Penny for them?' Vic said, against her cheek.

'Love you,' she said, leaning against him for a second. 'Now, let's get on.'

They passed ancient tombs, a knight and his lady lying side by side, the roll call of Prince Bishops and the great and good of the county. 'So this is Durham cathedral,' Vic said, blowing softly between his teeth. 'It's magnificent. Do they hire it out for weddings?' She laughed then and let him take her hand.

'Please God, let it be all right,' she thought again, before they went out into the sunlight. And then, quite suddenly, she remembered Anne Whittington, dying quietly in Darlasden. 'God help her, too,' she thought as she walked with Vic across the bright freshness of Palace Green.


'I made an excuse to get out for a while . . . I'm in a call box, so I can't be long. I'm frightened, Edward. Is there going to be a war?'

Edward could hardly tell Helen there was nothing to worry about. Parliament was meeting tomorrow, Saturday, an unheard-of move. Commentators were prophesying doom, and experts were talking war-plans. 'I think there is going to be trouble,' he said carefully. 'But I expect it'll be settled at diplomatic level. I don't think it'll come to a punch-up, if that's what you're afraid of. Besides, Michael is barely trained. They're not going to hurl him into a war-zone.'

He heard her sniff at the other end of the line. 'Oh God, Edward, you're such a comfort. I wish I was back in London now.'

'You're making too much of this Falklands thing, Helen. Every time the Argentine military government has economic troubles, it gets belligerent, to divert the peasants. You'll see, it'll all be over tomorrow.'

When Helen had rung off, pacified, he went to the sideboard and poured himself a drink. 'Father Confessor,' he thought, 'that's what I am. A shoulder to cry on, a prop, a stay, a nice man . . .' What had she said on the phone: *such a comfort*. He drank the raw spirit, enjoying its power. 'You, my friend,' he thought 'are too good for your own good.' He laughed aloud, but there was no mirth in his laughter. He was all things to Helen except a lover – and that was what he really wanted to be. He knew he was going to brood about Helen again, and took his coat from the hook behind the door.

As he entered the pub he saw his face in a mirror, beneath its bright slogan. Not much like Nigel Havers, not tonight. 'A pint of Fullers,' he told the barmaid, and took his usual stool. He looked up to find the barmaid's dark eyes on him, alive with interest. She was a pretty girl, a student probably. 'Can I buy you a drink?' he said.

## 34

Howard brought the car to the doorstep with the passenger door open on the house side. He went back into the hall, expecting to mount the stairs and help Anne from her room. To his amazement, she was half-way down already, her hands white-knuckled where they clutched the banister, her head covered in the heavy crocheted mantilla he had bought for her in Madeira.

'Anne, why didn't you wait for me?' He moved towards her, thinking with a flash of hysteria that her feet and legs were Minnie-Mouse like, the shins reed-thin, the shoes suddenly buckets for the shrunken feet. 'Let me help you.'

Her eyes still glittered, but this time it was not to repel. Her gaze was for the door and the car, her means of getting to church. She was being eaten away by something remorseless, and her cancer was only part of it.

She hardly spoke as they drove to St Mary Magdelene's, except to comment on the trees breaking into bud. He thought suddenly of how it must be to know you were seeing buds break for the last time. It would fill him with terror – thinking of it now frightened him enough. But Anne was calm, almost exultant.

He abandoned the car to help her into the porch and then there were a dozen helping hands to take her into the candled splendour of the church. He went back to the car and parked it, and then rejoined his wife.

He found her at the feet of St Teresa of Avila, eyes raised, face rapt. He knelt beside her and prayed as he had always prayed, for the power to make sense of it all, or the faith to see that sense had nothing to do with it. He thought of his son, perhaps sailing now towards a war-zone. 'Oh God, don't punish Michael for my sins. Please God, protect my children . . . and open your arms to Anne.' He felt tears prick his eyes and when he reached to brush them away he found his cheeks were already wet.

He stayed on his knees, and suddenly he could hear Anne's whispered, constantly repeated, words, familiar and comforting to join in. '. . . Holy Mary, Mother of God, pray for us sinners now and at the hour of our death. Hail Mary, full of grace, blessed art thou among women and blessed is the fruit of Thy womb . . .'

He turned to look at his wife, her lips trembling with fervour as the beads passed through her wasted fingers. She was praying for her children, and for him. He felt a sudden terrible tenderness overtake him, and when at last he reached to help her to her feet it seemed she welcomed his touch.

'Helen! How nice to hear your voice.' Diana sank into the hall chair and settled down to gossip. 'Well, fingers crossed, he's thriving. All in all, things are looking up – apart from poor Howard, of course. Anne is hanging on by a thread, and then of course Michael's ship has been diverted to join the task force. But you'll know that from Susan. Or Vic. How is my brother?'

She changed the phone to her other hand, noticing as she did so that there was thick dust on the hall table.

Things were going to pot in the house, but it seemed not to matter. The children were all that mattered, and they were fine. 'So when's he coming home? That's nice. You'll both have to come up here again soon.'

For some reason Diana couldn't quite fathom, Helen sounded rather forlorn. She was making a determined effort to be cheerful, but there was something in her voice . . . 'Are you all right Helen? You sound a bit, well, down. It's not Vic, is it? Good . . . Well, is it business? You can always come back and work here, you know. David moans and groans about there being no one like you.'

She listened as Helen assured her all was well, and brought the talk to an end, knowing it was time to pick up the girls from school. 'Well, if you'll take a piece of advice from me, you'll marry Vic . . . I know he's asked you.'

When Diana put down the phone she hurried upstairs to change her shoes. One day she would go down to London and sort the pair of them out. Helen must be thirty-six or thirty-seven now . . . if she wanted a family, time was ticking away.

She parked at the school gates and waited for her daughters to emerge. They came side by side, Tracy self-important, Barbara with her habitual furrowed brow. 'Get in,' Diana said, leaning to open the passenger door, 'and let's go home for tea. I'm ravenous.'

The girls stood, politely ushering one another into the back seat of the Fiesta so that they themselves could take the front seat. 'Who had it last time?' Diana said.

'Me,' came the answer in unison.

'Eeny, meeny, miny, mo – Tracy in the back,' Diana said. 'Come on, I want to go home and see Dad.'

'Go on, you can have it,' Barbara said, getting into the back. 'You'll only moan all the way home if you don't.'

As she let out the clutch Diana reflected on the wonder of the child-mind. When Barbara didn't have the front seat, it was vital to get it. Once she had it, she could give it away like an angel.

'I am going to make the most marvellous tea,' she said. 'Everything sickly, whatever you want.'

421

'Fish fingers and lashings of tomato sauce,' Tracy said promptly.

'Is that all?'

'And meringues . . . and cream cheese with pineapple.'

'Yuck,' Barbara said. 'I'll have anything but meat.'

David was getting out of his car when they drove in at the gate. 'Only two?' he said.

'Gary's gone out with Jenny. He'll be back for tea.'

David's arms were suddenly around her, his lips cutting off her breath. She kissed him back fiercely, wanting him desperately, loving him with all her heart because he was the father of her children. She heard cackling from the car and tore herself away. 'It's like Hollywood!' Tracy said, the gap in her front teeth showing as she grinned.

'Come on, Meryl Streep,' David said. 'Get into the kitchen and make my tea.'

But Barbara was ahead of them on the steps. 'We'll make the tea,' she said. 'We'll be careful. We'd like to, wouldn't we, Tracy?'

The eight-year-old's eyes rolled. 'I suppose so,' she said, 'but I'm not washing up.'

Helen tried not to look at the clock, hoping that when she did it would have moved round to lunch-time. She was going to walk in the park then: she always felt better in the open air. Suddenly she remembered the day on the hill with Susan and Michael. She had been so happy then, so thrilled to be with him as his friend. Now, if anything should happen to him, she would have no rights in him at all, not even the right to walk behind his coffin. If he came . . . when he came . . . back she would have tell him the truth. Straight away. It would be a shock, but he would understand, he was a thoughtful boy. Not for the first time she wondered why he had chosen the Navy when he did not seem the type. And to work with his hands . . . If she had not interfered, she thought grimly, he would be safe now, in some quiet chapel somewhere.

She was watching the street for Edward's return when the taxi drew up and a large woman in cape and turban stepped out, pushing coins at the cabbie and making for the shop door.

'Helen Clark? Zanna Black . . . I was given your name by Marcus Winter. He says you're *the* doll person in London . . . and I'm in the market.' She fished out a card with a New York address, and then looked around. 'I didn't realize you were interested in general trade . . . Marcus said you were a specialist.'

Her face was big and bold, carefully made-up and resolute. 'The dolls are over here,' Helen said, moving towards the rear of the shop. 'I don't keep a big stock, but I can get you most things. I'm keen on Bru and Jumeau myself, but I buy in anything interesting.'

The woman was casting a critical eye over the sedate rows of dolls Helen had revealed by twitching off some linen covers. 'I'm on a commission for a client . . . I want good orientals, boys and characters, also autos and googlies, of course, if they're good. They're getting very popular.'

'What about cloth?' Helen asked.

The over-painted eyes rolled. 'Not Lencie . . . they get moth . . . but I hear Katie Kruse will come good soon. I see you have a black Bébé there . . . original dress . . . very nice. How much?'

'A thousand,' Helen said, and the woman nodded.

'Yes . . . but to me? I'm talking real money here, honey. Say I take twenty at an average £750 . . . what's that? And of course phonographs . . . I'll take thirty if they're up to standard.'

'A collection of Jumeau phonographs is coming up for auction soon,' Helen said. 'I was going to bid anyway . . .'

When the American left, Helen had a tentative order for £20,000 worth of dolls, if they were to be found. Once that would have elated her; today it was simply something to be entered in the diary for attention at some future date when the world had ceased to tremble.


Lilian floured the haddock and dipped it in batter. It seemed odd to be frying one fish in her own kitchen – she was used to doing it on a big scale now. Still, he had asked for it so he was getting it. 'I love your batter, Lilian. I've tasted a few in my time, but you've got the knack.' She turned the fish in the pan, seeing tiny pieces of batter separate and turn to golden puffballs. She did have a good hand with batter, there was no denying it.

She shook his chips to rid them of surplus fat and added the green mushy peas he loved. Once he got that lot inside him, he'd be satisfied. She set the table with salt and vinegar, and put on the kettle for tea. The sight of the fish had sickened her and there wasn't a thing she could fancy. Still, you had to eat something – she cut herself a wedge of angel cake.

She was wiping crumbs from her mouth when he came through the door, and one look at his face told her the news was not good. He sank into a chair, his lip trembling. 'Well, the pit's had it, Lily . . . it's for the chop. I can go to Easington, or I can take me redundancy.'

She stood at the sink, churning the teapot full of hot water to warm it through, wondering why God always pulled the plug just when you had everything nicely arranged. It was no use her going on at Billy; he was no more to blame than she was. It was Maggie Thatcher – she'd sworn to put lids on the pits, and it looked as if she was going to do it!

'How will we manage, Lily?' Billy asked, expectancy in every word.

She tipped the water into the sink and spooned in dry tea. 'The same way we've always managed, Billy. One day at a time.'

'Are you vexed, pet?'

Lilian pondered. 'I'm utterly bloody furious, Billy, if you must know, but I'm not blaming you. You're a puppet . . . and as for your precious union – they've slept in, haven't they?'

She would have liked to embroider the point but Billy looked so miserable that she hadn't the heart. He would go down the hole and crawl on his belly, come home cut to the bone and never even whimper. She couldn't stand to see him like a whipped puppy now.

424

'Tell you what,' she said, sitting down opposite him. 'If you get enough of a golden handshake, we might go into business. How about that?'

His face brightened briefly, and then sank back into gloom. 'But what could we do, Lil?'

Her patience snapped. 'How the hell do I know? But I'll think of something when the time comes, Billy, you can depend on that.'


Tracy was playing the invalid again, and Diana was willing to pander to it. 'There now,' she said, 'I've done you a nice boiled egg and brown soldiers, and Barbara's only getting sandwiches.'

Barbara was nodding solemnly, entering into the game. 'I wish I was poorly,' she said. 'I wish I was brave.'

Tracy sighed slightly, as though to explain that virtue wasn't given to everyone, and proceeded to eat her egg. Barbara's brows were knitting, and she looked away from Tracy to whisper to Diana, 'What'll happen if there's a war?'

Diana had hardly given the Falklands a thought, but now she tried to marshal such facts as she had. 'Well, nothing much here, darling. It's on the other side of the world. I don't expect we'll even notice it.'

'Can we still go on holiday?' Barbara asked, relaxing at Diana's reassurance. That was what frightened Diana sometimes, the fact that as a mother she had such power to lift or put down.

'Of course we can. I mean, if we can't go to Spain we'll have to make do with Whitley Bay, but we'll definitely go.' And that was another thing, the way your children laughed at your feeble jokes.

'I had Auntie Helen on the phone this morning. She's coming up with Uncle Vic quite soon. I expect they'll be getting married, and you and Tracy might be bridesmaids again.'

'And Gary?'

'Oh no,' Diana said firmly, 'not Gary. He's quite capable of tunnelling under the wedding cake, or sliding up the aisle. Gary will be sent to stay with Grandma till the wedding is safely out of the way!'

Barbara smiled, her question answered. 'Grandma won't have him,' Tracy said, looking up from her egg. 'You know what she said last time!' They were still laughing when David came in and scooped Tracy up in his arms. 'Give me an eggy kiss.'

Barbara's eyes rolled at Diana, who grimaced in return. 'We're a family,' she thought, suddenly, 'I really think we are.'


'This is a nice place,' Phoebe said, looking round the restaurant.

Edward nodded. 'I like it.' He liked Phoebe too. She had come into the shop to buy a tortoiseshell comb set with agate and lapis lazuli, trying it in her sleek dark hair and posing before the gilt mirror to see if it became her. 'I'll take it,' she had said and then . . . 'that's my number, if you ever have anything else like it.'

He had phoned the next day and suggested dinner, and here they were. She loosened the georgette scarf round her neck and smiled at him. 'Now, tell me about your business. It seems fascinating.'

Edward talked for a little while about his passions and about Helen. 'Dolls,' Phoebe said, 'how absolutely marvellous.'

She looked like a naughty little girl but in fact she was a high-powered television producer.

'I'm impressed,' Edward said, when she named her programme. 'I watch "Line-Up" . . . it's good.'

Phoebe inclined her head. 'Thank you. I agree with you whole-heartedly.' They laughed and set about their *boeuf en croute*.

She had been married twice and had a son of fourteen by her first husband. 'What about you?' she said.

'I've never married,' Edward answered. 'Not for any particular reason: the people I wanted didn't want me, I suppose.'

426

'People?' She made it sound plural and promiscuous at the same time, and he laughed.

'Well, person.'

'And she's still around?'

Edward looked at her in amazement. 'How did you know that?'

She tapped the side of her nose. 'It's the journalist in me,' she said. 'I started on a small-town paper, the *Maysfield Gazette*. Then I went to the BBC regions, radio, then to television news. I did a spell with Granada and then I came back to the Beeb. I sniffed out an awful lot of stories along the way: I've got the nose for it.' She wrinkled her nose as if to prove her point and then continued.

'I'll tell you what I know about you. You're an only child . . .' He nodded. 'You adored your mother, were slightly uneasy with your father. You like men, but you get on better with women. You vote SDP . . .'

'You're a witch,' he said, admiringly.

Phoebe shook her head. 'Intuitive, like most women. Now, tell me what you think about this present Falklands mess . . . should it have been foreseen? I've listened to so many experts, actual and self-appointed, I'd appreciate an intelligent, even if uninformed, opinion.'

'Well,' Edward said, laughing and thinking what fun this was, 'if you insist on an answer . . .'


Helen ran a bath, poured in bath oil, and soaked for a while. Her eyes were sore from crying and the steam seemed to make them worse. In the end she got out, wrapped herself in a towelling robe, and was dialling Edward's number when she remembered he was out with his nice customer and replaced the receiver.

She switched on the television. There was a report of the day's proceedings in Parliament, and she curled up on the settee to listen. The government had frozen all Argentine assets. For some crazy reason she was thinking about corned beef, until she heard that Britain was to sell no more arms to Argentina. Had they already been selling arms? Would Michael die from a bullet made in Sheffield or Birmingham?

Was it for this she had watched and waited, schemed and dissembled – that he should die in Antarctic waters? She knew she was being over-emotional and stupid, but she was so overcome with regrets that excess seemed the only way. Why had she ever given him up? And having given him up, why had she sought him out? Having sought him out, why had she prevented his going to the seminary?

She poured herself a gin and tonic and drank it in gulps, swilling it around her mouth in an obscene gargle. If only Edward were here, or Susan . . . if only Vic would walk through the door and take her to bed.

She poured another drink and then, tasting it, put it away. This was stupid and, worse than that, it was an insult to Michael. She made coffee and put Gershwin on the stereo. Porgy and Bess, mournful, plaintive: 'Oh Lord, I'm on my way, I'm on my way to a heavenly land . . . .' She leaped to the switch and stopped the record with a screech.

When he came back she would tell him. But she would leave him free, no strings, no attempts to engage his affections. She would simply tell him the truth.

She riffled through the LPs till she found An American in Paris, and tried very hard to give the music her total attention.

## 35

They found him in the dining-room, seated at the table, an untouched cup of tea in front of him. 'Howard,' Diana said, laying her hand on her brother-in-law's arm, 'we're so sorry.'

David moved beside her. 'At least it's over, and she's out of her suffering, old chap. Now, tell us what we can do to help?'

Howard looked up at them. 'I think it's all in hand. They're upstairs now. Father Morris was with her, she died in a state of grace.'

'Have you contacted the children?' David asked, and

Diana could detect a note of irritation in his voice. She had long ago stopped trying to understand her sister and brother-in-law, so she was more able to accept Howard's somewhat exalted state.

'No, I was going to do it in a little while.'

Diana squeezed his arm, hoping for a chance to escape. 'I'll do it now, if you like? I have Susan's number. And presumably the Admiralty will help with Michael . . .'

'They won't let him come back,' David said curtly, 'he's part of a task force. In any case, he couldn't possibly get back in time. Have you fixed a day for the funeral yet, Howard?'

His brother nodded. 'Thursday. A requiem mass. Father Morris thinks the Bishop will want to conduct the service. If not, it will be the Monsignor.'

'Well, I don't think Michael should be told,' David said. 'Not yet. Time enough when he's on his way home. It would be different if there were a chance of his getting here.'

They both looked expectantly at Howard, but he simply glanced back at them, almost apologetically, saying nothing. 'It's up to you, Howard,' Diana urged. 'What shall I do?'

He still didn't answer and she heard David's breathing quicken with impatience.

'I'm sorry,' Howard said at last, shaking his head a little as though to clear his thoughts. 'I'm finding it a little difficult. I loved her, you see. She was a wonderful wife and mother. A *good* woman, in the very best sense of that word.' He looked first at Diana and then at David, his brother. 'How am I going to live without her? How will any of us manage without her?'

Diana could not find words, no matter how hard she sought them, and David was equally tongue-tied. She was grateful for this, relieved that David had not come out with the harsh and unattractive truth. But words would have availed nothing. All they could do was stand there, helpless and appalled, as Howard delivered a eulogy on his dead wife.

\* \* \*

Lilian watched Andrew go confidently through the school gates. She didn't want him to be a mammy's boy but a little wave would have been nice. Still, want would have to be her master: he never even gave a backward glance.

Today though, as though sensing her low spirits, he turned in the doorway of the Nursery classroom and smiled at her. Only a quick smile but it sent her on her way uplifted.

She would have to sort something out about their future: it would be up to her. Billy would work, break his back if need be, but if anyone was going to lift them up in the world it would have to be her. He would get about £10,000 redundancy if he was lucky. What if that wasn't enough? Their Helen had money but it would go against the grain to ask her for help, and no mistake. For a moment Lilian remembered how Helen had waltzed in and taken over Diana. She herself was still welcomed there whenever she went, but it was 'your Helen this' and 'your Helen that', even after Diana's bairns had been Karen's bridesmaids. Still, that was one area where Helen had not outstripped her: she had no bairn to get married, let alone give her a grandchild.

Mollified as always by this reflection, Lilian turned her thoughts back to the subject of Billy's redundancy. She was not having him bussing to Easington, so it was the golden handshake or nothing. Sometimes £10,000 seemed like a fortune, at others barely enough to keep the wolf from the door.

She saw a board outside the newsagents: '*Belgrano. Casualties mount*'. They had sunk an Argie cruiser, and there had been as much weeping and wailing on the telly as if it had been one of our own. The more Argie ships they sank, the sooner it would be over and the lads back. Diana's nephew was there, and his poor mother also in a bad way, by all accounts. Some people had worse troubles than her, far worse.

As she made her way towards the shops, Lilian began to rehearse how she would broach the subject of a fish and chip business to Billy. She already knew how to run one, so if she had enough money, buying one seemed the logical thing to do.

It was difficult to avoid mentioning the Falklands when the name was on everyone's lips, and radio and TV were obsessed with the subject. Edward tried manfully to keep up a neutral conversation with Helen, but sooner or later they would usually find themselves discussing Michael and the progress of the task force. Today, with everyone thinking of the *Belgrano* and its tragic loss of life, they had a particular unspoken mutual agreement to talk about anything but the war.

'So when do I get to meet this Phoebe?' Helen said. She was unpacking a job lot of porcelain, turning each piece to see the base in case of some rare and valuable mark.

Edward smiled at her diligence. The porcelain was filthy and the dust was rapidly transferring itself to Helen's face and hands. 'What are you hoping to find in there . . . Nymphenburg?'

She held aloft a figure of a young woman embracing a column. 'Belleek?' she said, pretending to make a wide-eyed face.

'Staffordshire,' he said. 'Keep looking.' Once, long ago they had turned up just such a figure and found the magic red anchor of Chelsea's finest period. 'As to Phoebe, the sooner the better. You'll like her. She's fun, intelligent, going white at the temples . . . She's rather – well, I suppose unusual is the word. She knows how to speak her mind.'

'She sounds like Germaine Greer,' Helen said, smiling at him. He had voiced his dislike of Amazonian Australians more than once.

'Not at all,' Edward said. 'She's much softer . . . rather nice, really.'

Helen had come to the bottom of the basket and looked down at her dirty hands. 'Good,' she said. 'About Phoebe, I mean. I detect a distinct note of enthusiasm in your voice which has been missing for far too long. Fix up dinner and

I'll come . . . or bring her to me. Remember I have a veto – if she's not good enough for you, she goes.'

Edward wanted so much to reach out across the piled china and kiss her eyes, her cheeks, her lips with the faint moustache of dust. He wanted to hold her while she cried out her fear and pain. He wanted to reach out and pluck her son from the sea, to deliver him safe into her arms. That was his real rival: it was Michael, not Vic, who held her heart, leaving no room at all for him.

'I'm seeing her tonight. She has some programme to record from six to eight, and I'm meeting her at Portland Place. I'll find out when she's free and we'll fix something.'

'Good,' Helen said, trying to rub her nose with the back of her wrist. 'Now, I'm going upstairs to clean up. I want to watch the eleven o'clock news. In the mean time, if you can do something about this chaos . . .' She gestured at the packing strewn everywhere . . . 'Debbie can wash the best pieces, in this pile, and repack the rest to sell on. There's not much. It wasn't one of my better buys – sorry.'

'Don't apologize,' he said. 'We'll probably double our money, so there's no need to cry.' He watched her as she went past the torchères and out of his sight.


'I think if you cater for thirty, it should cover. Make it more if you feel it's necessary,' Howard said. Elizabeth Fraser sat opposite him on the settee, knees neatly together, face concerned, pen poised above her notebook.

'What about flowers?' she asked.

'I've seen to those,' Howard said. He had ordered white roses and stephanotis, the flowers Anne had carried on their wedding day, and from Susan and Michael carnations and iris. 'There'll be flowers only from the family. Donations to Cafod from anyone else who cares to give. I think that's everything, Mrs Fraser.'

She pushed her pen into the spiral binding of her notebook and rose to her feet. 'I'll make you some tea.'

He felt agitation stir inside his chest. 'No. No, thank you, I had tea earlier . . . and it would be better if you went back to the office and made a start. People will probably be ringing about the arrangements.'

He saw that she was hurt but he couldn't help it. He disliked looking at her now, remembering how he had sat talking with her: harmless in deed, but not in thought. He had enjoyed her company, wallowed in it. And then there had been . . . the other matter . . . The horror of it rose again now to engulf him. He moved to the door and held it for Mrs Fraser to pass through.

When she had gone he began to mount the stairs, feeling a sense of peace overcome him as he neared the top. The bedroom smelled of disinfectant and flowers, an odour he could remember from other deaths, other darkened rooms. As a child he had been propelled into the room where his grandfather lay, seen the bandaged jaw, caught a whiff of corruption. This was different, though. Anne lay among lilies, smiling serenely in death as she had smiled in life.

'Pity they've been so heavily restored,' Edward said, pivoting the chair on one leg.

'Still, there are six of them,' Helen said. 'I know Victorian chairs are less desirable, but they ought to bring – four?'

Edward nodded. 'Minimum. We could have them re-restored, of course, but it's hardly worth it. Let's sell them on, they're not quite us.' He accented his last words in an effort to bring a smile to Helen's face, but she simply nodded.

He was about to suggest coffee when the doorbell rang. 'Susan!' Helen said, moving forward, arms outstretched. Edward watched them embrace and then came forward in his turn to kiss the girl's cheek.

'I've simply called in to tell you I'm going home now: Mother died early this morning,' Susan said flatly. 'Dad's on his own, so I need to get there as quickly as I can. But I wanted you to know, Helen. Will you be coming up . . . for the funeral, I mean? It's on Thursday.' Her eyes were suddenly beseeching, fixed on Helen's face.

'Of course,' Helen said. 'It'll be OK, Edward, won't it? But what about Michael – is he coming home?'

'We're not telling him,' Susan said, shrugging. 'He can't possibly get back from the Falklands in time, so it's pointless to worry him, specially just now. It was dad's decision, but to me it makes sense.'

'But it could have got him home!' Helen said desperately.

Edward looked at her sharply. She was going to give the game away and this was not the time or place. 'I doubt they'd have let him go, Helen,' he said quickly. 'There'll be plenty of time to tell him everything when he gets back.'

Helen had taken the hint, turning away to move a vase on an étagère a fraction to the left. 'He'll miss his mother. He was very fond of her.'

Susan was gathering up her bags again. 'Yes, Michael will be upset. But don't expect me to be a hypocrite, Helen. I'm sorry she died a painful death but I shan't miss her.'

Edward felt his skin prickle with embarrassment. 'From what I hear she was very reserved. Some people don't find it easy to show their love.'

Susan pulled open the door and turned to face them. 'My mother didn't withhold love, Edward. She simply had none to give.'


'Darling?' It was Vic, calling from Brussels, and Helen looked at her watch. Eight o'clock. He wasn't due to ring till ten, as he did every night when he was away.

'Hallo, Vic. Why the early call?' As he spoke she could sense the agitation in him, and her own alarm stirred. 'Is it about Anne? I know she died this morning because Susan called in on her way north.'

'No, no, it's not about Anne. I guessed you'd know, from Diana, if not from Susan. No, it's just that I've heard something on the radio . . . a foreign station. Oh God, Helen, I wish I was there with you now.'

She knew then what he was going to tell her, and felt suddenly quite calm and cold. 'What is it, Vic? I wish you'd tell me now. I'm perfectly all right. Just say it, whatever it is.'

'Helen, a British destroyer has been sunk, by an Exocet missile. They say it was *Sheffield* . . . but they can't be sure, there's so much confusion out there.'

'Are they all dead?' She felt a terrible irritation at the slowness of his delivery. Why didn't he tell her now and get it over!

'No. They don't know any figures but the majority of men are safe. There's a terrible fire, apparently . . . Look, Helen, you're not alone at home, are you? God, if I could get to you tonight I'd leave now, but there isn't a flight until tomorrow.'

'It's all right,' Helen said. 'I must go now, Vic. Don't worry.' She replaced the receiver and then, as an after-thought, picked it up and laid it down on the table.

She turned on the television and saw a diagram of ships and then a picture of ships at sea. 'And now a repeat of that news flash,' the announcer said. 'HMS *Sheffield*, a type 42 destroyer, was attacked and hit this afternoon by an Argentine missile. Fire has caused the crew to abandon ship and it is believed that most survivors have been picked up by accompanying vessels in the immediate area. Initial indications are that casualties will be low. Next of kin are being informed.'

She switched off the set and sank to the floor, putting her arms on the seat of an armchair. It was over. She could see his face now, rippling in water. It would be quick, death in the South Atlantic. 'I loved you,' she said aloud. 'Oh Michael, my son, I loved you so much.'


Lilian made one last survey of herself in the bathroom mirror. She looked quite nice, and her mouth curved into a smile at the sight. She was forty-three years old but it didn't show, especially since she had dyed her few grey hairs. She switched out the light and went on to the landing, pushing Andrew's door gently ajar to check his sleeping breath. It was quiet and even, just as it should be, and she smiled again. He was a good bairn, and bright as a button.

In the bedroom she opened the drawer and took out

her precious Youth Dew. Helen's gifts were always just for her, not for the house. It was awful to be given housey things; even if you needed them, it grated. But perfume, or the exotic body lotion she had just applied liberally to everywhere that didn't sting – that was a proper present.

She looked at the clock: she had been up for half an hour now, and Billy was still downstairs, with the telly going full blast. She was about to go down and give him a piece of her mind when she realized that it would do nothing for romance, and after all the flaming preparation she wasn't about to throw it away. 'Billy,' she called, keeping her voice low for fear of waking Andrew. 'Billy?' There was no response and she padded down to the half-landing, leaning over the banister to throw her voice. 'Billy!'

He came to the living-room door. 'Are you calling, Lily?' Was she calling! She resisted the temptation to wither him, and put on a smile: she would say, 'Come to bed, pet. It's getting late.' When she opened her mouth it came out differently. 'Haway, Billy man. It's nearly midnight!'

'I'm coming, Lily pet. I've just been listening about the *Sheffield*. As many as thirty dead, Lily. Isn't that the ship the doctor's nevvy's on?'

She sat down on the stair, looking through the banisters. 'I think you're right, Billy. And his mam's just died, I heard this morning. Eeh, what a carry-on.'

She mounted the stairs feeling heavy now, conscious of her fat body, her thighs slapping together beneath the frilly nighty. Some folks never got a chance to get their heads up, that was a fact. In the bedroom she knelt down and folded her hands together. 'Our Father, which art in Heaven . . . help that bairn. Help them all. No more wars. He's nothing to me, God, so I'm not asking for favours. Just do your best.'

She was in bed when Billy came up, and lay listening to the familiar routine, the chink of coppers on the glass-topped dressing-table, the sigh as he sat to unlace his shoes, the winding of the alarm, the sound of taps in the bathroom. When he climbed into bed she curled against him, slipping her arm round his chunky waist. Desire stirred briefly but was overcome by drowsiness. There was always tomorrow.

Edward rang the bell and then, impatient, rang it again. When at last Helen opened the door, he could see she already knew. 'Helen. I came as soon as I heard.' He had half-expected Vic to be there, Superman flown back from Brussels. But she was alone, alone and drunk. Tears and mascara had turned her cheeks to mosaic, her nose was running, and she wiped it with the side of one hand.

They moved in single file to the living-room, Helen swaying slightly, Edward struggling out of his mac and running fingers through his wet hair. 'When did you hear?'

She turned. 'Vic rang me . . .' She gestured at the television set. 'And then it came on. He's dead, you know.'

For a moment Edward was shocked, believing she must have some definite official news. But it was too soon for anyone to have heard.

He had been sitting in La Gavroche with Phoebe when the rumour went round, and had explained to her about knowing someone who had a son on the *Sheffield*. Phoebe had rung a friend in the newsroom at the Television Centre. There were no names yet, no real news – except that the *Sheffield* was burning. 'Apparently it's all changing from minute to minute. The Ministry are saying nothing till next of kin have been informed . . . other than to admit that there are casualties.'

Edward had signalled for the bill and she had reached to touch his hand. 'Of course you must go to her. Let me know if there's anything I can do.' He had leaned across the table to kiss her cheek, thinking what a nice woman she was and wishing with all his heart that he could love her.

Now he reached for Helen, holding her firmly by the shoulders. 'You can't possibly know he's dead, so stop saying it. How much have you had to drink?' An empty vodka bottle was uncapped on the sideboard, but the glass on the sofa table held dark spirit of some kind. He picked it up and sniffed. Whisky! He pushed her into a chair and went in search of coffee.

He was waiting for the kettle, two spoonfuls of instant in each mug, when he heard her stumble in the room. 'I'm going to be sick,' she said and lurched towards the door.

In the bathroom he held her while she vomited and cried, reaching for tissues to wipe eyes and cheeks and then, when it was over, mouth and chin. Was it really twenty years since that night in the squalid bedsit when he had saved her from the ten-pin bowler? He ran water into the basin and put in the plug.

'Sit down,' he said, guiding her to a cork-topped stool. He stripped off her blouse and dropped it on the floor. Her eyes were vacant, the eyes of the dumb beast in the abattoir. 'Oh Helen,' he said, and then, 'It's all right now. It's all right now.'

He sponged her face and neck and then her unresisting hands, slipping the face cloth between her thin fingers, turning her hands palm up, palm down as though she were a baby. Her hair straggled over her brow and he reached for a comb. 'Smarten up,' he said and smiled approval as she combed her hair into shape.

In the bedroom he found a nightdress and handed it to her. 'I'll be back in a moment.'

She took the nightdress from him. 'I need to go to the loo,' she said, like a child asking permission.

When he came back, carrying weak tea in a beaker, she was sitting on the side of the bed in her nightdress, shivering now, her hands clamped between her silk-covered knees as though to keep them still. 'Don't leave me,' she said.

'You know I won't,' he said bluntly and held out the cup.

She slipped between the sheets at last and he eased off his shoes and lay down on the coverlet. 'There now,' he said and switched out the light. He put an arm across her, holding her as close as the bedclothes would allow. In the darkness he smiled wryly: he really must talk to the scriptwriters. They didn't play fair with him.

'Edward?'

'Yes,' he said, his mouth against her hair.

'Will it be all right?'

He drew her closer. 'I expect so. Now go to sleep.'

He lay, listening, as her breathing slowed. Sometimes she hiccoughed slightly, the aftermath of drink and tears, but eventually he knew that she slept. He lay there, marvelling at the intensity of his own feelings. So this was love, this delight of intimacy that transcended lust. No coition could have brought what he was feeling now, a tenderness that made him weep until he had to turn away his head for fear of waking her.

At daybreak he slid from the bed and went to the kitchen. Soon she would wake and grieve again, and before then he must find out what had happened. He could ring Susan, but the girl was bright and shrewd – she would take Helen's concern for granted but not his. The snag was that Helen was in no state to enquire without betraying that her interest was more than that of a friend.

At seven-fifteen he heard her stirring in the bedroom and threw caution to the winds. He got the Whittington number from the address book on Helen's desk, and let out his breath in relief when it was Susan who answered the phone.

Helen was standing at the bathroom basin when he went to her. Beneath the satin nightdress her body was thin, too thin; her face, when she turned, was the face of a woman of fifty. 'He's alive, Helen. Your son is hurt, but alive!'

She cried then and he cried too, unashamedly, holding her close, their single image reflected in mirror and tiles.


# 36


Lilian couldn't believe how easy it had been. She had sat across the desk from the manager and given him the figures, and he had beamed and nodded as though she were Lady Muck of Vinegar Hill. Subject to Billy's redundancy money coming through as planned, they could have a loan for the shop. By the beginning of September it would be hers – well, hers and Billy's.

She had never dreamed she'd be able to buy the shop in which she had worked for so long; Terry and Evelyn had seemed set for life, until she told them of her intention to look for a shop of her own. 'Buy this,' Terry had said and now, ten days later, it was fixed. She walked out of the bank hardly able to believe her luck.

The coffee shop beckoned and she went inside, sliding into a cubicle and ordering coffee and cheesecake from a girl who looked half asleep and needed a toe up her bum. She would make changes when she got the shop. Teresa would go, for a start; and she'd go through to Shields for the fish herself, instead of taking what came. It would all have to wait till Billy learned to drive, but that was already in hand. In the meantime Karen's Brian would give them a lift if they needed it. All things considered, it was working out very well.

As she relished her cheesecake she pondered how lucky she had been – unlike poor Helen, who looked thinner and older everytime she came up. She'd invited them down to London when Billy was finally finished at the pit, and they would have to go before they took over the shop. She'd only been to London once, and wouldn't mind another look. Besides which, Helen could do with bucking up. She'd been lappy-tappying on with that Vic for so long now it would never come off – if you didn't land a man in a year, you'd never land the bugger. It had only taken Billy two months to propose to her.

Thinking of Billy, she found she was smiling foolishly and had to cover her mouth with her serviette. Under cover of the red tissue she permitted herself a small belch, and then waved to the gormless waitress. 'Same again please,' she said, 'and could you hurry up? I haven't got corn growing.'


They found a corner table and piled their shopping on the spare chairs. 'Let's have a glass of wine first,' Helen said, 'and then we can take our time about choosing.' They ordered a bottle of house white and one of mineral water, and began to study the huge menus. 'Crispy seaweed for starters,' Susan said. 'Then special fried rice and crispy almond balls, prawn crackers, and lychees to finish with.'

'Snap,' Helen said and gave the order. She enjoyed her occasional shopping days with Susan, and not only because they gave the opportunity to talk about Michael. She liked the way Susan was growing into an attractive, serene young woman, light years away from the sullen rebel who'd first stayed with her.

'Heard from Michael?' she asked when the waiter had withdrawn.

'I had a letter yesterday,' Susan said. 'He's going to be flown home . . . this week, he thinks. His burnt hands are doing well . . . only with Michael you don't know if it's true, because he never complains. He picked up some of mother's saintliness. A pity none of it rubbed off on me.'

Helen was smiling at the joke as Susan continued: 'Mother's been dead for six weeks, but in some ways it seems longer. Sometimes I feel I can hardly remember her, remember what it was like growing up in that house.' She paused while dishes were delivered to the table and set on burners. 'Why did dad marry mother? They never got on. I used to wonder what it would have been like if they'd each married someone else: would they have been happier?'

'I don't know,' Helen said, seeing an answer was expected. 'Remember I hardly knew your mother. As for why your father married her, people change with the years. She may have been very different when they met. I was just thinking about that this morning, when my sister phoned . . . yes, your Auntie Lilian. Do you know, I couldn't stand her when we were young? I used to feel so guilty about it. But she's changed . . . mellowed, I suppose, and I really like her now. She rang me last night to say she's buying that fish shop she works in, and she's so happy. "I'm going to be a bloated capitalist," she said.'

'She's a hoot,' Susan said, biting on a prawn cracker. 'Nice though. I mean, she's basically kind . . . and she loves her children.' There was a wistful note in her voice and Helen decided to risk a question.

'Do you ever think of trying to find your natural mother? You can do it now, if you're lucky.'

Susan nodded. 'I've thought about it . . . but then, I think, "What if I find her and she shuts the door in my face?" I'm better off as I am, not knowing.'

'What about Michael? Does he think of looking for his mother?' She felt her mouth dry at her own temerity.

'I think he's like me: he'd like to know, but he's scared. Actually I think he'd be keener than me: he worries, you see, about whether or not she's all right. Does she need him, that sort of thing. Typical Michael!'

'Well, you never know,' Helen said. 'One day you may both find out.' She had tried to sound nonchalant, and had failed. She saw Susan's eyes flicker, but she went on eating and gradually, as they gossiped about mutual friends and the latest fashions, Helen's panic subsided.

'I just phoned to ask how you all were,' Howard said, his eyes flicking around the hall in search of dust.

'Thank you, Howard, that's so kind of you and we appreciate it.' At the other end of the line Diana sounded faintly flustered. 'I was just saying to David that we hardly seem to see you now. Why don't you come to dinner one night? We tend to eat with the kids at tea-time, but it would be nice to eat later if you were coming?'

He tried to marshal his excuses, but in the end she made it easy for him. 'Well, when you feel like it let me know.'

After he put down the phone, Howard went upstairs. Ringing Diana had been the last chore of the day: now he was free. He went into his own room and undressed, putting his clothes into the used-linen basket and moving to the bathroom to shower. He loved this moment each day, when he washed away the grime of living and retreated to his quiet house. It was as though peace descended on him at the day's end so that he almost touched the nub of happiness, that indefinable core of living, so elusive and so well worth striving for.

He put on clean pyjamas and then crossed into Anne's room, closing the curtains before he lit the small bedside lamp. He touched the chintz-covered chair in which she used to sit in those last days, running his hand over the back, the arms, the wooden hand-rests. He moved to the drawers, fingering the piecrust edging, and then, trembling, pulled open a drawer, releasing the delicate fragrance of her presence.

How he had loved her. She had been the only woman in the world for him: the only woman! He found he was nodding fiercely to emphasize the point, and then he caught sight of himself, hollow-eyed and ghostly in the mirror, like a man who was weary after long, long travail.


Edward leaned on the bell, desperate to see Helen's face, the champagne held out of sight at his side.

She smiled at the sight of him and stood back to let him enter. 'This is nice. I was just going to do cheese on toast, but if you can stay I'll be more ambitious.'

'I'm staying,' he said, 'but not to eat. Tonight we celebrate!'

Helen's eyes widened. 'Not you and Phoebe!' She was about to say how pleased she was when he shook his head. 'You haven't heard?' he said and then, when she looked blank, 'There's a white flag flying over Port Stanley. They expect surrender any moment now.'

Helen ran to the television. 'I turned it off because all they seemed to talk about was the royal baby. I wish it would get itself born!'

'I'd try the radio,' Edward said, 'they're usually a jump ahead.' They switched channels, hoping for official news, and twice they heard the repeated statement that an officer had confirmed that a white flag was flying over Port Stanley.

'What does that mean?' Helen asked.

'It means it's over,' Edward said. 'It means no more war, no more death or separation. It means the fleet sails back up the Solent and your son is back for good, a little battered, perhaps, but otherwise safe and sound.' He took a sudden decision. 'I'm going to open this champagne now. It's only a formality, after all, the official announcement. Let's drink to all the returning warriors, especially those we love.'

The champagne foamed and cascaded; they drank, sneezed and laughed with that inexplicable gaiety champagne ensures; and then Helen was putting down her glass. 'Edward,' she said, cupping his face in her hands. 'How will I ever get even with you? You're always there at crunch time. I love you so much.'

Her lips were warm and moist on his cheek, applied again and again. He wanted to put his arms around her, to move this mouth towards her lips and return their pressure – but if he did the moment would be lost. 'Drink up,' he said, when his body threatened to betray him. 'We've got to empty this thing . . . it's too good to waste.'

At last it came, the Prime Minister's voice clear and proud. 'On a point of order, Mr Speaker, may I give the House the latest information about the battle of the Falklands? After successful attacks last night, General Moore decided to press forward.'

Helen had moved once more into his arms and stood there, mesmerized by the intensity of the moment. He locked his arms and held her, wishing the calm ministerial voice would go on for ever. 'The Argentines retreated. Our forces reached the outskirts of Port Stanley. Large numbers of Argentine soldiers threw down their weapons. They are reported to be flying white flags over Port Stanley. Our troops have been ordered not to fire except in self-defence. Talks are now in progress between General Menendez and our deputy commander, Brigadier Waters, about the surrender of the Argentine forces on East and West Falklands. I shall report further to the House tomorrow.'

'See,' Edward said as the House erupted in cheers and the commentator's voice returned. 'It really is over.' He bent to kiss her, and this time he might have taken it further if the phone had not driven them apart.

'Vic! Yes, isn't it wonderful! . . . Yes, darling, me too!'

Edward stood there, forgotten, while the bubbles popped against the sides of the glass and vanished into space. And then, outside the window, he heard the sound of someone cheering in a London street.

# 37

Lilian was thinking about the dinner as she put away the breakfast dishes. Billy would be in about twelve, ready to eat a horse, and she was debating the merits of corned-beef hash or stovies when the knock came. 'It's not locked,' she called, and turned to see who was coming in.

'There's been an accident, Lily, down the pit . . . someone in first shift.' The woman's eyes were out on stalks and it was easy to see what she was thinking. But there were 400 men on first shift. Why should it be Billy?

'What happened?' Lilian asked. She wanted to sit down but it went against the grain to show weakness.

'I don't know. They haven't brought him up yet, but the ambulance is at the pit-head. They're waiting for the manager, so someone's in for a shock. My man's abed, thank God, and I'll be glad when he's out of the hole altogether. It makes you think, something like this.' She looked at the range, where the kettle was gently steaming. 'Your Billy's on first shift, isn't he? Shall I make you a cup of tea?'

If the woman stayed, she might break down. 'I've had me breakfast, Jenny. And my Billy is on first shift, and he'll be in on time wanting his dinner, so I'd better get on.'

When the woman had gone off, discomfited, Lilian sat down in the chair. She knew it was Billy – had known from the first moment. Had been expecting it, in fact, for a week or two now. They had been too happy. It didn't do to be like that; it meant you got the eye of God on you and had to be brought into line. This morning, in the dark early hours before they left their bed, he had snuggled up to her. 'It'll be nice when I don't have to get up and leave you, Lily. I'm looking forward to it. The lads were moaning on yesterday, about being cooped up at home when they packed in. "I cannat wait," I said. "I cannat wait to be with our lass."'

'Oh Billy,' she said aloud. 'Oh Billy!' She had been a bitch to him . . . a thousand instances crept into her mind to torment her. The nights she had turned her back on him in bed to punish him . . . and for nowt. He'd never done a bad thing in his life. The times she'd given him his pocket money on a Friday night . . . and pinched what was left from his pockets on a Saturday morning, swearing blind he'd come in drunk and penniless. My God, she'd been a bitch. And the bairns – how would she tell the bairns?

Picturing herself at the graveside, the spades of earth thudding down on his canny bit face, she put her head on her arms on the pine table and allowed herself to cry.


'So where have you come from now?' As Vic detailed his tortuous journey to her door, Diana hugged him, thinking once more that her brother was as handsome as he was nice. 'Well, however you got here I'm glad you came. Coffee or tea? Or booze, if you like?'

He looked at his watch. 'It's a bit early, so I'll stick to coffee. How are my assorted nieces and nephew . . . and David? Well, I hope?'

'David's fine and the girls are blooming. Tracy still goes round like St Teresa of Avila, but she's as fit as a flea really. Barbara is top of her class and David already has her marked down for Somerville. As for our little lord and master, he's out with the mother's help. You'll see him shortly.'

She handed him coffee and he caught her wrist as she drew away. 'What about the mother?' he asked. 'How is she?'

Diana smiled and sat down opposite him. 'She is very happy, all things considered. Gary's illness clarified a lot of things. I love them, Vic – I think I probably did from the start, but I was scared to admit it. And then, when we were up against it with Gary, I knew they were mine, and that I loved them. Since then, it's been bliss – except that you're deadly afraid of losing them, and that scares you.'

He nodded his understanding. 'I've been thinking about kids lately. My girls are thriving, but you know how little I see of them. I want a child I can watch develop and grow, a child I can be important to. Is that egoistical?'

Diana shook her head. 'No, it's entirely understandable.'

'So,' he said, 'I'm going to propose to Helen one more time . . . and that's it. I love her, Di, a hell of a lot, but we've gone on like this for too long. It's either got to lead to something, or stop.'

There was a noise in the hall and then Gary was bursting through the door in his yellow anorak, halting suddenly at the sight of an intruder. 'Come and see Uncle Vic,' Diana said, hoping her pride in her tousle-headed son did not show too much. To cover it, she turned to other topics as Vic drew his nephew on to his knee.

'Michael comes home today, from the naval hospital. He's stopping in London overnight to see Susan – I've asked Helen to collect him. Howard has been so strange lately, and doesn't feel he can get away; I can't leave Gary; and David has the surgery. I couldn't bear to think of Michael coming out of hospital alone. His hands are still not properly healed.

'How is Susan?'

'She has exams . . . her first-year ones, and quite vital, apparently. She'll be with him tonight, but someone was needed to drive to Gosport. Helen said "yes" straightaway, bless her. And if she's to be one of the family soon, it's quite appropriate!'


Lilian had wanted to go out in search of news, but her legs would not carry her. She brewed tea, but it stayed, yellowing in the cup. They had been married twenty-three years and she had planned such a silver wedding as Belgate had never seen. She had intended to send him a kissogram, to see him blush and grin and say, 'Eeh, Lily, I don't know where to put meself.' And now he was dead, two weeks before his last day in the pit.

She knew what would happen. The manager would roll up to the door with the colliery nurse and they would ask permission to enter. She had tidied the room half an hour ago so that Billy would not be shamed.

She looked down at her flowered blouse, beneath her nylon overall. Perhaps she should take it off and find something less gaudy? She was pushing back her chair when the door rattled again and she heard her neighbour's voice. 'It's only me, Lilian! I've heard who it is . . . Leslie Johnson, him that moved from Shildon. They've laid the men off. Your Billy's coming up the street . . . well, he's stopped, talking to Grantham's lass. She's asking him . . .'

Lilian never heard what Grantham's lass was asking. She charged through the door, past the woman and down to the gate.

'Billy Fenwick! Get yourself in here . . . you've had me worried to death!'


When Diana had asked her to collect Michael from Haslar, the huge naval hospital, Helen had said, 'Of course,' and then had fallen to her knees, the receiver still in her hand, to weep her gratitude. She was going to fetch him, to bring him back to the world. She would have an excuse to fuss, to cherish . . . truly, the fates were kind.

In the weeks since she had heard that he was safe, life seemed to have narrowed to just one consideration. She went through the mechanics of working, playing her part with Vic whenever he was in London and giving him all the right responses. But always it was Michael who was uppermost in her thoughts – and now he was coming home, home to her flat, to sleep under her roof once again. She would see him in the early morning, smiling, accepting her . . . she tightened her hands on the driving wheel to still their shaking as she eased into the hospital car-park, and went towards Reception.

And then he was coming through the doorway, in civilian clothes, a breeze ruffling his hair, smiling down at the pretty nurse who carried his holdall, wearing his bandaged hands easily as though he had become accustomed to them.

'Hallo, Michael,' she said calmly, and reached to kiss his cheek, relieved to see that he welcomed her touch.

'It's so kind of you, Helen . . . this is Penny Riley. She's been bossing me around for the last few weeks.'

Helen smiled at the girl and saw her eyes fixed lovingly on Michael's face. Perhaps this was romance? 'I hope I see you again, Penny,' he said – and then they were in the car, together in a bubble of time, with miles of road to travel together.


Howard took off his glasses and rubbed his eyes. Now-adays he found the reading of documents a chore. He was fifty years old: in a year or two, when Susan and Michael were safely settled, he would give up law. He looked at the bracket clock on the mantelpiece below the photograph of the firm's bewhiskered founders. It was three o'clock: Michael had been due to leave the hosptial at two. A couple of hours to London – two and a half, allowing for traffic. He was staying overnight with Helen Clark. She had been a great help with the children over the years, and he must write her a letter of gratitude.

There was a knock on the door and Mrs Fraser entered. She was cool with him now, but still efficient. He would be sorry to lose her, but she was going at the end of the month. 'Miss Carrick is here, Mr Whittington. Shall I show her in?'

'Yes, please, Mrs Fraser. And would you stay? I'd appreciate your advice, since you know what qualities your replacement needs. Not that I expect we shall fully replace *you*.'

They exchanged the cold formal smiles of employer and departing employee, and she turned away. The phone rang and he reached for it.

'Michael . . . just a moment.' He looked at his secretary. 'It's my son. Hold things for a while, will you? Perhaps a cup of tea for Miss Carrick? He turned back to the phone. 'Sorry, I wanted to be alone. How are you? It's good to hear your voice.'

He listened as Michael outlined his plans for coming

home. 'So you'll be here on Thursday. Good. I'll see that your bed is aired. No, you're right, best to leave things till you get home. You know I'll help you in any way I can, whatever you choose to do. Till Thursday, then.'

When he had put down the phone Howard got to his feet and walked to the window, looking down on the crowds scurrying in and out of Dembry's and the other stores. Anne's son was coming home.


Phoebe looked beautiful tonight, the fine black sweater sprinkled somehow with tiny crystals, the white wings at her temples accented with tiny marcasite combs. 'You look lovely,' Edward said, and raised his glass in salute.

'Thank you.' When she smiled her face creased into folds of good humour. He liked her such a lot. There was an ease about her, a sense of being at peace.

'I've been thinking, Phoebe. . . . About selling the business, about moving from London, about a lot of things. I'm in my forties, which is young or old depending on where you're standing. Anyway, I don't want to get heavy tonight, but what I'm trying to say is that when I've sorted things out I wondered if you'd like a holiday – a month or two away somewhere? A gift from me, for the pleasure of your company? Anywhere you choose . . . you've seen more of the world than I have.'

Phoebe reached for his hand and stroked it. 'That's a lovely thought, Edward, and I know I'd like it very much . . . but I'm afraid I won't be around then. I'm going to the States, on assignment to CBS. I was going to tell you tonight. It's a wonderful opportunity for me – a whole new range of programming. Come and see me there. I'll be based in New York, and you're very welcome whenever you can get away.'

'How long will you be in America?' Edward was playing for time, trying to gauge his own feelings.

'I don't know. Two or three years . . . or perhaps for good. But, Edward . . .' Once more she reached for his hand. 'Don't feel you have to pretend to be desolated. I like you, you like me, and bed was good . . . but we're both in love with someone or something else. With me, it's my work: I really do love what I do. With you, well . . . you know best. But your heart has never been and never will be mine. So . . .' She raised her glass. 'Go and be happy . . . as I shall be.'


They had all lolled around Helen's flat, laughing and talking, avoiding any serious topic, drinking coffee and then, when it was nearly time for Susan to go, champagne.

'Well,' Susan said at last, 'time for Cinderella to make tracks.'

Vic stood up and fished for his car keys. 'Come on then, let's get you back to Guy's before you turn into a pumpkin.'

Susan looked from Vic to Helen, and then back to Vic again. 'Are you sure, Uncle Vic? I can get a taxi . . . brother here will pay for it out of all his back pay.'

'No, I'll take you,' Vic said, moving to put an arm around Helen. 'You need a lift, and I need sleep: I've been on the road since six this morning.' He turned to Michael. 'Nice to have you back, Mike. I'll be up your way again next week, and we must have a drink.'

Helen reached up to kiss his cheek, grateful that he was taking Susan safely home, even more thankful that at last she would be alone with Michael. She hugged Susan and tried to respond to Vic's final goodnight kiss without betraying how much she wanted him gone. And then the car was moving off and the last goodbye waves done with.

'Sue looks well,' Michael said, when they were seated again either side of the fire, the television murmuring quietly in the corner because he wanted to see the late news. 'She looks like a lady at last. Mother would have been pleased.' He looked at Helen. 'Have you seen dad lately? I've spoken to him on the phone, and he came once to Haslar, at the beginning. He seems strange to me . . . I don't know, perhaps it's mother's death. I haven't had much experience of the way these things affect people.'

Helen sought for words, not wanting to alarm him. 'Diana thinks he's . . . becoming a bit of a recluse. They don't see much of him, although he's on their doorstep.

But I expect he'll pick up, once you're at home with him. What are you going to do with yourself in Darlasden?'

He did not answer at first, apparently intent on the television. 'That's *Canberra*,' he said. 'She docked today.' On the screen an immense flotilla of small boats was following the stately liner into harbour. On shore people were cheering, waving Union Jacks . . . and then the men were descending the gangways into the arms of wives and sweethearts. Fathers were seizing bewildered children, weeping freely in the emotion of the moment. Helen felt tears prick her eyes, and when she looked she saw that Michael's face was rapt.

'Thank God it's over,' Helen said at last. 'Was it very bad?'

He was looking down at his bandaged palms, the emerging fingers flaky and pink with new skin. 'Some of it. Some of it was . . . an experience.'

She kept silent, knowing there was more to come.

'After *Sheffield* was hit I went towards the generator room . . . I had mates down there. You couldn't see anything, the smoke was in your eyes, your mouth . . . it stung! At first I was scared . . . I was so *frightened*! I found two blokes in a passageway, and I pushed one and pulled the other. When we got up we were choking. I wanted to go back, just in case, but someone held me back. They were trying to fight the fire, but the fire-fighting system had gone . . . we had no fire-main pressure. I wanted to go down again, but I knew it was no good. No one could have breathed in there. I could feel the heat of the fire coming through the deck, through my shoes. I kept thinking about holidays . . . I know it's crazy but I did. Hot sand on summer beaches. And then I saw the hull was beginning to glow and flames were coming out of the site of impact. We were all together on the foredeck waiting for the choppers. Someone started to sing and the bloke next to me said, "What does he think this is, the ruddy *Titanic*?"'

He looked at his hands suddenly, as though remembering. 'It was cold and somone put a coat round me. That's when I realized my hands had copped it. And someone said, "Not long now, mates . . . when this lot hits the magazine we're all for outer space."'

Helen thought of him, out there in the South Atlantic, a boy hardly out of the training school. She longed to comfort him, but she did not dare. 'You were brave, Michael,' she said instead.

He smiled. 'I didn't feel brave. All the same, I'd sooner go through that again than face Dad now.'

'Why do you say that? He's longing to see you.'

'It's what I've got to tell him, Helen. I knew before the Falklands . . . I think I knew as soon as I got to sea . . . that what I *really* wanted after all was to be close to God. I'm going back to the Church . . . if they'll have me. Not as a parish priest: I'm not up to that, helping people run their lives. But I think I might have a vocation for teaching. Anyway, I'd like to try for the Society of Jesus . . . the Jesuits. I'd like to teach in Africa eventually, if I make the grade. But I really just want to work for God, and love Him, so I'll do anything. Do you think Dad will ever understand?'

## 38

Helen slipped from bed before daylight, leaving Vic asleep. Outside impossibly cheerful birds were heralding a new day. She moved to the window and parted the curtain. Street-lamps, ghostly in the half-darkness; a single cat trotting purposefully along a wall; somewhere far off the whine and rattle of a milk-float.

She returned to the bed and felt for slippers and dressing-gown. In the kitchen she plugged in the kettle and brewed tea in a mug, sitting at the table to drink it. She still couldn't believe what Michael had told her the day before, could not take in the rapture on his face when he had talked of his plans. 'It isn't fair,' she said aloud and then looked guiltily towards the bedroom in case she had been over-heard. Was this what she had fought for, schemed for, lied for over all the years? That he should go Anne's way, meekly? No, that wasn't fair – joyfully: his face had been radiant as he spoke. 'It isn't fair,' she said again, addressing the soggy teabag bobbing on the surface of her mug.

She could stop it, of course. All she had to do was tell him the truth. It would change things, she knew that beyond doubt. He would be shocked at first, perhaps a little angry, but he would not want to lose her once he had truly found her. She was sure of his reactions, but much less sure of her right to speak out now, in order to sway him.

She lifted the mug in both hands, revelling in its warmth. Outside, above the London rooftops, the birds were positively euphoric about the dawn. 'The birds are brave,' she thought and envied them their courage.

Somewhere a door closed softly: Vic must be awake. In a moment he would come in search of her, his sleepy face concerned at her own wakefulness. He would reach for her and draw her back to bed. It had happened before, and she knew what would follow. She couldn't go on treating him like this, it wasn't fair. Edward had told her as much, and it was true. If only he were here now so that they could talk it through once more. She leaned back in the chair, closing her eyes against the harshness of the ceiling light. If only . . . if only . . . if only none of it had ever happened. Except that then she would never have known her son. She smiled suddenly, remembering that day in Dembry's, Lilian heavy with child and full of fury, and she running back to the Infirmary thinking that nothing would happen to her except to live happily ever after. What fools women were.

It would have to be resolved soon, one way or another. She wanted Vic, but she wanted her son too, wanted to lay claim to him so that she could watch him fall in love, marry, have children. But she wanted all these things because they meant happiness for her. She had not considered Michael at his birth, she had only considered herself. Now she must summon up that 'ultimate affection' the priest had spoken of, the depths of love that would let her choose for him alone.

454

'Darling?' Vic was there in the doorway, chest bare and still brown above the blue pyjama trousers, lifting a hand to smooth his ruffled hair, eyes flicking to the tea and then, concerned, to her face. 'It's the middle of the night, Helen. What are you doing here? Come on, come back to bed. You can have the radio on if you can't sleep.'

She followed him obediently, let him loose the belt of her dressing-gown and slip it from her shoulders, climbed into bed and felt him tuck in the sheet and rearrange the duvet. Her mother used to do that, years ago, only then it had been blankets, three or four of them, and the world had been Belgate and safety.

He was padding round to his own side, catching his toe on something and swearing softly before he climbed in and composed himself again for sleep. She held her own breath, waiting to hear his breath steady and slow, but he was raising himself on his elbow suddenly and then the World Service was droning away with talk of wars and diplomatic interventions.

'Darling . . .' He was turning to her, slipping a hand across her belly until his arm lay across her, warm and heavy. 'Love me?'

She smiled in the darkness. 'You know I do.' It was a relief that she could say that truthfully: there was a limit to how many lies you could support. But he was turning now, his hands alive suddenly, his mouth seeking hers. 'Marry me, Helen. I'm sick of this "your-place-or-mine" routine. We're not kids any more. I want to settle down. My job'll take me away from Britain soon, and I need the money. Don't make me go alone!'

She was kissing him now; it was more to avoid his question than arouse desire, but she was rousing him just the same. As soon as she had done it she regretted it. She could not make love, not now – she could not even fake it. 'I'm sorry, Vic. I'm out of sorts, I don't know why. Let's try and get some sleep.'

There was a second's hesitation, as his body urged him on, and then he was turning her from him, fitting himself around her and patting her arm in understanding. 'He's nice,' she thought. 'He's very nice, and I don't deserve him.'

There was still a pale moon in the morning sky when Howard went out into the garden. He sat on the wooden seat for a moment, surveying the neat terraces, ablaze now with lupins and marguerites, salvias, cornflowers and asters. He watched as butterflies skimmed the flowers, mostly humble cabbage whites but now and then a more exotic breed. Today he would buy a book on butterflies and find out which particular species he was harbouring. He rose from the seat eventually and went into the greenhouse, heavy with heat now, although the sun was still low in the sky. There was moisture on the glass, and he lifted the catches of the windows and raised them to let in air. He would have liked to stay there in the still, airless glasshouse, but there were things to be done. Michael would be home that evening. He paused on the terrace for a last look and then went into the house to get ready for the day.

He must go shopping at lunchtime. There was food in the house but Michael had favourites . . . it would be good to fill the cupboards again for a hearty young appetite. He felt a sudden joy at the thought of all the conversations they would have. There would be the boy's future to discuss – that was of prime importance – but there would be time to reminisce a little, recall the happy, happy times when all four of them had been together, all loving Anne, all being guided by her.

He was getting out of the car when Diana's Sierra drew up at the door. 'Howard, I hoped I'd catch you. I've just dropped off the girls . . .' Gary was already out of the car, his face expectant. Howard pulled down the garage door and led the way back into the house.

He set juice in front of the child and shortbread fingers. There were sticky chocolate truffles in the box . . . they had always been Anne's favourites, but were not right for a child, not this early in the morning.

Diana accepted coffee and sat at the kitchen table to talk

of Michael's homecoming. 'You must both come to dinner tonight,' she said. 'We don't see enough of you. I'll make something nice . . . David will love it . . . *do* say you'll come!'

Howard felt a surge of panic. He didn't want to leave the house tonight. Nowadays he enjoyed his own home more than anything. He picked up the biscuit tin and turned back to the cupboard. It was full of tins and boxes and he shifted them around aimlessly, trying desperately to think of a decent excuse.

'Let me help.' Diana was there beside him, making room for his tin, flipping open lids to see what could be amalgamated or stacked.

He found some words then. 'It's awfully good of you, Diana . . . and of course we will come. Some day soon . . .' He looked around the room helplessly. 'But there's an awful lot to do here still. Anne was so good . . . it's difficult to manage without her.'

He glanced nervously at Diana, but she seemed to take his refusal well, and he was relieved. He was fond of his sister-in-law and wouldn't like to hurt her.


Helen sat in the reference library, a book on the Jesuits open on the table before her. If Michael persisted in entering the order founded by St Ignatius of Loyola he would take vows of poverty, chastity and labour. There would be a six-month postulancy, and then two years of spiritual training in a novitiate. At the end of his novitiate he would take simple perpetual, public vows, and would then go on to take sacred orders in a Jesuit house of study. He would be, to all intents and purposes, locked away from the world, from her, forever. Eventually he would go to work in his chosen field of education, but that would not be for several years.

She pictured him, in her mind's eye, wearing the drab black of the Jesuit or the white robe of a priest under an African sun. If only she could be certain that it would make him happy, perhaps she could find the strength to hold her tongue? But what had religion ever done for Anne, except increase the unhappiness of those around her?

Outside in the street again, Londoners with blank faces passed her by, unconcerned. She looked at them, wondering about their origins. Were there any true Londoners? Or were all these people immigrants like her, perhaps with secrets that hung as heavy as her own? She was passing a garden now, surrounded by iron railings and dotted with seats. An open gate loomed up and she turned in and sat down, unwilling to press on, even to Edward and the shop, until she had cleared her thoughts.

An old man was sitting opposite, a Yorkshire terrier scampering in and out around his feet: he looked familiar until she realized he reminded her of the old priest, Father Connor. In the beginning she had been unable to think of him without a tiny frisson of fear at his remembered ruthlessness. Now, with the wisdom of hindsight, she could see that he had been not so much ruthless as committed.

He had dedicated himself to saving the life of an unborn child and to saving her from Purgatory: there had been no other course of action possible for him. The fact that she had been an individual with the right to make her own decisions had not weighed with him for an instant. A brief resentment surfaced – he had railroaded her to Northumberland! But her anger subsided as quickly as it had come. He had acted according to his belief, and who was to say he was wrong?

For a moment she pondered the question of abortion. Was it right or an evil? If she had given in to Alistair's pleas and allowed her pregnancy to be terminated, would anyone have benefited? It was impossible to form a rational opinion with Michael now so important a presence in her life.

Across the way the old man was rising to his feet, bending to kiss the cheek of the elderly woman who had joined him, taking her shopping bag and linking his arm in hers for the walk home. They were lovers still, probably had been for forty years or more.

She got to her feet and started walking, watching her

neat navy court shoes tread first the garden path and then the pavement, avoiding the cracks as she had done as a child a million years ago. 'She loves him, she loves him not, she loves him . . .' Her toe touched a line and she stopped her silent chanting. Did she love Vic? Not with an ultimate affection. She had not understood what that meant all those years ago, thinking the priest spoke of affection because he did not understand the meaning of love. But affection was more, a caring, a concern that transcended love. She did not have that for Vic, but could she find it? Or should she go north, once more, back to her roots? Back to the place where things had once seemed simple, and might do so again? When she turned into the Mews she had made up her mind not to think about anything but work until the end of the week. Then, and only then, she would decide.

Edward was busy with a customer. She saw him through the glass before she let herself quietly inside and slipped up the stairs. He had looked up and smiled to acknowledge her entry but his mind was clearly on the prospective sale, a rosewood smoking cabinet to which he was greatly attached. She smiled as she went into the flat, laying mental bets against a sale, longing for him to appear so she could tell him about Michael's decision.

'Well?' she said, when he finally appeared in the door-way. 'Did you sell?'

He looked faintly ashamed and avoided her eye. 'He wouldn't meet the price,' he said and then, as he looked at her at last, he laughed aloud. 'OK – so I asked an unrealistic figure. I'm entitled to a little foible now and again, surely?'

Helen paused, the percolator in mid-air as she looked at him. 'Oh Edward,' she said, 'I keep forgetting how nice you are.'

As they drank their coffee, they listened with half an ear for the shop door bell. It suddenly pinged, and Edward was rising from his chair when they heard pounding on the stairs and Sue's voice, breathless and impatient as usual.

'Hallo. Coffee, good! I've had nothing since I came off duty, and don't ask me how I'm still walking about after a ten-hour shift. Ooh, ta, Edward. And a bikky, please.' She sipped gratefully and then turned to Helen. 'Well, have you heard the latest? About Michael, I mean?'

Edward was looking curious, and Helen nodded. 'I was just going to tell you, Edward. Michael has decided he wants to go into the priesthood after all. The Jesuits. He told me the other night.'

Edward clearly understood at once what she was feeling. His eyes were full of compassion, and Helen felt her own eyes prick. She must be careful not to give herself away.

'Well, of course I think Mike's lost his marbles! After all the trauma of his change of mind, he has to be crazy.' Susan was munching away, colour returning to her face, white after a night spent on duty. 'He rang me this morning, before he caught his train, and I told him just what I thought. He's doing it for mother . . . it must be that! There is no other good reason for him to leave the Navy, except a crazy kind of loyalty to her. Even now, when she's dead, she's ruling us, Helen. Sometimes I think it'll never be over.'


Diana waited until the children had chattered off to watch television, and then she refilled David's cup and her own and launched into her subject.

'I called on Howard this morning, after I dropped off the girls. He was just going to the office, but he took us back into the house and was really sweet to Gary, getting him juice and biscuits and everything. But he's so strange, David. He looks awful – thin and old. His hair seems to be going; it's certainly turning white. Honestly, I know you think I exaggerate, but go and look for yourself. I don't think he eats properly, and you know he never leaves the house now, except to go to work. That really frightens me. It wasn't that he was just a bit reluctant to come to dinner here, it was that he was terrified I'd force the invitation on him.'

'Terrified?' David said quizzically. 'Literally terrified?'

'Yes,' said Diana firmly. 'Please take me seriously, David. He's my brother-in-law and I'm quite fond of him, but I'd feel just as anxious if he were a total stranger. I know it seems mad – I mean, she was anything but a loving wife – but he's pining for Anne, David. Really pining! His face lightens a little when you mention Michael, but he won't come out and see us, even with his son. You've got to do something.'

'OK, I'll find some excuse to call . . . but unless there's some actual medical condition, Diana, there's not a lot I can do. Bereavement does take it out of you, whatever the circumstances. It takes time . . . give him a year, and you'll see a difference then.'

'There's no way we can give it a year, David. But I'm not going to argue with you now – you go and see him and then we'll talk. In the mean time, I'm going to ring Susan. It's up to her to help, and Michael, too. They owe Howard something . . . and I'm going to remind them.'


It started to rain at five o'clock, a sudden squall that beat against the windows of the shop and sent prospective customers scurrying for home. 'You go,' Edward told Helen. 'I've got one or two things to do anyway . . . no point in both of us staying. There'll be no more punters tonight.' She was going to meet Vic and he wanted her out of his sight before she began to glow at the prospect.

'Are you sure . . . can I help tidy up before I go?'

He reached for her jacket with one hand and lifted the phone with the other. The minicab took only a few moments to arrive, and then she was dashing from doorway to cab, and he was alone.

He sat down at his desk and watched the streaming windows, trying not to think of the lovers moving even now towards one another. Outside the sky was black, and thunder rumbled dully a long way off. He ought to switch on the lights, but it was comforting to sit in the almost-darkness, like a creature taking refuge in its cave.

Suddenly he was afraid, feeling age come upon him, feeling the familiar shapes of the shop press upon him, dark and full of foreboding. When Helen went away to marry Vic, the light would go with her. Outside a flurry of rain struck the window as if to point up his misery. He was filled with a sudden, desperate longing for sunlight.

His fingers felt the numbers as he dialled his solicitor. 'It's Edward Portillo . . . I've come to a decision about the Mews. We sell. Get in touch with the developers and sound them out. After that, draw up whatever you need, and I'll sign it.'

It would have been different if he had had children: he would have kept this place for them in case they wanted it, as he had done from childhood. But there would be no children now. He would turn into an eccentric old man, pottering about in Menton or Le Touquet, dabbling in Oriental art or icons or carpets from the East. He moved about the shop, switching on lights, fingering the pieces that had been there half his life. This time, though, there was no pleasure in the touch. These were artefacts, no more, and he needed human contact. He moved to the phone and began to dial again, until his conscience smote him. He was ringing a woman, any woman, because he was in need of a sedative, nothing more. And the women who were his friends deserved better than that.

He paused at the foot of the stairs, looking at the gleaming black faces of the torch-bearers. 'Don't worry,' he said as he switched off the shop light and began to climb, 'whither I go, thou goest.' He smiled, going up the stairs. The sooner he retired to the South of France the better, for eccentricity was already upon him.


They dined at the Gay Hussar, talking of the carnage in the Lebanon, and then, for light relief, of the new royal baby and Prince Charles' chances of ascending the throne before the turn of the century. Vic was enthusiastic about Ian Botham's double century against India, but Helen could see that he was preoccupied underneath the banter. He had been at the head office of the firm of contractors who employed him, but if there had been bad news of some sort surely he would have mentioned it by now?

'Penny for them?' she said as they moved along the kerb, watching for a cruising cab.

'Tell you later,' he said and held up his hand.

He poured drinks when they got home and chose to sit in an upright chair. That was when she knew something was coming. Normally he would settle on the sofa and hold out his arm to make her place. Tonight was different: he was treating her home as though he were a stranger to it.

'I want to talk, Helen.'

'That sounds ominous.'

He didn't smile or soothe her fears. 'Not ominous. Serious, though. How many times have I proposed to you, Helen?'

'A couple of dozen, isn't it?' Even as she made the joke she knew it would fall flat.

'I'm not joking, Helen. I'm forty-four years old, I have a failed marriage behind me, and two kids I hardly know. They call another man 'pop' and I'm 'Vic'. It's not enough, Helen. I want a home and children, your children preferably.'

'If not?' Even as she asked the question she knew what his answer would be.

'If not yours, someone else's. I'll settle for that if you make me, but I hope you won't.'

Decision time. He was not going to be fended off again. Helen took a sip from her glass, playing for time, trying desperately to weigh the pros and cons. If she married Vic she would have children, something to fill the void Michael would leave if he went ahead with his plans. There would be a man to share her life, a good man, a man who would love her and laugh with her – and encourage her to have a life of her own into the bargain.

And she did love him. She looked across at him, looking at her and frowning a little as though to emphasize that he meant what he said – handsome, rugged, a man of the world. If she married him she would see the world. But she couldn't decide now: she needed time.

'Is this an ultimatum?'

Vic looked at her and she smiled, hoping to coax a smile in return. But there was no smile.

'Yes,' he said at last, 'I suppose it is. I saw the MD today, and they're sending me to Cairo in October . . . a twelve-month contract. I want to know by then, Helen. You have two months. If it's yes, we marry the first time I come back from Egypt. If it's no, you won't see me again . . . except for friendship's sake.'

Howard had listened in silence as his son spoke of his intention to re-enter the Church. Now he shook his head ruefully, amazed at the curious way life worked out if you left it to its own devices. Opposite him, Michael misinterpreted the gesture.

'I'll come home quite often, Dad. It isn't like the end of the world. I know you didn't want me to be a priest, but I hope you'll try to understand.'

Howard turned from the window to face his son. 'I was wrong, Michael. Your mother knew that it was right, but I wouldn't listen – and, God forgive me, I spoke harshly to her. Now it's all turned out for the best, and I'm very happy for you.' Inside him there was exultation: Michael had chosen Anne's road for him, after all!

'I have to go back to Haslar at the end of this month,' Michael said. 'My official discharge should come through before long, and I'll go into retreat for two weeks as soon as it can be arranged. The Jesuits advised that I should. They try very hard to dissuade you, you know. After my retreat I'll have to go to HMS *Nelson* for my formal discharge . . . and then I can go to a Jesuit house. I'm longing to go, Dad. It seems . . . infinitely desirable. Can you understand that?'

'I do understand, Michael. For a very long time . . . too long . . . I fought against all that your mother intended. I didn't understand how far-sighted she was. I couldn't grasp the depth of her spirituality. Now, I'm ashamed, but I know she has forgiven my doubts.'

He looked at Michael, seeing the unease on the boy's face, longing to reach for him and help him see the truth.

'Sometimes it was hard to take, Dad – mother's view of religion. For a while I was almost repelled by it. I know it affected Susan.'

Howard put out a soothing hand. 'I know. Sometimes we're not allowed to see things clearly . . . not at first. But your mother was right all along. She was stern with us sometimes, but you must see that it was because she *knew* what was best. Susan will come to understand that in time, you'll see.'

Howard knew that the boy was unconvinced, but it didn't matter. It was all taken care of, all part of the plan. In the end both Anne's children would appreciate how blessed they all had been.

'Will you be all right, Dad?' There was a look almost of puzzlement in the boy's eyes. 'That's my one worry, that I'm leaving you alone.'

'I want you to go, Michael. You do this with my blessing. You're doing it for me, in a way, because I want it with all my heart. And don't worry about me – I intend to retire at the end of the year. Susan seems happy in London, and you won't need my support. I would have provided for you if you'd chosen some other profession and needed my help. Now I want to do some reading . . . and there's the garden. It has missed your mother's hand. I have some catching up to do. She loved her garden, almost as much as she loved us all, and her Church.'

'I don't love the Church, father . . . not as mother did, anyway. It's different for me, a kind of certainty within me, a one-to-one relationship. I love God in spite of all the ritual and the rules, not because of them.'

Howard patted Michael's arm, but he did not speak. What he could never explain to his own son was that it was Anne, and Anne alone, who had saved him from that baser side of himself, the side that had been so quick to sin. He shivered slightly, remembering how it had been with Yvonne. Without Anne's understanding, he would have been doomed to perdition.

## 39

Helen shivered as she reached for her dressing-gown. October and the year was dying. She moved to the window and looked at trees half-stripped of leaves, moving now as though in agony as autumn winds tried to take what foliage remained. Time was running out for her, too. This afternoon Michael was leaving for his Jesuit house near Maidstone, and at eight o'clock tonight Vic would be leaving Heathrow. She had twelve hours . . . less . . . to go to Vic or let him walk out of her life forever.

She couldn't imagine life without him: the warmth of him in her bed, his laughter, the excitement of going places with him, or anticipating his knock at her door. She couldn't spend the rest of her life alone, nor could she imagine giving herself to any other man than Vic. Why did she hesitate? In an agony of indecision and irritation with her own vacillations, she clenched her fists and beat at her chest – until she realized the futility of the gesture.

Turning from the window she switched on the radio. Bloodshed in Beirut, rioting in Poland, a two-year old boy dead in an attack on a Rome synagogue, and a long list of honours for Falklands veterans. The war was being forgotten now, fading from most people's memories. The announcer was talking about raising the *Mary Rose*, King Henry VIII's flagship in a long-ago war. In 400 years, would someone seek out a Falklands relic, or was the loss of 250 men too slight to make an impact on history?

She got to her feet and made some toast, going back to the table to eat it. She had come to a crossroads in her life, a time for unbearable choices. Today Michael would retreat from the world – unless she spoke out. And Vic would leave her – unless, unless.

She went into the bathroom and turned on the bath taps, watching the cascading water as though it held the answers to her dilemmas. She was about to step out of her robe when she heard the front door bell. 'Vic,' she thought, torn between relief and apprehension. But it was Michael who stood on her doorstep.

'Helen,' he said, 'Sorry it's so early. I've been walking round for ages, I couldn't sleep . . . and then I thought of you. I didn't get you out of bed, did I?'

'No,' she said, stepping aside to let him into the hall. 'I couldn't sleep either . . . and you don't know how glad I am to see you.'

'London is full of Christmas,' he said a little later, as they drank their coffee.

'Yes,' she smiled wryly, 'and it's still October.' They were making conversation, both avoiding the thing they really wanted to talk about.

'Have you been having second thoughts?' she said at last, rehearsing her explanation as she waited for his answer: '*Michael, you must know I care about you*,' she would say, '*but you don't know why I care so much*.' That's all it would take. She felt her lips begin to form the words, and then Michael was speaking.

'About my future? No. About that I'm very certain – impatient, even. I can't wait for it to begin! That's why I couldn't sleep at Susan's place, and I slipped out so as not to wake her. She works so hard, she needs her sleep. I know it will be hard for me at times. I'm sure I'll waver occasionally. But it's the only way for me – I truly know that now. And I'm happier than I'd have believed possible.'

There was jubilation in his voice, and certainty, and the eyes smiling into hers were steady. 'He is at peace,' she thought, and at that moment all thoughts of revelation slipped away from her.

'I hope you'll be happy Michael . . . in your new life. I feel that you will be. I'm glad for you.' It was gone, the dream of having her son, his children, flesh of her flesh to carry on the chain.

'I'll see you again, Helen. It's not a prison, you know. The rules are quite relaxed now.'

She smiled and nodded but they both knew it would not be the same. He was going to a far-off country, and she could not detain him because it was the country of his dreams.

'Will you marry Uncle Vic?' he asked boldly, and Helen sighed.

'I don't know. Probably. Do you think I should?'

He didn't answer flippantly, but knitted his brow before he spoke. 'I've thought about marriage quite a lot. In a way it's the same kind of commitment as I'm making, one you hope will last for life. I think you should only give yourself to that relationship if you feel you'd die without it. Does that make sense?'

She felt her treacherous tears start, and fumbled for a hanky. 'It makes a lot of sense.'

When it was time for him to go she stood, smiling, as he stooped slightly through her doorway. 'You're very tall,' she said, reaching to touch his shoulder. 'I hope life brings you joy . . . always.'

He bent to kiss her – the first time she had felt his lips on her cheek except in a thousand dreams. 'Goodbye, Helen. Whatever you decide, I hope it works out well.' And then, as he moved away, 'Thank you for everything.'

As she watched him turn the corner and pass from sight, she cried out his name, but it was only in her head.


Edward slipped the bolts on the shop door but left the CLOSED sign in place. It was a pity to miss the mounting Christmas trade, but he had made his decision and the sooner it was over the better. A price had been half-agreed with the developer, Helen was half-certain to take the stock and would accept him as a sleeping partner if she decided to set up elsewhere. 'If' was the operative word, because she was almost certain to marry Vic, and perhaps that would be the best thing all round. If she was another man's wife he would cease to hanker after her and make a life of his own.

He got on with looking through his desk, a process that was already into the second week. He should simply have tipped the contents of the drawers into boxes and packed them away, but he had made the mistake of sorting through them and every dusty object he retrieved brought on an orgy of remembering.

He fingered a vesta case, its cloisonné enamel chipped, and remembered his father's hands holding the case, the thumb curving to open the hinged lid, the match extracted by the square fingernails, the flare as it was struck, and then the smell of cigars wafting through the shop. His father had sat there like a god while his mother ran hither and thither making everything work. But the old man had had an eye for the perfect object, no doubt about that.

They ran through his mind, those figures of his childhood: mother, father, Aunt Dorothy, the Stepinskis, the denizens of the Mews coming and going with the years. It was right that he should go now. There was nothing left to stay for.

He looked up as Helen came through the door. He could see she had been crying and the impulse to comfort her was strong, but that was not what she needed now. She needed space.

'I'm still going through these drawers. I hope you'll take this desk and all the rubbish with it, for I'll never clear it in time.' He moved to help her as she shrugged out of her coat.

'Edward . . . I want to go to Victoria this afternoon. I know it's crazy and I know Michael will have Susan with him. But I want to be there and see him off.'

'Of course,' Edward said, thinking ruefully of the bustle of Victoria. She would probably not even catch a glimpse of him. Still, though she might die of frustration if she went, she would undoubtedly die of her pain if she didn't. 'Want company?'

'No thanks,' she said, 'I'd rather go alone. Susan has told me their arrangements: they're meeting in that little café on the upper gallery, having tea and sticky cakes, she said . . . a kind of celebration. And then he's going off to catch his train, leaving her at the table because he doesn't want sad goodbyes. I'll be able to lurk somewhere and just see a little of him.' Her voice dropped as certainty deserted her. 'Won't I?'

He sat down at his desk and smiled at her as confidently

as he could. 'Of course you will,' he said. 'Now, let's get on with some work.'


'There's a table,' Lilian said, pointing to a corner. They carried their trays to the window seats and settled down with oohs and aahs of relief. 'I like Dembry's,' Karen said, 'and it's lovely to be without the bairn for once, much as I love him. Shall I pour?'

Lilian separated her éclair from its sticky paper and bit into it. 'I remember the day this place opened,' she said. 'You were with us, creating as usual, and I was six months on the way with our Diana. Poor little bairn. It's a good job we can't see the future.' They were silent for a while and then Lilian went on with her reminiscing. 'It was the day Kennedy invaded Cuba and we all nearly got blown up. You won't remember any of that, but it was a right scare at the time.'

Karen was looking distinctly unimpressed and it annoyed Lilian. 'I've lived through a few wars, miss, don't you forget that. I was born in a bloody war zone – they tried to blast Belgate in 1942. Talk about your Falklands, that was child's play!'

'They say the doctor's nevvy was a hero,' Karen said. 'There was a bit in the *Advertiser* about him being on the *Sheffield*. I can remember him when he was little. He was a funny bairn.'

'They say he's a bit potty,' Lilian said. 'Going into a nunnery . . . well, a monastery. It wouldn't do for me.'

'I don't know,' Karen said thoughtfully. 'There's times I wouldn't mind getting away from it all, kids and bills and keeping up with the Joneses.'

'Don't be daft,' Lilian said, reaching for her second éclair. 'You can't beat living. It's an uphill struggle, but in the end you make it. We've had our hard times, and look at us now. I never thought I'd have a business like your Auntie Hel. I used to envy her once because she seemed to have everything, but she's wound up with nothing except money. She'll never marry, now, too much to give up. Whereas I've got you and our Andrew . . . and your dad,

God help me. Still, I feel properly sorry for her. Blood's thicker than water when it comes down to it.'

'Could you have adopted a child?' Karen asked, between bites.

'Well, you never know,' Lilian said. 'I mean, if someone had come up to me with a bairn, green, yellow or black, and said it was for the chop, I'd've said, 'Give it here,' and I daresay I'd've come to love it in the end. Bairns is very much alike . . . watch those famine pictures, every one of them could be yours! All the same, like I said, blood counts. Your dad's been a headache to me, Karen, as you well know, but I like to think his bairns is my bairns.

'Mind, your Auntie Diana's as happy as a butterlowie, so it works sometimes. But that cracked one, . . . you know, Michael . . . the first time I looked at him I could see foreign blood. Your Auntie Helen was there as well and she said the same thing. And speaking of our Helen, I'm going to buy her something nice when we go downstairs. I don't know whether she's changed over the years or I have . . . but I'm going to buy her something nice to cheer her up.'


It had been a mistake to come. As Helen watched the scurrying crowds she accepted the sheer impossibility of seeing Michael unless she went up to the café, and that would be dangerous. Anyone sitting at the tables in the gallery could look down on the escalator and see who was ascending. If Susan and Michael were already there, she could not escape their attention. They would hail her and demand that she join them, and she was not sure of her ability to cope. It would be terrible if she broke down and cried . . . terrible and impossible to explain, except with the truth.

Temptation stirred, but she put it away. It was time to prove her love for Michael and that meant letting him go, unfettered.

In the end she found a staircase, deserted except for a boy burdened with cardboard boxes, and climbed up several flights until she reached her goal. She stood in the shadow of a pillar and scanned the tables on the opposite side. Pink tablecloths in the restaurant section; a boy carrying two huge knickerbocker glories on a tray; a business section with phones and writing desks; formica-topped tables where bored people read papers and sipped coffee. But no Michael and Susan.

She leaned against the pillar, feeling its edge against her cheek. So this was where it ended, that ultimate affection that had come to rule her life? Except that she would go on loving him wherever he might be. Motherhood was the longest and most unbreakable contract in the world, one that could never be rescinded. But in the end you were bound to lose. Perhaps it had always been a battle, a game to be won or lost. Had Anne won? She shifted her position slightly to ease her feet. No, if there had been a winner in all this it was God . . . and Michael, who was getting what he wanted most of all.

And then she saw them, at a table, heads together, laughing. She felt her own lips upturn in sympathy. She watched them, brother and sister, missing not a turn of the boy's head, a change of his expression, putting a hand to her mouth at times to press back the treacherous tears.

Then he was standing, hoisting a bag on to one shoulder, reaching for a case. He kissed his sister warmly, and moved away, returning to kiss her once more. '*I love you, Michael. I love you.*' But the words were still unspoken, merely inside her head, and all was well.

Helen watched him move to the escalator and lift his hand in one final salute as it bore him down and away. Susan's head dropped then, as though to signify that it was over and when Helen looked back to the escalator Michael had almost reached the ground. She saw his face lighten at that moment as though he had cast off the last burden of his former life. She put up a hand to dash away the tears, in case she missed one last glimpse, and when she looked again he was gone, lost in the crowds that jostled towards the trains.

She turned and moved towards the exit. 'It's too bad to cry,' she thought and was glad.

And then a hand was on her arm, slipping down to catch her fingers.

'Edward?' she said. 'How did you find me?'

'I knew where you'd be. I spotted you a while ago, but I thought I'd wait. Let's go and have some tea ourselves.'

Helen turned down Edward's offer of tea, but accepted a taxi-ride back to her flat. Edward watched her walk in alone, knowing it was what she wanted, then he sat back as the taxi carried him through the streets to the Mews. London was changing: perhaps that was the hallmark of a great city, that it could change and survive.

Edward paid off the taxi and let himself into the shop. For some strange reason he kept thinking of his mother, of the letter she had left him. '*I have no advice for you except that you should live life to the full.*' It was good advice, but sometimes impossible to put into practice.

He was about to mount the stairs when he heard fingers rapping on the glass. The girl was young and trendy and apologetic, dressed in black with striking enamel shields at her ears. 'I know you're closed, but I do love it so much. I've been trying to catch you . . . I live in the flats across the way. Is it fiendishly expensive?' She was pointing to a *plique-à-jour* pendant, and Edward opened the case to extract it.

'You're not a Londoner,' he said. 'What is that accent . . . Liverpool?'

She was nodding but her eyes were on the pendant. 'How much?' she said and took it with loving fingers.

He let her have it for £80, which was half its worth, and promised to visit the flat she shared with her boyfriend for a drink one night. 'I love London,' she said as she left. 'I really love it here. I'm so sorry you're closing down – the Mews won't be the same without your shop.'

He closed the door and bolted it, still thinking of the girl. She was a Londoner by adoption, like his mother and father, who had come from Cornwall to found their business in a London mews. Like the Stepinskis, who had came for sanctuary and made a home. That was London, changing and transmuting day by day, but always alive.

He thought of his mother's letter again. '*Live life to the full*,' she had said, '*but don't be afraid to stand still*.' He had wondered what she meant by that, she who had always urged him to explore. Now suddenly it was clear, and he was running for the phone. 'I've changed my mind,' he said, when he was put through to the solicitor. 'I'm sorry it's so eleventh-hour, and I'll come in tomorrow and explain. But I'm not selling, I'm staying put.'

He turned to the stairs, grinning back at the grinning blackamoors. 'So, my friends . . . we're in business once more.' On an afterthought he moved to the door and flipped the card from CLOSED to OPEN. Outside, the Mews had taken on a sparkle. There were people behind those bland façades, new Portillos and Stepinskis, Londoners every one of them. Why had he never realized that before?

It was five o'clock when Susan arrived at Helen's flat, white-faced but dry-eyed. 'He's gone,' she said. 'Can I have a cup of tea, Helen? He was so calm, it's unnerved me.'

She didn't speak again until the tea was poured. 'You know I thought he was quite mad? Shell-shocked, even? But I've changed my mind. He knows what he's doing.' She crossed her legs. 'I'm going home, Helen, back north. As soon as it can be arranged. I've been thinking about Dad. Auntie Di rang, and she thinks he needs me. At first I said, "No way," but I've changed my mind.'

'Have you told Michael?' Helen asked but Susan shook her head.

'Not yet. He's so happy, I don't want to spoil it. You know him . . . he'll think he should stay instead of me, and I can't spoil things for him.' Her eyes were suddenly moist above the cup. 'It's what Michael really wants. It's right for him, I see that now. Perhaps mother knew it all along. I don't know.' She was turning her back and walking to the window, still holding her cup and saucer. 'And it sets you free, Helen.'

Helen stood for a moment, a sudden heaviness inside her. 'What do you mean?'

The girl turned.

'I don't know what I mean, Helen. I don't really know anything . . . except that you've always loved us . . . and I think perhaps that's all I want to know for now. I'm not quite as together as everyone thinks, and I've had enough emotion for one day. But I want you to be happy.' She pulled a face to hide her embarrassment. 'I wish you'd stop gawping at me, and go and do something about your life. I know Michael would want that, too. Don't think, Helen, just go . . . thinking too much doesn't pay. It stops you from sorting the wood from the trees.'

It was starting to rain when Helen reached the pavement and as if by pre-agreement all the taxis in London had urgent business elsewhere. She began to walk in the direction of Vic's hotel, glancing backwards in the hope of seeing an empty cab. 'You're free,' Susan had said and it was true. For the first time in years she was free, and Vic was waiting. So why was there no elation?

Helen closed her eyes, trying to conjure up the image that eluded her, the image of happiness.

'Watch where you're going!' The woman's voice was harsh, her eyes beady beneath the dripping umbrella.

'Sorry,' Helen said and lifted her collar around her face. The rain had collected in her hair and now it ran down her forehead, a single Niagara-like stream. She wiped it away with a finger, thinking of what Susan had said about not seeing the wood for the trees. And Michael . . . he had said you should want something enough to die for it. What did she want? What would she die for the lack of?

Suddenly, she knew.

A taxi drew up beside her, the passenger flinging the fare at the driver and diving for cover. Helen stepped inside and gave the address, sitting forward on the seat as the driver cut across the traffic, as though to urge him to greater speed, marvelling at what she had just understood.

They were caught at every red light. Around them the rush hour heaved and finally ground to a halt.

'I'll walk from here,' Helen said desperately, but once

her feet touched the pavement she began to run, past the astonished faces of the crowd, the lighted store windows, until her breath came in gasps, and her feet were slipping on the cobbles, and she was beating on the glass of the door with both hands, oblivious of the key in her pocket.

'Hurry, Edward, hurry,' she shouted, half laughing, half crying until, as light streamed across the landing and he descended, she could see his dear, beloved face.

SIGNET

**By the same author**

## *The Beloved People*

The first part in a powerful new trilogy

In the Durham mining village of Belgate, the legacy of the First World War has far-reaching consequences for rich and poor, socialist and aristocrat, Jew and gentile alike.

**Howard Brenton**, heir to the colliery, back from the trenches with a social conscience, but robbed of the confidence to implement it . . .

**Diana**, his beautiful, aristocratic wife, afraid of her dour new world and fatally drawn to the jazzy gaiety of twenties London . . .

Miner **Frank Maguire**, and his bitter wife **Anne**, fired by union fervour as they struggle to survive the slump . . .

**Esther Gulliver**, to whom kindly Emmanuel Lansky shows new roads to prosperity beyond the pit . . .

And in the mid-1930s, the people of Belgate face together a new and terrifying crisis in Europe . . .

and forthcoming

**Strength for the Morning**
**Towards Jerusalem**

**SIGNET**

**By the same author**

## *The Anxious Heart*

As sunlight breaks into the first-floor flat at No. 13 Grimshaw Street, Julie Baxter, forever bright and irrepressible, gets ready for the mad merry-go-round of the day ahead. A single mum, she has plenty to keep her occupied and there are always the other tenants in the house to sort out. But Julie is so busy solving everyone else's problems that she has no time to think about her own. Until she goes to work for handsome, suave Graham Iley and the prospect of a whole new world opens up before her . . .

*and*

**Remember the Moment**
**The Land of Lost Content**
**The Second Wife**
**The Stars Burn On**